The Beast God Forgot to Invent

Also by Jim Harrison:

FICTION
Wolf
A Good Day to Die
Farmer
Legends of the Fall
Warlock
Sundog
Dalva
The Woman Lit by Fireflies
Julip
The Road Home

POETRY
Plain Song
Locations
Outlyer
Letters to Yesenin
Returning to Earth
Selected & New Poems
The Theory and Practice of Rivers & Other Poems
After Ikkyu & Other Poems
The Shape of the Journey: Collected Poems

ESSAYS
Just Before Dark

JIM HARRISON

The Beast God Forgot to Invent

Atlantic Monthly Press
New York

Published simultaneously in Canada
Printed in the United States of America

FIRST EDITION

Library of Congress Cataloging-in-Publication Data
Harrison, Jim, 1937-
  The beast God forgot to invent / Jim Harrison
  p. cm.
  ISBN 0-87113-821-2
  ISBN 0-87113-776-3 (Limited Edition)
  1. United States—Social life and customs—20th century—Fiction. I. Title.
PS3558.A67B42000
813'.54—dc21   00-038620

DESIGN BY LAURA HAMMOND HOUGH

Atlantic Monthly Press
841 Broadway
New York, NY 10003

00 01 02 03   10 9 8 7 6 5 4 3 2 1

To Joyce and Bob Bahle

CONTENTS

There is no road for the gods to offer you flowers.
—Yuanwu

The Beast
God Forgot
to Invent

I

The danger of civilization, of course, is that you will piss away your life on nonsense. The discounted sociologist Jared Schmitz, who was packed off from Harvard to a minor religious college in Missouri before earning tenure when a portion of his doctoral dissertation was proven fraudulent, stated that in a culture in the seventh stage of rabid consumerism the peripheral always subsumes the core, and the core disappears to the point that very few of the citizenry can recall its precise nature. Schmitz had stupidly confided to his lover, a graduate student, that he had in fact invented certain French and German data, and when he abandoned her for a Boston toe dancer this graduate student ratted on him. This is neither specifically here nor there to our story other than to present an amusing anecdote on the true nature of academic life. Also, of course, the poignant message of a culture spending its time as it spends its money; springing well beyond the elements of food, clothes, and shelter into the suffocating welter of the unnecessary that has become necessary.

So what? This is the question that truly haunts us, coming as it does at the nether end of any statement of consequence beyond the moment, as if grave matters must prove their essential worth in a competitive arena and not demanded of the meaningless activities that saturate human lives.

But I must move on because this is actually a statement offered to a coroner's inquest in Munising, Michigan, the county seat of Alger County in the Upper Peninsula, concerning the death of a young man of my acquaintance, Joseph Lacort. Locally he was known as just plain Joe, and he drowned thirty miles out beyond the harbor mouth near Caribou Shoals in Lake Superior. Everyone thinks he was looking for his fat Labrador retriever, Marcia, who swam pointlessly after ducks and geese and there was a large flock of Canadian geese in the harbor that day. But then what sort of madman would swim all evening and all night looking for a dog? Joe would. Myself, I think Joe committed suicide, though I consider this a detail mostly pertinent to myself as his remaining relatives doubtless feel well shut of this troublesome creature. But then the word "suicide" is a banality that doesn't fit this extraordinary situation. Perhaps he felt summoned by the mystical creatures he thought he had seen.

Before I forget, yes I do forget who I am, no longer a matter of particular interest to me, my name is Norman Arnz, and I'm sixty-seven years old. I'm semi-retired and from Chicago where I worked in commercial real estate and as a rare-book dealer. Not that it matters but I'm the only one in my larger family, none of whom I have any contact with—we share a mutual disregard—who re-adapted the family name "Arnz" after it was changed to "Arns" during the First World War when the Boche were a plague. My mother was mixed Scandinavian, so I'm a northern European mongrel.

I've spent summers in my cabin my entire life since my father bought the property while a mining engineer for Cleveland Cliffs in Marquette, Michigan, early in the Great Depression which has now filtered down into millions of little ones in our inhabitants. Excuse this modest joke, but then any product involved with de-pression has done very well on the market for those dedicated to this otiose poker game. When some clod begins a sentence with "My broker . . ." I immediately turn my back.

I told the coroner I couldn't come to Munising because of fail-ing health when, in fact, I avoid the village because of a melancholy love affair with a barmaid a decade ago in the last deliquescent flow-ering of my hormones. It was a love affair to me but a well-paying job to Gretel, not her real name of course, but then our miserable affair was public knowledge in Munising.

I took the precaution of phoning Chicago the other day to de-termine if whether Joe's death was suicide or accidental had any bearing on the insurance money due his mother. It doesn't. She's an attractive woman in her mid-fifties, deeply involved in her third abysmal marriage, this time to a logger over in Iron Mountain. I knew her first slightly in the sixties— she grew up here—when she ran off with a nitwit Coast Guardsman who became Joe's father for a brief time.

Before I get started I must say that the end of Joe's life was his business. Swimming north in those cold, choppy waters I can imagine his croaking laughter, the only laughter he was capable of after his accident some two years before. The aftereffect of the motorcycle accident was called a traumatic brain injury, or a closed-head injury as there was no penetration by the beech tree he ran into while quite drunk. It was lucky indeed for the tavern owner that Joe's last six-pack was consumed on the beach before he roared off on his Ducati. I could go on here about the pointlessly litigious nature of our culture but then would anyone listen? Of course not. Even my wife said soon after we divorced some twenty years ago that she looked forward to being married to someone who didn't make long speeches or lectures during dinner. In fact my local friend Dick Rathbone, with whom I've been close since we were children, actually turns off his hearing aid when I begin one of my speeches. Luckily certain old retired men on short rations will listen to me at the tavern as long as I continue buying drinks.

Until his accident in his mid-thirties Joe owned an interest in three successful sporting goods stores in central Michigan which enabled him to spend his summers up here. I've heard different figures but I'd guess his entire net worth, some seven hundred fifty thousand dollars, was spent on his unsuccessful rehabilitation until last May when Dick Rathbone and his sister Edna kept an eye on him for the welfare department. Dick had worked as a lowly employee of the Department of Natural Resources for thirty or so years and it was his idea, quite brilliant I think, to attach telemetric devices to both Joe and Marcia to keep track of their whereabouts. Certain newcomers to the community thought it inhumane (whatever that could mean in view of the past century) but then newcomers are generally ignored on important matters because of the essential xenophobia of the human condition. Due to his impact with the beech tree, the flubbery rattle of the brain within its shell referred to technically as "coup contracoup," Joe lost most of his ability at visual memory, even for faces such as his mother's and my own, a deficiency called "prosopagnosia." Joe's very least problem was boredom because everything he saw he saw for the first time, over and over. Each of his dawns began as a brave new world, to borrow a phrase from Aldous Huxley whose first editions have remained curiously stagnant in price.

Sometimes Joe followed Marcia but most often she followed him. His nexus was the rather ornate birdbath in Dick Rathbone's back-yard. Joe carried a good Marine-surplus compass and another was pinned to his belt. My cabin was a hundred seventy-three degrees northeast of Rathbone's birdbath, a matter of some five miles though this wasn't relevant to Joe. I have it on good witness that in June near the summer solstice he walked all the way to Seney and back to get a particular kind of ice-cream bar that Dick's sister had for-gotten while grocery shopping, a round-trip of fifty miles which took about fourteen hours, a double marathon though Joe viewed his pace as leisurely. A park ranger at the nearby National Lakeshore had maintained Joe walked up and down the immense sand dunes at the same speed. When I asked him about this he clumsily ex-plained that it was apparently due to his injury, and that he was helpless to change his gait which was a little problematical during his night walking due to the brush.

Frankly I didn't care at all for him before his injury. Despite his financial success downstate he would become immediately loutish up here, aping his local friends. It's hard enough to have your foot in one world, let alone two, and catering to egregious pricks out of child-hood nostalgia is a poor way to conduct your life. He used to drink rather vast amounts of beer, which caused pointless quarrels with whatever girlfriend was visiting. The impulse behind this kind of beer drinking is mysterious. Dick Rathbone has supposed they actually like to piss which they will do a dozen times in an evening. I called an old friend in Chicago on this matter out of idle curiosity. This friend is a true rarity, a gay psychiatrist of Italian parentage named Roberto.

I exclude his last name because the world is his closet, as it were.
Oddly enough Roberto agreed with our humble Dick Rathbone, but
I can't really imagine the nature of this impulse. We all have our limits,
don't we? The will to pee, indeed.

Fairly early one morning in July Sonia, a registered nurse from Lansing and one of Joe's girlfriends, showed up at my cabin saying she
had agreed to meet him there. It was already warm and she wore
an unnerving shorts and halter. When I brought her coffee I could
see her nipples and when she drew her leg up on her chair I caught
a glimpse of pubic hair. Unlike women in my younger days she was
utterly nonchalant about exposing herself and I felt the mildest of
buzzing sensations plus a certain giddiness I hadn't known in years.
Naturally I tried to determine immediately if this was a good or bad
experience and came up with something between the two. We are
mere victims, mere supplicants, in the face of what a Mexican friend
calls the "divina enchilada."

Her knees were more than a bit abraded and I retrieved some
Bactine and cotton which she allowed me to administer with a smile.
She said Joe had said he was walking up the small river, in the river
at that, to visit the grave of an infant bear he had buried in late May.
I asked her if she had fallen and she laughed heartily saying that
Joe had "fucked" her relentlessly "dog style" on the beach which
had been hard on her knees. Now I had met Sonia several times
before but one would think this kind of information would be shared
with only the closest of friends. I nodded and allowed myself a
chuckle. Nurses do tend to be matter-of-fact because of their con-
tiguity to death. After about fifteen minutes she asked if she could
rest on the couch and assumed an even more daring position before she began the slightest of snores. Here I was, a prisoner in my
own house, trying to read a previously fascinating botanical text

but unable to pass through a couple of sentences without another look at Sonia. I admit at one point I knelt rather closely with a devil-may-care attitude toward getting caught. After all, it was my house.

And thus the morning passed until near noon when I fell asleep with my face pressed against the botanical text rather than something more interesting. I awoke to the sound of the shower and Marcia, Joe's Labrador, barking loudly. I was slow to react, dreaming of all things of my favorite Chicago steakhouse, and damping a botanical plate with drool, when Sonia rushed past me in a towel. She stooped outside and petted Marcia who was obviously trying to get someone to follow her. My concern was leavened over the missing Joe somewhat by noting what a poor job the towel was doing covering Sonia. She was all for following Marcia which I advised to be a bad idea. Instead I called Dick Rathbone on my car cellular—there was no phone line to my cabin—and told him the problem. While we waited Sonia sat on a chair in her towel and began weeping. I stood beside her patting and rubbing her shoulders to comfort her. When a woman weeps I am desperately uncomfortable partly because neither my mother nor wife wept except on the rarest occasions. Sonia blubbered on about Joe's absolutely hopeless condition which she certainly knew as a nurse. I began, of all things, to get an erection which would be obvious in my summer-weight chinos. I tried to move away but Sonia grabbed my arm weeping piteously then, noting my erection, gave it the brisk finger snap that nurses do, laughed, and called me an "old goat." She dressed right smack in front of me with a boldly amused look, my heart aching with her insult.

Dick Rathbone arrived with his telemetric receiver and we set off down the tangled riverbank with Sonia and Marcia both choosing to wade and swim along beside us. We had gone perhaps a mile before we found Joe fast asleep on a sand spit near an eddy. Dick pointed out the cairn of stones upon the bank where Joe had buried the baby bear which its mother had destroyed, so said Dick, because one of its front legs was deformed. Joe had found this detail to be unendurable.

When Sonia shook him awake aided by Marcia's face lapping, Joe announced that he had seen something quite extraordinary, a brand-new mammalian species, a beast that he didn't know existed. Dick whispered to me about adjusting Joe's medication, then asked kindly about the whereabouts of the tracks. Joe said the animal didn't leave tracks but he knew the general area it favored, mentioning a location well to the south which I won't identify now to preserve it from curiosity seekers. For her good intentions, Dick gave Marcia a number of biscuits, which he kept for that purpose. Marcia's sole real fidelity was to Joe and anyone else was fair game. Once I met her near a woodlot on a back street of the village. She acted alarmed and enervated so I followed her and she led me persistently to the grocery store so that I might buy her a snack.

I wasn't inclined to sit there near the sandbar and watch Joe go back to sleep so I left the chore to Sonia, Dick, and the faithful Marcia. I was amused to note that every time Dick glanced at Sonia his big, floppy ears reddened. It was with relief that I silently handed over the burden of lust to my old friend and headed upstream toward my cabin for lunch and a hard-earned nap. Sonia reminded me of a miserable poem by Robert Frost called "The Road Not Taken."

Horrors! It's only July and we've had three days of dense cold rain with the wind northwest out of Canada. The life has drained out of me onto the maple floor. A business partner from Nebraska once told me that I kept my "lid screwed on too tight." Maybe so, but not that I've noticed except at times like now when the weather and my own contentious moods throw me for more than a loop. Dear Coroner, I loathe everything I've said but out of laziness I'm not changing a word. These are the first I've written in several days and I'll try to get more directly at the heart of the matter which, of course, is no longer beating. Right now I feel that my human tank is drained and I am the sediment, the scum on the bottom, the excrescence of my own years. It occurs to me that the memory of Sonia sitting in the chair a few feet from where I am now may have precipitated this funk. Nothing so much torments a geezer as the thought of the unlived life. For some reason she summons up an image of a steelworker shoveling coal into a blast furnace.

And I want to be fair-minded with Joe. This, after all, isn't about me but my departed young friend. There is ever so slight an aura around him now in my mind that must resemble the origin of some primitive religion. I just recalled one late June dawn when he arrived quite literally covered with mosquito and blackfly bites, muddy clothes, quite eager to show me the one-hundred thirty-seven water sounds he had logged in his notebook. What was I to make of this? Frankly it was interesting. Here was a man who quite literally saw everything for the first time every single day but had a quite extraordinary (a euphemism!) perception of the aural, if not the visual, though this is open to contention. The list of water sounds included the names of the creeks, rivers, lakes, also the morphology and weather conditions that had a part in their creation. I suppose all water may be perceived to be going downhill except in tidal situations where the receding tide is functionally going uphill to gather itself. There were a number of rubrics, squiggles, beside each item in Joe's list to remind him of the actual sound which he insisted over breakfast he could actually re-hear. Joe bolted his food like Marcia who was scratching the door. I made her a plate of several fried eggs in bacon grease, her favorite. Did I say that Marcia also disappeared the night of Joe's drowning? His body was eventually found, of course, dear Coroner. You have it, whatever it really is, in your possession. Marcia was never seen again and it's unthink-

able that a Labrador retriever could drown. Perhaps she joined his
imaginary creatures, if indeed they could be termed "imaginary."
More than likely this happy lady was carried off in a tourist's car.

I'm getting ahead of myself. The water-sound morning came
just before Joe's announcement about the discovery of a new beast.
I had asked my psychiatrist friend, Roberto, in Chicago about the
aural phenomena and he said closed-head injuries could indeed be
boggling because the brain itself (one is tempted to say "herself"
for a number of reasons) is so massively intricate. Roberto Fed Exed
me a brain text which I found largely unreadable in its complexity.
I simply couldn't quite believe "that" thing was in my head.

Joe's log of water sounds also made me wonder if nature, adequately perceived, is all that tame? I am perhaps not competent to
conjecture in this area but who is to stop me? Professors only police
each other and largely ignore the common man among which I number myself. Yesterday when the rain and blustery wind let up for a
few minutes I replenished my bird feeder and found a dead evening
grosbeak in the grass. For some reason I smelled its wet feathers
and determined that it had only recently died. I shuddered at its
lack of weight, though, of course, how else could it fly? I admired
its sturdy beak and the amazing yellowish and beige feathers, the
streak of white. I recalled the first time as a young man when I had
been fortunate to cup a girl's pussy in my right hand. A mystery
indeed. I'm sure every man remembers this encounter with a sense
of true "otherness."

Let's re-adjust again. I've added a log to the fireplace I could
barely lift. It was beech but not from the tree Joe struck so carelessly. I'm quite tired of being a querulous old fuck and I am
beginning to wonder if this persona isn't simply another cultural
imposition. Americans seem to love sporting metaphors and I have
certainly rounded third base and am headed for home plate, which
is a hole in the ground. Naturally I'd prefer to be "buried" in a tree

on a platform or in a little oblong wood hut like members of Native tribes. I'm only ninety-nine percent sure that this doesn't matter but the remaining one percent is troubling.

I can try to determine the nature of Joe by my observations and what he told me; also from the three notebooks he left me. Or so I think. But then it would be needlessly exhausting to defend the nature of my mind that creates the perceptions about Joe. These last three rainy days I have begun to perceive certain limitations I hadn't sensed before and am unwilling to defend as virtuous. I am possibly less nifty than I thought. This won't precipitate a depression as the rain has already managed that quite well, though I admit it has been a lucid, reductive pratfall, a threshold rain.

In July, for instance, Joe was visited by a young woman I found quite unpleasant for the first few days. This girl blew her nose more often than any other mortal due, she said, to an allergy of some sort. She was of normal height but quite slender, wearing the kind of floppy clothes that conceal the actual shape. She was a graduate student in comparative literature at Michigan State University, down in East Lansing, a school I know little about except that their teams are referred to as the Spartans and are in the Big Ten. I went to Northwestern myself and though it has an excellent scholastic reputation this fact did not reduce the torpor I felt as a student. There I go again. Who gives a flat fuck? I am scarcely interesting even to myself. I am the personification of Modern Man, the toy buyer who tries to thrive at the crossroads of his boredom.

Anyway, this girl, to whom I'll give the name Ann, had none of the physical vibrancy of Sonia. She was, however, bitterly intelligent and quite helpful to Joe in collecting botanical specimens for me, a meaningless hobby I've had since a child. Due to Joe's visual confusion he kept returning with the same specimens as the day or days before. I paid Joe five bucks apiece for anything new and one day with Ann's help he made two hundred dollars. Despite Ann's

obvious intelligence, not necessarily a pleasant item, she was irrationally in love with him no matter his hopeless injury. What in
God's name does this mean? How can you continue to "love" someone with this sort of injury, who doesn't physically recognize you
when you get up in the morning, though memory resonances are
there in conversation, touch, and probably odor.

My careless presumptions about her began to dissolve when I
was standing in Dick Rathbone's kitchen and he was describing
how Joe and Ann had walked the Lake Superior shore over the
Muskallonge Lake (twenty miles) and she had called him when the
afternoon had become unpleasantly warm. We were looking out
the back window into the garden, which surrounds the birdbath
which is Joe's navigational focus, when Ann and Joe came up from
the beach. She picked up the hose, turned on the faucet, and sprayed
the sand off Joe who did the same for her though the water had
obviously turned colder. Ann shrieked, stumbled, then jumped over
a stack of two sawhorses that Dick had left in the backyard near
the small cabin that served as Joe's quarters. Simple enough, but
then I checked them out later and the sawhorses were three feet
high. The mousy little girl was quite the jumper. What's more she
had the lithe power of a dancer which she turned out to have been
several years before. While Dick was busy at the grill with his hall-
mark barbecued chicken I spoke to Ann about this, having admitted that she had startled me. She said I was the type that spent
my life making false assumptions and presumptions about people,
though she said so with a smile. True, I thought, though I didn't
say so. Instead I told her that when I was a very young man my
mother hadn't allowed any books of a sexual nature in the house,
not even high-minded photographic books with nudes, but since
she followed dance there were any number of books containing
photos of ballerinas in the house and as the young used to say, these
books "turned me on." Ann was amused by this but then became

unpleasant. Had I followed up my early obsession with ballerinas? No, of course not. Was I still attracted to them? Well, somewhat in the limited way an elderly gent is attracted to anyone. Oh bullshit, she said, I should have followed my desires, ballerinas are relatively easy as most of them could always use "sugar daddies." Her own father had bored the whole family senseless by his "puttering." She would have preferred he acted badly like Picasso (he taught painting at a university). To Ann her father's maturity was a hoax and the fact that he gave up painting and drinking for home repairs was an impossible disappointment for her.

This made me uncomfortable enough to sidle over to Dick's homemade barbecue machine and affect deep interest in the chickens. Ann, who was now wearing what I think is called a sarong, was helping Dick's sister Edna set up the picnic for dinner. Joe was asleep on the grass using Marcia as a pillow as he often did. Ann sat down next to him and brushed his hair. It occurred to me then that she might be drawn to Joe because her father had apparently lost his wildness and that's all that comprised Joe's life. After a year and a half in and out of hospitals he had no intention of getting close to a hospital or a doctor again. But then it is presumptuous of me to say that he had any intentions at all other than what he simply "did."

Dinner wasn't pleasant for me except for the chicken and potato salad. Joe, as was his habit, ate an entire chicken in five minutes and went back to sleep. Edna covered him with netting to protect him from the early-evening mosquitoes. He twitched a lot and she wondered aloud if she should increase his medication. His pills made up quite a list, not that they had any positive effect other than to prevent something worse. Edna was amused when Ann began to pick on me over our dessert of fresh blueberry ice cream made with true unpasteurized Jersey cream Dick got from a friend over in Newberry.

Ann's first caustic remark came over the matter of my being a rare-book dealer, mostly retired but with a hand still slightly into the business. She thought of us as necromancers and how could I poke fun at the stock market when I was essentially in the same business. Her somewhat daffy mother had sold a first edition of Frost's *North of Boston* for fifty bucks to a dealer in order to buy her puttering geezer of a husband a special birthday present, a fraction of its worth. When Ann had found out she had gone to the dealer's shop, waited until there were several other customers, and then read the dealer out in the vulgarest terms imaginable. She managed to extract another fifty bucks which she tore into confetti and threw in the dealer's face.

This almost, but not quite, ruined my chicken. Guilty sweat trickled down my tummy over the memory of swindling a doddering academic wife out of her late husband's Faulkner collection to add to my own large holdings of this peculiar author who reminds me of botany in that there are so many shapes and permutations in his work. I took a fine vacation in Paris by selling a duplicate of *Soldier's Pay* for eight thousand dollars.

Meanwhile, I diverted Ann by guessing that she was a very late child so that by the time she reached adulthood she was very protective of her parents, in fact had probably become a parent to both of them. This wild, defensive guess electrified her to the point that the phrase "pissed off" was the mildest of euphemisms. She looked at me with the coldest contempt, woke up Joe, and led him into their cabin.

So now you've met Sonia and Ann and we've not seen the end of either. And there's one more coming in August. To make things up with Ann I had my part-time secretary in Chicago send her my own copy of *North of Boston*, a generous gift in monetary terms though I have no fondness for the poet. Ann replied by sending me five hundred pages or so of material she collected off the Internet on closed-head injuries. This was an unwieldy and ghastly manuscript which, along with hard, scientific information from doctors specializing in the field, included hundreds of testaments from the injured themselves. Some of the latter simply made the heart flutter and ache, woeful tales of years of therapy with small chance of total recovery, but then any little advances were cause for family celebrations. The sheer numbers of the injured, of course, reflected the frequency of auto and motorcycle accidents, the Newtonian principle that an object in motion (your head) tends to remain in motion unless acted upon by an unbalanced or unequal force (in Joe's case, a massive gray beech tree).

But why would I be so overwhelmed by these stories, a sophisticated student of language, of the best of world literature not to speak of legal documents, histories, the best newspapers and magazines? The answer I suppose lay in the charm of folkloric stories, primitive or "naïve" art, the origins of third-world music, the recorded oral tales of our own Natives. A trucker swerves to miss a school bus (of course!). There are massive head injuries and his head becomes a partially cooked rutabaga. His wife and five children bathe and feed him for years in their humble shack in southern Indiana. Gradual progress is made and after a decade of heroic effort by the family and doctors the trucker is able to give his daughter in marriage at a country church though his head lolls uncontrollably and he can only walk by shifting sideways. His grammar is poor indeed but he's able to send his valiant story to the closed-head injury Web site because the trucking company gave him a laptop! He is able by himself to catch catfish from a stream near their home. His family loves fried catfish, his only possible contribution to their welfare. Jesus Christ, this tale floored me!

That sort of thing. Reading these stories by the dozens reminded me how nearly all of our printed discourse is faux Socratic
and contentious, a discourse without nouns of color and taste, a
worldwide septic tank of verbiage that is not causally related to the
lives we hope to lead. It is the language of the enemy and politicians lead the pack, with this verbal shit spewing out of their mouths
on every possible occasion. Analogic, ironic, what we call common
usage leaking its viruses from between book covers.

Perhaps I'm being excessive but I doubt it. Anyway, after
carefully reading the five hundred pages I sent the packet back
to Ann saying I couldn't bear to have it in my cabin, but not before Joe saw it on my kitchen counter. His verbal memory is sul-
lied but not to the extent of his visual. To a certain minimal extent
he can recall nouns referring to trees, birds, water, that sort of
thing, but he can't directly relate, say on a walk, the nouns to the
actual people.

For instance he insisted in June on showing me a coyote den.
At first I refused because, unless it's quite windy, June walking
involves blackflies which will turn you into a mass of itching welts.
Of course I've noticed over the years that there have gradually been
more reasons not to walk: too cold, too hot, mosquitoes, horseflies,
deerflies, it's raining, it's too wet after a rain, or I'm too tired from
reading, thinking, eating, twiddling my big thumbs (genetic).

Joe said that we could drive within a half mile of the place
which was a fib. It was a full mile if not farther. The various bugs
were savage in the damp, still air. Joe pointed to a white pine stump
on a distant hillock that was partly surrounded by a nasty thicket
of thornapple, a bush covered with two-inch thorns so sharp that a
hunting friend had his penis speared to the hilt. I was using my
expensive binoculars and saw nothing noteworthy. Joe who was
without binoculars said he could see two noses poking from the dark
hole at the base of the stump, and then a third smallish figure scooted

into the hole. I missed this, too. The mother was watching us from beneath a chokecherry tree in lavish bloom. Joe stood behind me and I finally focused on the dim figure of the mother. Joe was upset because the pups evidently wouldn't emerge because of my presence. He directed me to walk back to another hillock about three hundred yards toward my car. I sniffed the unpleasant air and he drew out a plastic sack of rank stew meat from his pocket with a smile.

When I reached my assigned position I glassed Joe walking purposefully but zigzagging, jumping, and laughing. When he reached the den he lay down and dumped the meat on his chest. After a minute or so the three pups emerged and fed off his chest, standing on his body and quarreling over the food. The mother was now sitting about thirty yards away watching the scene. After the meal Joe crawled around playing tag with the pups, and at one point a pup rode on his back while chewing on his shirt collar.

I must say that though these animals were neither tame nor trained I didn't for some reason see the event as all that extraordinary. Coyotes owe their survival to their exceptional wariness. A naturalist acquaintance once told me that he suspected that for every coyote you see at least a dozen have seen you. So at the time it was amusing rather than impressive but then what did I really know about such matters? I had the slightest notion that the coyotes might trust Joe because he had become part of their world from which the rest of us are excluded for good reasons. And this particular species according to Native lore has quite the sense of humor. I might add that a Department of Interior game biologist I met told me that he had glassed Joe in early June walking alongside a smallish bear. This incident seemed troubling to him because the other two men who had accomplished this were professionals, like himself, in mammalian studies.

* * *

So much for this for the time being, dear Coroner. You wanted to know everything I know about Joe Lacort and I'm giving it to you in my own fashion. It's unlikely that anyone but the two of us will see this report. Since I don't know you how can I count on you? A burgeoning writer of sixty-seven must come to the conclusion that if no one will make use of me I'll have to make use of myself. The essential question of how did I live this long can be easily dismissed. The question of why I don't recall much of my life is more to the point. The placid convulsions of business tedium can last for months. Once in a Chicago restaurant an adjoining table was celebrating one of their members' one-thousandth autopsy in the city's pathology department which did not make them stand back from their porterhouses and strip sirloins. In Joe's defense, if I'm in a ruminative state, I can recall certain walks I took up here back in the 1960s. I suppose because they made a great impression on my senses. If I try to remember my business activities from that period I hear in my mind's ear the sound of shuffling papers, file cabinets opening and closing, the soft thump of one book being piled on another, police sirens from the street, the yawn or cough from my secretary and the clatter of her typewriter. I see the walls of my office, the somewhat grimy window, the comforting prints of eighteenth-century French and English landscapes. One saved the great ones like Caravaggio and Gauguin, our own Winslow Homer and Maynard Dixon for private moments at home. I didn't want my colleagues who were nice enough, but to whom the entire earth was zoned commercial, to see my favorites. My colleagues were predatory androids.

Ann came back up a short week after she left. The news was bad but then I was already aware of the problem. Joe had turned off his telemetric device two days before out of anger with the Department of Natural Resources. In late April, before the foliage was out, Joe had built a small shelter for himself on a hummock

surrounded by a large swamp, all on state land. The illegality of it
made Dick nervous as a former D.N.R. employee, though he drove
one smallish load of lumber to the nearest road, about four miles
from the site. It had taken Joe several laborious trips to haul in the
building material, from which he'd return muddy to his breast from
traversing the swamp. Unfortunately a D.N.R. spotter plane had
noted his shelter but it had taken until June for them to tear it down.
Dick had tried to interfere to no avail saying that he doubted anyone had been on Joe's hummock since the huge white pines had
been timbered off ninety years before. But rules, of course, are rules.
The law is the law. Shit is also shit. The government's central evil
is its willful failure to distinguish the quality of intent or motive.
Dick had driven over to Marquette to see the director who was a
new, young popinjay, a hotshot who despite Dick's thirty years of
service gave Dick only a scant five minutes before chortling that
the law was the law despite Dick saying that he doubted Joe would
last out the year. After all, what would they do with him when all
of the back roads are impassable with snow and the temperature
has reached as low as forty degrees below zero?

When Ann arrived about noon I had spent a sleepless night
worrying about the problem and there was also the mistake of calling Roberto in Chicago for advice. I was especially fragile because
the moon had been nearly full and a buck deer had snorted nearby
the cabin, a wheezing ghastly sound like the base note of a broken
harmonica. The only worse sound is when a coyote takes a fawn or
a rabbit and the death cries are those of a child.

In any event Roberto sounded bleak and hungover from God
only knows what perverse activities. He suggested that I was trying to control Joe as a substitute for my non-existent children. This
was unacceptable, also meaningless given the real situation. Roberto
also suggested that my motives were a concealed stew in that there
might also be some sexual envy, a sore point. A closed-head injury

is far more likely to cause impotency in the male than an increase in sexual activity. Was I jealous of Joe's tupping every heifer in range? Of course. When the beautiful Ann and Sonia weren't around he was capable of using the hard-earned money from collecting botanical specimens on any porcine tavern tart. One of them weighed at least three hundred pounds. When I teased Joe about this he merely said, "She excited me," then went on to something else, his attention span shorter than an average child's.

In other words when Ann arrived I wasn't in the best of shape. Though it was only noon she asked for a gin on the rocks and she stood there wide-eyed when I opened the freezer compartment for ice cubes because the freezer also contained Joe's "frozen zoo," a couple of dozen dead birds he had picked up on his interminable walks. Edna Rathbone had refused to store them in her freezer and I saw no harm in their being in mine. Ann plucked out a blackburnian warbler with its Halloween colors of orange and black, hefted its tiny weight, and then drew it close to her eyes, shaking her head in wonder. I explained that very few people find dead birds in any number, but mostly because they're not looking and their eyes aren't sharp enough. I told her that an ornithologist had once explained to me that a hawk would be able to read a newspaper's classified ads at fifty feet. At the time I thought his words quite homely. Why not a Shakespeare text, or even a bird book at fifty feet?

Ann caught me out, wondering if I was suggesting that Joe could see better because of his accident? I said I doubted it because I had checked with a neurologist friend of Roberto's and he said it was unlikely indeed but that he may have gained greater visual concentration and attentiveness of a peculiar sort. That certainly would be enough to explain his finding so many dead birds. She laughed and described how closely Joe had studied her body, then downed her gin in two swallows, perhaps out of embarrassment. I made us a little lunch of two veal chops I had thawed for my dinner, plus a smallish portion of *pasta al olio* with garlic and parsley. She politely held off on her desperation over Joe's absence until lunch was finished and then she became difficult indeed.

Obviously she had read too much on closed-head injuries what with a medical library at her disposal in East Lansing. I suspect such information is ill digested unless you are professional and can see the body's whole picture. For instance, I can read until the cows come home about the billions of synapses in the human brain and be amazed and at the same time not comprehend fully what precisely these neurons and synapses spend their time doing. Perhaps the layman is better off mutely accepting that the brain is the least fixable portion of the body. I do recall studying lamb brains in a butcher's shop on Rue Buci in Paris and wondering just how these little pink bundles are the reservoir of the lamb's character and function, the totality of its lambdom as it were.

Ann had gotten up at four A.M. to make the drive from East Lansing so I sent her up to the sleeping loft for a nap. I went outside and sat in a lawn chair on the deck overlooking the river as I have done when troubled for sixty years ever since I discovered riverine hypnosis as a child. The breeze off Lake Superior three miles distant was stiff enough to keep away free-flying noxious pests, and the river herself quickly absorbed the obnoxious pests in my brain. In Chicago Roberto has had to dose me with everything from Valium to Zoloft to Prozac but once I'm up north a few days I can abandon my chemicals in favor of river staring. I'm not saying that a river is a cure-all, only that your brain is unable to maintain its troubled patterns while in concourse with a river. I have supposed that this is the unacknowledged reason why so many people trout fish when most are so incompetent that there is little hope of catching trout on fly and fly rod.

I dozed off and suffered a ponderous nightmare about being lost in the woods, and having my limbs and trunk liquefy and be absorbed by the landscape. When the Gestapo (of all people!) found me I looked the same but I knew an essential part of my character was gone and I wept. Naturally I woke up weeping and then became quite lost thinking of my worthless dog Charley. Years ago in our divorce negotiations neither of us wanted the dog. At first we both pretended we did and both laughed quite heartily, strange behavior in a divorce, when we admitted how willing we both were to give Charley up. Charley's survival tactic seemed to be to have no character whatsoever, but to adopt the character and gestures he was called upon to deliver. He spent his life being non-committal, perhaps because I vastly overtrained him when he was young, gathering in my usual bookish way a dozen texts on how to properly train a pup. My wife insisted I had trained Charley so exhaustively that he had ceased being a dog and only acted doggish when not in my presence. We had a very large yard in Winnetka, a dreadfully monochromatic place, and if I looked out the window secretively just after daylight I might see Charley acting the dog. If he saw or sensed me at the window he would merely sit there come rain or shine. I was in my forties at the time, the true salad days of my illusion of control over my world. It was an unthinkable surprise when my wife said she wanted a divorce which proved her quite untrainable! Since I had willingly given her the house in the divorce she decided finally to keep Charley herself so he wouldn't have to move away from his friends, the other neighborhood dogs that stopped by for a visit. While with me Charley ignored other dogs as if I might not want him to recognize their existence. Much later on I perceived it was lucky we didn't have children.

Sitting there on the deck during intermittent periods of dozing I thought that it's really hard on a soul to admit how much of life we have spent being full of shit. In my case there has recently

been a certain amount of cynical laughter, but also mourning with
each year owning its tombstone. Time always appeared to be repe-
titious. Would that it were at this late date. Yesterday I went with
Dick Rathbone to visit a mixed-blood Chippewa who is reputed to
be the best tracker in this part of the Upper Peninsula. He knew
Joe slightly and pronounced him to be a "spooky fucker." This man
was not at all a drugstore or Hollywood Indian and we were made
as uncomfortable as possible standing there in the junky front yard
of his log shack. He said he would be glad to look for Joe if he was
lost but then that wasn't the problem. Dick insisted that Joe might
be in trouble without his medication and the man said, "There's
nothing to help that boy." He also added that since Joe was angry
he was better off being by himself in that if you're angry in town
you might end up in jail. He also said that no one, and especially
Joe, could be found around here except by his or her permission.
All you had to do to agree was look at the density of forest that
enshrouded the small clearing and shack.

I had told all of this to poor Ann right after lunch and she kept
repeating, "We could at least look." Fool that I am I finally agreed,
thinking it really doesn't get dark until after ten-thirty in the
evening at this northern latitude and it wouldn't hurt us to drive
around aimlessly and perhaps call out "Joe" into the greenery.

I left my beloved deck chair, went inside the cabin, and made
some coffee. I've always liked good hotels where they bring your
coffee to your bedside so I carried a cup up to the loft. She was sleeping on her tummy in her bra and panties, a lagniappe to say the least.
Her figure was quite boyish except for her bottom, which was definitely not boyish. She glanced sleepily over her shoulder and whispered, "You're such a dear." I politely averted my eyes but then
managed to hit my hip on the bedpost, slopping some steaming
coffee on my hand. Naturally it hurt but in a millisecond I decided
to pretend it didn't. I think she saw all this clearly and when I put

the coffee down on the bed table she swiveled into a sitting position and rubbed her eyes. I rushed off, though carefully in that my
legs seemed distant and I certainly didn't want to trip on the stairs.
My mind as an indiscriminate aperture had taken dozens of photos
of her in her pale blue (I think it's called "robin's egg blue") bra
and panties, her modest-sized rounded bottom, and when she sat
up, the diminutive bird's nest of her "mons veneris." Being several
years away from such perceptions I did not realize how vivid they
could quickly become.

     Of course what could a coroner care about an older man's
rather fitful lust? But then in the first place it wasn't my idea to
write this little report. Right now I'm trying to describe the change
in my perceptions that allowed me to unequivocally understand
what happened to Joe. I daresay no one else understands more than
the part of the story that is directly contiguous to them. For instance,
when Joe says in his notebook, "I have looked at my beech tree
from a hundred directions," I know both what tree he's talking
about (not the tree in his accident), and also his rather playful experiments in perception which, because of his injury, he was capable of making. In his notebook he is frequently talking to God,
or better yet, god. It took me a great deal of time to understand his
peculiar language partly because I did not yet truly understand my
own. For instance, in nearly all of our language we are emotionally
locating and making a case for ourselves every bit as much as we
do in the more childish forms of prayer. Joe showed me once, for-
tunately an easy walk, a particular enormous beech tree on the west
end of Au Sable Lake that he looks at from a hundred different
directions marked by sticks and five different distances in concen-
tric rings. To him the beech tree has a discerningly separate appearance from each of the five hundred points, so much so that it boggles
him, amuses him, makes him joyful, or did anyway before he drank
too much of Lake Superior. Multiply this by the thousands of places

he walked and studied, perhaps in a less structured manner, and you'll understand my initial problem of comprehension. Who is this man? He laughs like a baboon in the Lincoln Park zoo.

What a mudbath we had, literally and figuratively. We "moved out" at four in the afternoon, to use a military term. Ann packed a quart of water and some pathetic granola bars, the kind of hopeless yuppie food that even our dog Charley rejected, sulking off with his tail well under his belly. I have a fine four-wheel-drive vehicle, quite expensive but then I wished to counter unpleasant early memories of getting stuck with Dick Rathbone on our brook trout forays. We stopped at Dick's and Edna, kindly enough, packed us two pieces of chocolate cake, then asked me to point out on Dick's wonderful old detailed D.N.R. map just where we were headed. Edna is somewhat cynical about me in that we had a mild flirtation forty years before, and it's well known in the local community that I'm phenomenally incompetent in the woods, no matter my nearly sixty years in the area.

Of course I should have known better but then I never do. Once in Paris I was nearly in tears from not being able to find my hotel and when I received surly instructions I was only a block away. I had stayed at this hotel for years but then streets in the Varenne area look very similar except to locals, though this is a lame excuse. Besides, while looking for Joe I'd have Ann with me, though later it occurred to me that Ann was scarcely a licensed guide.

For Edna's benefit I made a tiny "x" on the map in a blank area which cartographers call a "sleeping beauty." There's nothing there except itself and two small crisscrossing logging roads, and a smallish creek that emerges from a large swamp that surrounds the hummock whereon Joe built his small shelter which the D.N.R. heroically tore to pieces. These are the same people who readily issue permits to Republican developers to defile the environment in every conceivable way. Edna immediately told us not to go into this area but I assured her we weren't getting out of our vehicle, which still stopped short of pleasing her. Everyone tries to please Edna. Joe even willingly accompanied her to the Lutheran church one Sunday morning so the congregation could pray that he be healed. This is not to be confused with the new American use of the word "healing" where the most terrifying human disasters are expected to be healed before the blood is dry on the pavement.

So off we went with light hearts considering Joe's supposed predicament. He was much more likely to be truly lost in town than in the woods. Someone saw him in a back alley checking his compass. For curious reasons having to do with intuition rather than circumstantial evidence I have suspected that Joe and old Edna have made love now and then. She's in her early sixties but why not? She's rather handsome in an odd Finnish way.

We were barely out of town before Ann began talking about things with a great deal of emotional content: love, death, art. I said I had to work into these areas slowly. She actually tweaked my ear before saying that maybe I was like the rest of the culture, especially the movies, where deep emotion is expressed by car crashes, gun shots, explosions, someone staring at a computer screen, meaningful glances, women on top in bed juggling around in a bow to the faux feminists. No one could actually talk about anything deeper than the cultural patina presumably because screenwriters and directors have no talent at meaningful human speech.

This put me in a huff, which in turn doubtless caused me to make my first wrong turn, the tip-off on one being that the road abruptly ended at the river. I pretended that this was on purpose though I could see Ann had her doubts. The river was in a gorge far below us and Ann stood close to the edge, which made me nervous what with being a victim of vertigo. On my countless trips up from Chicago I have to drive through Wisconsin rather than Michigan in order to avoid the vast Mackinac Bridge. Until the mid-fifties you could take a ferry across the Straits. Why war against my limitations? Those extraordinary individuals that appear to break through human limits frequently have unendurable lives. Or so it seems. Of course in Joe's case it didn't appear to be his choice but maybe part of it was. He had logged over a year in various hospitals. What better motive was needed to spend a life as a free-roaming primate? Why give up your life for doctors to toy with your head at vast profit when, according to his mother, Joe never had the slightest chance to return to what we wanly call a normal life. He had lost his functional intelligence or that part of it most valued in society, the ability to make a living.

After about fifteen minutes of pondering my next verbal move, and having my vehicle coming to yet another riverine dead end, I reached for my compass in the glove compartment, brushing against my companion which made me forget that you can't take an accurate compass reading in a vehicle because of all the metal. I decided to taunt her with piths and gists, fragments of excoriating wisdom from world literature. She asked for it, I thought. It became quite fun because I concealed authorship and pretended the ideas were my own and was intrigued when she caught me on two of the first three, even though I translated the thoughts into common, slangy language.

"I think that if you're really too conscious it's the same as being diseased," I said at which she replied, "Clumsy Dostoyevsky."

"Stare into a big hole in the ground long enough and it stares back into you." She paused at this one, then said, "Big hole is a bullshit version of 'abyss,' Nietzsche. Try harder." She also added that literary folks like us couldn't put together a whole picture because they were frightened at settling for less than the ultimate. She was amused when I butchered D. H. Lawrence's "The only aristocracy is consciousness" into "Oddly, the only unique possession we can have is the level of consciousness." I defended myself by saying that the reason I went into commercial real estate and book dealing was because at an early age, say nineteen, I admitted my mind was far too ordinary to become a writer, and that from an early age I had veiled my essential corniness by becoming prematurely querulous.

"Your parents must have stomped the shit out of you," she laughed. This was a bit too much for me to handle so I stared out my side window fearing that tears would form. Why hadn't I brought a thermos of martinis?

"There's a point at which the exposed heart never recovers." This was tit for tat and the Rilke nailed her through the heart. I could almost feel her throat swell and her tears begin to emerge. We were back smack-dab in Joe's territory, and consequently her own. She loved a man who had run into a beech tree on his motorcycle and she would likely think of it on her deathbed. One couldn't really presume that he loved her equally but that was now beside the point. I handed her a fine linen handkerchief, one of a dozen I had bought in London. She looked at it closely, handed it back, and took tissues from her purse.

"Goddamn the world," she screamed and I slammed on the brakes with sweat fairly bursting from my forehead. There's a lot of screaming in the media in general but you rarely hear a scream in actual life.

After about three hours when it was seven in the evening we emerged on a highway. This was puzzling because the highway number told us we were a full twenty miles off course. I was all for throwing in the towel and heading for a mediocre restaurant in the next town at the suggestion of which Ann became disgusted. I had a small

Xeroxed county map that they sell in local stores to tourists for a quarter. However, the map was poor and blurred and besides I hadn't packed along my reading glasses. I was able to show Ann our present location and she assumed the role of navigator with my heart sinking when I realized it would be a full hour on slow two-tracks before we could even reach the general area where we pre-sumed Joe to be. Meanwhile Ann was driving me batty by rambling on about medical details she had researched, all of which seemed to ignore the severity of Joe's injuries proven by dozens of tests that did not exclude the visual treats of the MRI and the CAT scan. Ann admitted she had read the three-inch-thick scrapbook of medical reports Joe's mother had collected, but then she had been through the scrapbook in late March and simple hope was begin-ning to overcome her rationality. She even mentioned a charismatic healer she had heard of who lived down on the Mexican border of Texas. Now she was close to touching my true "bête noire," the loathsome arena of the occult. All Joe needed least was to be hauled off to face some geek charlatan. The occult is always the excres-cence of our fear of death which is also the fear of the realities that surrounded us. I had dabbled a bit in the subject in a literary sense until in the late fifties when I began to read Loren Eiseley (sad that few, if any, scientists can write as well as this man) and also an article by the great Yale professor G. E. Hutchinson called "Homage to Santa Rosalia, or Why Are There So Many Kinds of Animals?" The mystery is in the products of earth herself not in the workings of vaporous goblins. Of course I went on and on until she demanded I stop.

It was at this point, about nine in the waning evening but still with plenty of light, that we thought we saw a partially nude figure cross the narrow road perhaps fifty yards ahead of us. The figure seemed to be in the act of leaping. I had just turned on NPR out of Marquette for music to soothe our abraded nerves, in this case

Brahms whom I don't care for. Even at this important juncture I must render my opinions! Anyway, I sped up until we reached the point we agreed on. She began yelling "Joe" and I closely examined the damp, sandy road for tracks, at first finding nothing but then on the far edge there was a deeply embedded heel print of the figure landing. I turned to see Ann running into the woods continuing to yell "Joe." I followed at a slower pace, tracking her by her voice. I wasn't very far into the woods before I sensed it was all a bad idea. I turned around, hopefully to determine the way I had come. The contemptible Reagan had said, "If you've seen one tree, you've seen them all." I immediately recognized eleven kinds of trees and shrubs but the predominant reality was the din of mosquitoes. Ann's voice faded in the distance and my insides quavered at the thought that we would both become hopelessly lost. Above the creepy whine of the mosquitoes I seemed to hear something else, almost like music. Of course. It was the despised Brahms on the vehicle's radio. I was saved but not so Ann. I walked back, the music becoming more fulsome and melodious, thinking I would pay ten thousand dollars for a Sapphire martini. It's all "dead money" anyway; money destined to nieces and nephews as my manner of living hasn't made the slightest inroads in the principal of my portfolio, an ugly word except where it pertains to the work of an artist. Why in God's name shouldn't I fork over an even ten grand for a martini, not that one was available in at least fifteen miles?

I honked the horn until I became tearful at this very bleak sound. The "beep, beep, beep" of children's stories doesn't do it justice. Beep a horn deep in the woods if you want to redefine your notion of the "forlorn"; the sound quickly baffles and muffles itself in the greenery. Lonesome Norm beeping the horn.

After about a half-hour Ann emerged from the woods asking why I had kept beeping the horn? When asked, she said she came out of the woods the same way she went in. Unfortunately I made a miscue when I turned the vehicle around. It was now getting dark and I backed into a ditch containing water. Four-wheel drive doesn't work when the car frame is on the ground and the hood is slanted upward as if it were a plane taking off. Luckily there was mosquito repellent in the glove compartment and Ann was kind enough not to call me a stupid shit. There was a full hour of Mozart on NPR before Dick Rathbone showed up and towed us out of the ditch which I knew he would. Show up, that is. While he hooked up the chain I was sure I saw a face in the woods where his truck lights were shining but said nothing.

Back at the cabin I made the dreamed-of martinis, also sandwiches because it was midnight and too late to cook dinner. When Dick had dropped us off he said he was going to return to Joe's area at first light and hang a little bag with his pills from a tree limb close to the old shelter. Joe had ditched his telemetric devices as he often did.

Ann was nearly asleep sitting up and I insisted she take my sleeping loft while I was content with a sofa before the fireplace because even the smallest wood fire on a warm summer night can soothe my brain. I recalled reading in William Calvin, a theoretical neurophysiologist, that most of the mass or volume of the brain is insulation for the countless billions of electrical impulses. Well, staring into a wood fire can slow these down to a manageable level. While waiting for Dick Rathbone to tow us out Ann said she had been awarded a partial travel grant from the university to go to St. Petersburg in Russia for a month in the coming winter. She had always wanted to go there in the winter and needed to visit some Turgenev scholars. She said idly while spraying on more mosquito dope that she might not be able to go because she was short of money. I had been to this splendid city back in the seventies before communism thawed into whatever and I insisted to Ann that I had a hotshot travel agent in Chicago who I'd get to put her up for the month in the Hotel Europa. I didn't want her to freeze her lovely butt off in some wretched student quarters. She teased that if I was after her "lovely butt" that was a very expensive way to go about it. We let the subject go over mutual discomfort. Staring into my beech fire I thought that if at my age you could buy a memory of this quality for ten grand or so it would be the ultimate bargain. What a bold thought, for me anyway. Is not Ann worth a portion of my dead money? If a martini was worth ten grand what improbable amount was Ann worth?

II

It was the hottest first week of August that anyone could remember, and these local folks are experts at remembering weather. Maybe all writers telling a story are in fact doing a coroner's inquest? For instance, this morning my left hand had an irritating tremble when I read the newspaper. I attributed it at first to the usual information that makes one livid, but then decided to admit the tremble might very well be another downward step in the aging process. As an experiment I concocted a glandular fantasy about tupping Ann on the picnic table and the trembling stopped. This is my kind of science. What magic potion could my brain have delivered?

Joe reappeared after five days in the woods, rather shameless over the worries he had caused us. He said he was sorry and then went swimming off the pier. He was pulled aboard exhausted by a cabin cruiser at least five miles out in Lake Superior on a warm but blustery day. The cabin cruiser folks were appalled and called the Coast Guard which dispatched a boat owned by the local Coast Guard auxiliary now that the local station is defunct.

Joe was gone five days because he was digging a cave near the site of his torn-down shelter. "They won't find my cave," he said to me in Dick Rathbone's backyard, then turned to Ann a few feet from me but evidently in a parallel universe in his mind and said, "They won't find my cave." Is he a sick dog who wishes to hide, a mammal who finds safety in secrecy, a wounded young man trying valiantly to sort out his confused mind? I must say I observed him closely for signs of unhappiness and self-pity but found none. Something in his bruised skull had accepted his condition in perhaps the same manner that his dog, Marcia, accepted his errant behavior. As a nickel-plated gourmand I asked him what he and Marcia had found to eat during their five days of absence. He said, "Animal meat" and left it at that. Dick later told me that when he checked out my cabin in April Marcia had managed to catch a large snowshoe rabbit. When the rabbit zigged and zagged at top speed, which it does to escape an ordinary predator, Marcia had run straight through the zigs and zags and was able to intercept the animal.

So he probably ate rabbits, presumably roasted, and God knows what else as he ignored further inquiries. When he returned, Edna remarked that both he and his clothes were relatively clean which could be explained by a creek nearby the site. This proved he remembered childhood lessons of hygiene though it should be noted that many species of mammals tend to bathe regularly.

Naturally Ann rejoined Joe at the tiny cabin behind the Rathbone's. The first evening without her I seethed with jealousy so Roberto's inept remarks were not totally off base. The tombstones of aging were coming up out of the earth like mushrooms or, better yet, toadstools. The old toad sits in his cabin with moist eyes, the first time he's been alone in five nights, though he's in training after having spent much of his life flying solo. His wife used to say, "I'm not really here, am I?" Joe was doubtless pounding away at poor Ann. Poor Ann indeed. Women are much more feral in their lovemaking than men, and despite a fire in the fireplace my brain kept raising images of their coupling and his evidently improbable potency, or so implied Sonia on her last trip.

When I awoke and made coffee I was startled to see Joe and Ann sitting out on the picnic table waiting for me to get up. At first I was irritated because I like to start the day with an hour of reading and I had reached a chapter in William Calvin's *How Brains Think* called "Syntax as a Foundation of Intelligence." There was also the problem that when my eyes first opened in that hypnagogic state between sleeping and waking my mind had concocted a dreamlike plan that was both generous and selfish. I own a small winter adobe in southern New Mexico left to me by my father from when he resigned from Cleveland Cliffs to go with Phelps Dodge whose questionable labor practices are maddening. I was thinking I could put Joe up in the nearby village, mostly Latino, and hire someone local to keep track of him. Latinos are traditionally more tolerant of people like Joe than we are. Of course this would mean that Ann would come for visits. In the Iago part of my impulse that was part of the plan. But then Joe wouldn't freeze to death or have to be locked up in the coming winter.

Now they were sitting on the picnic table at seven in the morning and I waved them in for coffee. I ended up frying Joe and Marcia a dozen eggs while Ann and I had dry toast. Ann drives one of those minuscule subcompacts, useless in this area, and she wondered if I was willing to drop them off as near as possible to the site of Joe's cave, still several miles from the nearest two-track. Joe needed to retrieve a present for me and Ann said she had to leave early the next morning. I've always loved even the smallest presents. Of course I would chauffeur them. We glanced over at Joe who was munching dog kibble from a sack I kept for Marcia's visits. Ann was horrified and slapped the dog food out of his hand. He burst into tears for the first time, or the first time I had seen him do so. She jumped up so fast she knocked over her chair and leaned over and embraced him. I could feel my face sadden because her lovely butt in her tight hiking trousers was inches from my nose and, at the same time, I was grieving over the embarrassing incident. He simply didn't recognize dog food. Marcia was having some with her fried eggs, why shouldn't he?

Off we went and I was proud that I drove directly to the place which was close to where I had backed into the ditch. At the last moment I decided to walk along with them, not for the childish motive of seeing my present without an undue wait, but from the ticklish idea that how can I understand the inside without going outside and taking a look from that vantage point. Besides, if I don't discover the earth in this life when am I going to understand it? This is admittedly a daffy notion but my brain was quite abuzz. Up and down I go, round and round I go, that is the human condition, but there must be a limited number of knots that can be tied in a single rope. Calvin quotes Sue Savage-Rumbaugh and Roger Lewin saying, "All organisms with complex nervous systems are faced with the moment-by-moment question that is posed by life: What shall I do next?"

I can't say my walk on the wild side went especially well. I fell down several times which in itself wasn't bad because I couldn't recall seeing the earth so closely. The third time it happened I began to wonder if it was partly why the Muslims do prostrations. I seemed to remember that the act of prostration also occurred in many cultures. Maybe bankers, politicians, and suchlike should begin the day out in their yards touching their noses to the Great

Mother. Of course, I haven't done so myself so my sudden reverence might be tainted. It simply doesn't exist in any viable form though often when I'm in the woods, say picking blueberries for pancakes near my cabin, I can sense the reverence creeping up my legs like standing in tropical waters.

I was falling down because during much of our arduous hike the ferns were as high as our waists or higher. Joe, without saying anything, demonstrated a more shuffling gait where you push your feet out close to the ground, insuring a certain balance when you run into an invisible dead tree limb or smallish stump.

I was quite impressed with the cave itself. I recognized Dick Rathbone's green-handled garden spade near the entrance, which Joe had concealed by transplanting viburnum and other shrubs. The cave itself was quite small with the floor covered with ferns and pine boughs which in turn were covered by untanned deer hides. People salt them down but tanning hides is laborious and to have them done professionally is expensive. There was a Coleman lantern, a cheapish plastic poncho, several bird and flora guidebooks, and a laminated map. I could imagine Joe reading the guidebooks even though his memory might recapture the information for only seconds in regard to the photos and drawings. He was, however, unable to imagine remembering the meaning of words but not the visual aspects they represented. None of us, not so afflicted, could cross this peculiar gap. I moved back quickly when a large, fat garter snake oozed out from under a deer hide. Joe croaked with laughter and Ann faked an untroubled posture.

Joe took the shovel and we followed him up a hillock and down a long, steep embankment to a creek. While Joe dug in the bank with the shovel I walked down the bank fifty yards, stripped to my undershorts, and sat in a pool of cool, rushing water to rinse off my sticky body. Ann took a bath herself near where Joe was digging and, ever the voyeur, I regretted moving so far downstream.

Joe shouted and held up an object I couldn't determine from that distance. He shouted again more loudly and I hastily drew on my pants over my wet legs and underpants. I hopped barefoot upstream and Joe handed me what seemed to be an enormous bear skull, very dark colored as it seemed stained by oil or tar or creosote-like substance. I only recognized it immediately as a bear skull because there is one above the fireplace in the tavern, though not nearly as large as this one. When he handed it to me it was so heavy I nearly dropped it, as if the skull had become petrified by its long burial. I was so nonplussed that I barely gave the wet, nearly nude Ann a glance though I discovered later my brain and eyes in their role of apertures took an adequate number of photos.

"What in hell is this?" I yelled, quite dumbfounded.

"Bear," Joe said. "Old bear." He pursed his lips and raised a finger to signal a secret, then pointed upstream where the creek emerged from a vast and foreboding swamp.

I smelled the oily tang of the skull with a slight shudder. I've always had an aversion to bones but in these woods you rarely see bones or antlers because we have so many porcupines that feed upon them. I recalled Jack London's phrase about always seeing "the skull beneath the skin" when he was drinking too much which was always. During summers as a boy up here I'd read and re-read Zane Grey and Jack London and felt quite manly with my hunting knife and single-shot .22 rifle, but even then I never went the extra mile into the woods but a mile less. A goofy friend back then, who became a renowned landscape painter, would always become lost and my parents drummed the terrors of the forest into my brain making me quite cowardly. When you paint the world with blame parents are the most convenient canvases. Of course later, in the fifties, I think, a little girl over near Brimley (east of here) was killed by a bear. Black bears have killed far more people than the fabled grizzly but then there are far more black bears. My mind whirred with irrelevancies because of the shock of the strange skull. Bones are certainly a lacuna in my education but I knew this skull couldn't have come from a black bear, but must have been from a creature before the glacial ice age some thirteen thousand years ago.

Joe struggled for words then did a dancing pantomime in the creek, showing how he had found the skull in the creek muck with his feet. He took the bear skull back from me, then scrubbed off the tarry substance with sand and replaced it in the hole in the bank for safekeeping. My present was evidently going to remain under his control. He reached in his pocket and handed me a massive, stained incisor tooth for reassurance. I almost didn't want the tooth but knew I had to be gracious.

Meanwhile, Ann stood there in wet undies with her brow furrowed, the human habit when the unknown is radically enlarged if only for a moment. Joe had obviously shown us something quite out of the ordinary but we were without the knowledge to perceive what it meant. Just moments after the skull was re-buried I was already questioning if it was as large as it seemed, and in my mind's eye I wondered at the shovel shape between its forehead and nose. I had visited the Field Museum in Chicago dozens of times during my childhood and right up until my last trip last year, but the skeletons of mammals weren't my favorites. I did realize that Joe's bear skull probably wouldn't fit comfortably in a bushel basket and I failed to remember anything that large at the museum. I mentioned to Ann that once on a trip to California my parents had taken me to the obligatory La Brea Tar Pits and it shared a similar odor to Joe's bear skull.

Well, there you have it. I was slightly knocked off balance and I've never regained it. It wasn't as if things went downhill after that day but they certainly took a different direction. On the way out of the woods toward my car I fell with a resounding thump on my ass, painfully bruising my tailbone. Joe carried me piggyback the last half mile which was, naturally, humiliating but then I didn't quite care. When we got to my vehicle Joe became more spasmodic than usual and Ann blamed the extra exertion. She was particularly worried because he was already at the maximum dosage of the pill intended to relax his considerable musculature. She rejected anything to eat and I dropped them off at her car downhill from the cabin. She embraced me good-bye, warmly with her entire body for a change, which momentarily alleviated my tailbone pain.

I made myself an overlarge pan of corned-beef hash and studied the bear tooth which was longer than my forefinger while I ate, recalling how Marcia had given the skull a quick sniff, a brief lick, growled, and retreated, then stared off into the greenery in displacement. I took a nap then and had dreams with striking images of Ann's body that unfortunately bled into a welter of botanical specimens of leaves that never existed so far as I knew. I awoke at twilight grinding my teeth and discovering I had broken a bicuspid. Oh fuck me, I thought, at least it doesn't hurt because I'd already had a root canal in the tooth, and thus the nerve was dead.

Just before dark Dick Rathbone arrived with a very irritated game warden who was investigating a crime. Two telemetric collars, one off a black bear and the other off a timber wolf, had been traced to a trash can at a tourist stop near McMillan, east of Seney. For an unannounced reason the game warden thought Joe was involved, no matter that Joe has a specific aversion to firearms since his accident, finding the sharp, loud noises to be unbearable. According to the game warden two game biologists were seeing a great deal of research go down the drain because now the animals couldn't be traced. Someone had obviously poached the animals and disposed of the collars. I asked the game warden, who was becoming a bit brash and cheeky for my taste, if he didn't think it was a bit coincidental that two species fifteen miles apart (he had said this) lost their collars in the same period of time. He said, "Don't tell me my business," and I asked him to leave at once, first demanding his superior's name who turned out to be the same nitwit that had had Joe's shelter torn down. This was supposedly Joe's apparent motive. I recalled in former times liking several old-time game wardens I had met but then the new breed were quite full of themselves as if they were the F.B.I. of the natural world.

My dream of Ann and all the flora she had become came back to me despite my irritable state. I "leafed" through a botanical text and decided that henbane (*Hyoscyamus niger*) most closely resembled what her dream genitalia had become. Maybe the witch's herb was appropriate to this solitary girl who, no matter her avowed rationality, seemed to be disintegrating over her lover's doomed condition. Melancholy as these thoughts were, these were far exceeded when my tongue tip hit my shattered tooth and I wondered what it meant mentally when you grind them so hard you break a tooth?

I had read somewhere that consciousness is predatory and when your consciousness becomes deeper and more complicated there are that many more layers you are obligated to process. This is definitely a discouraging notion. Since I was a young man I have frequently thought, and not all that unpleasantly, that I lived within a gray egg of my own making, an egg I had furnished carefully and selectively myself, and now it was beginning to crack. The fearful question, of course, is do all things that crack sink?

My ruminations were paltry compared to the yellow orb of the moon rising through the white pines and hemlock at the rear of my clearing in the forest. I sat on the picnic table, my butt still a little painful from its collision with earth, thinking idly that if Joe did have anything to do with the telemetric collars I doubted that he could have disposed of them some forty miles away, or would have had the sense to do so. But there was Ann who, if she had seen the telemetric collars aside from Joe's own, would have known something was amiss and surely would have wiped off the fingerprints before driving off to get rid of them at a safe distance.

I have small tolerance for mysteries, crime, and magic, that sort of thing. They aren't included within my gray egg but there was certainly the question of how anyone could get the collars off the animals without a tranquilizer gun or rifle. Since Joe had dug a grave for a baby bear only a mile down the river from my cabin he seemed a terribly unlikely candidate for killing a bear and a wolf.

The picnic table was too hard on my sore butt so I retrieved my sleeping bag and a large glass of very old Calvados I keep for special occasions. The Calvados had only been bottled a few years ago but it had been in a barrel since 1933, my birth year. I bought two bottles of it on Rue Madeleine in Paris for an inconceivable amount of money just after I retired. Now I held the glass up and looked at the moon through the amber liquid, dismissing the thought of what Joe and Ann might be doing at this hour. Sitting there on the folded sleeping bag, which was a fine cushion, I was stupidly amazed to realize how similar Ann's body was to my ex-wife's. The only way we had been truly compatible had been sexually and we had met several times in the year after our divorce for lovemaking. The divorce dug a three-year hole in my life but she had been much more resilient, re-marrying a prosperous man a few years younger than herself and, of all things, adopting two Oriental orphans from Laos. She had never acted very motherly around me but then I was scarcely a father type. My parents had been, in my view, cold, mean-minded Republicans so I thought of myself as a Democrat from an early age.

There was a whippoorwill calling from up the river, which seemed to make me drowsy. I stretched out the sleeping bag and lay back thinking how in Joe's case fate had reduced itself to an injury, how driven by the often malevolent god of booze a moment's carelessness had been a dramatic lesson against the concept of fairness, of course, but then history, if you're truly human, must reduce itself to the individual case. I still remember way back when waiting at the Drake to meet someone for breakfast and reading *The New York Times* in which Mao had said that China felt secure because she could afford to lose a half billion people in a war and still survive as a country, a statement of incomprehensive evil. Oh fuck history. I heard an owl and several bats crossed the face of the moon. A slight breeze from the swamp to the west smelled agreeably pelvic and then I slept, quite unable to rise and go into the cabin. We're not supposed to be trapped by our shelters but we are.

When I awoke at daylight it was raining softly but not enough to penetrate my sleeping bag. I traced a finger across my wet forehead and said, "This is me" as if to remind myself. The first sunlight was peeking through the trees in the same place that the moon had risen the evening before. The nature of the clearing around my cabin, which is normally brutally fixed in its sameness, looked peculiar. Through a hole formed by two adjoining branches of a birch tree I could see a raven in the sky but only for a moment. A chickadee, a somewhat pathetic little bird, stared at me from the handle of my barbecue grill not three feet away, but then maybe he thought I was a pathetic life-form. When it rained I had seen Joe looking upward as if trying to identify single drops. My skin tingled when I heard a noise and saw movement in the bushes just beyond the edge of my clearing. Several times this summer I've had a mother bear and two cubs visit my large plastic garbage can, usually just before dark or at dawn. When the garbage can is empty they swat it and bite holes in it. At that moment I didn't want a visit so I sang out, "*O solo mio*" and was amused at my choice. There was a crashing in the brush that sounded like a solitary deer, which you can determine by the brief space between the sound of the landing and the leaping.

I felt mildly vertiginous getting out of the bag and off the picnic table. It was pleasurable in that it was a fresh sensation. The vertigo is that if I'm not going to continue doing what I'm already doing what am I going to do? There was the idea of setting fire to the cabin but then why should I blame it? There was also the idea of selling the approximately ten thousand volumes of my book collection in my Chicago condominium or running away which is childish because it presumes there is someone to look for you. I could fall in love like the great Picasso did over and over, buy a hundred Viagra pills, and blow out my heart making a sensual stew, which sounded like the best plan yet.

For the time being I fetched a bucket from the cabin and set off to pick blueberries to make pancakes for breakfast. There was a fine patch of the berries only several hundred yards from my cabin and my plan was to pick the berries, drink a cup of coffee while making the batter, and drink a large glass of good Sauternes with the pancakes, and then back to bed.

I had the bucket half full when Ann came thumping down my rumply two-track in her miserable subcompact. She said she was on her way home to East Lansing and simply wanted to say good-bye, which was a transparent fib. Her face was cold and her arms were crossed tightly on her chest, all in contrast to her white sleeveless blouse and short, blue-flowered summer skirt. The great Picasso would have leapt on her like a flying squirrel, or so I imagined. She was just standing there so to treat myself I knelt and picked a cluster of berries next to her left calf. Her knee was definitely a knee. Blue flowers on blue skirt, blue berries. I held out my palm and she ate some blueberries, then in a staccato rush poured forth her torments. She was trying to become pregnant by Joe! But then her mother was terribly religious and there was a burden in bearing an illegitimate child. Dick Rathbone was a mean bastard as Joe's legal guardian and wouldn't allow them to marry. Maybe I could marry her, with of course no legal obligations, assuming she was able to get pregnant. I tried to divert her by saying that marrying Joe would be an inter-species marriage. She yelled "Fuck you," and jumped in her car, taking off so fast she spun some sand in my berry bucket. I meant to rinse them anyway.

According to Joe he first took note of the beast he had mentioned the month before while standing on various high hills either overlooking large expanses of woods or Lake Superior. It took a full afternoon for me to interpret what he was saying, aided to some degree by his notebook which was mostly gibberish. I have no doubt that he thinks he is writing something quite different from what he actually writes, just as when he is speaking he often is saying other than he intends. Anyway, this so-called "beast" reveals its location when your vantage point has altitude by a specific patch of stillness in the woods or on the water on very windy days. There are a number of other details I will add later on the nature and various shapes of this beast.

Well, Mister Coroner, don't be ready to assume that I took Joe seriously on this matter, but then I've always found why a man believes something to be so more interesting than what he believes. This is not a fine point but something big as all outdoors. You have doubtless sawed a hole in Joe's skull to determine the condition of its contents. At least I'm told this procedure is "de rigueur" in an autopsy, but surprise (!), what you discovered is what we've already known. What I am telling you is how that bruised gray matter drew him so far north on the watery night, very likely swimming after his beast, whether real or imagined. Of course, I asked Joe what the creature looked like and he bumbled out that it had three different appearances.

I can't say that all this was pleasant to think about over my pancakes and Sauternes, a Château d'Yquem of a moderately good year. There was the question of why drink a three-hundred-dollar bottle of wine for breakfast but why not? I was simply enough celebrating having slept outdoors for the first time in thirty years and I meant to do so again. And astoundingly enough, I didn't go back to bed after breakfast. I assumed I had slept poorly outside but not so. Almost as a joke, but also to soften my forever-nagging sense of insecurity, I strapped on my pistol and set off for a hike.

I hadn't gone more than a few hundred yards when I was stopped by the thought I had read somewhere to the effect that our perceptions are our only internally generated map of the world. I wondered immediately about the map generated by the hawk that can read the classifieds at fifty feet, or the bear whose preposterous skull signaled that he or she had no natural enemies, or better yet the map generated by Joe's wounded brain and how different it might be from that of the rest of us. This made my tongue probe my broken tooth. In one of the books Roberto sent from Chicago it said that every single brain differs significantly from every other brain. In the simplest terms it takes a lot of training to make them behave the same. Some of Joe's training was obviously destroyed by his injury never to be regained. What, if anything, took its place? Was there even a shred of the compensatory? It is obvious that he spends a great deal of time enjoying himself but that seems to be in areas in which he is least like us. He appears to have a freedom of a different sort that slips off the edges of the definition.

I looked around at my surroundings closely and determined I was on a horseshoe bend of the river in an area where the brook trout fishing used to be particularly good. I got on all fours and crept up to the mossy bank seeing several fish in the category we used to call "keepers." These trout spent their entire lives underwater except for the briefest forays into the air for flies. I stared absurdly at the dozen or so species of trees in the vicinity. None were perfect or near-perfect specimens of their kind. I was aware from my botanical dabblings just how many tree diseases there were, literally hundreds. People generally only think of such matters before Christmas when they are quite bent on the "perfect" Christmas tree, but these species are scarcely wild, tended and trimmed as they are in vast plantations which are mostly biological deserts. There are no perfect trees any more than there are perfect human beings.

Upstream from where I knelt on the bank I knew there was a very large section of a white pine log that didn't reach the mouth of the river during logging days. It is at least seven feet in diameter. When we were very young Dick Rathbone used to concoct ways that we might drag the log out and sell it for a large sum, though to whom was in question. Somewhat like Joe's prehistoric bear the log was a relic of another time.

My location had become eerie with memories of fishing expeditions of more than fifty years ago. I looked longingly at the high-forested banks on the other side of the river. I checked up and downstream and selected the shallower spot, wading across the water which was only thigh deep though quite cold. It was exhilarating to do something so totally out of the ordinary, at least in my own life. I meandered around in the forest for an hour or so catching brief sight of the pileated woodpecker which is nearly as large as a crow. Naturally I was quite lost but quickly settled my emotions when I determined I was walking the wrong way from the sun, an easy enough perception if you avoid panic. When I reached the river again it seemed to be flowing in the wrong direction rather than my own. I calmed myself, opting for the river's sense of direction. Now I was headed again toward my cabin and stopped on the bank for a rest near where Joe had buried the baby bear who had never seen the light except for a few months of spring. Sentimental tears formed but perhaps this sort of mourning really isn't sentimental. As a geezer I had a perfect right to empathize with a creature whose life was truncated barely past its beginning. Mortality indeed. We're always standing on a trapdoor with wobbly hinges. The little bear perhaps had only been out of its birth den two months. Joe was probably at least halfway there at the point of his beech-tree collision. Of course he was still technically alive, but I was beginning to think that in some ways he might have a distinct edge on the rest of us. At sixty-seven I was doubtless seven-eighths "there," a matter on which it is impossible to draw conclusions.

I had long since evolved a system wherein I was always right but of late there have been tremors where the very concepts of right and wrong in the conduct of one's life recede into the ready-made, off-the-rack past. Life seems so unlike, in certain moments, what I expected it to be, and I have begun to question Joe's effect on me.

Sitting there against the warm bank of the river I could lay back and see the protruding roots of trees, bushes, grass. Turning on my side I could see Sonia's butt prints on the sand spit where she had sat a few weeks before. Across the river a smallish trout was rising to midges in the cool shadow of an undercut bank, then was joined by others, one apparently of large size. There was the ever so slight urge to drag my jumble of fly-fishing equipment out of the closet, unused for a decade in favor of nothing in particular.

I had noticed something troubling which quickly became amusing, on recent trips to the grocery store, or the saloon for my occasional Sapphire martini. The populace at large, and especially his old friends who were now distant from him, had begun to talk about Joe in somewhat mythological terms as if he weren't quite part of the human community, or had ceased to be. Often the descriptions or gossip referred to "sightings" as if Joe were a rare ornithological or mammalian specimen. He was seen crossing the highway in a swampy area after midnight on a moonlit night. In June he made love to a big fat woman on the beach for hours. He was a millionaire (not quite true but close) whom the doctors had bilked (possibly). He was seen by an old Finn and a park ranger walking next to a bear (hard to believe). Beautiful women (Sonia and Ann) liked him because he was weird. He slept in a cave (how did this get out?). He had become a religious nut (a park ranger had glassed him gesturing at the sky).

You really couldn't blame the locals. I had a greeting knowledge of nearly every one of the four hundred souls in the village and in the summer they gossiped most often about the foibles and idiocies of their lifeblood, the tourists. There are utterly natural resentments here. In the winter they could talk about each other or the weather. Since I had been around before most of them were born I was in a category best described as "odd rich guy." I admired the ingenuity and intelligence of many of them who, strangely enough, would have become great successes in the outer world about which they never showed much interest. They were all experts in human limitations, and knew their own in a way city people rarely do.

Joe was snoozing on my sleeping bag on the picnic table when I returned. Marcia was full of the kind of wriggles of which only a Labrador retriever is capable. I fetched her an ample chunk of cheddar cheese, her favorite snack. While Joe was asleep I looked closely at the indentations is his skull above his hairline with a momentary admiration for doctors who have to deal with such matters. When I was younger many older folks still referred to doctors as "sawbones," a graphic name indeed. I caught sight of Joe's notebook near his left hand, feeling a touch of dread at its presence because it always entailed the struggle for questions and answers. I was scarcely a therapist, and it was impossible to imagine a professional capable of doing him any good at this point. Still he came to me occasionally carrying the notebook when there was something especially bothering him. A few weeks ago I found myself trying to explain the idea of color and the nature of the spectrum. Also, why don't animals have six legs! Why were all the huge white pines cut down at the turn of the century? Why were the stars colorful? I assumed with the latter that he had seen some of the Hubbell photos in a magazine at the Rathbones' but wasn't sure.

I flipped through the notebook and was quite startled to find a risqué Polaroid photo of Ann taped against a page toward the back. The angle was from the rear and she was on her hands and knees in the briefest blue undies and turning her head with a flashing smile. "Land sakes alive," as codgers used to say. I knew Dick Rathbone had a Polaroid camera from just before his retirement when he was on a project for trapping and examining fish populations. He had shown me photos of the largest specimens. I could imagine Joe holding the camera for this particular photo. It was obviously Ann's attempt at a reminder since he tended to forget all faces but evidently not the sense of touch, smell, the sound of her voice, and scarcely her unique taste.

Joe awoke abruptly with a shudder and reached over the edge of the table and scratched Marcia's head which quickly grounded him. Since I was already caught I handed him his notebook but then he didn't question my snooping. He showed me Ann's photo as if it were a precious, religious relic, then turned to a page where there were four clumsy drawings, the kind you might expect from perhaps a second grader. The first was of a fish, which he demonstrated to be longer than the outsized picnic table, say about ten feet. The drawing reminded me of a lake sturgeon I had seen in the fifties along the beach north of Harbor Springs. The second drawing was clearly a bearded male raven but Joe held out his arms to show that it was somewhat larger than the usual raven. This wasn't alarming in itself because I have learned over the years that maybe one raven out of thirty is demonstrably interested in me so that I feel warm to them. The third drawing was a bit off the charts in that it didn't illustrate any animal I recognized. It somewhat resembled a very round bear but with a largish curved proboscis, and Joe held a hand midway up his chest to show its height. The fourth drawing was the raven superimposed on the bearish figure with the big nose so that they were a single creature.

I was at my wit's end and it took a sweaty half-hour to figure out what he meant by the drawings. It turned out that the beast Joe had mentioned that afternoon down the river when Dick Rathbone, Sonia, and I had found him supposedly changed shapes. In the middle of the day it was a fish and from twilight to about midnight it was the round furry creature shaped like an enormous bowling ball, and then in the middle of the night until mid-morning it was the overlarge raven.

This all filled me with the densest lassitude. My mind cried out for lunch and a long nap. The company of a madman is exhausting, even though you somehow have grown to like him very much. In short, I wanted to be alone but for a change I overcame this banal impulse. It's not like I see myself as a Romantic Hero brooding in solitude on matters of enormous import, if in fact there are any. It's probably more connected to my accumulated wealth and the obvious fact that rich people are usually cagey, wary, suspicious, guarded as if the world were quite set on a uniform effort to get their money, which is also true but so what? The fact that I'm not really a member of any family, group, or community is something I no longer see as virtuous. "I wandered lonely as a cloud" is not necessarily good thinking.

So I indulged Joe's chatter. When he becomes excitable about one out of ten of his words is on the money. When serene he can be as close as one out of two. His animals which, of course, were ridiculous raised him to a pitch I hadn't witnessed before. He was actually trying to convince me not only of their existence but also of their most frequent whereabouts. I was forced to affect an attitude of gullibility to calm him down. Even Marcia had become restless and worried over her master's anxiety. In fact, he was so passionate that for the briefest moment the back of my neck prickled at the idea that this trinity beast might exist, no matter how patently absurd the idea. I have read so many novels with preposterous plots that I end up believing if the writing is of sufficient quality. Maybe we're all fools in this way except for the most redoubtable epistemologists.

Joe's aphasia, his language difficulties, were normally quite endurable and certainly understandable, somewhat on the order of a stutterer whom you like very much, and whose speech difficulties emphasize the importance of what is being said. In this case Joe had lost the trace of humor usually present and his face bulged with veins sticking out in a hopeless effort to explain himself lucidly. He sputtered, paused, wheezed, mumbled, and keened with spit flying through the air. It finally became apparent that he wanted me to see his beast in whatever form, which was the last thing I intended to do.

"O *deus ex machina!*" I was saved by the bell in the form of Dick Rathbone driving into my cabin yard with a large, rather bovine girl I'd guess to be in her late twenties, the third of Joe's girlfriends, and not one to give you that faintly ominous buzz to the testicles. Shirley was plain as day, noon to be exact. She was spontaneous as barbed wire, a young woman of Norwegian extraction, who lived on a farm near Ovid, Michigan, where Joe used to pheasant hunt. She obviously was as stricken with him as Ann. Only Sonia, being a nurse, showed any good sense. Nurses are specialists of the present tense, in reality, as it were.

Shirley had driven north with a splendid, fresh peach pie, which was on the level of some of the best desserts I've had in France. Before we ate the pie she had taken Joe into my cabin toilet and washed him up, then brushed his tangled hair at the picnic table. This all reminded me of the public grooming of chimpanzees. I must say that though Shirley was quite large, nearly six feet and thickish to my taste, her big figure wasn't lumpy in the least and she resembled any sturdy, well-built girl only larger. When at her insistence she and Joe took a river dip (she told him he smelled "gamy") I noted that she was perfectly symmetrical. She had also picked up Marcia as if she was cuddling a kitten and I'm sure Marcia weighed seventy-five pounds. Farm girls!

It's amusing, and I'm sure an anthropologist can explain it, the way men prate and yap how a woman or girl is formed no matter how sloppy and ungainly we men are. I've seen the ugliest bastard in the world rating some poor woman on a one to ten scale, but then I'm sure women must have some vaguely commensurate behavior, largely secret from us.

When they left I was a limp noodle with the identifiable dread that I was going to traipse around in the wilds looking for non-existent beasts. Joe had left his notebook on the picnic table and I was alarmed over the idea that Shirley might have picked it up and seen the garish photo of Ann. Only she hadn't. How often we are alarmed by something that didn't happen. I had once gone to a Chicago Bulls game with Roberto who, rather than merely lusting after the players, was an astute student of the technical aspects of the game and a season-ticket holder. The renowned Michael Jordan had leapt clean over the head of a referee who had suddenly

stopped at mid-court. There had been a sudden moment of silence
in the crowd. No matter how astounding the feat was, for hours
after the game I dreaded that he hadn't succeeded at what he already had done.

I treated myself to an ample martini and leafed through Joe's
notebook, trying but, of course, failing to avoid the photo of Ann.
This geezer trembled again, wondering at the power of a simple
photo when all forms of normal pornography left me cold. Evidently
scientists now know the exact part of the brain where these emotions generate themselves. This pushed me to think of Joe in terms
of "who cares what is wrong but that it is wrong and can't be fixed."

His prose, as such, didn't exist. It was mostly a jumble of
nouns, colors, smells. The bearish figure smelled of "horseshit and
violets." It takes real ability to smell a non-existent beast. "Mud.
Rain. Orange bus. Elephant cloud. Gull cloud. Rock cloud." What
is this but the shapes of things?

I delayed dinner and took one of those truly wonderful hour-
long naps when your body becomes at one with the bed. I awoke
at twilight with all the birds around the cabin saying good night
and the sound of distant thunder coming from the southwest. Both
Joe and Dick Rathbone love a rain because it wipes away older,
blurred animal tracks and everything becomes new again. The year
before, right after a fine late-July rain, Dick had showed me a very
large set of bear tracks in the sand not fifty feet from the door of
the cabin.

When I lifted myself off the bed, glancing habitually at my
watch, part of an insight I had had just before falling asleep returned. Joe's consciousness is totally predatory, hyperthyroid,
because he senses the end, that he's going to die. The injury, and
the massive medical portfolio that attests to this, altered his sense
of time, or destroyed the sense of time necessary to conduct the
business of a culture, a "civilization," as it were. Joe's sense of time

has become hopelessly round while ours is linear. His time is the duration, immediate, of what his senses feed him. Thus a bird's song is time, so is the wind, the slow passing of a particular cloud, trees giving way to other trees, growing hunger or thirst. It is not a clock. His individual universe is totally holographic, so that he moves dimensionally within time's enclosure but quite unrelated to it. In his natural world death is child's play. Of the million and a half living species (some scientists now speculate it is closer to eight million) everything that has lived dies.

This had become a bit heady for me so I made the simplest supper available, a sandwich of Italian sausage fried with green pepper and onions, opened a bottle of Côtes du Rhône, and took my supper outside to enjoy the very last of the light and to watch the moon rise. How upset my parents would have been at such an idea! They permitted themselves nothing out of the ordinary. Unless we were here at the cabin, my father invariably wore a tie for dinner and, what's more, he never spilled on it. He died with a closet full of clean ties, which I gave to our Winnetka yardman, a Jamaican named Cedric, along with fifty or so dress shirts and twenty suits. I even paid to have all the pants shortened two inches. This rather elaborate wardrobe enabled Cedric to become the manager of the yard-grooming service rather than a laborer, though when I saw him over a drink many years later he had become rather bloated and unhappy, complaining that in the old days he used to fuck every day and now that he was behind the desk and well out of shape it was once a week. Success again.

I had a night of intermittent sleep in the cabin, quite upset that the rain was keeping me from my picnic table, my outdoor nest, as it were. At three A.M. I got up and searched through my gear closet for a tarp and used safety pins to wrap it around the sleeping bag. I went out in the rain, naked except for my slippers, and got into the bag only mildly wet. To the east of me there was a thunderstorm

creeping violently north where it would reach the cold air above
Lake Superior and be repelled, re-gather its strength and try again.
For a moment I had the wonderful illusion of seeing a little sign-
post in the sky that said "This way lies madness," and quite like a
college student who feigns instability to simply catch his breath, I
was willing to take this route.

A modestly troubling thought arose in the rain over Ann's
Turgenev research which at first made me wonder if I'd grind another tooth to death when I fell asleep. Sad to say I could remember all too clearly Turgenev's *Diary of a Superfluous Man* and its
wretched hero, Chulkaturin, who was obsessed with his gestures
rather than his contents. It is a bitter, hopeless little novella written in the mid–nineteenth century and signals the literary birth of
the alienated man who now, of course, seems to number in the
millions. Ann doubtless knew this novella very well and I wondered,
or, more explicitly, suspected, that she saw me as an aged Chulkaturin in the same manner she viewed her father.

But of course, as the French say, I am cranky at times, querulous, guilty of lassitude, strangled somewhat at an early age by brutally insensitive parents just like Chulkaturin, but then, as I've
implied, there must be millions of us lapsing into old age in a state
of irritable melancholy. Above all else, at least according to this
culture, I am a not especially noteworthy success. As far as I know,
there's nothing on earth I could do to make Ann care for me.

The rain increased deliciously, bathing my face as if I were an
oceanic "lacrimae Christus." I could not help but laugh at the ordinariness of my condition. January loves May who naturally is bent
on wounded July. I tried to recall for amusement the details about
another Chicago boy's aged affection for a young woman. Hemingway's love for Adriana Ivancich was absurdly delusional which
didn't slow down the wonderful old fool for a moment. Like the
rest of us he was trained rather harshly by his parents to be a good

boy, a good man, a good old man, and demonstrably failed at good-
ness. He instead became a courageous fool though there is evidence
he drank far too much from his twenties onward and probably had
no firm notion what a preposterous fool he had become. In any
event, there is nothing in him that requests our forgiveness. Luckily the young woman escaped his palsied clutches though someone
told me she eventually committed suicide and won a *New York Times*
obituary, a sign of success in life. But then the tidy bourgeoisie (am
I a member?) is always "tisk-tisking" about those few who struggle
out there on the borderlands, though the feeling of moral superiority while suppurating within your investment portfolio is also a
struggle. I remember as a boy when my father drove me past the
Hemingway house in Oak Park and I thought I sensed a specific
doom that I also felt about our own home. Everything is up in the
air, thus our vertigo.

I looked up into the night unable to see the tiny raindrops falling against my face. It was a simulacrum of blindness. I thought
idly that we are trained rather idealistically in secondary school, high
school, at college, but with little enough to do directly with this
idealism except to become drones, good citizens, make money, and
die. This struck me as comic. There had to be millions of men like
myself who thought likewise, at least on a rare occasion. I recalled
an English professor, an elegant but misshapen oaf at Northwestern, who liked to quote Wordsworth's "getting and spending,
we lay waste our powers" or something to that effect. We all knew
that he had married well and collected rare sherries and port, and
would shoot his cuffs so we could see the links made of Elizabe-
than coins.

I turned slightly and could make out the dark but comforting
shape of the cabin. My shelter, as it were. Was Joe somewhere in
a fifty-mile radius milling around in the light rain? Maybe he was
inadvertently right. Inside and outside are a little confusing. I sup-

pose that in anthropological terms shelter was what you resorted to when you were "done" with your hunting, gathering, tilling, and whatever, outside. I've spent the vast proportion of my life inside, of course, dealing with my livelihood. If you go outside in a relatively unpopulated area you are immediately a little less claustrophobic though, of course, there are no miracles because you carry your civilization in your head. I suppose if you simply spend your entire life indoors as many do you are lost within the confines of a maze with no solution. But then I recall taking a day hike with my nephew, truly one of the burgeoning swarm of eco-ninnies, and he spent the entire hike whining about his father, my brother-in-law, who was admittedly a nasty item. The point is that my nephew was outside in his body but not in his mind. Luckily his father dropped dead in a sand trap on a golf course and the young man is now chasing fossils in peace in South Dakota.

O Christ but our minds move so quickly that our emotions can't quite follow. Years ago I met a Frenchwoman in Paris who maintained that you could only be truly alone in Paris when you were in the toilet, but then one day in late May in a light rain I viewed twelve hundred varieties of roses in the Bagatelle Gardens of the Bois de Boulogne and I was quite alone. The other day on NPR I heard that since atmospheric conditions are "inexhaustibly chaotic" it was difficult to predict the weather. Joe immediately came to mind.

III

We waited overlong at the neurologist's office in Marquette. I became irritated in part because neither Joe nor Dick Rathbone were irritated. Dick scanned a year's worth of *National Geographic* while Joe turned his chair around and stared at the street below as if fascinated by the sparse traffic in this neighborhood of the city. After about a half-hour, a dowdy middle-aged woman brought a girl in, probably about thirteen or fourteen, whose head was bandaged in the manner of a skullcap with a flesh-colored bandage. Joe turned his chair back around and he and the girl stared at one another, obviously recognizing each other as the patients in the room. The girl became a bit flirtatious which made me quite nervous because of her age. Dick ignored the display while the girl's mother seemed not to mind. The girl's left hand began to shake as if palsied and she grabbed it with her other hand as if embarrassed. I picked up a *Harper's* magazine to quell my nervousness, but then Joe went over and sat by the girl taking her palsied hand and holding it. They both laughed and the mother smiled happily at me. The girl kissed Joe on the cheek and he kissed her back. This fairly burst my noggin with anxiety but then I scarcely knew what to do about the situation so I stared at a page of *Harper's* until my eyes blurred. Dick Rathbone began to talk with the woman in the casual way of the Upper Peninsula, starting with locating each other. She was from over between Trenary and Chatham. Her husband drove a logging truck. I glanced at her feet, which were a bit swollen so her shoes were only loosely tied. I did not raise my eyes above her feet or the feet of Joe and the girl.

"They tell us Prissy's a goner. Priscilla's her name. She's my number six. The last one. Tumor way inside her head."

"Mother, I'm not looking for sympathy." Priscilla announced she was going to show Joe her dog that was down in their pick-up and when they left the woman burst into tears. Dick Rathbone went over, sat down, and tried to comfort her. The whole scene was so wretchedly Dickensian, or from our own Steinbeck, that I was full of ire despite the fact that I could scarcely swallow from melancholy. Unlike her mother the girl was rather pretty. I stood up then and out the window I could see Joe and the girl petting a mongrel that sat in the back of an old pick-up with rusted fenders.

I felt generally desperate and grilled the receptionist for the third time about the doctor's whereabouts, receiving the identical message that resembled a telephone answering machine to the effect that the doctor was in surgery and would be here as soon as possible. Of course it's quite pointless to get angry with doctors who resemble the small captious gods that cursed the Greek peasantry.

There was the briefest urge to strangle the receptionist but I doubted my strength. At least Dick had calmed down the woman and they were now busy talking about the "good ole days." I went back to the window only to discover that Joe and the girl were now hugging each other on the grass while the dog was scooting in circles. It occurred to me with a dagger of fear that it was not totally beyond Joe to "close the deal" right there on the office lawn. As luck would have it our wayward neurologist pulled up in a spiffy BMW and when he got out to greet his embracing patients he was wearing what looked like golf clothes. Surgery indeed. You could almost smell his sun block a hundred feet away. But then I felt a tinge of empathy as he actually sat down on the grass with Joe and the girl. I had met him twice before and he really wasn't a bad sort. My mind whirled for a moment at the idea of a doctor's job what with having to say good-bye to the living whereas an undertaker didn't have to listen to the response.

On the way home from Marquette we stopped for a hamburger at the Brownstone. Joe had been sleeping sitting up in the backseat with his eyes open, an ability unnerving to others, mostly to me as Dick Rathbone was in a state of rapture over Mozart's *Jupiter* which I was playing on the tape deck. Earlier, and instead of me, it had been Dick Rathbone who had been vexed. The doctor, I suppose properly, had refused to slip a telemetric device under Joe's skin, and this after telling us that any increase in Joe's complicated medications would only disable him to the point he couldn't walk or navigate. He insisted that what Rathbone suggested certainly wasn't an "approved procedure." When we got back in the car Dick was so pissed off that he told me he knew an alcoholic retired veterinarian who lived near Seney who might

do the job. Joe, meanwhile, was studying the hand-drawn map
the girl had given him locating where she lived. Dick hadn't noticed this yet but my heart sank a bit thinking of the eighty or so
miles between home and the girl's place between Chatham and
Trenary.

Mozart soothed Dick's ruffled feathers but then I was off on
another disturbing tangent. Roberto wouldn't stop sending books
despite my requests that he do so. And I couldn't stop dabbling in
the books. It was the simple matter of my inability to resist opening a new book with that peculiar new-book smell. Early this morning it had been Slobodkin's *Simplicity and Complexity in the Games of
the Intellect*. It had been the single sentence to the effect that no or-
ganism responds to the full complexity of its environment that had
thrown me out of whack. Over my underdone blueberry pancakes
I had wondered what if a great naturalist like E. O. Wilson, whose
Biophilia I had revered, also had the penetrating insights into human
behavior owned by Freud or Jung or Dostoyevsky.

Dick interrupted my thinking by asking, "How did Mozart
make that up?" A simple enough question to which I said I hadn't
a clue. He rewound the tape and started it over. Meanwhile, I was
back to my naturalist genius to whom I had added, in the manner
of Dr. Frankenstein, an equivalent ability to probe into human
behavior. Maybe toss in musical and other artistic ability. Caravaggio, Yeats, García Márquez. Of course the banality in my thinking was the old time trap. My invented genius had to go to meetings,
seduce women, raise unruly children, drink wine and perhaps martinis, make a living. His own true character would be too expan-
sive to adequately develop.

Joe startled me by saying he was hungry. There you have it.
Our genius would have to cook, eat, defecate, take showers, and
possibly make love. All human activity would be distracting. Or
maybe ultimately supporting?

* * *

It was certainly time for my annual hamburger which turned out to be so delicious I thought I might compromise and have another this year. The waitress at the Brownstone was trying to flirt with Joe but he, of all things, kept sniffing the map that Priscilla had given him for a trace of pheromones and when we went back out to the car Dick Rathbone had to explain the directions to Joe since he was without his compass. Lake Superior across the road was to the north. East and west could be determined by the traffic on Route 28. On the near side the traffic was headed east. Joe looked at Priscilla's map again and turned until he faced south. He apparently felt naked without his dirty brown shirt with its dozens of pockets and his compass, jackknife, fish line and hooks, insect repellent, and maps. It occurred to me at that moment that we better get him in the car before he escaped.

Which is what he did at the rest stop near the Driggs River when we stopped to pee an hour later. Dick has prostrate difficulties and I was bent on overhearing a quarreling tourist family at a picnic table (since my youth I have felt I might pick up a dark secret in overheard conversations).

In any event Joe was across Route 28 and into the Seney Wildlife Refuge before I vainly called out. Dick heard my somewhat plaintive voice and rushed out of the toilet tugging at his zipper. "Goddammit," he said. I glanced at a map in the car trying to estimate how long it might take Joe to cross the Refuge, after which there was a wide swath of the Hiawatha National Forest, at least sixty miles as the crow flies from where we stood to Trenary and Chatham. Of course you know you're not a crow when you run into creeks, wide marshes, lakes, dense swamps, rivers. Dick immediately worried that Joe didn't have his humble survival gear. We certainly didn't bother discussing what Joe had "in mind" other than the obvious Priscilla.

✵   ✵   ✵

That night, unfortunately, it turned very cool for August. I sat with Dick Rathbone in his kitchen while he got very drunk. I had a few myself but he basically finished a fresh bottle of whiskey. His sister became quite furious by midnight, coming out of her bedroom and shrieking incoherently. Dick yelled back, "Batten your gob you old bitch," and she retreated weeping. Our conversation delaminated. I've always overvalued the friendship of Dick because he prefers the more relaxing surface of things. Now, however, he wondered aloud that we might be mutually worried about Joe because we had no children of our own. I had just enough booze to indulge in the sentimentality I normally loathe. I had years ago gotten a vasectomy to relieve myself of the threat of paternity suits, not that I was a Lothario but that at the time I was sunken in the disease of money. Roberto cured me a few years ago by asking suddenly over dinner what the first image was that came to my mind when he said "money." My reply surprised me. "The soiled toilet paper you sometimes see near campsites." He was delighted.

About midnight the sheriff of Alger County called to say that neither his people, the D.N.R., nor the Department of Interior employees at the Wildlife Refuge had seen Joe. We hadn't expected anything and Dick reminded me of what the Chippewa tracker had said to the effect that if a competent person wanted to disappear in this area there was nothing anyone could do but wait. Waiting and drinking. Stewing.

I awoke at dawn on the Rathbones' couch and Edna was already frying sausage and potatoes. She was one of those people who truly believe that "breakfast lays the foundation of the day." She also was one of those women who seem to feel better to the degree that she senses you feel badly. She looked through the open double door from kitchen to parlor and cheerily waved and sloshed the remnants of the whiskey bottle, then brought me a mug of coffee which I drank hastily and fell back to sleep. I was disturbed again that I found her attractive in an old robe and her hair wet from a shower.

I awoke again at nine quite upset to discover that Dick was up and gone down toward the Hiawatha on the track of Joe. I had clearly been left behind. Edna said that though Dick was just a month short of my age he could still walk a good dozen hours in a row. This somehow clamped my throat enough that I couldn't swallow the second bite of my breakfast. Edna tried to cover her insensitivity by saying her brother didn't have a dime in the bank and their mutual pension checks barely stretched a month and taking care of Joe had been quite a financial windfall. Naturally this didn't help and she errantly dug the hole deeper by calling up my envious position far in the past when my family would come up from Chicago in our "great big Buick." She remembered I wore the "white buck" shoes later made famous by Pat Boone. All the local girls knew that by the time I was sixteen I would be a "prime catch" and that's why I had my way with them. In fact, Edna added with a prolonged giggle, the girls called me "Johnny Fuckerfaster" after a famous dirty joke of the time.

I put my plate of breakfast on the floor for Marcia, petting her head while she ate. I had plainly been knocked off my pins by Edna's initial inference that I would merely get in the way in the search for Joe. And then there had been a flood of memories of the half dozen local girls I had made love to with my high-grade Chicago condoms before I went off to college and began working summers. Staring into a pool of cooling egg yolk I could recall their names, also the moment of the hopeless attempt at camaraderie when my father had told me right after my sixteenth birthday to use condoms, "safes" he called them, because girls would know we were "well-heeled" and might wish to trap me into a "shotgun marriage."

O Jesus but I fled the house, stumbling so that Edna caught me at the door. I managed to push her away, my hand recoiling at the jiggle of an ample breast. By the time I reached my car in the yard I had calmed down in the manner of a movie zombie. It was unthinkable not to stop at the grocery store and post office. For some reason I bought my first can of Franco-American spaghetti since college (surely an early sign of profound confusion). At the post office there was yet another book bag from Roberto and a letter from Ann, which I read immediately, not a good move. She wasn't pregnant by Joe yet but still insulted me roundly for not consenting to marry her when she became "with child," a curiously literary way of putting it.

At the cabin I ate my canned spaghetti on toast and was quite swept away by unhappy college memories about a girl in my French class who I adored but would have nothing to do with me. She pretended to be intellectual but was pinned to a basketball dork who was also the president of his fraternity. Come to think of it this girl also looked like my eventual wife and Ann. My father was obsessed with hard work and thrift, those Calvinist curses, and all of my spare time was spent helping my uncle get commercial properties ready to sell. Often they were small factories and I'd go in with a crew of blacks to scrub the place clean and then do a cheapish, cosmetic paint job. I often wondered later how we could have such a grand time doing something so clearly unpleasant. My uncle had a very rare theory that if you paid your men well you made a better profit for yourself so those who worked on my crew had very high morale. My uncle was also a trencherman, though quite finicky, and the lunches he had sent over were always a treat, usually gigantic sandwiches from an Italian delicatessen.

How could I now wax sentimental about scraping grease off the floor of an empty, unheated factory on cold January mornings or on blistering July afternoons? Frankly my black friends at the time made my college acquaintances look shallow, puling, emotionally shabby.

This week's book from Roberto, Edelman's *Neural Darwinism,* shoved me over the edge into a prolonged anxiety attack that my poor soul had evidently been spoiling for. Here I was spreading the spaghetti on toast and as smart as I was supposed to be (157 on one I.Q. test) I simply couldn't seem to comprehend a single paragraph. I smelled the new book and that didn't help. I quaked and the room became blurry at the edges. Tears formed. My lungs wouldn't fill. My mouth became dry. There was the quick image of my cousin Laura showing me her rear end when we were twelve in this very room. Over where the windows nearly met in the corner. Under the antique brass fish scales with her left hand on the windowsill. "See my butt," she said with a ladylike lilt.

As I was flipping pages in *Neural Darwinism* in a vain search for a sentence I could understand Laura's lilac scent entered the room despite its fifty-five-year absence. My own wife didn't care for bugs, in fact couldn't tolerate them, thus was rarely here. It actually approached a phobia that evidently began when her cousin dumped a sack of bugs he had collected into the tub when she was bathing. Or so she said. The details were good.

I met Roberto right after the last details of my divorce were settled over teatime at the Drake. How very amiable until everyone left except my personal lawyer and I went to the toilet which began swirling in a mockery of movie versions of whirlpools and vortexes. Roberto's office was just down the street and he gave me drugs that dumbed me down for a few months. What are we to make of the vast hole that divorce shovels in one's life, at least a three-year hole?

Roberto insists that it's because we're essentially monkeys, primates, and grow hopelessly absorbed with one another. Obviously people wouldn't have anxiety attacks if the particulars (a million possibilities per human) were all known. Few know their own minds and we are all suffocated by psychologisms, I reminded myself.

I stretched out on my sleeping bag on the picnic table at ten in the morning and was still there at dark with little movement except to roll over and pee off the edge. I had no real desire for food or drink, not enough anyway to get me to move. My brain fluttered and pounded, my body twitched. Tears came and went. My blood pressure spiked the passing cumulus clouds. It was a delight when my left foot cramped and drew me away from the rest of my body. My life unrolled like a torpid newsreel. My condition kept reminding me of an uncle, a gruff man, I didn't care for who returned from a four-year Pacific stretch in the Navy in World War II, looked over the Chicago arm of our family for a few scant months, and then moved off to Corpus Christi in Texas. Moving to Texas was truly a breach in family taste. Anyway Carl was an old-fashioned manly man in the manner of the movie actor Robert Ryan. My father had mysteriously said that the war had "cooked Carl for good." I wasn't sure at the time what he meant but Carl certainly followed his own counsel. I, of course, had never been to war but that was how I felt. Cooked to near death, as if my life in our culture had been some wretched and meaningless war in which the economy had become the only acceptable reality. I didn't in the least feel entitled to whine or complain about this. I was at least a one-star general in this life-long conflagration. Of course, there had been the temptation all along to pursue the hundreds of self-improvement schemes that afflict us, then convince us with their ultimate silliness. At one of my former geezer clubs in Chicago we used to be carelessly amused about the joggers among us who had dropped dead, conveniently ignoring those who dropped dead from physical sloth.

A screeching blue jay brought me back to the core that I had spent the day so relentlessly avoiding. I shut my eyes, which enabled the bird to approach the feeder for the last time in the twilight. What did a blue jay understand about my eyes, I wondered, re-opening them to perceive how the twilight seemed to have advanced toward darkness within the few minutes I had been giving the blue jay a feeding break. If I could notice this how much more securely could I notice that there was no time left for another life. This was the source of the terrifying anxiety that had kept me glued so absurdly to the picnic table for more than twelve hours.

The next step was even more harrowing to deal with because it was so logical. What had made me so foolishly wish another life when I had been reasonably contented with my own? Age sixty-seven was obviously not appropriate timing for this question but it seemed that the biggest pratfalls in my life had been deemed quite appropriate. Both my own and my ex-wife's families thought of our marriage as overwhelmingly appropriate. Of course within this sort of state of exacerbation it is easy to become sidetracked into less threatening items in our personal histories. My ex-wife was basically dead to me and I suspect I was even "deader" to her.

Luckily I recognized the white light in the forest as the rising moon, a few days into its waning state but certainly bright enough to help Joe who, given his improbable physical condition, might be nearing his outrageous destination, not certainly outrageous to Joe because those considerations must have fled his brain. I could imagine him gliding through the forest toward his too young girl in the manner of those terribly corny Zane Grey novels of my youth that featured improbably heroic woodsmen and cowboys.

Dick had had the sense to call Ann when we returned without Joe. She was taking an exam but would be up tomorrow. We had immediately thought of Ann as, at the very least, a decoy to get Joe

off the track of the girlish tumor victim. The problem was not the
less poignant for being so absurdly vulnerable to sentimentality.

The moon was slipping up through the trees and my body and
brain were finally, after nearly thirteen hours, in a state of rest. Of
course I didn't have time for another life but at least I could take a
look. It is easy enough to discard the possibilities gotten from a
thousand good books but the nature of Joe was close at hand. And
it was also easy for me to assume that my little torments were caused
by Ann in the obvious manner of an older man with a virtually sex-
less life running head-on into a young woman for whom he felt a
powerful attraction. This was predictable and somewhat comic. It
always is. How often with my Chicago friends, really acquaintances, had we spoken in comic derision when one of us had been
silly enough not to act his age, sometimes disastrously, and certainly
very expensively. But then just when you are quite confident that
you have stored your hormones up on the shelf they are capable of
suddenly leaping down at you. I suppose in contrast to the youthful it is a matter of frequency and intensity.

I got off the table, my legs deadened, and fell rather softly on
my face in the grass. The earth felt reasonably solid in contrast to
earlier in the day. Maybe the world doesn't really look like the one
I've been seeing all along. That was one of the questions Joe offered. The timing had to be right in that even last year I might have
ignored Joe despite my closeness with Dick Rathbone, or at least
kept my distance. I had to be in a state of vulnerability, somewhat
pathetic in that my interest in life at large seemed to be evaporating, and I sensed that I wanted to see what Joe sees, even if it's a
brutal sensory overload. The anxiety comes from the "going, going,
gone" chant, the much bandied "unlived life," the sense of occlu-
sion that arrives quite naturally to a stifled curiosity, or a curiosity
that has buried itself in a familiar hole. I readily admit that the particulars of the effects of Joe's injuries are unknown to me but then

I've read that eminent brain researchers at their conventions are inclined to make jokes about when they're finally going to be ready to attack the problem of the "nature of consciousness."

As a worthy follow-up of my somewhat sententious day I cleaned out and sorted my spice and condiment shelf. I rarely make curry but found nine containers of curry powder, some of them god knows how old. Dick Rathbone jokes that I'm the "king of condiments." The tiniest vermin possible thrive in ground chilies but not in brown sugar! Without training there are limits to how far you can take this. I heated some frozen tamales Fed Exed from a friend in New Mexico and opened a bottle of Domaine Tempier Bandol.

With the shelf cleaned and a crisp sense of accomplishment, and while waiting for the tamales to steam, I opened the most recent of Joe's notebooks. I puzzled over a page of near gibberish, then noted a tearlike moisture in my eyes, quickly tracing it to the evening of my father's death over forty years ago when my mother had irrationally spent most of the night washing her many sets of dishes. My cleaning of my condiment and spice shelf held a fragile similarity but then no one had died. I shivered a bit as I rejected the temptation to shine a flashlight out onto the picnic table to see if my body was there. It was now after midnight and I was counting on the wine, which hit my empty tummy rather directly, to return me to the solid earth or maple chair where I belonged.

Joe's prose was a code with a seemingly infinite number of variables. Wolves were occasionally spelled "wuvs" or just "wo" while bears could be "bears" or "brs" but then all the connective language tissue, the articles, verbs, and adjectives, tended toward pure mud. Edna Rathbone had told me that in Joe's quarters there was a large crock of bird feathers, dried flowers, dead insects, snake-skins, bones, parts of mammal skulls. A park ranger, an officious nitwit, told me that he had followed Joe's tracks out into the fifty or so square miles that comprise the Grand Sable Dunes along Lake Superior, and in a thicket he had discovered a half dozen coyote skulls arranged on a low-slung birch branch. The ranger wondered if I thought this comprised some sort of "hocus-pocus."

Further on I was able to parse that he often spent nights in the "sky." I took the word "humock" to be hummock, a raised piece of land in a marsh, then thought he probably meant hammock. I knew he was given to climbing trees, which aroused modest fears in all of us, though not to the degree of his swimming. I also knew the ancient hammock was missing from my woodshed.

While eating my tamales well after midnight it occurred to me that once more I might be a victim of my envy. Since my youth I've always felt I was missing out, doubtless because I was. I've dabbled enough in my reading in remote areas of botany, anthropology, history, geography, even physics, to name a few, and have been exposed to brilliance that made me feel like a simpleton, a proper feeling in that I was a simpleton in those areas. This admission did not decrease the level of my envy which fairly hissed through my pores. I was, however, hesitant to take the usual step in our culture of totally discounting acts of genius. For instance, very early on in my book collecting when I was still in my late twenties, my uncle who was my mentor in the area cautioned me against scorn and egregious comparisons. I was flippant about Langston Hughes and Richard Wright in favor of the recently published Ralph Ellison. I had wisely bought a whole carton of fifty of *The Invisible Man.* My uncle chided me that I was treating literature like a sack race, and that my humility in the face of any good work was appropriate. Of course the literary community at its worst, such as it is, *does* treat it like a sack race but that is collective stupidity.

My weakest characteristic, and this is perhaps where Joe was a goad, was in my paucity of imagination. Once in Barcelona while in my early thirties, I actually tossed a bilingual anthology of Spanish poetry off the balcony of a fine hotel down onto the Ramblas, peeking furtively over the edge to see if I might have struck one of the masses of promenaders on the avenue. I had reassured myself many times that the three most wildly imaginative acquaintances of mine had come to nothing, but stopped doing so when I realized I had come to relative nothing without being imaginative. The Spanish poetry made me seethe with jealousy because I couldn't create a metaphor. Not even a bad one.

Ann arrived about four A.M. shortly after I finally fell asleep. She looked a bit like a photo of a Treblinka survivor with red eyes, flat hair, all twitches and blowing her nose. I was fatigued and quite cross, poured her a few ounces of Calvados, and went back to my bed in the loft, refusing to sacrifice my comfort to her like a sexual toady. On my way up the stairs she choked out that Edna had told her on the phone that Joe was off chasing a fourteen-year-old. Good old Edna. I whispered through fake drowsiness that I'd talk to her in the morning. Before I slept, and while I listened to the drumming sound of Ann's shower, it occurred to me that Joe might need his tripartite beast or monster for the reason that Claude Lévi-Strauss pointed out, to the effect that the creation of such mythological beasts was as necessary as nest building. To take it a step further, in the terms of my ill-digested *Neural Darwinism*, maybe Joe's beasts were similar to our own impulse in the creation of our early religions, a map of gods. I also wondered if there were monsters for genetic reasons left over in a few of our twelve billion neurons. Our monsters are now quite abstracted but earlier in our

collective history they were very real. I imagined (for a definite
change) some cave dwellers down near Sarlat in France struggling
to defend themselves against a two-thousand-pound cave bear. God
knows what they had to defend against two million years earlier in
Africa.

About five A.M., not all that long after first light, Ann took it upon herself to join me in the loft. It was ultimately comic because I was deep
in R.E.M. sleep and dreaming of a night with my wife in Palm Beach
back in the seventies when we had stopped to visit her aunt after a
pleasant week in Key West (by luck I got Tennessee Williams to
sign most of his opus). The aunt was a loathsome Republican crone
who drove her half dozen Latin American servants witless. She
bitched about Democrats over dinner in one of those horrid "con-
tinental" restaurants that many rich folks prefer where you can't
tell the veal from the fish because it is laden with "Chef Pierre's
Special Sauce." After a nasty quarrel over the minimum wage (the
aunt had soap money from Cincinnati) I stalked out and checked
into The Breakers close by because I'd left the car with my wife.
All the hotel had available was a revoltingly expensive suite but I
was too pissed off to care and ordered up a Côte Rôtie I favored.
Anyway, my wife found me there and we were both so hopelessly
exacerbated we made the best love of our marriage. "Go figure," as
they used to say.

    Anyway, I was having a splendid though distorted dream of
this marital fuck feast and when I awoke Ann had "covered" me
for what I'd guess was a five-second sprint. She murmured that her
gesture was "a thank-you note" for all my kindness. Still in a dream
state where I wasn't sure if Ann was my ex-wife I merely looked at
the rough board ceiling, grimacing at a pain that shot through my
prostate like a hot hat pin. When the pain subsided I began to go

back to sleep but then she began weeping. My five-second coupling was beginning to look like one of the lesser deals of my life when by a grand stroke of luck a family of ravens arrived in the yard. I moved quickly to the bench by the windows because the ravens visit me rarely and usually about this time in mid-August. I croaked softly which didn't alarm them because they were accustomed to my silly attempts at inter-species communication. Ann was at first pissed off that I found the ravens more interesting than her grief but then she joined me on the bench. There was one very outsized bearded fellow, an Ur-raven as it were, certainly the largest raven I had ever seen, but then I distrust my mediocre vision and the bird was partly in the shadow of a clump of cedar trees. The group of a dozen pranced, hopped, chortled, squawked, and whistled. The blue jays and evening grosbeaks that were normally at the feeder at this hour fled except for one brave female grosbeak. I admired her lovely Roman nose, which reminded me of Ann's. There was the lingering jolt that the grand fellow in the cedar might be Joe's bird. I turned to Ann who had her elbows resting on the windowsill, which drew her bare breasts upward. She was kneeling on the bench, which gave the inanimate bed a view I would have loved. I took courage from the ravens and said that I had to get the small pair of binoculars I keep on the nightstand for bird and beast occasions. So I caught the view of her upraised bottom at the window and there was the urge to howl "Praise God" but of course I didn't. My member was becoming swollen again, a matter of some pride to this geezer, but when I returned to the window she laughed, gave it the briefest squeeze, and went downstairs.

Sleep was out of the question after having had only a mere hour or so. I was so much dead meat when I cooked and served a small breakfast to Ann. She pointed out that she had had as little sleep as my-

self and I let pass the simple fact that there was forty years' difference in our ages. If she wasn't dwelling on the fact maybe I'd have
another shot, though at the moment sex was way down the list with
anxiety attacks as desirable. She also made a little joke about the
possibility that she might be pregnant with either me or Joe and I
cagily withheld the fact that I had had a vasectomy. Just why this
was tactically smart on my part escaped me but in both commercial real estate and book dealing there is the temptation to be pointlessly shrewd just to keep in practice.

On the way to Dick Rathbone's Ann further irritated me by
referring to Joe as noble. I slowed my vehicle for one of my special
speeches, noting that the absurd concept of the "noble savage" can
scarcely be extrapolated from Joe's condition when, in fact, it was
a brain injury that appeared to make him his own sub-species of
Homo sapiens. She then shrilly called me a "tiresome old asshole."

At Dick Rathbone's there was a huge cab of a logging truck
parked in the yard. Inside we were introduced to Priscilla's father,
Henry, a middle-aged fellow smelling of grease, diesel fuel, and pine
bark, and obviously of French-Canadian descent. Despite his somewhat brutish appearance he shared some handsomeness with his
daughter.

He was, unfortunately, a taciturn man and I had to piece bits
of the story together because Dick was drowsing in his breakfast
chair and not all that communicative. Joe had reached his Trenary-
Chatham target area in about forty hours, not bad at all for sixty
miles or so of this country, in fact well out of range, I suspect, of all
but the sturdiest physical-culture nitwits our civilization has produced. Henry, Priscilla's father, had found Joe sleeping under
the porch with the dog Joe had met in the back of the pick-up at
the doctor's office in Marquette. Priscilla hadn't returned from
Marquette because her tumor was growing like "all get out" and
she had been sent over to the hospital. I couldn't help being dis-

appointed at the slight wave of pleasure that passed over Ann's face
when she heard Joe hadn't seen Priscilla again. Sexual jealousy
thrives even in the face of the death of the unwitting competitor.

Anyway, Henry said Joe wouldn't leave but then Henry's wife
had called from Priscilla's room at the hospital and the "lovebirds"
got to talk a moment though Priscilla was "real doped up." Joe
had then comprehended the situation and Henry had brought him
home, though down by the juncture of Adam's Trail and Route
77 Joe had gestured that he had to pee and jumped out before the
truck even stopped, heading east into the woods at a dead run.

When Henry got up to leave we thanked him and I tried to
give him a C note for his round-trip which he proudly refused. He
evidently came from an affectionate family because he gave us all a
hug, which, of course, made me feel awkward. It was odd indeed
to embrace such a powerful body. Out on the porch, Henry said,
"This whole thing ain't hardly fair," an ultimate Dickens reverbera-
tion and my throat clutched.

The sky was still reddish when we set off at eight in the morning.
Edna packed us a food basket and water and at the last minute we
decided to take Marcia along for her tracking abilities. The problem at hand was that Joe hadn't had his medication in two days
and the effect of this was problematical. Ann was irked when we
stopped at the Bayshore so Dick could pick up an emergency bottle
of whiskey. When she chided him he said, "Mind your own fucking
business," a word he only used under the direst circumstances.

Since our collective mood (except for Marcia's) was a bit shabby
I began to sense the beginning of the end, at the same time chiding
myself for this questionable sense of pre-recognition. I swerved to
avoid a ground squirrel or chipmunk and failed, hearing the almost
imperceptible thunk of its demise. This further distracted me and

Dick asked me to stop so he could take over the wheel. I got in the backseat with Ann, and Marcia gladly got in the front seat with Dick. She somehow prefers this illusion of keeping a watch out for us. I avoided looking at Ann who still seemed to be smarting from Dick's whiskey comment. And then without warning I fell asleep as a child might, waking only when Ann pushed away my head which was half on her lap though I hadn't been sufficiently conscious to enjoy the position.

Dick had parked my four-wheel drive on the two-track with the closest access to Joe's cave and was stuffing the food and water in his daypack. I drowsily watched Marcia scoot into the brush on the track of Joe while Dick and Ann laughed about something out of my earshot so Ann must be over her snit. They both looked at me as if questioning whether I was going along and I scrambled out of the backseat with all of the energy of a half-drowned worm.

I had been smart enough to use a walking stick to poke ahead of me after my former pratfalls and was able to keep up with them without too much trouble, concentrating on Ann's butt a few feet ahead of me. How could such a functional thing be a source of so much anguish, I asked myself, mulling over the usual biological answers. I was amused to remember that Edelman had quoted Darwin saying, "But then arises the doubt: can the mind of man, which has, as I fully believe, been developed from a mind as low as that possessed by the lowest animal, be trusted when it draws such grand conclusions?" There was an image of randy Shakespeare lapping at a low chambermaid like a street cur right after creating his greatest sonnet. And libidinous Einstein, he of the enlarged hippocampus, retreating from cosmic considerations to the pleasures of a dampish adulterous bed. We won't include our beleaguered president who seems to make the most otiose pundit and graft-sodden congressman feel superior.

Off course I ran into Ann in my reverie when she stopped to tie her boot. I picked her up as she hissed, "You asshole," then congratulated me on picking her up so easily. I'm reasonably strong from the aimless calisthenics that start my day, the only self-improvement scheme I haven't abandoned. I want to continue being able to open wine bottles, jars, climbing stairs to my bed.

When we reached Joe's cave Marcia was waiting for us, then scooted off into the brush which Dick took as a sure indication that she knew Joe's location. I was a bit miffed thinking I'd take a rest on one of the deerskins I intended to pull from Joe's cave. Ann handed me one of those trifling squirt bottles of water used by hikers, joggers, and bicyclists and the stream of water sent me choking. Ann dashed off after Dick and Marcia and I labored to follow, refusing the heavy heart of the kid who couldn't keep up. My heart actually seemed to flutter and chatter and I was windless but I kept up, almost anyway, at least to the point I could hear them thrashing through the brush ahead of me.

When I emerged along the high bank above the creek where Joe had found the huge bear skull I could hear Marcia barking. Well down the bank Dick and Ann were looking straight up into two very tall white pines and Marcia barked with her forepaws against one of the trees. I could see nothing from my vantage point and rushed to join them. Ann turned, hearing me, and pointed straight up. At first I could see nothing but then within the bows of the two tops of the trees that were nearly intertwined there was a hammock. It was at least fifty feet up and obviously contained Joe though he wasn't moving. It is indeed a euphemism to say we were nonplussed. "He's arboreal," I said, rather stupidly. We sat down to wordlessly think it over. After a bleak few minutes Ann took some pills from the bottle in Dick's daypack and stuffed her small squirt bottle in a side pocket of her hiking trousers. "Don't

fall," Dick said lamely, which she didn't respond to before she
started up the tree.

It was easy climbing, not that I'd do it myself. White pines have
nicely spaced branches but when Ann reached the hammock we
could clearly hear the kind of keening wail you used to hear at old-
time Irish funerals in Chicago, or in the tapes ethnologists make of
Native American ceremonies. The sound made my very innards
blush and I began to grind my teeth and hit the ground with the
palm of my hand. Marcia forced herself onto Dick's lap and closed
her eyes. Dick stared down at the meandering creek for the smallest comfort. There was no point in trying to imagine Joe's poor
bruised brain gone quite amok until its vocals became so berserk
that the forest herself refused to absorb it. I frankly began to weep
which I hadn't done since my father disappeared from earth and
even then I waited until the next morning when I saw his briefcase
on his desk in the den which held his large rock collection. Then I
wept. And now I did.

When the keening finally stopped, Dick tipped himself backward until
he was supine and Marci stood beside me wagging her tail. Ann
came down the tree, gathered some food, and went back up without saying a word. I shared a pot roast sandwich with Dick, laden
with Edna's homemade horseradish so hot it cleared the sinuses.
Dick took out the bottle of whiskey and we stared at it a moment
as if finally figuring out what whiskey was truly for, then each had
a swallow.

It was early evening before Ann came down again. She looked absolutely haggard, fairly hissing "thank god for drug companies." It
seemed to me also that certain romantic illusions had fled her, at

least for the time being. Dick made her a cup of instant coffee into which she poured a goodly bit of whiskey. She exuded a sense of powerlessness that we all shared.

The smoke from our campfire drifted straight up in the windless air, a burnt offering that lightly enshrouded Joe's hammock in a silken mist. Our sole comfort was our rationed sips of whiskey though you had to count the rather tender burble of the creek. My mind drifted back to our collective ineffectuality though if all those genius authors of my stack of brain books, or at least say Edelman, Damasio, Slobodkin, Calvin, et al., had been here they couldn't have done much except greatly deepen the level of conversation. It was akin to an oncologist possessing vast knowledge about melanoma except how to cure it. Dig it out with your miniature shovel, the scalpel. The man in the tree above us was as far out of reach as the moon that gave the illusion that it was nestled in the treetops beside him, but the moon had been one of his greatest comforts according to the frequency in which it appeared in his journals, which were somehow his brain's effort to re-map itself after the losses incurred in the injury. You had to think of his neural correlates of perception, the struggle of those infinitesimally thin sheets of brain tissue to map the woods and water, the birds and mammals he felt drawn to, his utter and direct intimacy with his senses unmitigated by our usual concerns. And what "self" he had left would largely be considered nominal to many of us, possibly not worth living for but then there was my perhaps goofy suspicion that he had crossed over a line into an *otherness* of perception that was unavailable to the rest of us.

Just before dark Dick went up the tree with an additional bedtime pill, perhaps a slight overdose but also a chemical insurance policy against Joe having a major seizure in the night. It was impossible

not to wish to avoid that wailing which would be explosively disturbing in the dark, even worse than in the afternoon when the
sound left the mind scorched of anything else.

The speed at which Dick climbed the tree belied his age which
was practically my own. I recalled a dreary meeting with my accountant last spring when he happily reminded me that my life ex-
pectancy was now eighty-three. The blessings of wealthy desuetude,
I thought at the time, nearly walking into a speeding Rush Street
taxi. I impulsively went over to Gibson's and had a porterhouse with
a full bottle of Pomerol, thinking that I may as well knock a month
off the end. Poor Dick and Edna only bought cheap lean cuts. Years
ago I had sent them twenty shares of Ford Motor for Christmas
and it arrived back with a thank-you note to the effect that it was
"too late in life" to own stock because he didn't want to have to think
about it. This year I intended to have a Newberry dealer deliver a
new yellow pick-up and doubted he'd have the craw to return it
because he greatly valued pick-up trucks. Dick never had the least
interest in money beyond what he and Edna needed to get along.
Once he used a whole week's salary to buy me a fly rod but mostly
because he loathed the old "whippy" rod I was using.

Her back was turned and I listened to Ann eat an apple as Dick
climbed back down the tree. A crisp crunch and apple-wet glisten-
ing lips in the firelight which grew in the darkness. Dick laid out a
survival item he called a "space blanket," which protected a body
from ground moisture, for Ann to rest on. He had earlier tried to
talk me into leaving the woods and picking them up in the morning. I doubted my ability to navigate the hour's walk back to the
car but also at heart I didn't want to leave. Instead, I made myself
useful gathering a large pile of firewood, proud that I was doing so
while Dick snoozed.

I had envisioned a long evening talking by the fire but we each
had only a single nightcap before we began to snooze sitting up.

Ann patted the narrow room on the space blanket on each side of her and suggested we "cuddle," adding that we "geezers" should keep our hands to ourselves. Dick joked that "that shouldn't be difficult" as Ann was a bit "thin in the withers" for his taste. She faked irritation and cupped herself against me as if I were a superior choice, then promptly went to sleep.

I stared up at the moon which was sliding slowly away from Joe's treetop perch. I wondered if he might be looking down on us as a raven might, that is with curiosity but ultimately impassive because it wasn't one of us.

Dawn was an abrupt and unpleasant surprise. The eastern sky was a furious red and the wind had arisen precipitously from the northwest, chill and brisk. It wasn't all that far before dawn when Dick had heard the wind and fed the fire. We could also look up and see Joe's empty hammock flapping in the wind. Ann predictably burst into tears, and then we noted that Marcia was also gone. Dick immediately trotted off in the direction of Joe's cave telling me to put out the fire. Ann shrugged off my consoling hug and followed Dick. I looked at the blazing fire with its flames fed by the wind and quickly boiled water for coffee. I felt awful indeed with aching bones, a tight chest, and sore throat. I got close enough to the fire to stop my shivering. I poured some medicinal whiskey in my coffee and noted that at some point during the night Marcia had finished off the food.

The idyll was clearly over, brief as it was. It is often difficult to start a fire and even more difficult to put it out. I had no container for water except a tiny camp coffeepot but there was a great deal of sand just below the lip of the creek bank. I scooped away painfully breaking a fingernail on a tree root. For some reason I diverted myself with thoughts of claws versus fingers. At one point

I had the unnerving sense that I was being watched from the dense greenery across the creek. I had seen a large sturgeon once in my life and then there was the seemingly outsized raven yesterday morning with Ann in the loft. Now all I needed in my cold, clammy mood was to have the third and most preposterous beast to slouch out of the tag alder across the creek. I studied the greenery with shortened breath before I came to my senses or, more accurately, dismissed my dubious senses in favor of putting out the fire.

I became reasonably ill for a week and, more importantly, so did Joe. I had a violent chest cold but Joe's medication had become less effective than it had been during the summer. When I reached the others at Joe's cave that morning, after trying arduously to put out the fire during which time I didn't give a flat fuck if the whole world burned, Joe looked gaunt, miserable, groggy, remote, and a little disoriented. He was cooking some rather large trout on a flat board near a large bed of coals which meant he had descended from the tree in the night. Dick was quite curious about the trout which we ate with extreme pleasure with salt. I was feeding Marcia some fish skin when she looked off toward our night campsite and growled. Joe made some peculiar animal sounds I hadn't heard before and Marcia romped and scooted in a circle then dove into the cave for shelter. Ann spoke sharply to Joe asking him not to repeat the sounds and Joe turned pale and shaky as if on the verge of fainting. His eyelids fluttered and his eyes rolled back until we saw total white. Ann embraced him and broke down at which I fled toward the car, stumbling along in the most complete, sick exhaustion of my life. Curiously, I had no trouble navigating on the hour's walk and it occurred to me that to the degree I had given up on my interior quarreling after the anxiety attack I had begun to notice better the "outside," or all that took place exterior of my mind. Of course this is obvious, nominal, and rather silly but it was, nonetheless, interesting.

I spent a full week in bed and bribed a nasty old critter of a doctor to make a house call from Munising, a hundred-and-twenty-mile round-trip. He was unimpressed by my illness, gave me some antibiotics, and had the cheekiness to tease me about my unpleasant affair in Munising a few years back. It turned out the wretched, gold-digging girl was his niece. One must be wary up here where nearly everyone is related. "Why should anyone screw an old fool except for cash on the barrelhead?" he quipped, giving me a shot.

Joe was another matter. Dick visited several times during my week in bed, bringing in and stacking a pile of wood near the fireplace. The pre–Labor Day weather had become unnaturally cold, driving most of the tourists and cottagers home early, or so he said. Joe and Ann had spent three days in his quarters only coming out for food. Joe hadn't really recovered and Ann had made a number of hysterical calls to the doctor in Marquette who had Fed Exed over an additional experimental sedative. Dick had talked separately to the doctor who was not optimistic because they were running out of drug options. However, Joe had disappeared in the middle of the night and when the new drugs arrived the next day Dick and Ann hadn't been able to find him at his cave until the following day at which time he grabbed the new bottle of pills and flung them off in the woods. Ann and Dick crawled around for an hour looking for the pills but then Marcia retrieved them. Ann cajoled Joe into taking one of the pills after which he became a somnolent "zombie" for several hours, an unacceptable condition for him.

On the last day of my convalescence there was further bad news that required me to take some action. Dick rushed out and said the D.N.R. game warden had stopped by and said that he had found three illegal set-lines, a method of continuing to fish when you are absent, on a portion of the Sucker River some two miles from Joe's cave, though he was not privy to its location. The warden had lain in wait several hours and when Joe had appeared, and the warden had tried to arrest him, Joe had run for it. What's more, some bear hunters were tracking a large bear and when their dogs temporarily cornered the beast it was wearing a set of cowbells on a collar. This constituted some sort of violation of "tampering with wildlife" much more serious evidently than shooting the beast although they were licensed to do so. The D.N.R. was smarting over the missing telemetric collars from earlier in the season and still had their sights on Joe.

My first impulse was to call my hotshot law firm in Chicago, but then Dick said he had already called a lawyer in Marquette who was capable in the area of fish and game violations. Since Joe was also charged with fleeing arrest, the situation was dire indeed. Dick was without the necessary retainer so I got out an old dry-fly box where I store cash and took a sturdy sheaf of hundreds. Much of the rare-book business is transacted in cash and it's fun to outwit the IRS on smallish sums when I've forked over millions over the years, having paid max income tax since early in my thirties. However, Dick shied away from the money saying he hoped I was well enough to meet the lawyer with him early in the evening at the tavern.

There is the vague notion that you can't escape the shit of life because you are also shit. I had spent a marvelous week simply being ill, at times uncomfortable but utterly diverted from problematical thinking. I ignored my large stack of brain books. A little knowledge is not so much dangerous as useless. Nothing that god and man have invented can help this young man. He's literally taking bites out of the sun, moon, and earth which is metaphysically illegal.

Instead of thinking I stared at the red sky every morning through the east window, planned minimalist meals, and read my collected Chekhov, a cheapish paper edition put out by Ecco Press. A well-made book can't live through the winter up here and any book with a nice binding goes with me when I close the cabin in mid-October.

Unfortunately on the last true night of my petty convalescence I was harried by animal dreams, ranging from my own pathetic mutt Charley to immense and distorted wolves and bears, strange sharks, and bear hounds in my yard where, in fact, they did occasionally arrive during the hunting season. I rather like these hounds, usually Walkers, who were quite sweet and docile except when chasing their prey. Hopefully the dream meant nothing.

Late in the afternoon while making myself spiffy to meet the lawyer a D.N.R. official showed up, a man who evidently was a supervisor of the more ordinary game wardens. I immediately took a liking to him because he was appreciative of the unique construction of my log cabin. My warmth cooled slowly when he began talking in a series of otiose clichés. He hoped there wouldn't be a big "brouhaha" over Joe's infractions. He somehow had found out about the lawyer we retained, evidently a fearsome creature. The official said that he felt "between a rock and a hard place" over Joe because "the law was the law." He was being "pressured by superiors" to shoot the bear wearing cowbells because they were sure the bells and collar would yield Joe's fingerprints. I retorted that a "pre-emptive" strike against the bear was a ghastly idea, and that slowed him down into a moment's contemplation, but then he said his department needed to "tie up the loose ends" on the missing telemetric collars. He proposed that if Joe would confess to the cowbells and telemetric collars they wouldn't have to shoot the bear and Joe might get off with a brief time in jail for the charge over the set-lines. I had a hot red flash in my brainpan and said that if Joe spent five minutes in jail I'd spend a cool million making the lives of him and his buddies politically miserable. He got up to leave saying that he guessed "we were at loggerheads."

Occasionally, as many of us know, our government can be quite literally an instrument of torture. I had to caution myself a bit here as I've always felt more confidence in the civil service than the collective citizenry. The upshot of the whole officious mudbath was that I lost the trail of a fantasy I was having about Ann where we were snuggled in bed at the Hotel Europa in St. Petersburg on a snowy night with my Viagras on the nightstand gleaming like jewels.

Ann as a sex object quickly dissipated when I reached the Rathbones and both Ann and Edna were sniveling at the kitchen table. Ann and Edna had gone grocery shopping in Seney and Dick was supposed to be keeping an eye on Joe but he didn't do so because Joe was in the little guest hut and Dick figured he was fine there. Well, they chorused, wait until I see the damage done. Dick now had Joe out for a dune walk trying to calm him down because Edna had "over-reacted" by screaming.

I followed the righteous ladies out to the guest cabin, not all that enthused about viewing something disgusting. The ladies were infuriated when I began laughing so hard my stomach muscles ached. What Joe had done was to totally take apart a dozen nature guidebooks—mammals, insects, birds, wildflowers, trees, etc.—and had covered walls, ceiling, and even the floor with the colorful photos. Unfortunately, Edna said, Joe had used something called Krazy Glue so his decorating job was there to stay unless it was all entirely re-done. I said I rather liked it which sent them away, but then I finally noticed that there were also a few risqué photos of

Ann included, and some decidedly meat-market-type photos clipped from men's magazines, more pronouncedly visceral than erotic. A photo of an actual beaver was pasted near a very distant cousin. Oh well, I thought, it could be worse. A photo of Ann's butt was surrounded by those of daisies and Indian paintbrush. No conclusions were required.

We had coffee until Dick and Joe returned, my mind still trapped by the room-sized collage, the improbable wild profusion of the natural world visually concentrated. While the ladies dithered on I began thinking that perhaps 99.9 percent of us have no idea where we are in the terms of Joe's decorated world made large. Books and television can't really extrapolate a world you must learn on foot as our ancestors learned it. True comprehension requires all of the senses. Joe was simply trying to surround himself with "beloved objects" as the Austrian poet Rilke put it. My mind fairly crackled with the possibilities offered by both the natural world and poetry. Typically I wondered if something was wrong with me. I had sat in this kitchen more than fifty years before and now Edna had replaced her mother. Who was this Ann with the beautiful neck? A new girl in town.

Dick and Joe came in the back door from the beach. Now the sky was reddish in the early evening through the screen door behind them. I normally wouldn't bet a penny on my talent for intuition but looking at these two men I sensed the middle of the end.

Dick and the lawyer sat with their backs to the window in the front booth of the tavern. I was facing them so I could look out the window at the street and harbor during the inevitable tedium of legal chat. We talked for a few minutes with a nearby table of old bear hunters, having known them for decades. Everyone in town by now knew about the bear wearing cowbells and these old woodsmen thought it quite funny, speaking with great admiration of anyone who could manage the trick. These men simply ran bear with their hounds and didn't shoot them because over the years each had taken a bear and in the ethic of their region, they were from Tennessee, a man was only entitled to one bear in his life. One of them talked about an old game biologist over in Ely, Minnesota, who was able to put telemetric collars on bears without "doping" them because the bears had known him so long. Dick told about a friend of his who lost fifty chickens to a toothless old bear who simply gummed them for their questionable juices.

We had just begun talking about the legal ramifications of Joe's stunts when I saw Joe and Ann walking down the far side of the street in front of the Bayshore Market. Two burly hunters had finished gassing up their truck and were entering the store when Joe stopped to pet the bear hounds tethered in the truck, not necessarily a smart thing to do, as tethered dogs, not able to escape, are often ornery. Dick and the lawyer turned in their seats to see what I was watching just as the two hunters came out of the Bayshore. I could hear one of them shout at Joe who turned, startled, and the second one pushed Joe roughly away from his dogs and Joe tripped over a gas hose falling flat to the cement. Ann slapped the hunter in roundhouse fashion and he pushed her violently away.

Dick yelled "Jesus" and then the three of us were up and rushing out of the tavern followed by the old bear hunters, but by the time we hit the street Joe was wrestling half in a mud puddle with one of the hunters and the other was on his knees slugging at Joe. Ann jerked him by his hair and ear and he screamed holding a hand to his bloody ear. He lunged at Ann but by this time Dick had reached the scene and gave him a good boot to the side of the head. The very large hunter had Joe in a bear hug as they rolled in the middle of the puddle but Joe bit off the tip of his nose, the only thing in reach. The gouting red blood contrasted oddly with the dark brown mud. He released Joe with a bellow and they both stood with the man rubbing his bloody face. Ann and Dick pulled Joe away as he spit out the man's nose tip which looked very odd on the cement.

What a mess, a grim euphemism at best. Someone had inappropriately called the town deputy. Such fisticuffs up here are generally treated as a private matter. The hunters wanted to press charges but there were ample witnesses to the first shove and there was the xenophobic advantage that Joe was local. Besides we had a lawyer at the ready. Meanwhile, Joe and Ann had walked down the grassy bank to the beach and harbor. Joe dove in to rinse off the mud and by the time I got there he was sitting in the sand with Ann. Marcia had arrived with three town dogs and Joe was back petting dogs where it had all started. He was laughing and, if anything, looked better than he had earlier. I was utterly nonplussed and sat down beside them thinking that he really couldn't belong in this world. He might have had a chance fifty years earlier, or further back in time.

After Labor Day the weather warmed up again. Another aspect of xenophobia is that every locale seems to think its weather is particularly interesting. Three days after the fight Dick had come out with an assortment of news with possibly legal consequences. The D.N.R. had claimed to our lawyer that they had a legal right to keep Joe out of both state and federal forestlands in areas where any game-management experiments were taking place. Our lawyer disabused them of that idea in that no charges had been brought due to insufficient evidence on the telemetric collars and the cowbell matters, and the set-line infraction was a paltry misdemeanor. When Dick had tried to explain to Joe that he couldn't put out set-lines Joe had ignored him at first, then pointed at his mouth as if to say,

"I have to eat." The plot had thickened at noon today. A logger had told Dick he had seen many armed D.N.R. officers in Joe's area which evidently startled Joe because today the collar and cowbells were found by the game warden's wife in their rural mailbox. For some reason this didn't make the posse happy.

Ann stopped by yesterday to say good-bye on her way back to East Lansing. Joe was with her but disappeared with Marcia while we were having coffee. He looked fine and she looked both exhausted and exasperated. She simply couldn't bear their redecorated quarters but anyway had to get back to her schoolwork. Joe spent hours going from glued photo to photo, she said, even staring at them when she thought it was far too dark for him to be able to see them. Was it possible, she asked, that he could see in the dark better then she could? I said that I had no idea. I sensed that her romantic feelings for Joe were finally being crippled by her inability to imagine any sort of future for them. I certainly didn't bring up the subject of pregnancy but she did just before she left. At this state of her desperation it didn't hurt me to be kind so I said I'd marry her if she was pregnant in order to make her life easier with her parents. I'd even send her off for a year's solo trip to Russia and Europe whether or not she was pregnant, quite a honeymoon! This improved her mood and she was kind enough to say that I was welcome to come over for a visit.

Joe arrived at dinnertime today with two brook trout, one about a pound and a half and the other a trophy-sized three pounds. There was still enough of the fisherman in my past that I got out my topographical maps and he pointed dead center in a five-square-mile swamp not all that far away, certainly an unavailable location to a geezer. While I was grilling the trout over a wood fire Joe and Marcia took a skinny dip in the river and I noted that Joe's legs

were even more extremely muscled than those of the NBA basketball players I had seen. I idly thought that maybe Dick would con-
sent to dropping Joe off in northern Ontario and I would pay a
Cree family to look after him. Life in the present-day Upper Peninsula no longer seemed possible. The day for the freedom he required
was past in the United States.

The early evening was warmish but somehow still autumnal.
I gave Joe back his notebooks but when he tried to throw them on
the still-hot coals I took them back. When he left for town, refusing a ride, he shook hands with me for the first time since before
his injury, a civilized good-bye gesture. My throat thickened a bit
as he and Marcia walked off down the two-track.

It was well after dark when Dick drove out to tell me that Joe had
disappeared at sea. A group of brain-damaged older folks who live
at what is wittily called our limited-care facility were walking down
Coast Guard Point when they saw Joe dive into the harbor. Marcia
was already out there swimming after geese who amused themselves
by staying a dozen feet ahead of her. The chaperone of the group
hadn't been too alarmed when he saw Joe swim out of sight in a
half-hour or so. By the time he called Dick it was dark and several
boats were launched for a desultory search because it was everyone's conviction that Joe had probably returned and headed into
the woods.

It was about eleven when Dick first arrived and I asked him
why he seemed to think Joe had kept swimming north to Canada.
He said it mostly was a matter of thirty-three dollars tied up by a
red ribbon on the table in Joe's cabin, not exactly a suicide note
but a gesture in that direction.

We had a few drinks of whiskey until about two in the morning questioning ourselves on why we assumed the worst, coming

up with not all that much that was specific other than feeling that
Joe himself had sensed that the arc of his life was over. We chided
ourselves about this flimsy conclusion but couldn't come up with
anything else. As an old fish and game pro Dick came up with the
dubious notion that Joe had run out of suitable habitat. I said, "But
he's a human being," without a great deal of conviction. Perhaps
inspired by the whiskey I rambled on with a mishmash drawn from
the brain books and my own dimmish experience with the absolute sense of dislocation felt by many comparatively normal folks
let alone those with closed-head injuries. It had occurred to me that
Joe had lost a lifetime of habituation and conditioning when he hit
the beech tree on his motorcycle. After nearly a year of insignifi-
cant help by the medical community through no fault of their own
(there are limits to optimism not felt by the financial community)
Joe set off on foot to re-map the world, or the only world his senses
could tolerate. Ultimately there was not enough of this world to
make his life tolerable. I had read that such people in New York
City often live in subway tunnels if they are not confined in Bellevue.

I was losing Dick in my pompous droning. I said, "Oh fuck
it" and our mutual tears fell. "He was a wild one, that boy," Dick
said, pouring us what he called "a final nightcap." He began to talk
about our own youthful antics in the woods but stopped himself.
The simple and obvious fact was that we always had a return ticket,
that we hadn't suffered any metamorphoses by fate. Dick somewhat
comically began to massage his head as if questioning its true contents. We laughed over his gesture. He decided to walk the five miles
home in the middle of the night, not wanting to run into a tree and
wreck his head and pick-up. Dick always said that walking for him
was not much more tiring than sleeping.

When I went to bed I fretted over who would have to call Ann.
Me, naturally. When nearly asleep I consciously watched dream
images arise from my gray matter, from stray dogs to the time my

wife, after two gin fizzes, climbed a tree in our backyard. This isn't permissible, I yelled up to her. Clouds rolled. The moon shone. Joe laughed. Ann cried. Joe shook my hand with his hand. My dad died yet again. I looked down in the water and couldn't see the bottom.

Some lake trout fishermen found Joe at Caribou Shoals at noon the next day, thirty miles out in Lake Superior, certainly not an impossible swim as Joe had proven. One of the fishermen claimed Joe was "nearly alive" when they pulled him aboard but the two others weren't sure. I called Ann immediately and she said, "No, he isn't" and hung up.

Now it is early October, dear Coroner, and I have finished my chore far beyond the call of spurious duty. His mother agreed with me that his remains should be cremated and I will go with Dick Rathbone and Ann out to his cave and scatter the ashes. Ann is angry, of course, that she isn't pregnant. We figure some adoring, late-season tourist has packed up Marcia who would never tolerate a collar and will be quite happy with anyone who feeds her properly. Like any other mammal I am trying, moment by moment, to think of what I should do next. Joe had left us to ourselves.

Westward Ho

In Westwood Brown Dog recognized a cloud as one he had seen several years before over two thousand miles to the east out near Fayette on Big Bay de Noc. The cloud was sure enough the same one, no question about it. The question was what route did it take to California, to Westwood in particular? This cloud sighting was not remarkable in itself. In a lifetime in the woods he had witnessed three different birds (a raven, a red-tailed hawk, and a lowly robin) drop dead off their separate perches, and once while illegally pillaging a shipwreck in Lake Superior at a depth of a hundred feet or so, a very large passing lake trout had picked that moment to drop, wobbling slow and lifeless to the lake's floor. There was a moment's temptation to pluck it up and stow it in his diving bag with some brass fittings from the sunken ship, but then it occurred to him that the fish had achieved a peaceful death and it wouldn't be quite right to fry it up, douse it with hot sauce, and eventually turn it into a turd. As a child his grandfather was wont to say when B.D. was sullen or depressed, "Keep your chin up, Bucko. We all end up as worm turds."

The cloud passed away, replaced by blue. B.D. stretched in his nest beneath the immense leaves of the taro bush (*Colocasia esculenta*) in the U.C.L.A. botanical gardens, a bush, he decided, that was one of God's most peculiar inventions, so unlike his native flora in Michigan's Upper Peninsula as to be from another planet. But beautiful as his dome of vast green leaves was it did not help Brown Dog locate himself as was his habit on waking. This was to break the thrall of his vivid dream life, a spell that dissipated easily when you said, "I'm in the cabin where it's about forty degrees. The wind out of the northwest at thirty knots. November first and if I hadn't had the extra poke of whiskey I would have got up in the night and fed the stove and it would have been fifty in here instead of forty, a weenie-shrinking dawn." That sort of thing. How can you start the day without knowing where you are?

Or, perhaps more important, why? The answer to which is bound to be lengthy, imprecise, blurred by the urge to think that where you are is bound to be the right place on your short and brutish passage. Seven days ago he had been in the Upper Peninsula and now he was under a taro bush in Westwood in what is euphemistically called greater Los Angeles (what with lesser Los Angeles throbbing to be released on a moment's notice and frequently springing free).

Frankly, Brown Dog was on the lam, having flown the Michigan coop with Lone Marten, an erstwhile though deeply fraudulent Indian activist, after a series of petty misdemeanors and relatively harmless felonies. His original crime had been pillaging

Lake Superior shipwrecks, even removing a Native body from one, a corpse he had eventually decided might have been that of his dead father, though this conclusion was based on circumstantial evidence. Like the proverbial collapsing dominoes, this first crime seemed to lead to others, though in his own mind he was altruistic because his abrasive brushes with the law had come from his efforts to protect a secret Indian graveyard, the presence of which had been betrayed in a pussy trance with a lovely young anthropologist. Concurrent with these legal problems was the fact that Lone Marten had abandoned him in Cucamonga two days before. Brown Dog had gone into a rest room to pee and when he came out Lone Marten was gone, and when Brown Dog had asked the attendant about Lone Marten's whereabouts because his precious bearskin was in the trunk the attendant had said, "Beat it or I'll call the cops," not a very friendly welcome. He persisted, asking directions to Westwood whereupon the attendant merely pointed west. Brown Dog was a bit transfixed by the attendant's large hoop earrings which seemed inadvisable if you were going to get in a fight. Your opponent had only to grab your earrings and you were dead meat, or so he thought as he set out for the west with a somewhat heavy heart but down a road with a comforting name, Arrow Highway.

The walk from Cucamonga to Westwood is some forty-seven miles, not all that far for a man often referred to in his home area as a "walking fool." It took Brown Dog a rather leisurely thirty-six hours, making way for short cheapish meals and naps which he accomplished with the true woodsman capability of dozing with his eyes open. This didn't seem the area in which you could safely close your eyes. When he had asked Lone Marten just how many people were in Los Angeles and Lone Marten had said, "Millions and millions," the amount proved mentally indigestible. Not since the student riots in Chicago that took place while Brown Dog was a very casual student at the Moody Bible Institute had he seen this many people going to and fro. It was apparent that there was a lot going on but he wasn't sure what. Another big crowd in his life had been the Ishpeming Bugle and Firefighters Convention a few years before but there the purpose had been quite specific. Brown Dog had stood in the garage parking lot waiting for the head gasket of his van to be replaced and had watched several hundred buglers take turns doing their best. This turned out to be more than enough bugling to last a lifetime.

A forty-seven-mile walk offers plenty of time to think things over but it is the walking rather than the thinking that calms the spirit. Brown Dog had none of the raw melancholy that the well educated often feel when first encountering Los Angeles. His frame of mind was a great deal more functional with the single purpose being to retrieve his bearskin and head back to the country, wherever that might be, though he had pondered Canada as a haven that might be safe from the arm of the law, and not the lovely strip club in the Canadian Soo where the girls got down to no clothing at all, but perhaps way up on the Nipigon River on the north shore of Lake Superior. Sizable brook trout were said to be plentiful there and he could always go back to the obnoxious job of cutting pulp.

B.D.'s last walk of this length had taken place a few years before when two Grand Marais girls he had driven over to Munising had ditched him there when he had drunk too much at the Corktown Bar and walked down a grassy knoll near the harbor for a snooze. He thought himself deeply in love with one of the girls, innocently named Mary, who originally hailed from Detroit and it was she with her own dark past who had hot-wired his van and taken off for a weekend in Iron Mountain. So deep was his grief and anger over this betrayal that he walked back to Grand Marais, taking a leisurely full two days, over forty miles and sadly, or so he thought in the present, about the same distance as Cucamonga to Westwood. But much of his Munising–to–Grand Marais hike had

been cross country and except for a stop at the small store in Mel-
strand to pick up a few cans of pork and beans he had not viewed
another human being. It was mid-May and warmish with a big
moon and by the time of his first campfire he had largely gotten
over Mary. Frank, his true friend and the owner of a local tavern,
had warned him that Mary was "fast," the evidence being the morning that B.D. had sunk himself in Frank's bathtub, the water to
which had been added a potent anti-crab medicine. There weren't
any fleas that far north and Brown Dog had been puzzled by a
buggy feeling all over his body, even in his eyebrows. Frank had
worked construction way down in Florida and made the expert
analysis from experience.

A few hours out of Cucamonga he suddenly remembered
where he had heard the name before. His grandfather had listened
to the Jack Benny program on Sunday evenings on their battery-
operated Zenith and Jack Benny himself had often traveled through
Cucamonga on the train to Hollywood. Jack Benny's buddy
Rochester would sometimes yell "Cucamonga" for no apparent
reason and one summer evening when there was a very small bear
rummaging in their garbage pit at the far end of the garden the bear
had suddenly looked up on hearing Rochester's voice. He and his
friend David Four Feet, who died in Jackson Prison, were full of
envy at Rochester's voice though they were incapable of imitating
it and when they tried Grandfather would yell, "Batten your gob."

The memory of Jack Benny lifted his spirits and B.D.'s vision
expanded from the cement beneath his feet and the narrow tunnel
in front of him that his emotions up to this point had allowed. Before Jack Benny he had been trying to remember the gist of the
biblical story about Ruth among the "alien corn." During his brief
period at the Moody Bible Institute in Chicago the pastor from the
church back home had sent a letter about Ruth among the alien corn
to assuage Brown Dog's possible homesickness. Unfortunately the

church had mistakenly sent B.D. the entire tuition check rather than directing it to the institute and he had squandered the money on a black waitress. The expression "head over heels in love" had always puzzled him because, though love could be physically rigorous, it didn't seem quite that acrobatic.

As his vision widened somewhat his native curiosity, surely the most valuable thing one can own, took over and he began to observe this foreign country of Los Angeles more closely and certain things became clear. For instance, millions of new cars were supposedly sold every year but you saw few of them in the Upper Peninsula except on Routes 2 and 28 during tourist season where they were collectively parked in front of the more expensive motels in the evening. Here in Los Angeles there were countless thousands of new cars which meant the locals must be making money hand over fist. But standing on an overpass stretched above the San Gabriel River Freeway and staring down at six lanes of jam-packed traffic going bumper to bumper in both directions, he wondered why the drivers on each side of the highway just didn't trade jobs and avoid the mess. B.D. also read the sign twice but couldn't find the San Gabriel River and there were no other pedestrians to ask the river's whereabouts.

Hours before he had stopped in a small park and had been rather amazed at the flora, none of which he recognized, though he knew the names of hundreds of trees and bushes in the Upper Peninsula. The birds were also a mystery and he wondered idly at God's messiness in inventing so many species, then decided it was the messiness of nature that gave it such beauty.

He tried to extend his pursuit by the law into a gentler region of his mind to avoid the sensation that he should be looking over his shoulder even though the scene of the crime was two thousand miles to the east. He had burned the tent of two evil young anthropologists to protect his Indian graveyard, also with Lone Marten had lobbed cherry bombs and M-80 firecrackers into a protected archeological site, the graveyard, in an attempt to drive away the despoilers. This was scarcely a high crime but his probation had dictated he could not enter Alger County though the attack engineered by Lone Marten had strayed only a few hundred yards from Luce County into Alger. The point in Brown Dog's mind was that if only the law imitated the gorgeously messy aspects of nature the judge might say "Let bygones be bygones" or something on that order. And then he could go back home, assuming that he recovered his bearskin. Delmore had mentioned that a bearskin should never be taken away from the region in which the animal had been killed because the skin sometimes still contained the spirit of the beast though B.D. suspected that Delmore often made up Indian lore when it suited his purpose.

The biggest problem on the long walk had been water. They weren't exactly giving it away in this area. He had been charged fifty cents at a fast-food place for a large Styrofoam cup of water and hadn't been able to drink it because it seemed to contain some weird chemicals. The girl behind the counter had been sympathetic to B.D.'s startled look when he tasted the water and pointed out a cooler that contained quarts of the stuff at over a dollar apiece. It was a warm day and he had no choice. He wasn't quite prepared for this experience but recalled a quarrel in Frank's Tavern over the matter of bottled water that had recently entered the Upper Peninsula. At the time he had been struggling to hear his all-time favorites, Patsy Cline and Janis Joplin, on the jukebox and Ed Mikula, the chief of the local Finns, was hollering that God's own precious water was now being sold in bottles for more than beer or gasoline per ounce. Who was behind this crime was the question at hand? When asked his opinion B.D. said that water, gasoline, and beer were equally important but not interchangeable, and he was up to walking to any number of springs he knew of to get first-

rate water even in the dead of winter, a fine notion though springs
in Los Angeles were unlikely so he paid the full price for a quart of
water that the label said had been shipped all the way from France,
a boggling idea. He imagined some secret enormous burbling spring
in far-off France and wanted to question the store clerk but she was
now busy. There was the immediate notion that when he got back
home he need only bottle twenty quarts of water from one of his
springs to make a living wage. He had stuffed a fifteen-foot pole
down in one of them and it had shot back up in the air from the
force of the water. If you had a hangover you could just lie there
on the soft green moss, drink plenty of the cold water, and after
you were still for a while the brook trout would begin swimming
around again.

    After the first twenty-four hours of walking the map he had
bought for yet another dollar at a service station had turned soft
from his sweaty hands. He had passed the confusing place where
César E. Chávez Avenue became Sunset Boulevard and had bought
a black lunch bucket and a green janitor's uniform at a secondhand
store, the lunch bucket to carry his water and any leftovers from
his snacks. He was down to forty-nine dollars but then forty-nine
was also his age so this collusion somehow appeared fortuitous at
least for the time being. The problem was that he was beginning to
stink and needed a place to suds off before putting on the clean
clothes. The janitor's shirt had the name "Ted" stamped on a pocket
but then he felt it was unlikely that he find a shirt with his own name
on it. He made his way up to Silver Lake Reservoir, clambered over
the fence, and had a short swim. A number of hikers and dog
walkers had hollered at him because swimming was forbidden in
the city's water supply but he ignored them. The objectors had
withdrawn for the same reason that two unfriendly Mexican fel-
lows had withdrawn back near Monterery Park when Brown Dog
had asked for directions. First, to all he looked rather goofy, and

second in modern terms he was quite a physical specimen from his lifelong work in the woods. He didn't have the big breasts of the many bodybuilders he had seen on the streets in their tight T-shirts, but he could unload a four-hundred-pound iron wood-stove from a pick-up all by himself and other men tend to notice those capable of such feats. But more important, B.D. lacked a single filament of hostility in his system. Even way back in his teens when he was a champion bare-knuckle fighter in the western U.P. he was not prone to anger unless an opponent poked him in the eye. Even his anger over the soon-to-be-desecrated Indian (Anishinabe) graveyard was directed more at himself for betraying the location. In addition, he had what used to be called a "winning smile," though that wouldn't be true as he drew near the Pacific and the more prosperous areas because two teeth were prominently missing.

Under his poi or taro leaf in the botanical gardens there were a number of things to take pleasure in. He had had enough sense not to discard the neatly folded garbage bag in his back pocket. "Just when you think you won't need it anymore you will," old Claude liked to say. Claude would get in his garbage bag when he was out in the backcountry and it began to rain, or if the wind was cold he would step into his, hunch down, and pull the drawstring and have a nice curled-up snooze. Claude insisted the garbage bag was one of the great inventions of modern man along with toilet paper and galvanized buckets. Brown Dog tended to agree but mostly when he needed one. The Westwood night was tolerably warm for a northerner but the laid-out garbage bag made a nice ground cloth to protect him from moisture. His pleasure was not diminished by the fact that Westwood didn't seem to have much in the way of woods, and just before dark he noted that the small pond with a feeder rivulet contained only a dozen or so lethargic orange carp. It might have been nice to cook one on a bed of coals but a fire would doubtless draw attention and the botanical park was officially closed for the night.

A good share of his pleasure under his leafy blanket came from his grandfather's notion that you had to make the best of it wherever you were, and throughout the long hike from Cucamonga he had been pleasantly boggled by all the colors of the people he had seen who must come from many lands. Way back in school he had never been quite taken with the idea of America as a boiling pot, partly because his grandpa had used a boiling pot to scald pigs at butchering in order to scrape off the hair. Despite his hard knocks he felt a specific pleasure in all he had seen, especially along the busy part of Sunset Strip as he had continued heading west late in the afternoon. There had been literally hundreds of beautiful women though they tended to be uniformly quite thin in his terms. Delmore liked to say that you should avoid women who don't enjoy their food because that means they have real problems, but even old Delmore would have had his head turned by this plenitude. To be sure, not one of them gave him a glance but he suspected this was because of the green janitor's suit and the black lunch bucket which had the good quality he noted of making him invisible to the many police he had seen.

In fact he had become quite invisible to everyone except for a few other menial workers who nodded in greeting. When he had made his way farther west into the swank residential area of Beverly Hills he fairly had to wave in the face of a girl selling star maps which he quickly perceived had nothing to do with the constellations. He repeated his question about the whereabouts of Westwood three times before she deigned to take notice. Her eyes focused past his neck as she said that a few miles farther on he should take a left on Hilgard. There was something distinctly familiar about her and he remembered that last winter when a tree he was cutting had kicked back and injured his knee, during his convalescence Delmore had rented him a video called *Butts Galore* and this girl sure looked like one of the "butts" in the film. He couldn't help but ask her and she replied, "Maybe yes, maybe no," but a slight tinge of blush entered her cheeks. He would have tried to continue the conversation but a carload of older tourists pulled over wanting to know where Fred MacMurray lived so Brown Dog moved on. You couldn't say *Butts Galore* was a top-drawer movie but it was certainly amazing to just get into town and meet an actress you recognized. The fact of the matter was that Brown Dog hadn't seen many movies. The closest theater in one direction was in Newberry and that was over fifty miles distant, and in the other direction Marquette's theaters were over a hundred miles to the west. Delmore played old westerns on his VCR because they were cheap to rent and he hated them which gave rise to a much needed emotional life. There was also the additional shortcoming to Brown Dog who lived on a subsistence level that a price of a movie was a price of five beers at Frank's Tavern. Once as an early teen he and David Four Feet had hot-wired a Plymouth and gone to a drive-in theater to see what was advertised as a daring sex movie. Part of it was a cartoon showing a phalanx of sperm traveling up into the womb and David had hollered out the car window, "That's me in the lead," to much general laughter and horn beeping. The movie ended with a rather skinny woman giving birth in a rather frightening close-up that could not readily be distinguished from any of the farm animals they had seen giving birth. They both agreed they could have used the fifty cents apiece to see the genitals of a classmate, Debbie Schwartz, which is what she charged, a buck a look.

After finding his botanical-garden nest Brown Dog drifted through the greenery in the last of the twilight. There was a slight evening breeze from the west, clearing the air which had all day long resembled a sheen of yellow snot with the heat close enough to body temperature to emphasize the exudate nature of the air.

B.D. found a patch of bamboo and lit a match to see it more closely, noting with pleasure that the bamboo was a giant version of the cane poles he had used as a child to fish inland lakes. This bamboo was a half foot in diameter and he supposed that it was capable of landing a fish the size of a Budweiser Clydesdale. The breeze picked up further and rattled the bamboo. He thought the breeze must surely come from the Pacific Ocean and his body fairly shimmered with delight at the prospect of seeing this body of water. He had spent enough time with maps, his favorite school book being the world atlas in the library, and he remembered clearly what this ocean looked like on paper. While he arranged his Hefty garbage bag on the ground his thoughts of the Pacific wavered into the image of a girl getting out of a Mercedes convertible on Sunset, and as luck would have it he had been blessed with a clear view way up her legs to her pale blue undies and slightly visible fur pieces. She had trotted down the sidewalk and into a store and he had marveled at her grace of movement, the fluid lubricant that fills such a body and makes it move so beautifully. He whispered a very old song, "I'd love to get you on a slow boat to China," something on that order, before he slept, quite unmindful in his ordinariness that his straits were dire indeed, or that some in this immediate area of a great university, not to speak of the film business, would mistake this ordinariness as extraordinary.

Those who sleep outside a great deal know that this sleep can't aspire to the comatose aspects of hibernation that so many seem to crave from night. You might wake up a hundred times for a moment or two, allowing your senses of hearing or smell or sight in the dimmish light to test your surroundings. This is unconscious enough not to deter from rest. Brown Dog was visited by a single curious cat for a short time, and also the stars which finally made an appearance

as the ambient light of the city diminished. The few times he became conscious enough his thought processes settled on simple
things such as he would not be able to continue spending seven
dollars a day on water. The air was quite sweet in the garden, a wonderful contrast to the fungoid odors of the motel rooms he had
stayed in with Lone Marten who was armed with a dozen phony
credit cards. Brown Dog had suggested that a couple of cheap sleeping bags would cost less than a night in a motel and Lone Marten
had called him a fool and a "blanket ass," a pejorative term for traditional Natives. Lone Marten insisted he needed a desk at night
to work on the "colloquium" he would perform at U.C.L.A. Lone
Marten called him a fool so often that in Laramie B.D. had to run
him up the wall by his belt so that he flopped there while B.D. asked
him to stop using the word "fool," that in biblical terms it was a
terrible thing to call your brother a fool. Of course from his uncomfortable position Lone Marten agreed, thinking at the time that
if he weren't David Four Feet's brother he might actually be in
danger with this simpleminded fool who hadn't the sense to do
anything to his own advantage.

About an hour before dawn a siren howled down Hilgard
Avenue and through the foliage B.D. could see the flickering amber
lights of an ambulance, the yowl the most ghastly of all human-
produced sounds, which had barely subsided when a Medevac
chopper fluttered and whacked overhead landing on the roof of
the medical center that adjoined the gardens. Rather than being
irritated B.D. had the feeling that these local people had the
wherewithal to immediately take care of their sick or injured. A
few winters before a logger friend had had some of his ass literally
frozen off when he had been trapped by a fallen log for about eight
hours before help came. Of course, he reminded himself, he had
seen a great number of the miserably poor on his day-and-a-half
walk who might be advised to walk in front of a car for a change of

luck. There was an owl with an unfamiliar call directly above him and moments later the first stirring of dawn birds which always brought on an hour or so of the deepest sleep the outdoor sleeper can have, maybe a genetic remnant from a time when the predatory enemy was always nocturnal and first light meant the sweet dream of security.

Having finally figured out where he was Brown Dog was on his knees neatly brushing off and folding his garbage bags when he was approached by two garden workers, a young man and woman, who told him he wasn't allowed to sleep there. "But I already have," he said, adding that it was a truly wonderful place. They were botany graduate students and the lumpish girl tried to give him a dollar which he turned down saying he already had forty-nine dollars. He asked a few questions about the flora which they referred to as "Pacific rim," a new term for him though in his mind's eye he could see the black ink outline of the ocean in the atlas. He also asked if there was a nice woods in the vicinity where he could camp out and they thought not, though the young man added that he might check out Will Rogers State Park farther out Sunset. A mountain lion supposedly lived there, right smack-dab in Los Angeles, also lots of coyotes, not to speak of rattlesnakes and birds. This information made B.D. think that this wasn't a bad place after all. He asked the whereabouts of the "Indian office" at the university in hopes of a starting place for tracking down Lone Marten. They only said that there might be one but they didn't know where it was. They said good-bye then and when they walked off with their pruning shears the lumpish girl had begun to look pretty good. B.D. thought they could sit naked together in the carp pool near the bamboo thicket and it would be like some old movie set in a tropical island. On the way out of the garden he looked at the top of a very tall palm tree and it reminded him of one of Delmore's favorite movies, *Sands of Iwo Jima*, which B.D. didn't care for because of the endless gore. The stealthy Japanese hid at the tops of coconut trees because, according to Delmore, their heads looked like coconuts. Delmore's own head looked like a beige bowling ball, size nine, in fact, on the top of a small wiry frame.

When B.D. emerged from the garden his heart jumped and his stride quickened. What luck! Right there across Hilgard, parked illegally, was the five-year-old dirty brown Taurus station wagon, Lone Marten's car, and a rumpled and burly man was unlocking the car. Brown Dog dodged the early-morning traffic with difficulty and when he looked back at the Taurus a squad car had screeched up behind it and the burly man was leaning against the car in despair. Brown Dog's momentum, caused by a leap to escape a yellow Ferrari, was such that he was nearly in between the burly man and the cop before he could stop himself. This was a collusion of fates that afterward would stun B.D. For lack of a better thing he opened his lunch bucket and swigged the last of his water, noting too late that it definitely wasn't Lone Marten's brown Taurus. Shit, he thought, as he smiled lamely at the burly man and the cop. At the very moment a half dozen U.C.L.A. coeds, definitely sorority girls, flounced up the sidewalk singing a merry tune, all with uniformly tan brown legs and trim bottoms. While the cop glanced at the girls the burly man winked frantically at B.D. and flashed a wad of bills from his pocket. The cop looked back at the man and then at Brown Dog with irritation.

"I think you were going to drive. I could take you in," the cop said.

"I was getting a manuscript out of the car while I waited for my driver, Ted. You really shouldn't arrest me for my supposed intention. Besides, Ted drives me everywhere."

"Get in the car and start it," the cop said and Brown Dog took the keys from the man and started the car, so obviously not Lone Marten's though it was even more of a mess. It didn't, however, smell of Lone Marten's main fuel, cannabis. The car phone, the first of his life, began to ring and the man jumped in the passenger side, saying, "It's the coast."

"We're already on the coast, fuckhead," the cop said and then demanded B.D.'s driver's license. "You're the driver. Where's your license?"

"Yes, sir," B.D. said, knowing with cops that politeness was the primary move. He was somewhat proud that he kept his driver's license current though in fact the renewal form constituted the only mail he ever received, not being a member of any organization or even owning a social security number. The cop appeared as if he were going to return to his squad car to check the license, then changed his mind saying that he was originally from Livonia which was part of Detroit and had been up deer hunting around Curtis which wasn't all that far from Grand Marais. The cop had also fished perch at Les Cheneaux and walleye near Rapid River, two species that bored B.D. though he didn't say so. B.D. asked him why he had moved to L.A. and the cop said he had always wanted to become an actor. As they shook hands the cop stooped and looked over at the burly man who was in the middle of saying on the phone, "If you think I'd do a rewrite for a hundred thou you can suck a Republican's dick."

"Bob, shut up and listen to me. Don't ever in your wildest dreams try to drive a car in this city again. You're grounded forever, Bob. You'd do a year minimum no matter what lawyer you got. If you so much as touch a steering wheel you'll be eating and shitting with beaners and jigs for three hundred and sixty-five days."

"You shouldn't talk to me like that, you blue-belt pansy. I was a United States marine," Bob said, hanging up the car phone.

"You were never a marine, Bob. We know your record. You're only a writer." The cop walked off as if he had won the day and B.D. turned to Bob wondering how he dared call a cop a "blue-belt pansy," so he asked him.

"The U.S. Constitution. Also he wants a part in a movie. He tried to get my last D.U.I. reduced but lower-echelon cops can't swing anything. I went over the curb on San Vincente onto the median because it was hot and I wanted to park under a tree for shade."

"What did you blow?" Brown Dog asked. Driving under the influence was a big-ticket item in the U.P., especially around Marquette and Escanaba.

"I blew a point two three which is slightly major." He gestured for B.D. to get moving and they headed north up Hilgard toward Sunset. "The name's Bob Duluth. Where do you want to go?"

Brown Dog said "the ocean" but the question was puzzling in that he had supposed Bob had places to go for meetings or whatever. There was also the unnerving idea that this was the most unlikely way he had ever gotten a job and there was the question of whether life should be changing this fast. He explained to Bob his theory about not driving over forty-nine and Bob said if you did that on the freeways you'd get your basic tailpipe up your ass. Bob's language was a strange mixture to B.D., half the low-rent vulgarity of pulp cutters and construction workers, and half the peculiar kind of elevated talk B.D. identified with woods yuppies, as they were called, richer people that built in remote places way up north in order to be close to nature. These were often nice enough folks but their conversational patterns were quite intricate. B.D. had cut firewood for a couple in their thirties who had had a top-rate crew come all the way from Minnesota to build them an elaborate log house. They overpaid him for firewood and he had tried to give them some venison (illegal out of season) in return, but they were devout vegetarians. This was quite odd to B.D., one of whose ambitions was to eat a porterhouse every day for a week if he ever had the wherewithal. The couple had even invited him to take a sauna with them and the woman was absolutely bare naked and a knockout at that. He feared he'd get an erection but then he had a hangover and they raised the heat level to an unbearable degree to "purify their bodies." They fed him a vegetarian meal with some vegetables and grains dressed up like meat which was pretty good though later in the evening he had one of Frank's special half-pound burgers. They had become distanced when he had run into the woman outside the I.G.A. grocery store and she had said, "I feel good about myself." B.D. had simply asked, "Why?" and she had totally delaminated and started screeching that he was a "thankless bastard" right there on the street which made the locals think he'd had an affair with her. Sadly, this was not true. Once when he had delivered firewood the couple had been doing their yoga exercises on the sun deck and the woman who was wearing a bikini had her heels locked behind her neck when she waved at him. He unloaded and stacked two full cords of beech while they were flopping around on the sundeck and he was quite amazed at their contortions.

Bob fell asleep in the car after using words as varied as "etiolate," "shitsucker," "fractious," and "motherfucker." Brown Dog turned off into the Will Rogers State Park out on Sunset just to check it out as he had a feeling the job might not last and he might need to set up camp. The park fairly made his mouth water as there were few people around and the hills looked endless. Just the idea that there was a mountain lion roaming around made all of the multimillion-dollar homes in the distance look rather toylike and puny. The yoga couple never had any houseguests at their "retreat," or so they called it, and the locals wondered why they had two bathrooms.

Before Bob dozed off B.D. had heard a few items from his past that seemed a bit jumbled and possibly fibs. Bob said that he initially meant to be a scholar of real old literature from England, had taught in Ashland in northern Wisconsin, then at the University of Wisconsin in Madison which he considered his home. His wife and the son and daughter attending college were all fatally ill. This raised a lump in B.D.'s throat though only moments later Bob said his son was a Big Ten gymnast and his daughter a long-distance runner who had placed high in the Chicago Marathon, and his wife ran her own landscape gardening business. B.D. tried to imagine them all plodding to their strenuous activities shot through with mortal illness. No matter how well they were doing Bob felt that it behooved him to make money to insure comfort in their doomed futures. In successive summers Bob Duluth had written three mystery novels that did very well that featured a midwestern professor who was alone among all men in sensing the true and pervasive evil in the world. For the past few years Bob had been in and out of Hollywood to make the vast sums of money required to pay for the treatment of his gymnast, runner, and businesswoman. He dared B.D. to ask how much and B.D. asked, "How much?" and Bob said, "Over a grand a day," an inconceivable sum to B.D. It was, however, in this matter and Bob's current occupation as a "screenwriter" that B.D. sensed the skunk in the woodpile. Back in high school there had been a teacher fresh out of the University of Michigan, rather than one of the state's many teachers colleges, who was much disliked by the other staff for being too smart for his own good. This young teacher knew how everything in the world worked and, what's more, could explain it to his students. He cut up a bunch of movie film and somehow developed it, put it on a wind-up roller and spun it, showing how moving pictures worked. It was still as impressive to B.D. years later and the teacher hadn't made any mention of anyone writing the spinning film. Even though Bob

Duluth said he only invented the entire stories for films he still
seemed on thin ice. Unfortunately this beloved teacher had been
caught tinkering with Debbie Schwartz on a woodland field trip,
the same girl who made pin money showing her underpants. Debbie
was fifteen at the time, though in most respects older than the teacher.
The students widely protested the teacher's firing but the school
board was adamant. Brown Dog and David Four Feet did their part
by throwing dog shit and Limburger cheese in the blower down in
the school's furnace room which evacuated the school. B.D. heard
that years later Debbie and the grand teacher had been married and
were living in a mansion near San Francisco, the teacher having
invented new functions for computers.

As they continued on toward Malibu, Bob Duluth was still
asleep, snoring in fact, with an unattractive bubble of sputum on
his lips. B.D. figured the man must work pretty hard because there
were bags under his eyes and he twitched in his sleep like Grandpa
used to when he worked two straight shifts, sixteen hours, at the
sawmill.

B.D. wasn't quite ready for one of the signal experiences of
his life. He had been following a slow-moving green Chrysler driven
by a blue-haired lady when he looked up on a rise in the road and
there was the Pacific Ocean. He drove off on the narrow shoulder,
got out, and leaned against the car hood, at first with his face in his
hands and peeking out between his fingers because the view was
far too much to be absorbed wide open. He felt choky as if there
were a lump of coal beneath his breastbone and his body buzzed
in a way not unlike the minutes before sex. If he had known
Beethoven's "Hymn to Joy" he would have been hearing it, and
the vast, rumpled bluish green water drew on his soul so that his
soul only spoke the language of water, forgetting all else. He simply couldn't wait to touch it with his hands, so he jumped back in
the Taurus and sped off with Bob Duluth opening one eye in care-

less non-recognition Who is driving me and who cares? I've been
up all night eating what's left of my heart, over an actress at that. A
Brown Dog driving a brown car.

In Malibu, B.D. parked in the nearly empty lot of a restaurant, locked the car, and made his way down to the beach. He knelt
and felt the water, colder than he expected, about like Lake
Superior in May. A wave submerged his shoes with a delicious
feeling, his feet, so unused to cement, still sore from the jaunt from
Cucamonga. A big sailboat came by, its rail nearly buried in the
water. B.D. waved and two folks in yellow slickers waved back,
which gave him a good feeling about the human race. He sat on
the beach for an hour in a state of total forgetfulness about his new
job, watching seabirds that resembled the rare piping plover but
were a bit larger, no doubt cousins. His mind was a peaceful blank
other than thinking that after he retrieved his bearskin and before
he headed back to Michigan to face the music, or better yet northern Ontario which was the U.P.'s cousin, he'd spend a couple of
nights on the beach wrapped in his bearskin, and also a couple of
nights on the ridge he had seen up in Will Rogers State Park. Of
course there were many signs that said "No Camping" but then the
world had become full of signs that said "No Something," so to avoid
suffocation you generally had to ignore them. In the Upper Peninsula such signs were generally filled with bullet holes from those
acting out of resentment or for convenient target practice. During
the worst of the bug season, late May and June, when the mosquitoes and blackflies could be irritating, B.D. on breezy nights liked
to sleep on a stretch of fifteen miles of deserted shore of Lake Superior, a different place each time, though most of the routine was
invariable. First he'd get a loaf of homemade bread from an old lady
he cut wood for, catch a few fish, buy a six-pack, start a driftwood
fire, fry the fish in bacon fat in an old iron skillet, and eat it with
the bread, salt, and the bottle of Tabasco he always carried in his

old fatigue jacket, wrapped in duct tape so it wouldn't clink against his pocketknife. He'd finish the six-pack in the late twilight near the summer solstice that far north, nearly eleven in the evening, scrub the pan with sand, then get naked and scrub his body in the cold surf. A lady might come ambling along though this had never happened and it wouldn't do to be unclean.

When he reached the car and unlocked it Bob Duluth was still sleeping and now sweating profusely because the car was very hot in the mid-morning sun. B.D. started the car but the air conditioner made a weird noise and wouldn't work so he opened all the windows. Bob had begun to make a keening noise in the midst of a bad dream and his hands flapped and clutched his face. At first B.D. couldn't think of what to do other than run for it, but opted for turning on the radio real loud. Luckily the dial was on a Mexican station and a woman's voice was full of passion and deep lyrical sobs, then she would lilt off into high beautiful notes. The music seemed to go with the wordless, verbless immensity of the ocean thought B.D., though not in that specific language.

"I was never the man I used to be," Bob said, opening his eyes and mopping his face with a handkerchief, looking out at the water. "When I die I will disappear at sea. A hot sea."

"In a boat?" B.D. asked, a bit unnerved by memories of choppy, rolling Lake Superior.

"I'm not at liberty to say. Let's have a beer. This fucking car is a steam bath. At a garage in Ensenada some fucker stole some parts from the air conditioner."

"It's not open until eleven," B.D. said, having checked the lounge door after his beach-beer reverie. B.D. followed Bob around to a service entrance where Bob banged at the door and gave a kid in dirty white kitchen clothes twenty bucks for two Tecates. B.D. was pleased to drink his first foreign beer while looking at the ocean.

❊   ❊   ❊

"Feminine ambrosia. Seaweed trace. Nipple taste. A bit of tire," Bob said, tasting the wine.

"Oh Bob, you big dork," the waitress shrieked, tapping him on the noggin with her ballpoint.

The first beer seemed to have given them a certain momentum. B.D. thought other people might join them when Bob ordered five complete meals plus bottles of both red and white wine. B.D. stuck with Mexican beer, his wine-drinking career having ended young when he and David Four Feet had stolen a case of Mogen David which made them quite ill though they had drunk it all so as not to be wasteful. The very long lunch required seven beers which B.D. had always thought was a perfect number. Bob liked the number seven, too, noting that he had ordered five lunches rather than four because odd numbers were better than even. He had sworn, or so he said, during his impoverished youth never to get stuck with the wrong lunch which would leave you depressed the rest of the day. By ordering five you vastly increased the odds of getting something good to eat. B.D. raised the issue of the expense of this custom and Bob replied that his agent had negotiated a per diem of a thousand dollars a day which was peanuts compared to what certain actors and actresses required.

"We'll check the set tonight. We're night shooting. This bimbo actress has a hundred-foot trailer with a full Jacuzzi. She eats caviar on oysters which should only be eaten separately. Her hamburger must be ground from prime sirloin right in front of her eyes or she won't eat it. Her tuna fish must be made from scratch. She changes her underpants a dozen times a day, all at studio expense. I've heard that the best barber in Beverly Hills charges her five hundred bucks to shave her pussy because he's gay and doesn't like the job. Don't quote me on that because it might not be true."

This wasn't quite the kind of information B.D. was likely to quote though Frank back home might enjoy hearing it. His mind had been somewhat seized by the idea that this nutcase got a grand a day to live on and that before he ordered the food he had consulted his "food notebook," telling B.D. that he preferred to avoid eating food prepared the same way during the same year, adding that on New Year's Day the slate became clear again.

"What about eggs?" B.D. had asked.

"There are a thousand ways to cook eggs," Bob had replied, reeling off a manic string of egg recipes, many of them in French which B.D. recognized because he had met French Canadians over in Sault Ste. Marie. He rather liked the way they talked for the same reason he liked to listen to the older, traditional Ojibway (Anishinabe) talk, say when Delmore was speaking to a friend on the phone. Delmore explained to him that all that language was comprised of was agreed-upon sounds. And now he was listening to this batshit writer talk about his incapability of repeating meals within the same year. He wondered idly what his anthropologist lover, Shelley, would have had to say about it? She regularly visited her mind doctor for a tuning up and when Brown Dog looked at the wide array of food before them there was something crazy about it though it didn't deter his appetite. They ate Dungeness crabs, clams, oysters, and three kinds of fish, including sea bass and fresh yellowfin tuna.

"Can you offer me a recommendation for the job?" Bob asked, putting down his fork for a split second and taking a monstrous gulp of wine.

"Nope. I'm here on a secret mission. I didn't bring my paperwork." B.D. was pleased by his fib. No one could be expected to cart around all their paperwork though he, in fact, had none save the aforementioned driver's license and a twenty-nine-year-old selective-service card.

"I'd have to guess you were on the lam and trying to bury your identity in a big city," Bob said. "Don't forget that I write detective novels and am widely admired by professional criminologists."

"Tell it to someone who gives a fuck," B.D. said, studying the ornate carapace of the Dungeness crab, thinking that the creature carried around his or her house much in the manner of the way old Claude carried his Hefty garbage bag and taught him to do so. "I'm thinking of heading up to Oregon to cut timber, or maybe Chapleau up in Ontario. If you want to do a readout on me drive your own car and end up in the hoosegow playing with yourself."

"Calm down. I could easily jump on the computer and get your records."

"If you knew my name." B.D. took Bob's car keys out of his pocket and slid them past a bowl of *vongole* with a rich hint of garlic. Two women at a nearby table were eating lunch with their sunglasses on which seemed awkward to him.

"Chill out," Bob said, pushing the keys back toward B.D. and twisting a forkful of pasta and spearing a clam from the *vongole* bowl. "My own origins are unknown, even to myself."

"Mine too," said B.D., spooning up garlic and oil from the bottom of the bowl. Few tourists understood that a diet that included lots of garlic was useful as an insect repellent, though right now he was suddenly lonesome for his mosquito-infested home country, the lakes and bogs, the ceaseless cold rain, the pockets of snow in swamps that persisted into late May, the shelf ice buried in the sand and rock-strewn shores of Lake Superior that often lasted well into June. You could dig down and store your beer there and it kept wonderfully cold.

"I often pretend I'm a dark orphaned prince but the truth is my mother was promiscuous. It's brutal to accept that your mom was loose with her body." Bob was sad for a split second, then slurped down several oysters.

"I heard mine was too but I figured she must have had her reasons. Grandpa said we have strong bodies and can always earn our bed and grub, and sometimes women have to play it a little looser to get by. He might have been trying to save my feelings from anything I might hear when he raised me. You know, local gossip." B.D. felt that oysters were more interesting than the past.

"We left my dad and older brother who didn't look like me up on the farm near Cochrane north of La Crosse," Bob said. "We lived in Eau Claire, Fond du Lac, Oshkosh, and ended up in my high school years in Rice Lake, which incidentally has the best pizza in the world, a place called Drag's. Ever since I've not been much of a pizza buff. It's hard to step down. It's like going back to a waitress after sleeping with beautiful actresses and fashion models."

"I've always favored waitresses myself." B.D. had noted that the bones and meat of saltwater fish had a density that suggested they must work harder for a living than freshwater species. "Of course I don't know about magazine models much less actresses though I met one yesterday who starred in the film *Butts Galore.*"

"I've seen it. Intriguing but not much of a story line. Most of our porn is shot through with our collective tit fetish. If only the money spent on tit jobs around here was devoted to the five million children in America that go to bed hungry every night. Meanwhile, I grew up as a waif, moving from pillar to post, from dingy apartments in one Wisconsin suckhole city to another. But I was a bright lad and by dint of hard work became successful."

"What happened to your mother?" B.D. watched closely as Bob struggled a bit for an answer, B.D. recalling another radio program his Grandpa listened to after Jack Benny. It was called *Fibber McGee and Molly.* Fibber fibbed a lot.

"I support her lavishly in a posh retirement home in Milwaukee. My older brother and dad both wrote me notes to say that they didn't care for my detective novels. It hurt deep." Bob seemed pleased with this detail that should increase his credibility, or so he thought.

B.D. pushed himself back from the table, chock-full to the gills, and wondering why Bob never took note of the ocean right out the window in front of them. "Some of your lingo strikes me as far-fetched, Mister Bob. Maybe it just comes from the locale which doesn't seem like the rest of our country."

At this tense moment the waitress reappeared and asked if they needed anything more. Bob affected a heartfelt lust: "Only you, darling, can satisfy a need far deeper, far more basic than food. All this food we've eaten is dead. You're living food."

"Sure thing, Bob. Eat me and you don't get fat or drunk or have to spend an hour a day on the toilet." She slapped down the bill and flounced off.

Back outside they snoozed for an hour but with the car windows open, a sweet sea breeze wafting through the windows, keeping most of the flies away from their snoring mouths. They awoke on the same cue, a bit thick and grumpy. Bob opened the glove compartment and insisted they both take megavitamins, the capsules as big as horse pills, then directed B.D. to drive south to Santa Monica where he had a late lunch meeting.

"You mean you're going to eat again?" The thought of another bite made B.D. feel gaggy.

"Eating at its best has nothing to do with appetite." Bob took a small Dictaphone from his pocket and said, "Not call me a cab, but get me a cab," with the air of someone who had accomplished an important project. Bob then glanced over at the ocean for the first time and said, "Roll on thou deep and dark blue ocean, roll."

In Santa Monica they stopped at valet parking for Ivy by the Shore. Bob pointed at the pier on the other side of Ocean Avenue and told B.D. to be back in an hour, looking at his non-existent watch as if puzzled.

B.D. was pleased to be out of Bob's range and have a chance to walk off the lunch which would only be justified by an eight-hour hike. There was the untypical fragile feeling in his mind, a fluttery sense that forbade him from getting his true bearings which, like the currently popular notion of "situational ethics," were not set in stone. The wanderer is vulnerable, and no matter that he hadn't been inside a church in twenty years except to mop up a flooded basement, certain almost religious feelings began to arise, the first surge caused by the overwhelming merry-go-round music coming from a big shed at the foot of the pier. Swank autos were parked in front and a group of natty chauffeurs were sitting in the shade. There was some kind of party for rich little boys and girls and their lovely mothers. B.D. stood there transfixed by the music which was just about his favorite kind, recalling all of his many trips to the Upper Peninsula State Fair in Escanaba though through the ornate shed's glass he could see that this was the most gorgeous merry-go-round in the universe. Once again he noted that because of his green janitor's suit he simply didn't exist in view of the others on the somewhat crowded pier. Three attractive nannies were around the corner smoking cigarettes and they looked right through the invisible B.D. He was pleased to have found the ultimate in disguises but if he was going to come across any affection in this town he'd better buy some extra duds.

The merry-go-round music had begun to increase a lump of homesickness in his chest, certainly a primitive religious feeling where the home ground is sacral, so that when you're on a foreign shore you recall the hills, gullies, creeks, even individual trees that have become the songlines of your existence. B.D. fought against the homesickness by looking north along the Pacific's shore up toward Malibu and the green hills sloping toward the ocean and the almost unpardonable beauty of the seascape. This place was not exactly the prison he was destined toward back home, or the Alger

County jail where they couldn't scramble eggs at gunpoint and the sheriff cheated at cribbage. Not far from him in a moment of sheer good luck a lissome girl dropped her skirt though there was a bathing suit under it. The suit was drawn up a bit into the crack of her butt and she deftly used her thumbs to adjust the blue strap edges. His heart lurched as her hands gave her thighs a rub and when he sat down on a bench behind her he could see the blue ocean between her thighs. She reached playfully for a gull that flew swiftly by barely beyond her reach.

This vision was too much to deal with and B.D. moved farther out the pier where old men were fishing, turning several times to look back at the girl receding in the distance, unmindful of Nietzsche's notion that if you stare into the abyss too long it will "stare back into thee," but nevertheless feeling the admonition as a physical presence by the somber nut buzz in his trousers. Unavailability increases desire into the arena of dull incomprehension, and you can feel dowdy to a point that you may as well sit down, let out a sob, and eat your own shoes.

Despite all of this he was still capable of compassion both to others and himself. He did an abrupt about-face and hastily returned to the bench immediately behind the girl, picking up a stray newspaper and tearing a small hole in the crease. That way he could hold the paper up as if reading it and stare through the hole undetected. It was a counterspy technique he had read in a stack of old *Argosy* magazines in Delmore's woodshed.

The girl was now talking to a friend, a chunkier version of herself, and they were both sipping soft drinks through straws in plastic cups, making a noise that reminded B.D. of a very crude joke about a local woman back home who reputedly could suck a golf ball through a garden hose. He dismissed this witticism as unworthy of the vision through the hole in the newspaper, which already was producing an altered state, removing him from the

mundanity of his problems. A great artist might be able to capture
the ocean between her tan thighs, a distant swimmer's head bob-
bing through the frame. His concentration was absolute though it
did not disallow certain thought of revenge against Lone Marten.
This was only his second full day in town, and though he was currently feeling vaguely religious and lucky, he was mindful that his
only other city experience in Chicago so many years ago was not
exactly admirable. A fly landed and the girl twitched her butt like
a horse shimmied a flank A gay blade sat down on the bench a few
feet away but the green janitor's suit repelled his interest. B.D. had
to readjust his focus as the girl turned slightly sideways, a hand on
her jaunty haunch. On their long escape drive from Michigan to
L.A. they had stopped for a snooze beside the Wind River south of
Thermopolis in Wyoming. B.D. had stretched out on his bearskin
rug but hadn't slept, watching the river transfixed, the smooth sheen
of an eddy showing several dimpling trout rises. Now the girl was
facing him with her slightly puffed "mons veneris" clear in the
newspaper's hole. Suddenly two cups full of ice rained down on
him and the gay blade quipped, "You've been caught, buddy."

B.D. dropped the newspaper and tried to smile. The girls
laughed and gave him the finger. At least they had a sense of humor.
He got up and bowed deeply, then made his way out toward the
end of the pier where on a lower fishing deck he redeemed himself.
An old, particularly wizened man had snagged his fishing rig on
the bottom and whined loudly that it was his last rig. B.D. quickly
stripped to his skivvies, made his way partly down an iron ladder,
then jumped in after first telling the old man to hold on to his trousers and wallet. B.D. easily followed the taut fishing line down about
thirty feet to the bottom. The visibility was poor and the water
suprisingly cold, but he quickly untangled the old man's rig from a
piece of rebar, cement reinforcing rod, jutting from a pier piling.
When he came back up victorious from his charitable baptism a

small gathering applauded, but there was Bob Duluth looking a little angry.

"B.D., you fucking moron, I've been waiting an hour. You could have drowned."

"Sorry, sir, just trying to help a poor old fellow out." He checked his own non-existent watch as Bob had done earlier. "I'm an experienced diver."

"Fuck you, big shot," the old man said to Bob.

On the way east on San Vincente, a street B.D. found remarkable for its beauty, Bob had him pull over so he could point out the spot of his fatal D.U.I. There was nothing remarkable about the location except for the peculiar xenophobia of the one man showing it to another. Their stations in life couldn't be much further apart but Bob was from up in Wisconsin and B.D. from the Upper Peninsula, so that rather irrationally meant something to both of them as if they had together been cast up on the wilder shores of Borneo.

"Tell me about it, son," Bob said, at least affecting a stone-serious mood of concern.

"Tell you about what?" B.D. felt a little quavery when Bob used the authoritative "son" though Bob couldn't be more than ten years older.

"Tell me what you're running from. I'm sure I can help. Occasionally I like to alleviate suffering, to remove my venal blinders and do a good turn."

That threw the raw meat on the floor. They got out of the car, crossed to the wide grassy median strip, and talked under the very same tree where Bob had been rudely handcuffed, then hauled away. Somewhat in the manner of the ruthless interrogators created in his fiction Bob put B.D. through the exhaustive paces of his story, his three brushes with prison, the first when B.D. was a

salvage diver and found the dead Indian in full regalia down in fifty
feet of water for fifty years, perfectly preserved in the icy water of
Lake Superior, then stealing an ice truck in an attempt to trans-
port the body to Chicago for profit, followed by arson of the
anthropologist's tent and camping equipment, all to protect his
secret Indian graveyard from certain excavation, the only Hopwell
site in the northern Midwest. B.D.'s so-called anthropologist girlfriend, Shelley, was right on the money as Eve in the original Garden, tempting the secret location of his graveyard with her body
and that of her friend, Tarah, whose body was somewhat slimmer,
a detail Bob drew from B.D. to get the whole picture, including the
color of Tarah's undies. The third felony had been the recent attack on the site where a group of archeologists and anthropologists
from the University of Michigan were doing preliminary work. B.D.
and Lone Marten had mostly lobbed fireworks from a relatively safe
distance while the rough stuff had been left to Rose and a group of
Anishinabe warriors. The main problem here is that B.D. had been
enjoined from entering Alger County for a year to let the university people work without interruption.

    B.D. tried to continue on with the flight west after swapping
the hot Lincoln for a Taurus across the border in Canada, all engineered by the highly skilled criminal mind of Lone Marten. Bob
held up his hand and rushed to the car to make a call. Out of sheer
thirst they then went into a fancy Chinese restaurant in Brentwood
where Bob was well known. Bob had a quick bottle of Puligny-
Montrachet for a hundred bucks and B.D. drank three bottles of
Kirin beer. Was there no end to the foreign beers available in this
area? He did point out to Bob that L.A. lacked the wonderful bar
life of Chicago where seemingly every street had its neighborhood
tavern, or up in Wisconsin where apparently anyone could turn
their home into a bar. Once over near Alvin when he had been fishing the Brule River he had sat drinking beer in such a house, took

care of a pile of kids while the barmaid grandmother had cooked burgers for a crowd, and what's more, he had eaten four burgers for free for helping out, which included carrying the town drunk back to a shack over his shoulder like a two-hundred-pound sack of oats.

Bob wasn't listening. He was all business though B.D. reflected Bob could handle a bottle of wine as fast as an ordinary mortal could drink a beer. When Bob rushed out to fetch his I.B.M. laptop B.D. looked at the notes Bob had been making but they were scrawled in what must be a secret code. The Chinese waitress brought him another beer and bowed, so he stood up and bowed back which she found amusing.

"Welcome to our country," B.D. said, with what he hoped was a seductive smile. She was a real peach, as exotic as the flora in the botanical gardens.

"My family has been here since the 1870s. We came over to help build your railroads and mine your mines," she said with a twinkle. There was a slit in her skirt that ran halfway up her thigh. She didn't seem to mind the liability of his janitor's suit but he guessed that was because Bob was a high roller. With Bob's bankroll he probably got more ass than a toilet seat though there was the idea that it didn't seem to be doing him any good.

"Voilà!" Bob roared, rushing in with the laptop and tapping out some codes in front of B.D. Right there on the screen was the record prepared by Michigan State Police Detective Schultz on Marten Smith, a.k.a., Lone Marten, ex-member of the American Indian Movement (purged for embezzlement), expert at getting National Endowment funds for dissident films that didn't eventuate, wanted for credit card fraud, larceny by conversion, a dropped charge for manufacturing crystal methamphetamine, and having raised funds for a supposed Native radical group called the Windigos of which he was the only proven member, his main hench-

man a local fool with the unlikely name of Brown Dog, to be considered unarmed but nevertheless dangerous due to an early career
as a bare-knuckle fighter.

Tears nearly formed at the sight of the word "fool." B.D. pointed
out that Detective Schultz had been removed for illegally spying
for political purposes which the state police had been forbidden to
do. Bob countered that there had been the not so small item of sexual
photos of Schultz and Rose, B.D.'s ex-girlfriend. A frame-up engineered by Lone Marten.

B.D. was amazed and disgusted that Bob had all of this information at his fingertips. Up until two years ago when he had met
Shelley he had led a totally private life, mostly because, he now
supposed, nobody was interested. There was a specific sorrow and
yearning to find a truly remote deer cabin, and trade the off-season
rent of it for some maintenance. He had re-roofed many deer cabins, liked the smell of tar paper and shingles, and the bird-level view
of the world a roof offered. Now tears of frustration actually did
form which made Bob nervous indeed in this city where actual
emotion is indeterminate.

"Stiffen up, bucko," Bob said, signaling the waitress for another bottle of wine. "We'll nail this miserable fuck to the wall."

"I just want my bearskin back."

"Of course you do. You didn't view Lone Marten as dangerous because he was the brother of your boyhood friend David Four
Feet. Few of us will admit it to ourselves when our friends are evil,
or maybe that all our friends are evil, including our parents such as
my beloved though promiscuous mother, or all of our forefathers
and foremothers back to page one in human history. You know the
Bible, right? I've read the Gideon Bible in a thousand hotel rooms
because television repels me except, say, Mexican or French television because I don't know what the fuck they're saying. Then
it's okay. You tend to blame your erstwhile anthropologist lover,

Shelley, for leading you astray but she didn't do it, your weenie did. Weenies and vaginas are the heart of the great mystery of life. They are our glory and our doom. Some eminent theologians have suggested that Adam and Eve didn't have genitals when they entered the original Garden but we must discount this as the thinking of dead-pecker old suits like we have in Congress. It's my contention that life as a whole might be much less than the sum of its parts and its most reliable content is evil. Right now we are sitting here having beverages in what may be thought of as the heart of the Evil Empire. Out here we stretch people's dreams and leave them only with stretch marks. Of course we're just making a living like anybody else, only more so."

Not surprisingly B.D.'s attention span had weakened though he affected concentration. The lovely Chinese girl was setting up tables across the room of the empty restaurant. The question was partly why people from all foreign lands, including America, looked so different. Frank had told him it was climate, referring to the hot sun in Africa, but B.D. was suspicious of that explanation. None of the Orientals he had run into in Chicago years back had looked yellow, nor did this girl. And none of the hundreds of Native Americans he knew looked red. A veterinarian from Charlevoix had told him in Frank's Tavern that if all of the dogs in the world were left in free concourse, down the line they'd all be medium-sized and brown.

Bob Duluth was waving his hands in the face of B.D.'s reverie, and sliding over the laptop for a closer view. A friend of Bob's at the L.A.P.D. had run a check on Lone Marten, and his local record was mostly concerned with wholesaling Formosan-made Navajo jewelry as the bona fide goods. This had pissed off the real Navajo. As a radical dissident Lone Marten was also under "light surveillance" in Los Angeles where it was also illegal. But hadn't these people taken over the empty prison, Alcatraz? There were also a number of addresses and phone numbers where he stayed when in the Westwood area, usually with other Native dissidents connected with the basketball powerhouse U.C.L.A. Bob suggested that he had an Italian friend named Vinnie who might retrieve the bearskin but Brown Dog said no. He'd do it himself. All of this stuff was going much too fast for his taste. Lone Marten would give him the skin if he hadn't already sold it.

Now the waitress brought a platter of ribs for a snack. Bob fell upon them but B.D. was capable of only a few, however delicious. Bob had claimed at lunch out in Malibu that he had pioneered the concept of multiple entrées, doubtless because he hailed from the Midwest where overeating is frequently regarded as an act of heroism. The waitress returned and asked Bob shyly if B.D. was famous? Her name was Willa and Bob said "definitely not" to her question. At the introduction B.D. dropped to a knee and kissed her hand, something he had seen in a movie.

They found B.D. a not so cheapish room between Westwood and Culver City at a place called the Siam, a motel with a modestly Oriental decor which made B.D. ponder the odds of getting Willa over for a visit. On the way out of the restaurant she had mysteriously refused to give him her Chinese name, much less her phone number. Bob said it was because he wasn't famous. They stopped at a convenience store and bought two cases of Evian for what Bob called B.D.'s "water fetish." When he drove Bob back to the Westwood Marquis, Bob told him to pick up some duds and gave him a five-hundred-buck advance on his salary which, though a great deal of money, didn't alleviate B.D.'s unrest.

Before he headed back to the Siam he took another quick walk in the botanical gardens. Bob had said one of the main secrets to his success was the nap he took every afternoon of a minimum of

four hours duration. Deep in the foliage near the bamboo thicket
he wondered if there were any possible secrets in his own life or
was he simply an open, used paperback? This self-doubt quickly
passed when he noted that the orange carp invariably swam
counterclockwise in their miniature shaded pool. The carp were
definitely more interesting to watch than the vagaries of doing a
rundown on yourself. Like the rest of us B.D. didn't know what
life was about, and now the lead carp made a graceful U-turn and
slowly drew his school clockwise. That had to be one of the answers
to the millions of questions life didn't really ask.

Before returning to his room at the motel B.D. picked up two
nice outfits at a used-clothing store, colorful Hawaiian-style shirts
and brown chinos, plus an attractive but dusty old fedora that reminded him of the hat his Grandpa wore to the fair and funerals.
Bob had taught him how to use the car phone so he called Delmore
back home and immediately wished he hadn't. Old Doris was in
the Escanaba hospital with a heart attack and Rose was in jail for
biting off the finger of a cop in the mayhem B.D. and the "evil" Lone
Marten had started at the graveyard archeological site. Delmore
was taking care of Rose's two children, Red and Berry, the latter,
however charming to B.D., a retarded and unmanageable victim
of fetal alcohol syndrome. Delmore had hired a full-time baby-
sitter for the kids and he described the young woman as a real
"peach," a white girl who wanted to devote her life to helping Natives. She even tried to get Delmore to eat yogurt. The upshot,
though, was that B.D. must come home immediately and act the
father for Rose's children. Rose would have to do a couple of years
for the missing finger even though she claimed the officer had
bruised her tits. "But how can I come home," B.D. asked, an unpleasant quaver rising in his chest. Delmore had a lawyer looking
into whether B.D. was actually over the Luce County line into Alger
when he lobbed the firecrackers. With the recent advent of laser

surveying many county lines were in question, especially in this
particular locale which was a dozen miles from any human habita-
tion. B.D. insisted that he'd die of heartbreak in jail like Delmore
had told him had happened to incarcerated Apaches. Delmore said
that he could at least come as far as the Wisconsin border and call
in for instructions. The conversation had all the disadvantages of
the telephone where there's no time to digest the information before the next load arrives.

Back at the motel the desk clerk, a tiny man from Laos, was
apologetic over the fact that the television in B.D.'s room didn't
work and when he was told that was fine because B.D. hated television the man laughed long and hysterically. It was a morale raiser
to tell a successful joke, even though you didn't know what the
joke was.

In his room he chugged a bottle of water to try to tamp down
the troublesome remains of the huge lunch. This was his darkest
hour in most respects and he had only his twenty-three bottles of
water for solace. He intended to try Bob's secret of success and take
a long nap but first a shower was in order. Just before he turned
the water on a slight noise caught his attention. He checked the door
and peeked out the window at the parking lot blazing in the sun.
There was a muffled scratching at the wall near his bed and the
sound of a woman singing softly. It sounded like the French of the
strippers in the Canadian Soo, all of whom came from Montreal.
How nice, he thought, then returned to the shower. Five minutes
later he heard the neighboring door slam and again peeked out the
window, seeing a trim girl in a cream-colored outfit getting into a
Mercedes-Benz convertible.

This did not help him sleep. He was outside of his tolerance in
terms of time for lack of affection. Perhaps the new clothes, not to
speak of the slick fedora, would help. The janitor's outfit was neatly
folded on the dresser in case he needed to disappear again while

stalking Lone Marten. The fact of the matter is that he felt utterly dislocated, a rapacious modern disease. The only familiar part of his surroundings was when he raised his hands from the bed, stared at them, and said "hands." The slump was a palpable weight on his chest and forehead. Grandpa used to say that life wasn't a bowl of cherries which was okay by B.D. because he didn't like cherries. Bob had flippantly asked him if he was afflicted with "dementia pugilistica," then explained the term by asking him if he was punch-drunk from his early fisticuffs. "Nope," B.D. had replied. He had rarely been hit in the face and that's why he always won. A good face blow disarms all but the most experienced. Now he flipped through a short list of assessments. Money. With about four hundred seventy bucks separated into several pockets and one sock for safety he was nearly as rich as he had ever been. Someday he hoped to buy a used yellow pick-up, a simple Ford 1500 would do. He would like a nice girlfriend but assumed so would everyone else. It really came down to the bearskin which was his single prized possession. Early in life Delmore had given up his bear medicine and turned to turtles, giving the skin to B.D. with ceremony.

He tossed and turned on the bed, ripping the thin sheet beneath him. They'd probably charge him an arm and a leg for the torn sheet. This was not the proper time but he was tempted to look at the nude photo of Shelley in his wallet for strength. A different kind of strength was needed for L.A. and it was scarcely a stiff pecker pointing at the snarling leopard lamp on the night table. Indeed, what power could the lonely wanderer summon that would be adequate for this vast tormented city sprawled around him, with its ten thousand laminae of sophistication and wealth, its venality and hatred, the million attractive women whose peculiar language he did not know? What he did know, though he had never collected his thoughts on the subject, which Shelley had him do on other matters, was that he was ill suited to leave the "back forty" as they

used to call it. It had long ago occurred to him that the woods only
prepares you for more woods. His expertise as a subsistence hunter
and fisherman did not ready him for anything other than eating fish,
venison, or grouse and woodcock. The end of that story was a full
tummy and the memories of the splendor of the day.

In a way you didn't enter the woods, the woods entered you,
and its presence did not make you more operable at the business at
hand. Up until a few years ago game biologists had visited him to
get the locations of bear and wolf dens in exchange for a six-pack
or, in the case of wolves, a whole case of beer. He had given up this
practice when Frank warned him that all the biologists were going
to do was put telemetric collars on the animals so that they could
keep track of them without effort like animal police. In other words,
though Frank didn't say it that way, perhaps B.D. was betraying
the creatures without knowing it. Naturally it was hard to turn
down a six-pack or a case but he was full of enough remorse to meet
all future biologists with a "get the fuck out of here" and a slammed
door. And he had graduated in terms of human failing to gambling
his knowledge on the Native graveyard for sex. It was certainly time
to act noble but the training wasn't quite there, and perhaps nobil-
ity wouldn't help get back the bearskin.

Jesus H. Christ, he thought, hearing the roar and beeping of
rush-hour traffic. How can they live with this fucking racket? He
got off the bed and tried the radio built into the broken TV and
had a thrilling moment when it worked. He tuned in some Mexican
music loud enough to drown out the traffic noise. The yoga couple
with whom he had had the parting over questioning why the woman
felt good about herself possessed hundreds of records they played
day and night, drowning out the birds and coyotes, and even a
possible wolf. She was a tad thin for his taste but back in bed he
recalled how pleasant she had looked when he had taken them on
a day-long hike at their request. They had become a little lost on a

series of ridges above a swamp that formed the headwaters of the
Two-Hearted River and her husband, who had been irritated all
day over the fact that the cellular phone attached to his belt didn't
work in this location, totally lost his composure. B.D. claimed that
they weren't lost, they just couldn't find their vehicle and said that
he had happily wandered around a couple of days in this sort of
situation. He knew the area well in May before all the foliage was
out, and October when most of the leaves were down, but now the
thickness of the greenery and the dull overcast hiding the sun's true
position had made the route difficult.

On the bed B.D. realized why the experience had come to
mind, first discarding the beauty of the woman's butt in her pale
green trousers. It was because he feared falling apart now in L.A.,
delaminating as the man had done that day, including falling back
and eating the rest of the sandwiches they had intended to share,
hogging all the remaining water so that finding a creek or spring
was immediately more important than finding the vehicle. The
man's five-hundred-dollar custom hiking boots were turning his feet
to purple jelly and late in the afternoon he had burst into paranoid
sobs, claiming that B.D. and his wife were trying to kill him so they
could become lovers and get his money. All of this on a simple ten-
hour walk, B.D. had thought, quite puzzled, though amazed that
the wife remained curious about the flora and fauna and had pretended by mid-morning that her husband didn't exist. They were a
full two hours from the car when B.D. figured out the specifics of
where they were but he didn't let on, wanting to stick it to the guy
for his bad behavior. When nearly out of the woods the man had
thrown his cellular phone out into the middle of an algae-laden pond
covered with the white and yellow flowers of lily pads. "How ugly
of you to throw your phone into the beautiful pond, darling," the
wife had said. A scant hundred yards from emerging the man had
clutched his head and yelled, "I hear a roaring," which was only a

log truck on the road just ahead. Afterward the man had acted self-righteous rather than embarrassed, blaming the whole thing on an organic purge he had taken the day before to clean out his system. His wife and B.D. had watched in amazement as the man hogged nearly all the remaining water in the car and stuffed down two high-energy bars from the glove compartment without offering them a bite. For B.D. it was an incredible lesson on how you don't want to act in your brief time on earth. She had dropped B.D. off at his tarpaper deer hunter's shack, pressing a sweat-dampened fifty-dollar bill in his hand while her husband snoozed and moaned in the backseat. "Thanks for the wonderful day," she had said, staring straight ahead as if windshield wipers were the most interesting things in the world. B.D. had eaten a three-pound canned pork shoulder for dinner, then hoofed it the five miles to town in the twilight. The carburetor in his van was on the fritz and he was a little weary, but who could resist Frank's tavern when you had fifty bucks free and clear?

The upshot of the memory was something biblical on the order of "gird up thy loins," that is, stop your quavers and act like you know what you're doing. Anyone could become a slobbering asshole, even a guy who could do yoga and owned a hundred-grand log cabin with two bathrooms. He had been on a seven-day fandango, covering two-thirds of the country, and it was high time he get his bearings. He didn't know, of course, that by the time you truly felt the heartbreak of dislocation it has become the deep itch of getting better. And as the ceiling above him, speckled mauve, grew foggy and distant he entered sleep and the largely ignored arena of dreamtime wherein the simple little carp pond in the U.C.L.A. botanical gardens gradually became a mighty river on which he was floating on a log. Evil men in black uniforms followed in a boat shooting at him and forcing him toward an immense waterfall. At the last moment before being pushed into the thun-

derous cascade his body lifted up and he could hear the heavy creak-
ing and flapping of his wings, his neck craned outward. He felt very
heavy but maintained altitude and his flight pattern took him downstream far above the raging torrents. His wings became tired and
heavy and he descended, landing at great speed but somehow
clutching a large white pine tree at the edge of the river. Puzzled
by his escape he looked down at his body and saw he was half bear
and half bird.

The phone rang and it was a paw that lifted it clumsily from
the cradle on the nightstand. "Hello," B.D. said in a throaty growl.

"What the fuck's wrong with your voice? It's Bob reminding
you that you're picking me up at eight, about an hour from now.
You got it?"

"Of course. I just finished my yoga and I'm doing my hair,"
B.D. said, clearing his throat of any bear remnants.

"You're fucking kidding. You're doing yoga?"

"Yoga and a gallon of yogurt a day keeps the doctor away,"
B.D. said, thinking about how Shelley and her friend Tarah lived
the life of health, though they had had a weakness for cocaine and
champagne.

"Cut the bullshit. Just be here. We have to go to the set. We're
night shooting."

"What set?" B.D. asked, looking at his erection and wondering if there was bear power in it. Bears were notorious for endur-
ance fucking.

"Just be here you goddamned fool." Bob sounded a bit speedy.

"Use the word 'fool' again and I'll give your Taurus to a poor
person of color."

"I'm sorry. I apologize. Anyway I got Lone Marten pinned
down to a speech he's going to make tomorrow evening. I'm hoping that they'll find out where he's staying. It's better if the show-
down isn't public."

"Thanks, Bob. I better get my tux on."

"Don't wear a tux for Christ's sake."

"Okay." B.D. hung up, still feeling strongly the power and in-souciance of his dream. Who's going to fuck with you if you're half bear and half bird?

In the lobby of the Westwood Marquis both guests and staff nodded and smiled at him under the careless assumption that he might be an important rock musician, many of whom stayed at the hotel, while B.D. was confident that it was the combination of the tropical shirt and his natty fedora. When he found Bob in the lounge drinking a martini out of a beer mug Bob looked at the hat and said, "Nifty." The hat had the extra advantage of hiding his stiff and unruly hair. During his childhood visits to the barber for his twenty-five-cent haircut the barber would whine that it would take a quarter's worth of Brylcreem or butch wax to mat down B.D.'s hair.

The hardest thing for a rural stranger in a huge city is to figure out the relationship between what people do for a living and where they live. On home ground you can drive down a street and say butcher, baker, candlestick maker as you pass successive houses. In Los Angeles, of course, you immediately give up to the nagging grace of incomprehension, as you do in New York City, with its layered oblong onions of life, its towering glued-together slices of separate realities held together by plumbing pipes and brittle skins of stone. In New York you can at least imagine you are way up in a childhood treehouse and those far below are not woodland ants but asthma-producing roaches. But then a pretty girl walks by with nine goofy dogs on tethers and you can get the feeling that these folks know what they're doing. In Los Angeles any sort of comprehension is out of the question for the initiate, though after a number of visits there are certain buildings, streets, and restaurants that become comforting landmarks. This is also true of the locals, most of whom become quite blind to their surroundings, like, say, the citizens of Casper, Wyoming. The sophisticate, the student of cities, soon understands that Greater Los Angeles resembles the history of American politics, or the structure of American society itself. The connection between Brentwood and Boyle Heights is as fragile as that between Congress and the citizenry though the emotional makeup of both resembles the passion and power of the *Jerry Springer Show.*

Thus it was on the way between the Westwood Marquis and the Sony Studios in Culver City that Brown Dog could bark out fondly on passing the Siam Motel, "That's where I live," to Bob Duluth who had his nose in his brightly lit laptop computer.

"Ah, yes, the wonderful Siam. Beware of a faux-French girl who lives there. That means she's not actually French. She's from Redondo Beach. Real French girls find it impossible to get green cards, you know, permits to get work. I was deeply in love with Sandrine for about three days. I introduced her to a couple of friends from Paris and they were amazed. They thought Sandrine was more French than the French with an impeccable Auvergne accent to boot. Whenever any filmmakers have a bit part for a French girl Sandrine gets the call. Her scam is to plaintively ask a gentleman to help her get a green card. Of course I tried. A lawyer charged me a grand to look into the matter for ten minutes. The immigration people told him that I was the thirty-seventh person trying to help Sandrine get a green card. Be careful about your wallet if you meet her."

"Not if you keep your money in a sock," B.D. quipped.

"A sock is an obvious place to hide money. Ask any girl in Vegas. She checks the socks first."

"I mean the socks you are wearing. You tend to limp a little so you don't wear out the money."

"What if you need to buy a hot dog or a drink?" Bob closed the computer top. His mind thrived on doses of inanity.

"You keep a little spare in your front pockets. It's close enough to your weenie so no one can get at it. It's a real sensitive area. My old girlfriend Shelley told me it's like my religion but she was dead wrong. I keep my religion secret."

"Not a bad idea, I mean secrecy in this town. With actresses I recommend talking about religion as a sexual ploy. Just ask them what God's specific purpose was in creating the movie business, and I don't mean it cynically. Stay earnest and a bit above the idea of sex. Probe for their deepest hopes and fears and tie it into the higher purpose, whatever that might be."

"Is my neighbor Sandrine religious?" B.D. wanted to bring it closer to home.

"She claims to be a French Huguenot. That's where the Arcadians, or Cajuns, come from. More to the point, she doesn't allow entry which at first made me think she was a transvestite. A closer look told me no. She seems to deeply enjoy sixty-nine, though I think she uses a thin plastic liner in her mouth. Once when she was in the bathroom I saw a packet of them in her purse."

"You don't say." B.D. was a little unnerved by this information. It smacked of the *Twilight Zone* repeats that Delmore occasionally watched at dinnertime. "You mean you snooped in the poor girl's purse?"

"Just checking for a pistol or switchblade. I have trouble performing the sex act if I feel threatened in any way. We grow up haunted by the tales of easy sex that don't eventuate. If you're in Eau Claire they tell you all the girls in Oshkosh fuck at the drop of a hat so you drive your old Plymouth to Oshkosh where they say it's Milwaukee, and in Milwaukee they say the college girls in Madison will leap on your head if you whistle, but in Madison you're assured that Eau Claire is stuffed to the gills with dumb secretaries who will fuck you silly for a three-course meal at McDonald's."

"You just went in a circle," said B.D. who was a student of road maps. A cabin owner had given him an old Rand McNally and B.D. had spent many an evening studying it.

"That's what I mean. Now I offer girls modest scholarships which keeps it on a higher plane. Before I forget, don't admit to anyone you're my driver. It has to do with labor relations. The teamsters might slit my tires."

"What will I say I am?" B.D. pulled up at the Sony security gate which protected Tri-Star and Columbia from Greater Los Angeles.

"*El don Bob*," said a Mexican security officer poking his face in the window.

"*Qué pasa*, baby?" Bob waved. "Give my aide-de-camp here a badge for the set."

B.D. pinned on his "VIP" badge, not quite remembering what it meant. Also "aide-de-camp" seemed a step up in the world from "driver" which he had also done for Lone Marten in the semi-hot Lincoln Town Car which they swapped even up for their escape vehicle, the brown Taurus.

At the set, the front of a fake small hotel, Bob was met by the director and producer and he handed over a paper with the new line. B.D. was standing close enough to hear the director summon over the star actor who was darkly tanned but looked a bit like a bloated peanut. Now instead of the actor saying to the doorman "Call me a cab," he would say "Get me a cab." The reason behind the change, Bob was explaining, was because the actor was a distraught and impulsive lover and would not be in the mood to be polite to a hotel doorman. It didn't seem a very interesting point to B.D. but both the director and the producer liked the idea and Bob beamed. The actor wasn't quite sure but after an initial frown he prepared himself emotionally for the next take.

B.D. was amazed at the hundred or so people working on the set, the grips and gaffers, makeup people, continuity girls, assistant directors, wardrobe ladies, and a few important studio executives who stopped by for a few minutes before driving home from work. Everyone seemed to greet Bob as if he were a big shot, and smiled at B.D. as he drifted toward the caterer's table, as if the VIP badge might mean something. Bob, still beaming, slapped him on the shoulder, "All in a day's work," he said, grabbing B.D.'s arm as he reached for a hot dog and soft drink. "Save your appetite for dinner, plus we got work to do." Another fucking food bully, B.D. thought as Bob led him to the entrance of the fake hotel. Shelley had been like that, forcing him to eat a big bowl of Tibetan boiled grain that you had to chew on a long time like a cow does its cud. Don't eat a hot dog kiddo, it will rot your insides out.

The next shot would be in a mock-up of a hotel room, Bob explained, stepping over tangles of cables and wires that looked dangerous to B.D. who always felt nervous over something so simple as plugging in a lamp. This was doubtless due to all the ranting his Grandpa had done about the destructive powers of electricity and automobiles. B.D., however, was pleased when a gaffer said, "Great hat" and a makeup man screeched "I *love* that hat, darling." It was a little disappointing, though, when he found out that the actress they were about to meet wasn't the one who demanded that her hamburger be ground before her very eyes, and had her parts exhaustively shaved. This one was named "Shoe" which seemed odd, but then he had gone out with a barmaid over in Neguanee whose last name was Foot who was first-rate, if a bit on the hefty side.

And there she was sitting on a rumpled bed in a bra and a half-slip, a bottle of whiskey and a full glass of the precious amber liquid on the nightstand beside her. While she talked to the director a makeup girl further tousled her blond locks. She stood up and gave Bob a peck on the cheek, nodded at B.D., and said, "What an adorable hat." He flushed deeply and bowed, then stepped backward toward the door, well behind the huge million-dollar camera, at least that was the price Bob put on it. Bob and the director and Shoe were discussing the upcoming scene and then went through the actual paces. She stood grief stricken at the window as her lover drove off in the cab, came back to the bedside where she tossed off a glass of whiskey, screamed, "Goddamn you, Richard," then threw herself sobbing on the bed. B.D. quickly made note of the idea that movies were made of discouragingly small pieces and also, what kind of stupid shit could walk away from this woman? His eyes bugged in alarm when she tossed off the full glass of whiskey in rehearsal and the assistant cameraman whispered that it was tea. It was beautiful indeed when she threw herself on the bed and her sobs were so convincing that you wanted to rush to her side and comfort her. The slip nudged up the back of her legs so far that you could almost see her fanny and a smallish lump arose in his throat when he realized that such beauty was not for the likes of him.

After five of the eventual nine takes of the scene B.D. drifted back outside because the hot lights caused sweat to trickle down his back and legs and from beneath his magic fedora. The hundred or so employees were still milling around outside and when he emerged from the hotel several of them asked him how the scene was going. He said, "Swell" as he stared out over the assembled crowd from the foot-high vantage of the hotel's steps which he noted were not real cement though they looked like it. Oh sons and daughters of man, under the vast and starry night though the stars are invisible, what are you doing here while your histories moment by moment trail off behind you like auto exhaust, he thought though not quite in those words. What wages did they draw to endure such torpor, though he couldn't say they looked more miserable than most hard-working folks. At least they could feel there was glamour in the end product, which was hard to envision cutting pulp on a cold snowy day, somewhat stunted third-growth timber that might very well end up in a newspaper after being extruded from the mill. Maybe these workers felt like those in an absolute assembly line in an auto factory and though they were remote from the end product they were confident that out would pop a Cadillac. Cast in the best light, B.D. decided, this work could be likened to his years as an illegal-salvage diver, bringing up antique booty from the depths. Some people would pay top dollar for a binnacle brought up from an old freight schooner resting in peace in the depths for over a hundred years.

Brown Dog stared out at the crowd for a long time with the non-conceptual attentiveness of a child. In terms of local social mores such stillness was extralegal and many in the crowd found themselves staring back. Was this fucking goof really important they wondered? They all knew from common gossip that the screenwriter, Bob Duluth, wasn't dealing from a full deck, didn't have both oars in the water, but they were bright enough to also know that he was the origin of their employment. In the parlance of the industry, screenwriters were an unfortunate necessity, or "just writers" as the executives tended to refer to them.

Finally a very large black security officer approached B.D. and asked him if he needed anything and B.D. whispered, "A beer, sir." Off to the side, but fairly near, two wardrobe girls were skipping rope and smiling at him as they went through intricate, hyperathletic moves. They must be more accessible than a famous actress he thought, recalling the intimidating beauty of the woman as she glugged her whiskey tea and, after the shot, wagged her butt at Bob and the director.

The security man returned with a beer enclosed in his big paw. B.D. stared at the label. St. Pauli Girl all the way from the land of

Germany. He wondered if they could come up with a Goebbel's or a
Stroh's from Detroit. Probably. He thanked the security officer who
followed B.D.'s line of vision to the wardrobe girls skipping rope.

"Watch out for those two ladies. They're not twins but they're
known in the business as the Terrible Twins. There are no snakes
in the world as dangerous as those two, not even the dreaded fer-
de-lance of my home country."

On further conversation it turned out that the security man,
Harold, came from Belize, and his crisp elocution was explicable
because he was not a victim of our educational system. Harold gave
B.D. his card in case he needed any after-hours "protection," then
withdrew with a slight bow when Bob reappeared mopping his face
with a handkerchief. When they had shaken hands it had occurred
to B.D. that Harold was as large as the federal officer that had arrived in Grand Marais to arrest three men for shipping illegal otter
skins across state lines. When the officer, who was also black, got
out of his car "he just kept on getting out" an old Finn had said. He
was at least six and a half feet and about three hundred pounds,
wore a cowboy hat and a silver-plated long-barrel .44 on a hip holster. The trappers had offered no resistance.

Bob waved a hand in B.D.'s face to catch his attention at the
same time the wardrobe girls, the Terrible Twins, approached wondering if they wanted any after-work company? Bob said that he
and B.D., who was given yet another card, were booked solid for
the rest of their lives. The girls gave him the finger and strutted
away.

"Gee whiz, Bob, they're cute." In addition to being real hungry the twins had given B.D. a nut buzz just by standing there. One
of them wore soft cloth trousers that pulled right up in the fold of
her genuine article.

"A grief too deep for words," Bob said. "There's a lot wrong
with me possibly but I'm not some sort of toe-freak masochist."

✾   ✾   ✾

On the way to the club on Santa Monica Boulevard Bob's dialogue was rather manic and B.D. turned him off, his hunger pangs now so severe that his mind flitted to and fro between other great hunger situations in his life, say the time he was lost from dawn to dark on a cloudy day while deer hunting and when he reached his battered old van there was a precious can of emergency Spam in the toolbox. His cold hands shook and he struggled to open the can, dropping the contents when he cut his finger. He had hastily and unsuccessfully tried to scrape pine needles, leaf fragments, and his own blood off the meat before cramming it in his mouth. It lasted three bites and there was nothing to wash it down with except a few ounces of banana-flavored schnapps in a dusty bottle, given him because it was too repellent for the purchaser. In the ensuing indigestion he felt the inventor of banana schnapps ought to have his ass kicked. Spam alone, however, was a reliable staple for the weary white trash of the northern forests, or that was what Shelley called them.

"Did you ever notice how often you look at the clock and it reads eleven-eleven," Bob asked loudly to get his attention.

In truth B.D. had never noticed this but quickly figured it only happened twice a day and said so.

"It's not reality but our perception of reality that counts," Bob said, finishing off one of those little two-ounce bottles of airliner booze. "When you ride first-class for thousands of extra dollars they give you these free. Maybe it's because eleven-eleven is when I get up, and when I eat dinner."

It had just turned eleven and B.D. was wondering why there was so much traffic. In most places night and day aren't so different in emotional content and rather rigid patterns are followed. There were long lines and youngish people outside of clubs, and a movie theater playing something on the order of *Fungoid Fat Guys Must Die*. He didn't realize it was Friday night since what day it was

never had any importance in his life. His mind wavered back to his
hunger and Grandpa's contention that even saltines were a feast
for a hungry man. It didn't take all that many years for him to figure out that Grandpa was frequently full of shit, sitting there before the woodstove eating stinking Liederkranz cheese and pickled
bologna with his saltines, talking grandly about how much hemp
they had smoked at the government-sponsored C.C.C. camps during the Depression in order to save their pathetic pay for beery
weekends. Now this same hemp, B.D. thought, could get you locked
up real tight for a long time.

When B.D. pulled up in front of the club he asked if Bob might
send him out a sandwich, say liver sausage, sharp cheddar, with a
thick slice of raw onion, plus a Budweiser if possible.

"I'm a liberal democrat with populist roots. You're coming in.
I've already figured out your meal. I just hope you love spinach."

"I can handle it with pork products," B.D. quipped, handing
the keys to the dirty car to the reluctant valet, who then grinned
when Bob got out and handed him a twenty.

Inside the club the air was thick with smoke what with smoking being the main reason the private club existed. On the way to
their table Bob explained quickly, if loudly, that since the politically correct fascists in California had banned smoking even in bars,
certain intelligent radicals had joined together to form clubs in honor
of freedom. B.D. thought that the swank club wasn't exactly remi-
niscent of the Chicago radical explosion but then he wasn't in a
critical frame of mind over such matters. He only smoked when
drunk but that was because cigarettes had become too expensive.
Throughout the club folks were puffing away with panache. They
were the nattiest group B.D. had ever seen in one place, all gathered in rebellious smoking friendship.

When they reached their booth blood rushed to B.D.'s face.
Bob's date, Sharon, whom he had mentioned earlier in the day,

turned out to be a junior high girl, or so he thought. Sharon sprawled in the red leather booth in a short pink dress, white anklets, and black patent leather shoes known as Mary Janes, looking thirteen at the outside. She batted Bob with the Sherman Alexie novel she was reading when Bob slid into the booth beside her and cupped her ass. B.D.'s mind spun, thinking it was odd that California banned smoking and then allowed this sort of thing. He sat down hesitantly at the scene of yet another crime and on a closer look figured she might push eighteen but was dressing real young for private reasons. Bob chuckled at his discomfort and said that Sharon was a recent graduate of Radcliffe on the East Coast, which raised in B.D.'s mind the image of a building on a cliff above the stormy Atlantic.

"You're real lucky to go from one ocean to the other," B.D. said, shaking her small soft hand which made him quiver.

"I've never thought of it that way." Sharon was wondering if this asshole was for real or putting her on. "Bob talked about you on the phone. I have great sympathy for you and the plight of your people."

"The road is both long and short. I have my hopes in my heart." B.D. was a little confused by a woman in the booth behind Bob and Sharon whose monster tits were literally falling out of her blouse. She flashed him a dizzying smile.

"Well put," Bob said. "The struggle is both in the moment and in the long term." He grabbed the arm of a passing waiter. "Why don't you miserable fucks bring us some drinks?"

"Do many Natives wear such wonderful hats?" Sharon ignored Bob's impatient anger, not being an alcoholic herself though she was mildly wired on Zoloft.

"A few of us in the brotherhood," B.D. said, wondering at the same time why he was spilling bullshit. Sharon was like Shelley who seemed to demand it. If he had had a pencil or pen he could have used the old trick of dropping it on the floor to look up her legs but then, however pretty, she was a tad scrawny. Bob, who had just gotten up to track down drinks, must be trying to recapture his youth or something like that, but then again he might just be trying to help Sharon out.

"Bob's a swell guy," Sharon said, glancing across the room at Bob at the bar demanding service. "I just worry he's going to blow his tubes with booze like my dad did. Sure, he's a good writer but ninety-nine point nine percent of all writers are forgotten within a month after their last book."

"Why would anyone want to be remembered?" B.D. asked. "We're all worm chow." He felt cozier watching Bob approach followed by a waiter with a tray containing two bottles of wine and a martini, the other hand holding an ice bucket with three Buds.

It wasn't really a swell evening except to B.D. Sharon only picked at a plate of two oysters, two shrimp, and two cherrystone clams on a bed of radicchio while Bob had a double order of veal chops and pasta. Lucky for B.D. Bob's spinach joke was only a side order that accompanied a prime New York strip that weighed nearly two pounds. He had noted it on the menu but then it cost thirty-eight dollars so he had settled on spaghetti and meatballs which only cost the astounding price of eighteen dollars. There was a restaurant in Iron Mountain where the same dish was only four dollars and a single meatball was the size of a baby's head and a side order of half of a roasted chicken was only two bucks. Bob stepped in and insisted B.D. have the steak saying that in L.A. a man requires power food. Sharon's pathetic dish irritated Bob so much that he began choking. B.D. agreed on the idea of power food, describing the sense of well-being he felt after eating five deer hearts. Sharon impolitely pointed out that they were both full of shit.

"Only partially full, darling. But then so are you. From birth to death the primate colon is never completely empty." Bob's voice carried strongly and two couples at a table across the aisle from their booth didn't seem happy.

Sharon giggled and playfully lifted a leg and kneaded Bob's ample tummy with a shiny, patent leather shoe. As B.D. worked methodically on his steak, eating the delicious fat first, he noted Sharon was a pretty smart gal. She and Bob had a high-minded argument about whether the media, *in toto*, was in reality the main weapon of mass destruction in the world since it irretrievably warped the minds of the collective citizenry. According to Sharon TV, the movies, newspapers, and nearly all books were actually a nerve gas dumbing down the world. Bob countered by asking, "Then why do you want to enter the movie business?" Naturally, she said, "To improve it."

"You lame fucks from New York and your itty-bitty art films," Bob said. "You xenophobic dweebs think that New York is the world. Everything is cold and sooty and everyone shivers in leather jackets at dawn. You see a bridge, buildings, and pigeons. Then more bridges, buildings, and pigeons. Throw in a dog or two and a Chinese restaurant and a bum picking his nose." Bob was carried away but not so far that he neglected his meal.

"You liberal romantic novelists come out here thinking you're going to do good work and what do you come up with?" Sharon talked so softly you had to stop chewing so your mandibles didn't drown out her voice. "You think you can apply your lame sensitivities across the board to every situation and what do we get? Shooting. Everyone shoots everyone. You think that the paradigm of life is crime. You fall back on your limp penises which take the form of guns. Bang. Come. Bang. Come." Sharon wiped her spotless lips with her napkin, a prim gesture. She pouted at B.D. who had finished his steak and was loving the spinach which swam in olive oil and garlic. "What do you think, Mister Noble Savage?"

"I was thinking that this was the best steak of my life and that I want to get my bearskin back." He eyed her uneaten cherrystone clams and she pushed them over. This was another adventure in the making because he had never eaten a raw clam. "I know I'm missing out a lot where I live but I don't have a TV, the movie houses are far away, and I don't care for newspapers because the pictures are in black and white and the world is in color." He felt weak in the face of her onslaught.

"But sweetheart, you get the nerve gas in the discourse of everyone you know." She stuck her tiny foot out under the table and gave his pecker a polite nudge.

Just then Bob's cellular buzzed and he portentously lifted it from the belt holster. He said, "Yes. No. Yes. No. Great," writing down an address from his jacket-pocket notebook and clicking off the phone. He eyed B.D. and affected the voice of Joe Friday. "I've got Lone Marten's address. We should move in now." He was clearly in his cups and smirked with a sense of mission, picking up a veal-chop bone and gnawing at a difficult piece of gristle.

"It would be better to move out at dawn," B.D. said, sensing that caution might be a better tack.

"Tomorrow is Saturday which makes dawn around noon, at least in L.A. Bob always sets his alarm for eleven-eleven sharp." Sharon turned to Bob who was staring blearily at the bar then waved at a couple.

"It's Sandrine and her big-shot NBC stiff. He saddle-soaps her boots with his tongue. I can imagine what that might do to your taste buds. Take it from me, your palate is a big part of your future. Once your palate goes the rest of your sensory apparatus dries up like a cow pie in the noonday sun, under which only grubs and maggots can thrive—"

"Oh for Christ's sake, Bob, shut up." Sharon nudged him so hard that only superior balance in such matters saved his glass of wine.

"Sandrine de la Redondo, this is your neighbor Brown Dog at the Siam," Bob said, ignoring the TV executive in his English bespoke suit and amber steamed glasses, and very clean ears, when they approached.

"*Êtes-vous célibataire?*" Sandrine asked, placing her hand cheekily on his neck. B.D. stared deeply into the bare midriff of her outfit, smelling the pleasure of lilac bushes on a May morning.

"That means, Are you a celebrity?" Bob translated.

"It means, Are you single?" Sharon corrected.

"*Pouvez-vous venir prendre un verre chez moi ce soir?*" Sandrine asked, running her little finger behind his ear which made him shudder.

"She wants to know if you'd like a drink later." Sharon yawned.

"Yup. Don't mind if I do." He figured if this woman were immediately interested in him there must be something seriously wrong with her. Just what it might be was the intriguing question. If she wanted a green card he'd promise her one by dawn. He waved a bit limply as Sandrine and her limp boyfriend departed.

"She wants a part. Everyone wants a part of some sort. Including me. I'll take him home. We're stopping by a very important party where he's going to introduce me to people who might give me a job." Sharon shoved Bob out of the booth with her heels, straightening her legs made strong by tennis and whatever. Bob merely signed the bill and tossed a C note on the softening pats of butter on which a single fly was mired.

Nothing, for the time being, could be other than it was, B.D. thought, stretched on his bed at two A.M. back in his room at the Siam. He thunked his drum-tight tummy. Perhaps late in the evening was too late for a two-pound steak? On the way home he had bought a six-pack of Grolsch for ten bucks with a devil-may-care attitude to tamp the steak down while he listened to Mexican music. There were ap-

parently only so many parts and jobs in the movie business and a
lot of people wanted them, but then he recalled that when United
Parcel Service had had an opening in Escanaba over two hundred
men had applied. There were a lot of *benefits,* everyone said. If you
stayed on the menial level you could avoid this mad struggle. If you
needed some dough you showed up with your chain saw, a can of
gas, and a few quarts of oil and you could always cut pulp. If you
needed a place to stay there were hundreds of deer cabins in the
Upper Peninsula you could stay in for doing some fix-it work.
Through his friend Frank at the tavern he was always in demand.
He'd live-trap the porcupines and red squirrels that were damag-
ing a cabin and let them loose near another, say at the cabin of the
yoga couple to see if the critters liked expensive dwellings. The
present was hard enough to deal with so that you couldn't very well
handle the notion of the future. He had noticed that it arrived in
daily increments without any effort. The more central struggle in
life was between water and beer. Too much beer, he knew from
many years of experience, tended to be hard on the system. The
yoga couple had told him that Elvis Presley need not have died had
he consumed enough water. All of Presley's pain and drug taking
were due to constipation caused by bad diet (cheeseburgers and
grilled peanut-butter-with-banana sandwiches) but mostly by a
failure to drink a lot of water. B.D. had been concerned about his
love for Frank's cheeseburgers and the yoga couple had given him
a ballpark of four twelve-ounce glasses of water per cheeseburger.
You had to get up and pee a lot in a cold cabin but luckily there
was a window near his cot. He ultimately did not scorn these wood
yuppies because, at this moment, they would obviously better know
how to deal with Los Angeles than he did. He found it hard to counsel himself against impatience though he had only been there two
days. And the third day looked like it would bear fruit, as the Bible
people say.

Sandrine knocked at his door at three A.M. adding a muffled
French greeting. B.D. was ready with a rule that she had to talk in
American. He had also dispersed his four hundred and seventy
dollars in a half dozen places, including a fifty in each sock. Someone said that you had to give a little to take a little, the kind of confusing homily life is built on. Sandrine's room was very pleasant
indeed, papered with French posters that included a sublime river
gorge in the Midi that might hold lunker trout. I should be back
home fishing at this very moment, he thought, because timewise it
was six A.M. in Michigan and he could imagine dawn mist curling
on the surface of this favorite beaver pond that had yielded a three-
pound brook trout on a No. 16 female Adams with a soft yellow
belly. Sandrine had decided B.D. was at least a minor rock musician, though never on the cover of *Rolling Stone,* from his absurd
outfit and because she knew that Bob wouldn't be hanging out with
nullities. When they smoked a joint as an alternative to a drink B.D.
saw problems coming, in that it was by far the strongest pot he had
ever experienced. It miffed him when she turned on the television
but she said, "The walls have ears" and that the immigration people
were hot on her trail. In France she had lived in a château but in
"Amerique" it must be the Siam for concealment from the neo-fascist
government. She was incapable of dropping her entire disguise, and
her central motive, rather than the green card, was getting the thousand bucks Bob owed her for a sexual favor. Perhaps B.D. was
gentleman enough to cover his friend's debt for a poor girl? "Let
me think it over," he said, speaking into a clenched fist as if it were
a microphone. The pot smoke had begun to swirl around his brain
pan and the yoga couple's advice to "listen to your body" was at
the moment not very attractive. Right in front of him Sandrine had
changed into something more comfortable, a soft cotton shift leaving her legs bare to the mid-thigh. His tummy beef became restless
and began to moo. She took off his fedora and leapt back as if hit

by a cattle prod, proclaiming his hair to be the ugliest in the cos-
mos. Luckily for him she was an experienced cosmetologist. She
led him to the bathroom, had him bend over the bowl, and sheared
off close to the scalp his bristly skullcap, a matter of no importance
to him though when he saw the lid of water covered with his hair
he thought of biblical Samson being shorn by Delilah. When she
flushed the toilet the swirling vortex of hair looked like a cow's ass.
She finished his head off with a bluish rinse at which point he recalled Delmore's portentous dream that he would return home with
a weird haircut! My God, but life was mysterious. They embraced
in front of a large bathroom mirror with Sandrine releasing his
weenie from captivity. It seemed far away as it prodded her warm
cotton outfit seeking out the bull's-eye. *"Non, non, non,"* she whispered, heading for the bed. They flopped into the age-old upsy-
downsy position, a practice Bob had advised she preferred. In his
pot haze anything was fine by him and this delightful lass had obviously been there before. Without the stealthy effects of beer, steak,
and marijuana it would have been over in a trice. The world seemed
dark so he opened his eyes and there between the two orbs of her
bottom he could see Vincent Price on the television. It was the very
old horror movie about parachutes that didn't open, an apt metaphor for his life. Delmore had complained that modern airliners
weren't equipped with parachutes. She thwacked away at his chin
and he felt her hands run up his calves and shins to the only thing
he was wearing, socks. Her hands played over his insteps as Vincent's airplane cradled through the clouds between her butt cheeks
and she gargled, "A present for Sandrine, *merci.*" At his moment of
release she shrieked, "You fucking cheapskate," having peeled off
the socks and found the two fifties. She leapt up with tears in her
eyes, shaking the paltry bills that he hadn't exactly given to her.
While he quickly dressed she threatened to call the Mafia which
he had only dimly heard of, though post-dope paranoia had set in

and any harm was possible. Up until this point, and he was well
into his forties, he did not believe that the aftermath of sex could
depress him. When he pulled on his trousers she grabbed for his
wallet which he had wisely left in his room and they tumbled backward onto the bed. While she kicked and emitted fake sobs on her
belly he stood and decided hers was actually the top fanny of his
life which did a lot to lift his momentary depression. When he
reached the door and took one last look she held out a hand im-
ploringly for more cash, every bit as winsome as the divine actress earlier in the evening. Back in his room he drank a quart and
a half of his valuable stash of water and went to bed without a single
thought.

The phone rang at eleven-twelve in the morning. B.D.'s eyes were
already open and he was thinking of Frank's wise saying "No matter where you go, there you are." How could anyone quarrel with
the depth of this statement.

"We have a rendezvous with destiny. I feel great. How about
you?" Bob said loudly enough on the phone that B.D. had an ear
buzz. After Frank's wisdom he was trying to think of what the yoga
couple had told him to the effect that all over the body are hands
and eyes, or throughout the body are hands and eyes, which means
there are a lot of resources if you want to use them. The couple were
big on quotes. They had them tacked and taped up all over the place.

"B.D., are you there?" Bob could hear breathing but that
was it.

"Yup. I was lost in thought."

"Did you get together with the lovely Sandrine?"

"In a way. Do you believe in evolution?"

"Everyone does if you watched *Planet of the Apes*, but what the
fuck are you talking about?"

"I was wondering if you could be descended from a bear rather than an ape?"

"I don't think so but then science is not my long suit. Are we still on?"

"Yes. If it's okay we move out at dawn. Sharon said that's in a half-hour hereabouts."

"Come up to the room and we'll strategize. I'll order breakfast."

When B.D. washed the sleep from his face he was startled by his haircut and its bluish cast. All the more reason to own a fedora. That Sandrine was a real pill. His socks felt deeply the lack of the two fifties so he redistributed his three hundred seventy. At this rate blow jobs were going to get priced out of the range of the common man and inflation alone would insure marital fidelity, assuming you had a wife.

As an afterthought before getting into the car B.D. slid a crisp dollar under Sandrine's door as a teasing tip, affording her one-third of a cup of coffee to meet the day which showed signs of a terminal smog alert. His eyes and nose itched like they did around a dump fire where tires were burning, but then perhaps it was the right kind of weather for the mission. The yellowish sky looked ominous and he ran a finger along his badly chapped lips remembering the source of the ailment. Frank had told him that before Native warriors entered battle they liked to say "Today is a good day to die," but that seemed a bit much for the current situation. A modest injury would be appropriate but he didn't want to bite the big one, as they say. Not that he wanted another go at the brunette bombshell Sandrine, at least not at that price. For a hundred bucks you could get by a whole winter month if you were careful. A couple of old World War II veterans at the tavern had told him that in wartorn Europe or Japan a fellow could get sex for a candy bar but that hadn't seemed like an admirable transaction. The least you could do is fry up a chicken and make mashed potatoes for the poor girl, bake up an apple pudding with brown sugar and lots of butter.

Up in Bob's room B.D. was impressed with the set-up in that there was a living room and two bedrooms with one full of books and used as a study. It hadn't occurred to him that this was possible in a hotel. In the living room beside the table full of food there was a telescope on a tripod aimed down at the swimming pool. There was the question of if you wanted to see the ladies why not go down to the pool and take a look but Bob said, "It's safer this way." B.D. was a bit played out on women and focused the telescope on a flock of pale green parakeets in a flowering tree. He was disappointed when Bob didn't know the name of the tree, also when Bob said that the hotel was trying to get rid of these lovely birds because they sometimes shit in flight on guests around the pool.

"What are they supposed to do? Birds don't have toilets." B.D. was irritated. These birds were as pretty as orioles.

"The manager thinks they're doing it on purpose."

"I hope so." B.D. sat down at the amply laid table. The steak had now left quite a hole in his stomach.

"I ordered you country ham, country eggs, and country fried potatoes. The menu doesn't say if the toast is country, maybe suburban."

"I could use some gravy but I'm not complaining. Catsup will do." B.D. fetched his Tabasco from a pocket and quickly learned that it burned his chapped lips. He speared a piece of Bob's smoked salmon and judged it not bad. As a joke Bob had ordered B.D. a large glass of carrot juice which he poured in the toilet when Bob went to his bedroom to dress. The carrot juice wasn't pretty in the swirling toilet any more than his hair had been the night before. At least Bob had been kind enough not to laugh at the blue haircut. Bob just said, "You're in Rome and you have done as the Romans would." When Bob came out of the bedroom he wore a nifty camo T-shirt under his Italian sport coat in honor of the mission.

"Sharon said that we keep trying to paint the world with our own colors when it already has its own," B.D. said.

B.D. took one more look through the telescope, having noticed a non-birdlike movement beneath the parakeet tree. It was a woman in a white string bikini and adjusting the telescope he could see a hint of short hairs emerging from one of the greatest non-bran muffins in the kingdom. Bob took a peek and said that it was Nina Coldbread, the Italian television mogul, set to give her skin a good scorching. When Bob had offered her a villa for her company she had only yawned and burped, or so he said. While Bob looked overlong through the telescope B.D. sensed that he had been given an over-exposure to beauty, that in the Great North a lifetime could pass without seeing such a woman, and if it happened it would become a precious memory. Perhaps a man was better off if his experiences were more limited, and did not even include the velvet battering ram of the night before that made his face sore and tender. Perhaps the experience had knocked some sense into his head, perhaps not.

Bob became more than a little nervous when B.D. pulled their vehicle up to a security gate off Benedict Canyon, the address where Lone Marten was supposedly staying. Bob knew from some alcohol-suffused memory that it was the home of a studio honcho which would fill any screenwriter with fear but he couldn't remember which one. He rattled off a list of studio names, then remembered Universal and was relieved because he had already burned his bridges there with a not very exciting project, *Some Called It Tuesday*, about the sexual adventurism of a Republican wife. Bob had B.D. hit the buzzer and when a voice asked, "May I help you" Bob

yelled out, "We are of the people" and the huge gate magically opened.
Bob told B.D. that the woman of the house was active in civil rights
specializing in Natives. They drove through a brick-lined tunnel, the
ultimate in security from God knows what, and emerged onto a large
green sward in front of an English Tudor house. In the middle of the
huge lawn but near the driveway a woman in a lilac peignoir was
playing croquet with three obvious Natives, all with long black pony-
tails. Another man was sleeping beneath a pine tree.

"Irony scratches her tired ass. Redskins playing croquet," Bob
chuckled.

"Not really. The Ojibway invented croquet though they only
used balls hand-carved from the boles of a diseased oak that had
been struck by lightning." Under pressure B.D.'s mind had become
antic. He knew that the man beginning to sit up under the pine tree
was none other than Lone Marten.

They got out of the car and the woman rushed over saying,
"Bob, Bob, Bob, welcome aboard." Bob flushed with pleasure that
she remembered his name but then he realized she might not have
a memory suffused in alcohol. They embraced as is the custom of
the area and she made a bow to B.D. whom she took for a Native,
but B.D., intent on his purpose, was already striding through the
wickets toward Lone Marten. A large Lakota, at least that's what
it said on his T-shirt, stepped in B.D.'s path when Lone Marten
screeched and began climbing the pine tree. B.D. eyed the Lakota's
general musculature, then looked over the big shoulders at Lone
Marten still screeching up in the tree.

"I have no quarrel with you, chief. He stole my bearskin. At
one time I was the best fistfighter in many counties. I haven't forgotten it all."

"He stole your bearskin?" The Lakota turned to stare at Lone
Marten up in the tree, then back at B.D. "I saw the bearskin yesterday. I think he might have sold it."

"My Uncle Delmore gave it to me. His was bear medicine and he gave it to me because after he moved south he had to go over to turtles."

"We never got along with you Chippewa people which is putting it mildly, but times have changed. Even nowadays you can't be stealing a man's bear medicine." The Lakota nodded and stepped aside, though by now everyone had followed B.D. to the pine tree. B.D. picked up a couple of croquet balls and hefted them, firing the first into Lone Marten's ass which was hanging over a branch. Bob tried to grab B.D.'s arm but without success. The Lakota and Bob explained the problem to the hostess who was wringing her hands in horror at male anger, something she had seen in her husband though in a more subdued form. She grasped B.D.'s arm as he was ready to fire the second croquet ball at Lone Marten's head.

"Lone Marten, I can climb up and tear you out of that tree like a bear would!" he yelled, though he turned politely to the woman grasping his arm.

"Lone Marten sold the bearskin to Lloyd Bental at our fundraiser here yesterday. He's going to donate half the proceeds to the cause. If that's not good enough I can pay you for it." She took the cellular from her gossamer waistband and shrieked, "My checkbook please."

"No you can't." B.D. slumped to the ground with his face in his hands, not noticing that on hearing the name Lloyd Bental Bob had shrunk back, his face becoming as pale as dirty snow.

An impasse had been reached. The Lakota and the two other Natives sat down on the far side of the tree from B.D. and were eventually joined by the woman who assumed there was something sacramental going on and she should probably join in. Her maid came running with the checkbook and was shooed away. Meanwhile, Bob had returned to the car where to his dismay he could only find three little airline booze bottles. The very name Lloyd

Bental, by far the most powerful producer-director in Hollywood, shrank all his blood tubes with fear. If you crossed Lloyd you'd never work in Hollywood again. No one had dared count how many writers had been sent back East with jellied brains and shriveled nuts.

Finally Brown Dog stood up, raised his chin, and stared hard up in the tree at Lone Marten who now felt like a fired writer sent back East. For the first time in his life Lone Marten knew he had gone too far. When the chance had come to sell the bearskin to the mogul he had known it was the wrong thing to do just as he knew it was wrong for poor dumb Brown Dog to let the fucking "wasichus" know the location of the graveyard. But then Lloyd Bental had been accompanied to the fund-raiser by two young actresses who had made Lone Marten's skin steam and itch, not to speak of a roll of hundred-dollar bills that would choke a pig. White women and money, not to speak of drugs, had always wrung his smallish petty-criminal heart.

"Lone Marten, if you don't help me get my bearskin back I'm going to track you down and tear out your heart." With that not very ambiguous statement B.D. walked slowly back to the car, using a sleeve to wipe away his tears. The woman followed him to the car and asked where he was staying and when he said "Siam" she naturally thought of Yul Brynner and Anna. She patted Bob, who was a slobbering mess, through the window, and she really didn't mind when B.D. did a U-turn in the yard, digging up long divots as he sped off. This was real emotion.

It was his darkest hour and his hands felt numb on the steering wheel. Traffic was tied up on Sunset due to an accident and B.D. felt poignantly the utter crush of civilization. An eighty-year-old Finn he had known well had flown out this way to see his son and had warned B.D. that "the world is filling up." No shit. B.D. wanted to turn turtle like he did when he and Lone Marten had driven through the profound ugliness of Las Vegas, and where he simply raised his shirt collar and sank into its dark confines, preferring his own rank air.

It didn't help that Bob was in his bibbety-babbety-boo state, blabbing away about Lloyd Bental's seven Oscars, his hundreds of millions of dollars, his homes in Beverly Hills, Palm Springs, Palm Beach, Acapulco, his brownstone in Manhattan, his grand apartment in Paris, not to speak of the beach house in East Hampton. These details wavered B.D. a bit from the purity of his righteous anger wondering if the guy had the pipes drained to avoid freezing up when he moved from place to place and the way the fixtures within unused toilets tended to seize up. Then the phone rang interrupting Bob's interior and exterior monologues and it was as if Bob didn't recognize the phone so B.D. answered it. It was the croquet hostess who called to say that she had gotten in touch with Lloyd Bental but that he was unwilling to give up his rug which, even at the moment she had called, he was stretching out on because it made him feel spiritual. She had also phoned her husband, waking him up in London, but he was calling the head of the prop department of his studio and a bear rug would be delivered to the Siam. B.D. was on the verge of telling her to go fuck herself but a dimmish idea began to emerge so he only said, "Thank you, white woman, and let me say you looked good in that lilac gown." Despite his anger at the time he had made a record of her attractiveness.

Meanwhile, Bob had continued rattling on and the upshot was that he could no longer help B.D. try to recover his bearskin because if he were caught crossing Lloyd Bental he would "never work in this town again."

"You could work in Nebraska," B.D. said lamely, eyeing the traffic congestion ahead for an escape route.

"He'd have me followed there, buddy. His vengeance is sure and swift. He even takes it out on animals. A few years ago, someone gave him a wolf hybrid as a pet. She shit on the floor as animals will do. Lloyd had her dyed solid pink and she expired from embarrassment. The Humane Society was called in but even they were frightened of Lloyd Bental. I've got a family to support, a sick wife and two sick kids. They need groceries and milk. I need to send home five hundred grand a year."

"What about your promiscuous mother?" B.D. asked, without irony.

"Her too. She's in her mid-seventies but she's probably still hitting the streets. Mind you, my heart's with you."

"No car?" B.D. could see a life on foot returning. Walking anyway cleared the mind.

"No car. My car's my trademark. Everyone in town knows my car, especially the cops. I could rent you one." His voice trailed off into bleating.

When B.D. parked at the hotel Bob was racked with sobs of grief and fear. They embraced in front of the puzzled doorman and Bob stuffed some more money in B.D.'s pocket. He turned away as Bob tripped up the steps and walked kitty-corner over to the botanical gardens, needing a big dose of nature to gather his thoughts. A little dose would have to do.

B.D. hoofed it back to the Siam in an hour. In the garden there had been an Oriental in a white suit sitting by the carp pool and since he had his heart set on it B.D. sat there too. After about a half-hour of mutual silence the Oriental smiled and got up. They talked for a few minutes and B.D. learned that the guy was composing himself to do an eight-hour brain surgery on a little girl. B.D. wished him good luck, thinking of Rose's little girl Berry, back home, whose head was severely cross-wired, which came from Rose's heavy drinking when she was pregnant and now the condition was hopeless. All the way back to the Siam B.D. felt the peculiar, damp heaviness of homesickness swelling in him. He actually craved to get bitten by mosquitoes and freeze his ass off on one of those cold summer mornings when the wild huckleberry crop was in danger and he had gone out to pick a few to make pancakes. He always used way too many berries so the pancakes were a mess but, nevertheless, good. Afterward a beer would cut the sweetness of the maple syrup and then he'd take a stroll of a few hours or go fishing.

Back at the Siam he had a shower, throwing his fancy Holly-wood clothes aside with disgust. It was time to return to the cool, level-headed humility of his janitor's suit with the unknown Ted's name on the pocket. With his ear to the wall he could hear Sandrine singing, certainly the most noteworthy experience he had had in town though the reviews were mixed. The view had anyway been wonderful despite the occasional intrusiveness of Vincent's dour face between the smooth cheeks. He had barely finished a quart of the expensive water when there was a knock on the door. He took the precaution of peeking through the curtains and there stood Lone Marten holding a bearskin rug with a green felt liner. He opened the door and the rug looked even more pathetic than it had through the window with a slight cinnamon phase to the fur and rubber non-skid gizmos on the liner. It might not be possible but the skin looked like it belonged to a very gay bear.

"This car I borrowed cost a hundred thirty grand," Lone Marten said, gesturing at the Mercedes convertible behind him.

"Tell it to someone who gives a shit." It did occur to B.D. that the amount probably surpassed his lifetime income. "That bear rug looks like it came from the prop department at Universal."

"How did you know?" Lone Marten looked quizzically at the rug in his arms.

"I have my ways." He swiveled to see Sandrine peeking from her door wide-eyed.

"Lone Marten!" she exclaimed.

"Sandra, the French girl! How strange to see you in humble circumstances, including B.D."

"Sandrine's the name, kiddo. I bet you thought of fencing that car in Tijuana for a lot of bucks. I live here because it's free rent. I can't live with a man because you guys are the spawn of the devil, maybe worse."

It turned out that her NBC exec boyfriend had taken her to the fund-raiser up Benedict where he had bid on some ersatz turquoise jewelry.

"Sandrine, darling, I need a pair of scissors." Everyone seemed to use the word "darling" and he might as well join them. He took the bear rug into his room, intending to somehow sneak into Lloyd Bental's house and switch the rug for his bearskin. He'd probably end up dying in a California prison but so what? Maybe they'd let him out in a couple of winters so he could go home and hear the delicious sound of crunching snow beneath his feet.

Sandrine and Lone Marten sat on the bed smoking a joint while B.D. cut loose the lining with the scissors. Lone Marten discussed several ways he might help B.D. get his bearskin back, including the highly creative way of blowing up the house with a ton of nitrogen fertilizer, some kerosene, and blasting caps. Sandrine yawned when she heard Bental's name.

"Think smarter and try to remember that I'm otherwise going to tear out your heart." B.D. had finished with the rug noting that someone had shampooed and softened the fur and given the bear marble-blue eyes. There is no end to blasphemy, he thought.

"I know Lloyd Bental real well," Sandrine bragged, which really got their attention. "I've blown him a few times. I won't fuck him because he's not a star, only a director and producer."

✻   ✻   ✻

It hadn't been real hard to strike a deal for Sandrine's help. Lone
Marten started at five hundred bucks but she held out for the usual
thousand, glaring at B.D. and reminding him of the measly two fifty-
dollar bills in his socks. Lone Marten took out a wad and peeled
off the ten one-hundred-dollar bills, explaining plaintively that this
was the people's fund-raising money and now they'd lack money
to repair their leaking tepees. Sandrine made a fake yawn and went
to get Lloyd's number from her five-inch-thick alligator-skin personal phone book. The moment she left Lone Marten whispered to
B.D. that the money was bad counterfeit he'd bought for twenty
bucks for a thousand, useful in such occasions. B.D. agreed and
when Sandrine returned she said that Lloyd only had a thirty-
minute "window" at nine before going to dinner so they had to be
on time. That meant they had two hours to stew in their juices.
Sandrine was hungry so Lone Marten took her out for something
to eat, tooling out of the Siam parking lot with unbelievable speed.
B.D. requested that they bring him back a liver sausage on rye with
onions, cheddar, and hot mustard but wasn't too hopeful they'd
succeed. This was as close as he could come to power food from
back home. A deer heart or liver would be more proper to ready
himself for the momentous night ahead but either of them would
be hard to find in the neighborhood. A number of times hunters
had given him and Frank bear meat, wanting to keep only the hide.
They quickly discovered that you had to get all the fat off older bear
or there was a predominant flavor as if you had mixed axle grease
and saddle soap. Younger bears, especially female, had fewer pu-
rines in the blood and on slow nights in the kitchen of Frank's
Tavern in late October they'd make some experimental bear stews
using lots of garlic and red wine, but sometimes varying the recipe
with garlic, hot pepper, and dark rum which Frank said is how they
cooked old goat down in the sunny Caribbean. The downside of

bear meat for Brown Dog was that it always caused remarkably vivid bear dreams. It was pretty frightening to make love to a sow bear even in a dream, and the male bears, the boars, made Mike Tyson look like Mary Poppins. Delmore had teased him that in the old days it wasn't unknown for a man to become a bear if he ate too much bear meat or generally fooled around with them too much. Down near the headwaters of the Fox River one evening while fishing he had sat with his back against a big white pine stump and a sow bear had come along and sat down no farther than twenty feet from him. It was a real attention getter and they both averted their glances, knowing that in the natural world a direct stare is considered at the very least impolite. Even ravens don't like to be stared at and if you look off to the side a bit they're much more likely to stick around.

The slam of a car door jogged him from his bear trance which had only served to increase his homesickness. His heart leapt at the idea of his liver sausage sandwich and he sniffed the air as he opened the door. It was Sharon driving the brown Taurus with Bob snoring away beside her. Now she was in adult clothes, a tank top and Levi's, rather than a pink dress and shiny black shoes. She leaned against the car door with an attractive twist to her hips and her nipples were perky beneath the tank top.

"Bob insisted I drive him over to apologize to you and now he's asleep."

"Let sleeping dogs lie," B.D. said for no reason at all.

"Don't be too hard on him. He's just a big kid."

"I'm not. He's got his own problems. It must be pretty hard when your whole family is sick, not to speak of your mom loose on the streets."

"Oh, that's all bullshit. Our families are friends from way back and there's nothing wrong with his wife and kids except the usual neuroses, dope, and alcohol."

"You don't say." B.D. couldn't figure out if he was startled, surprised, or just plain diverted for a moment from his own problems. "I thought you were his lady friend."

"I admit I have to lead him on a bit. I really want a career in the movie business and after last night's party I think I might have a job with the great Lloyd Bental. He reminds me of a pear with lipstick but I liked him a lot. He quoted poetry to me in five languages."

"Well, congrats to you." Now B.D. was startled. Within this big town there was obviously a small town. The last thing he was going to do was tell Sharon he was forming a plot against the versatile Lloyd.

"Did anyone ever tell you that you're weirdly attractive?" Sharon had glanced over to make sure Bob Duluth was still asleep.

"Can't say that it never happened." Their eyes fixed deeply on each other unlike what's permitted in the other part of the animal world. B.D. bowed and swept an arm in a gesture to his motel room door. Sharon entered with a pronounced blush. Not a little while later he would have a perplexing moment thinking about how fucked up the relation between time and people can be. He and Sharon had fairly collided behind the door. Her jeans were half down and he was kneading her bare bottom while she yanked a bit roughly on his weenie as if starting an older-model outboard motor. Their tongues were sweetly entwined when Lone Marten screeched up outside yelling, "Liver sausage from Nate and Al's." It was simply heartbreaking, so near but so suddenly so far. Injustice spread around him like an elephant fart. He quickly cinched his pecker under his belt and went outside, followed by Sharon who for some reason whistled "The Colonel Bogie March."

"Here it is, blood brother, and with double meat." Lone Marten handed him the lunker sandwich just as his pecker fell in his trousers like the reverse of the famous Hindu rope trick. He turned abruptly, hearing an audible hissing. Sharon and Sandrine were faced-off a mere foot from each other spitting out their words.

"Trying to cop another of my boyfriends, you string-bean Ivy League bitch," Sandrine shrieked.

"I'll kick you in the cunt, you gold-digging faux-French street slut," screamed Sharon.

B.D. leaned against the passenger side of the Taurus, looking down in embarrassment at the sleeping Bob. This range of female anger horrified him. He took an enormous bite of his sandwich, feeling the possibility that since he had just been cheated of sex, it was also possible to lose his sandwich. Lone Marten moved quickly between the women and in perfect unison they both slapped him for reasons of their own. Sharon stalked to the Taurus and B.D. reached in the window and patted Bob on the head. Bob woke up smelling the sandwich and quickly took an offered bite. B.D. had to jump as Sharon backed up.

"Good-bye, old pardner." He waved. Bob looked something like a wizened child who had fallen asleep after a tantrum.

Zero hour. Sandrine drove the car expertly up Beverly Glen, what with her NBC boyfriend owning the selfsame vehicle. The front seat was rather small and Lone Marten had to sit on B.D.'s lap. Imagine paying that kind of money for just two seats, B.D. thought, noting that Lone Marten's bony ass lacked the charm of either Sharon's or Sandrine's. The plan was that Sandrine would go into Lloyd's house and before she did her job she'd leave the door ajar, presuming she could divert him from whatever room held the bearskin. This was less than a guaranteed plan and when Lone Marten said something about "giving it the old college try" it meant nothing to B.D. who was irked that Lone Marten and Sandrine were sharing yet another joint so strong that the secondhand smoke addled him.

"*Je suis ici,*" Sandrine warbled, pressing Lloyd's gate button, "*Je suis là.*" There was an immediate mellifluous, baritone "Goody" from the other end, and gates as large as those in a prison movie began to open. B.D. and Lone Marten slid down until they were out of sight. Sandrine slapped at Lone Marten as he lifted her short-cotton dress for a peek. B.D. couldn't help but feel a little smug over the time he had spent in Sandrine's nether regions notwithstanding the now permanent image of Vincent Price. Just as she stopped the car he grasped the substitute bearskin which felt feminine, albeit dry. Sandrine got out and he heard her throaty laughter, and her saying something more in French and the man's hearty laughter which sounded something like the Escanaba newscaster's on TV when some tourist insisted on watching the news at Frank's Tavern. B.D. couldn't help but take a stealthy peek out the car window. The man wore a short yellow robe and did look like a pear with lipstick as Sharon had described him. B.D. had to admire how fast he worked because he already had Sandrine's skirt above her waist. B.D. was thrilled to see that after they walked up the wide, palatial steps she was able to leave the door slightly ajar. Above the ticking of the Mercedes engine B.D. listened for her voice which would call out "Moola" if she managed her intent of getting Lloyd out the side door and into a rose garden, or into a bedroom, anywhere at a safe distance from the bearskin should she be lucky enough to note its location. Lone Marten looked a bit glazed and drooling under a bright mercury-vapor light above them. And then B.D. heard the high clear call of "Moola" and eased himself out of the car, the cinnamon skin with blue marble eyes in hand. When he reached the steps he turned and saw that Lone Marten was following him like a zombie. B.D. grabbed him, carried him back, and threw him into the car, looping a seatbelt around his neck. He would have to go it alone.

❀   ❀   ❀

❄   ❄   ❄

And it was easy as pie, though he was first diverted by the splendor
of the home, thinking it must be the kind of place where the king
of the world would live. He tried to run silently on his tiptoes which
proved unsuccessful, but then he quickly found the bearskin which
was predictably on the floor of a den lined with hundreds of photos and testaments to the greatness of Lloyd. B.D. swiftly folded
his bearskin and stuffed it into the black garbage bag that was still
handily in the back pocket of his green janitor's trousers. He carefully arranged the ersatz skin, looking up for a moment at the line
of Oscars on the fireplace mantel and suspecting they must be pure
gold. The only close call was when he heard a female voice with a
Mexican accent calling out, "Mister Lloyd, is that you?" but by then
B.D. was in the foyer near the front door and at that moment the
great Lloyd himself groaned out mightily from the garden, "Mom,
Dad, success," which made B.D. pause a split second while tripping down the steps to the car. He recalled one night in Munising
while making love vigorously to an actual lawyer's wife he had
slapped his own ass and yelled out, "Ride 'em, cowboy," and she
had crossly jerked his ear.

Lone Marten was sitting upright dead asleep and B.D. shoved
him down, climbing on top of him and pushing him into a ball on
the passenger-seat floor. He decided not to take another peak when
he heard Sandrine and Lloyd calling out their melodious *au revoirs.*
He was unnerved by the thumping of his own heart and fear that
Lone Marten would let out another movie-Indian *Ugh!* He searched
out Lone Marten's face and firmly pressed a foot against his mouth.
And then Sandrine was in the car which roared to life and he could
not help but press his own face against her lap and give her a hearty
kiss. Her fingers tapped a rhythmic tattoo on his neck as he pushed
up her skirt. She sang a little French ditty and there was grace in
not knowing what the words meant.

❖   ❖   ❖

The only real reason to go back to the motel room was the full remaining case of expensive water plus a few spare bottles. He had debated whether to head to the airport or a bus station but then at least four days on a bus would increase the chances of someone stealing his prize. He felt he probably had enough money for a plane ticket, at least partway, though no specific figure offered itself. He asked Sandrine if he might have a loan if he ran short on ticket money and her *no* was explicit.

"I went down on you all the way from Beverly Hills to Santa Monica and you won't pony up a cent." He found this discouraging.

"Here's the buck you slid under my door, asshole." She smiled.

They stopped at Sandrine's exercise place in Santa Monica so she could pay her bill with her earnings from Lloyd. Lone Marten wandered off to buy a five-buck cup of coffee and there was the question of borrowing some counterfeit but that seemed touchy. He had never been on a plane before except a small Cessna with a logger checking out territory and it hadn't been too pleasant other than seeing the bottoms of rivers and lakes from the air. Now he stood looking into the open front of the gym with growing amazement. The rock music was quite loud and there were rows upon rows of exercising women following the movements of a sleek, young black instructor. B.D. did a little body count and figured not one out of fifteen women needed exercise and here it was shortly after ten in the evening and they were pumping and jerking themselves into a froth. Would the wonders of this place never cease? He noticed again that those passing on the street utterly ignored him in his green janitor's suit. Earlier there had been a temptation to pick up both the water and his fancy Hollywood outfit but where would he wear the outfit up home?

When Lone Marten returned with his quart of coffee he seemed hyper. B.D had previously wondered how whatever the man put

in his mouth always caused some immediate effect. This time Lone
Marten had also scored some speed at the coffee place and was
offended when neither Sandrine nor Brown Dog wanted any. All
the way to LAX they wrangled about one thing or another center-
ing on Lone Marten's idea that they fence the expensive vehicle in
Tijuana and then he and Sandrine could fly off to a South Sea island with the proceeds.

"I have to live in this town," Sandrine said, rather righteously.

"Maybe I could use you in a documentary I'm going to do for
the National Endowment of the Arts about Cheyenne dancers,"
Lone Marten suggested.

"What's the part?" There was a trace of interest in Sandrine's
voice.

"You'd be a lamprey eel in a wig that sucked out men's souls
through their peckers," Lone Marten shrieked with laughter.

"Cut that shit out. This lady helped us." B.D. placed a hand
firmly at the back of Lone Marten's neck.

On the car phone Sandrine had found out there was what she
called a Northwest "red-eye" from L.A. to Minneapolis leaving at
midnight, which didn't sound all that encouraging to B.D. but then
he sensed that fate was beginning to be kind to him. When she
dropped him off B.D. walked around to the driver's side to kiss her
good-bye.

"Good-bye, darling. You're fab. Come see me again," she said.
It was nice to end it on a high note.

While sitting at the gate and waiting to board B.D. rehearsed his airport troubles. The attractive woman at the ticket counter was at
the same time so daffy and crisp he figured that she too must be
trying to get into show business. It was Memorial Day weekend
and the only seats left were in first class which would take nearly

all of his money, about nine hundred dollars which included what
Bob Duluth had kindly stuffed in his pocket. There would be no
money left to take the feeder flight to Marquette. Or he could take
his chances at the gate with *standby tourist class*, which would also
entitle him to the flight at seven in the morning. There was a real
ugly sound to *standby* so he turned over all of his crumpled money
except eleven dollars, reassured by Delmore's dream of picking him
up in Minneapolis with what Delmore had called a "weird" haircut. It was clear that one should try to fulfill a mentor's dream.

   There was a worse mess at the security check when the bear
skull showed up on the monitor screen and a black woman in a nifty
tight uniform screeched, "What's that?" Two security agents took
B.D. aside and there was the question of whether he had the proper
papers for the bearskin as required by United States Fish and Game.
This was a real impasse but luckily the shift was changing, the
agents didn't want to be involved, and B.D. used a line Frank had
used when the cops had pulled them over on the way home from
the Seney Bar. "I fought in Vietnam to keep this country free. My
body looks like someone went over it with a big leather punch. We
took a lot of incoming mortars on the Mekong Delta which really
fucked up the fishing." That was enough and he proceeded to the
gate not knowing that only the most ardent officers want to deal
with a crazy.

   When he called Delmore from a pay phone the news was mixed,
but tending toward the median strip of the good side of life, except
for old Doris who was still in intensive care. To B.D.'s surprise he
hadn't wakened Delmore at the late hour in the Upper Peninsula.
Delmore had been chatting with a man in Uruguay on his ham radio
and described it as an "up-and-coming country." Delmore demanded that Brown Dog come home immediately, not only to see
Doris before she "cacked" but to take over the raising of Rose's
children, Red and Berry. The erstwhile white nanny who loved

Natives only lasted three days because Berry had done such things
as put a baby snake in the girl's cereal and had eaten hamburger
raw with salt and pepper. There was still some controversy over
whether B.D. was actually in Alger County when the fireworks
were lobbed at the archeological site. The real crime still garnering
news was the fact that Rose had bit off a police officer's finger,
though a feminist lawyer had come up from Lansing to help because
of Rose's contention that the officer had manhandled her tits.
Whether B.D. liked it or not Delmore and his lawyer were working on a deal for which Delmore had signed an affidavit claiming
B.D. to be the true father of Rose's kids. Since the new prosecutor
was a Republican who believed in family values he wouldn't want
to put the father in prison too, which would cost the county a fortune in foster care. Raising the kids also had the virtue of keeping
B.D.'s "nose to the grindstone," not really an appealing idea but anything was better than confinement behind iron bars. B.D. had never
felt that Frank's idea that we all spend our lives in a cage included
him. Finally B.D. told Delmore that he better start driving now because the plane would arrive at six-thirty in the morning in Minneapolis and there wasn't enough money for the Marquette flight.
"I told you this would happen, you goddamn numbskull," Delmore
crowed, adding, "Be at the curb. I don't want to pay no parking
charges."

When B.D. took his seat near a window at the front of the plane he
stowed the bearskin under the seat in front of him, then took off
his shoes so he could place his stocking feet against the fur, making it impervious to theft. A prominent Minneapolis businessman
sat down beside him and was obviously unhappy to do so. The man
wore a tailored pin-striped suit and made B.D. feel more invisible
than he had felt before which was some pretty stiff competition.

When the stewardess came around for drink orders B.D. asked for the price and was delighted to find out they were free, though later he figured out the nine drinks he consumed in the night were actually a hundred bucks apiece. His composure was pretty firm except for the improbable land speed of the takeoff and the ungodly noise of the engines. Soon afterward his skin prickled at the beauty of all the lights of Los Angeles, drawing their vision within as an uncritical child does. And later, when the altitude reached over thirty-five thousand feet he had to say to his seat partner, "We're seven miles up in the air, the same distance so I'm told of the deepest part of the Pacific Ocean." The man quickly closed his eyes, feigning sleep. And later yet, far below, he could see small thickets of lights that marked villages and cities that blurred into lovely white flowers.

When the snack of a seafood salad was served B.D. quickly determined the food wasn't of the quality of Bob Duluth's Malibu restaurant, took his bottle of Tabasco from his pocket, and turned the contents of the plastic dish into an appealing pink. The man then looked at him longingly and B.D. passed the hot sauce.

"How bright of you," the man said.

"Can't say anyone ever called me bright," B.D. said, savoring his burning tongue.

"Fuck 'em, you're bright." The man had finished his third drink and was warming up.

It turned out the man had done some rather fancy kinds of hunting and fishing and was quite pleased to find someone to listen to his self-aggrandizing tales of salmon fishing in Iceland and Norway, duck hunting in Argentina, dove hunting in Mexico where in one fabulous afternoon he had shot three hundred white-winged doves. Coming down to earth he also admitted to simple grouse shooting up near Grand Rapids, Minnesota, where Judy Garland had been born and not all that far from Bob Dylan's birthplace. The man took out his computer and showed B.D. moving pictures of his two Brittany bird dogs and the dogs actually barked rather loudly which turned the heads of passengers who were trying to sleep. Since men are men, whatever that means, the man also showed him several different photos of his Los Angeles girlfriends. He traveled to L.A. and back once a week and though he was happily married, attested by earlier computer photos of his wife and children who came right after the dogs, the road was a lonely place and a hard-working man deserved affection. If B.D. hadn't dozed off for a few minutes he would have seen the photo of a poor French actress the man was helping to get a green card. B.D. also didn't take note that during the entire four-hour flight the man hadn't asked him a single question about his life. The final transfiguration was the shimmering dawn on the greenery far below. "This is the shortest night of my life," B.D. said too loudly. Even time herself didn't stand still in a way you could count on.

Nine drinks is quite a bit on earth let alone in a cabin pressurized to a mile high, a dangerous height for drinking in volume. When the plane landed on a cool, wet, and windy Minneapolis dawn the other first-class passengers gave the prominent businessman and Brown Dog meaningful glares which were not recorded. The businessman conked a fancy lady on the head while dislodging his briefcase from an overhead bin, tried to kiss a stewardess good-bye, and brayed he was now headed for work in his brand-new Land Rover. The co-pilot, peeking out from the cockpit with a tired smile, chided the stewardess for giving the asshole too many drinks. Even B.D. dimly knew that it was time for their friendship to end and let the man go ahead while an older woman across the aisle told B.D. that he was an "enabler."

He was well down the long corridor and emerging into the main terminal while clutching his full garbage bag to his chest when he stopped to ask himself why the ground, the endless carpet and now the hard floor, felt so strange beneath his feet. He had forgotten his shoes and when he turned to retrieve them he saw that he would have to go through security again which was definitely a bad idea.

Outside he sat on a bench near the curb and was soon wet and cold but dared not retreat for fear of missing Delmore. Finally he unwrapped his bearskin and enshrouded himself in it, violently hungover but warm. Two eco-ninnies fresh out of Boulder, the kind that piss off left, right, and middle, stared down at him with anger from the height of their elevator Birkenstocks but he was nonchalant, safe and secure in this citified version of the north country.

Finally, after more than an hour, Delmore beeped his horn repeatedly from a scant five feet away and B.D. roused himself from a beautiful dream where he and Sandrine were whirling through the universe attached tails to teeth like Celtic dogs. He opened the car door and spread out his skin.

"I got the bearskin back," B.D. said, near tears.

"I didn't know you lost it. It's a good thing you got those clothes because I forgot to tell you on the phone there's a chance you can get Rose's old night job sweeping the casino. So help me navigate out of this goddamn suckhole." Delmore passed B.D. the map but he was already asleep, having heard nothing at all.

They were halfway across northern Wisconsin on Route 8 when Delmore stopped the car at a roadside park that abutted a lake east of Ladysmith. He had bought a loaf of bread, mustard, and a can of Spam as a welcome-home lunch for Brown Dog who still hadn't awakened. The sun was out now, and though it still was only in the high fifties Delmore felt warm and good to have his relation back even though the simpleminded fool wouldn't wake up. Delmore made the sandwiches, set out an ice chest with a six-pack for B.D. and iced tea for himself. He became a little irritated, went back to the car and turned on a Sunday morning Lutheran church service at blasting volume. B.D. sank deeper in his bearskin and Delmore opened a beer and dribbled some on his lips. B.D. fumbled for the door, got out and fell to his knees, got up and took the can of beer from Delmore. He drank deeply, blinking his eyes at the landscape, rubbing his stocking feet on the soft green grass, drained the beer and handed the can to Delmore, then half-stumbled down through a grove of poplar, cedar, and birch to the lake where he knelt in the muddy reeds and rinsed his face in the cold water. On the way back up the hill he took a longer route through the woods, half-dancing through the trees like a circus bear just learning his ungainly steps, slapping at the trees and yelling a few nonsense syllables, dancing back to the picnic table where he popped another beer and picked up his Spam sandwich, looking out at late spring's deep pastel green with the deepest thanks possible.

I Forgot
to Go to
Spain

You know me but then you don't know me and why should you? I have never had the slightest interest in riddles of any sort which is partly why I wrote my even three dozen Bioprobes, those hundred-page intrusive biographies that fairly litter bookstores, newsstands, novelty counters in airports — I even saw an assortment of my life's work in a truck stop near Salina, Kansas. Marilyn Monroe and Fidel Castro sold the best, Linus Pauling and Robert Oppenheimer the worst. True intelligence has little time for the vulgar preoccupations that generate good life stories.

Twenty years ago my publisher charged three dollars for my little Bioprobes and now they cost an even seven which really isn't all that much in this extended, rampaging bull market, not to speak

of the fact that my chief researcher's wage has increased from twelve
grand in 1979 to one hundred grand in 1999. She's a brutally
crippled librarian living in Indiana. I've only met her once and the
sight of this unfortunate soul put me off my feed for months. This
is a lie. She's reasonably attractive at fifty-two and is my sister. What
makes her metaphorically ugly is that she considers herself my
conscience. In fact she has thought of herself as my conscience since
she was a precocious ten-year-old and I was a slow-learning thirteen. She began as unbearably acerbic and has remained so. She
files her teeth listening to Schoenberg and Stravinsky and doing
crossword puzzles in a half dozen languages while I struggle along
with solitary English and foreign smatterings. It hasn't been officially diagnosed but is quite plain to everyone who knows her that
she is agoraphobic. She mostly only leaves our childhood home for
the porch that surrounds half the house. You couldn't prove it by
me but she insists that everything she needs is available through
her computer and the daily visits of various deliverymen. Certain
quarrels have arisen because of this machine despite the fact that
my livelihood emerges directly from it. One is tempted to use the
old word "lifeblood." I flunked out of regular graduate school at
Northwestern and was forced to take the less rigorous M.F.A. elsewhere at a school that will be unnamed for reasons to be revealed
later. My failure at graduate school was due to the closeness of
Evanston to Chicago and, more germane, I simply couldn't do what
is called "research" and still can't, thus my sister is worth every
penny of her enormous salary which is based on a percentage of
my annual gross, as is that of my younger brother Thad, who puta-
tively takes care of my business affairs. My sister Martha and I have
carried Thad in the manner of doomed sailors with albatrosses
around our necks. Thad mans our little office in Chicago when it
would be altogether more convenient if the office were in New York
near the headquarters of my publisher which, not oddly, is owned

by a German mogul so eccentric that he makes the late Howard Hughes look like Mary Poppins. Thad loves to travel back and forth between Chicago and New York at least once a week, though once a month would be adequate. Neither my sister nor myself are particularly venal but Thad is a chiseler. He's also a clotheshorse which makes New York a perfect destination. He uses limos for the airport while I've always settled for taxis. Like many Thad uses an air of condescension as a masquerade of intelligence. By arrangements made by my sister Thad's secretary receives a sizable annual bonus for warning us in advance of any of his financial shenanigans. All of our corporate checks must now be signed by two of us. At one time the double signature wasn't necessary for anything under a thousand dollars but Thad managed to pocket an extra one hundred thousand several years back through a witless swindle. I used to think Thad might be gay but my sister Martha insists he is only the world's leading narcissist.

Why do we put up with this thoroughly modern monster, this thorn in the mind and flesh? Because he's family, as they say. He's our little brother and we're still wiping his nose, tying his shoes, telling him rather explicitly not to shit in the sandbox.

I was eighteen, Martha fifteen, and Thad a mere twelve when our father, a botanist, died on a small research vessel anchored in the Galápagos, after the boat turned turtle from improperly balanced ballast tanks. Six months later our mother, who taught history at the University of Indiana, took her own life under the absolute conviction that she had a fatal brain tumor and it was pointless to go to a doctor. An autopsy revealed that she did have the sort of brain tumor that is invariably fatal. When her batty sister from New Jersey arrived to take care of us I quickly perceived that I would not be able to go off to college as planned. It was the spring of my senior year in high school and I had been accepted at the University of Chicago, but I couldn't very well leave my sister and brother in the hands of this woman who resembled in every respect the cartoon character Daffy Duck. Instead I enrolled at my hometown University of Indiana and became a perhaps premature adult.

There. I've laid things out but have I? "Nope," as many midwesterners say. Even the most wise among us strike others from the East and West as vaguely corny. Who better than I should be aware of the essential nature of the biographical hoax? I admit I'm off my feed a bit because it's late April and I'm on the lip of a garden-variety depression, but then some of them have been almost enjoyable because they are a relief from work. In both my small studios in Chicago and New York I have banks of fluorescent tubes that emit artificial sunlight. They almost do the job for a man in a habitual spring funk but not quite. My own father was an unwitting victim of the seasonal affective disorder but determined early in his career that all of his "slumps," as he called them, could be cured by a trip to the tropics, if only for a week or so. He was lucky indeed to be a top research botanist for Eli Lilly & Co. which didn't mind funding his trips, as certain of his discoveries in the realm of tropical botany were profitable indeed.

To be frank I've lately had a pratfall of a double nature, an enormous one at that. My sister sent me one of her countless faxes, this time quoting a poet named Gary Snyder who said, in effect, that all of our biographies are essentially similar, it's our dreams and visions that count. She appended a "Ha!" Of course I had read Snyder but not for nearly thirty years when I entered the feckless voyage of becoming a truly professional writer. If I spent a whole week reading poetry I'd get a blasting attack of eczema. In 1969 when I wrote and published a book I now refer to as *Murgatoyd in SOHO*, I was nearly crippled with eczema, so much so that I came to a publication party at my alma mater with my clothes literally pasted to the various salves on my body. *M.S.*, to use the book's nickname, was a vaguely avant-garde intermix of poetry and prose, a faux autobiography of a young New York City suicide who, scorned by the young woman he loved, flung himself from the Empire State Building in a Buddhist orange cape. It was a *"succès d'estime"* which means you get good reviews but no money. Sad to say it was nearly a true story, thus the eczema. My marriage to my own true love had lasted only nine days, annulled at the insistence of her parents. She was eighteen, an undergraduate, and I was twenty-four, just finishing my M.F.A., and teaching freshman comp on a nasty graduate assistantship. She was my student and though eighteen she looked fifteen. It was legal back then to make love to your students. I had very long hair and wore a pair of velvet bell-bottoms to parties, difficult to admit but then so are so many of the contents of one's life.

Anyway, I was sitting in the Cajou last night eating my "raie au beurre noir" after a dozen oysters, admitting that my taste for seafood in blackened butter depended quite a bit on blackened butter. A woman down the row was leaning over in her chair, her butt a bit off to the side so the crack was on the chair edge with one half compressed and the other half hanging. A jolt to the brainpan. My fork tingled my chin as I missed a bite. Tears nearly formed. It was a clone of Cindy's butt. If our marriage hadn't been annulled we were going to change her name which wasn't appropriate for the wife of an artiste. That intention was one of a list of items that, perhaps properly, enraged her parents.

Of course I couldn't commit suicide way back then because who would look after Martha and Thad, my sister and brother? I should add that my mother didn't mention the responsibilities in her elaborate suicide note. What peerless grammar.

The girl with the Anjou pear fanny got up from her chair, straightened her skirt, and went to the toilet. Her sallow boyfriend smirked like a weasel with a fresh pullet. To avoid his glance I looked at the ceiling where Cindy's image blazed in her gardening shorts. I had met her in my class, acknowledged her attractiveness, but when I saw her poking around in her dormitory's flower beds I was poleaxed. She was kneeling there talking to an old Italian, one of the college's gardeners, and a lecher to boot, and her butt was flexed skyward as she diddled with the flowers.

And that touched on the other side of my double pratfall. The first, the implication of my sister that my life's work was worthless because it is our dreams and visions that own true significance, not our petty biographical details, was difficult to handle but the second was more poignant. On a morning American Airlines flight (I have three hundred thousand Advantage Miles!) the day before I had picked up the airline's magazine and there smack-dab in front of me were a number of photos of Cindy in an article titled "A Woman of Many Flowers," a hundred acres of them to be exact on a farm along the Mississippi just north of La Crosse, Wisconsin. She was fifty now but rather handsome in that Palm Beach way of women who have spent too much time in the sun. She had been married several times, "thrice divorced" in the usual magazine prose, with "two grown children" of indeterminate sex. Had our nine-day wonder counted as one of the marriages? She was bent on preserving rare "heirloom" flowers, and she and her assistants had traveled far and wide to gather seeds from flowers that had passed out of current gardeners' fancies. When I left the restaurant after my habitual sorbet I was so distracted that I nearly said to the proprietor that my meal had been "a triumph of the human spirit," as I had said a few weeks before to Mario Batali at Babbo, where I eat at the far end of the bar on Wednesday nights when I'm in New York. Mario had looked at me and repeated, "A triumph of the human spirit?" These are the petty details of life. I assume that I loathe ironies but it is easy indeed to become a victim of them. Ironies are a way to shield ourselves from the obvious life-sucking vulgarities of our culture. You could say that they make life more endurable but not better. They are mental heroin. To say "a triumph of the human spirit" is merely the sort of thing that comes up when you write three dozen Bioprobes. If only it were true but under the most diffident scrutiny it's not, or extremely rarely, in public life. Private life is another matter but the separation between the two has become problematical. Pick up and feel the heft of a *National Geographic.* Read a supposed article, say, "Greece: A Country at the Crossroads," and try to remember the smarmy blur the next day. You'll have the feeling that you're on a television program because you are. Your thumping little heart is a boiled offering.

What fun it was to try to call Cindy on the phone, a crisp, indomitable thing to do, so unsoiled by irony. Of course she wasn't there. Her house sitter said that it was spring (so easy to forget in a city) and that Cindy was off in Kansas as "busy as a bee" investigating early spring wildflowers. Why not, I thought, neglecting to leave my name and number.

How clearly I remember the evening in Hinsdale, Illinois, when her father and teenage brother threw me off the porch of their fine home. I'm not a shrimp so it took some doing. She was restrained by her mother and could not run to my side if, indeed, she made the attempt. They were wealthy people and I had falsely assumed a certain level of manners. Her father had been sure I was one of those "Chicago radicals." Her brother was on the Yale crew, one of those big boys who row a boat until they become a sizable knot of muscle. Never had I felt more like an orphan than when I was sprawled there in their yard, nose down in a flower bed Cindy had doubtless planted.

❖   ❖   ❖

For a number of specific reasons I awoke at dawn laughing. This comes closer to a triumph of the human spirit for a fifty-five-year-old man. I recalled a dream early in my eighteenth year that the closet in our old Indiana farmhouse, which had slowly been surrounded by a suburb, contained all of my future unlived life, everything I wouldn't get around to doing. Even at that time I thought this might be a case of premature aging. My parents, of course, were on the verge of dying but hadn't yet done the job so I couldn't blame the dream on their absence. I had no dream clues to the content of this unlived life, just that it was there in the closet. The simple conclusion about this dream that kept reoccurring over the years was that we are partly defined by what we draw back from, by what our temperament decides to exclude before it has a chance to happen. Years ago when I had been working on my Bioprobe of Barry Goldwater I met a ninety-year-old German woman who had been living in an Airstream trailer in an Arizona desert since 1946 for obvious reasons. My dream would have indicated that she should have moved there earlier, say in 1934 or 1935. She was a botanist and by professional happenstance knew of some of my father's work in wild-plant genetics. When I answered her question about my own livelihood her eyes dismissed my profession as if I had said that I spun cotton candy at county fairs.

The main source of my laughter, however, had been my long walk the evening before from Cajou near Nineteenth Street up to and far east on Seventy-second where I have my New York studio apartment near the river. For the cognoscenti, I live near the George Plimpton compound. We've never formally met but have nodded at each other at the embarcade while we watched passing tugboats and other craft. Anyway, on this long walk home I watched limousines and town cars loading and unloading small groups of wealthy businessmen at expensive restaurants. I'm not sure what struck me as suddenly so funny about my own "class," say those who made over three hundred thousand a year, though perhaps over five hundred thousand would be closer. I don't mean from inherited wealth but actual working, mostly white men, and excluding actors, musicians, and professional sports players. The highest echelon of working stiffs is peculiar indeed but I can't say that up until this moment had they ever seemed profoundly comic.

Curiously, my brother Thad wishes dearly to be one of these creatures but he simply doesn't know the secret of how to effec- tively offer up his entire life. Not incidentally, Thad blew the hun- dred grand he stole from me on day trading and a ten-percent share of a sure-thing filly at the Keeneland Sale in Kentucky that year. I can't bear to describe these men *in extensia,* the members of my fraternity at large, my fellow alpha canines who when at their kind- est are still baring the teeth of total self-interest. The usual self- referential potato cannot clearly describe his potatohood. And on this long walk home, more clearly than ever before, I could see my brethren as lucidly as you could spot a diplomat in a dime store. These folks were going to micro-manage, truly an ugly word, their after-dinner farts.

I was laughing when I turned on my coffeemaker, invariably prepared the evening before, and laughing that I had arisen at nine- thirty rather than the habitual seven. I'm certainly not a cold- hearted prick. I'm just not at all sure of what to do except work. There are some interesting clouds out my window, rather pretty cumuli on the warmish morning. How do they adhere to themselves rather than fall apart? A call to my sister would get me the infor- mation quickly but this morning the very idea of useful informa- tion gives me an un-comic tremor. While watching the clock reach ten, I wondered what I could summon up from my life that is pri- vate, but dismissed the question by calling my favorite local wine store and ordering a case of the Gigondas I had favored the evening before, plus a pack of cigarettes, an item I hadn't touched in a full decade. I was tired of being on the correct side of every issue that arose on *The New York Times* editorial pages. I was in full possession of my senses which are anyway quite intractable. The fashion in recent years for early, mid-, and late life crises among white men always seemed an indication of a shabby emotional I.Q., a failure to see that there is always another corner around the next corner. Primitive societies had circles. We have corners.

It was obvious to me that I knew I'd try to call Cindy's house before it became a conscious act. My morning laughter was a shot of oxygen from a not so simple phone call, no matter that the phone call hadn't worked. There is the current notion of "closure." I stopped seeing an attractive and intelligent ex-model this winter in Chicago because she couldn't stop using such words. There are dozens of these verbal turds in our common usage and I'm not about to demonstrate them, though the worst is the time of "healing" that is called for right after some schoolkids get their guts blasted out with automatic weaponry. I talked one evening to an eminent translator at Café Select on Montparnasse in Paris and he said these sorts of tainted nodules can also be found in current French, usually by people who are consumed by a fatuous sincerity.

The wine-store deliveryman, Rico, arrived with the Gigondas and a raised eyebrow at the cigarettes. I've known Rico for years and he's a veritable mine of information about strange food practices available in the New York area. One February evening he picked me up in his ancient Corolla and we drove out to Queens and ate a goat-head stew at an African restaurant. I hedged at the eyeballs but not Rico. Rico used to teach high school biology in Brooklyn but cracked up when his wife left him for a soccer coach. By delivering wine Rico believes he is bringing beauty into people's lives. I agree. It's impossible not to get sentimental about these true New Yorkers. One of my favorite taxi drivers is an Inuit, an Eskimo of sorts. Rico is about my age and keeps in good shape by trundling cases of wine. He admits he could live on the life insurance left him by his father but he simply loves to talk about wine and deliver it. We had a small glass of wine with our coffee, a mid-morning French tradition. He enjoyed watching me smoke a cigarette and cough. He also coughed sympathetically. Before he left he showed me a discreet Polaroid of his latest conquest, a slightly plumpish but attractive secretary who worked at the World Trade Center. She was fresh in the city from the Adirondacks and he had cooked her an elaborate Tuscan dinner which had done the "trick." I've been slightly jealous of his sexual energy for years which he attributes to red wine, garlic, the physical exertion of his job, the reading of erotic classics, listening to Brazilian music, and the simple fact that unlike myself he avoids mental exhaustion.

When Rico left it was the French and three ounces of their wine that gave me a sneaky idea. I called Cindy's flower farm and announced myself as Jacques Tourtine from the Jardin des Plantes in Paris, a botanist curious about the availability of certain wild-flower seeds. I was advised to ready myself for a call back within a few minutes. Now I was rather too nervous to laugh and sat there watching the kitchen wall clock moving. I limit myself strictly to one bottle of wine a day for specious reasons. I'm scarcely the sort to get out of hand. After seven minutes the phone rang and it was Cindy on her cellular from the tallgrass prairie near Wichita, Kansas. I began with a fake French accent but she wasn't fooled for more than a few seconds. "You asshole," she laughed. Feminist women who used to refer to us as "needy" frequently now call us "assholes" which is endearing.

The conversation was pleasant, though afterward I was a sweaty puddle in the kitchen. Keep your studio at sixty degrees and you'll work harder. Yes, she could scarcely help noticing my many Bio-probes. I could hear the prairie wind over her phone and the way it modulated her voice made me envision her at sea in a gale.

"How in God's name could you write about Kissinger?" she asked. "You were so anti-war, so terribly radical."

"It's a living," I said lamely. "The book did very well. You don't have to agree with someone to write about them."

"Oh bullshit," she said. She never used to swear. "I always thought you'd be a poor, noble poet living in Spain. I liked your Linus Pauling but when I looked at Newt Gingrich I wondered how a man I once loved would jump headfirst into a fucking pigpen."

"I'm still supporting my brother and sister. Unlike yourself I didn't inherit enough to live on."

"Neither did I. My father went bankrupt. Luckily my last divorce made me able to buy a farm. I did fairly well on the second one, too."

I didn't know where to go with this peculiar feminine logic that allows them to win the point even when they're wrong. It was, however, easier to take in her next blithe chatter in which she asked how I, as a former poet and ex-fictioneer, could write prose that sounded like that on a network news program or in a newspaper or, of all things, in the *National Geographic*. I used to be so imaginative and read her the poems of Dylan Thomas, Lorca, and Yeats, and even my own lovely "stuff."

"You're stomping my balls," I said.

"I'm sorry, but first I got stuck in the mud earlier this morning and then I had a flat tire. There's sharp flint rock buried in the mud around here and I'm not finding the blooming flowers I expected. I'm a few days early."

What she had to say was not the less hurtful after she mitigated the circumstances. You step on a tack, then you shoot someone in the head. When I asked if I could see her the following weekend, it was now Wednesday, there was a longish pause and then she said, "Why not?" I told a gratuitous lie saying I had to be in Minneapolis anyway and would reach La Crosse by dinnertime on Friday.

❧   ❧   ❧

I took one of those hopeless showers where you have the illusion it will do you some actual good beyond destroying noxious bacteria on your skin. It was tough enough to have the early love of your life belittle your prose and its subject matter. Assuredly biographical prose tends to be like old-time midwestern football, three yards and a cloud of dust. Another three yards and more dust. More immediately painful was her vision of me as a poor noble poet in the Spanish countryside, possibly leading a donkey carrying my belongings. In truth Spain had been my central obsession at the time of our nine-day marriage, but when I finally had the wherewithal and the freedom I forgot to go to Spain.

Coming out of the shower I did have the suspicion that the language I was using to describe myself to myself might be radically askew. I could doubtless extend this to the language with which I describe the world. My word tools, as it were, are cool, analogic, slightly ironic, as if there were a more wholesome backdrop onto which I might paint my language decals. Metaphor, for an instance, is illegal in my Bioprobes. Metaphor is largely illegal in any "for profit" prose in the media at large. And back when I was acquiring my desperately valueless M.F.A., metaphor was fast becoming proscribed in our prose fiction. I find this is predominantly true now when I flip a few pages of novels in bookstores. If metaphor can't be taught, then it must not be very important, that's at the very least a logical conclusion. Poor Shakespeare, perhaps looking in the mirror when he said, "Devouring time, blunt thou thy lion's paws." Oh well.

I keep a ball bat near my door in case of any intruders. If they're armed with a pistol you would naturally hand over the money and whatever, but a mere knife is no good against the swing power of a mint Louisville Slugger. At the moment I felt like breaking something valuable. If only I had a Ming vase. For the lack of anything else I set a bottle of my Gigondas on a kitchen stool and swung heartily, watching it cast its purple spell around the room in irregular drips and splotches. Time for a walk.

By the time I hit the street I was, of course, laughing at my childish behavior, but then why should I evaluate all my gestures? It is as feeble as lovers asking "Was it good for you?" after desire has drained off into the void. I will only give a flat fuck when I clean up the mess.

It was a more than fair day as I headed up First Avenue, as sure of my first stop as Admiral Byrd was of the Pole, whichever one it was. I was going to stop at Schaller and Webber for a one-dollar slice of head cheese which I often do. Head cheese was one of my father's few food passions. Another two blocks across Eighty-sixth and I would arrive at the Papaya King for two dogs with sauerkraut and mustard. I had been eating oatmeal every morning for seven months to "combat" cholesterol and at this moment I'd rather gobble a steaming dog turd than look at another bowl of oatmeal. I certainly remembered that I had an appointment with my editor and publisher, the same editor I've had for thirty years who is now the president of the publishing company. I have never forgotten an appointment in my life. This time I was going to leave him hanging, probably at the bar at Four Seasons with his club soda and lemon twist. He used to order a cup of hot water during the brief period when this heady drink was the fashion in Gotham. I tried it once and thought it was like coffee without coffee. Some-one massively famous must have begun this fad, though it never appeared to have crossed the Hudson.

I very nearly walked into the path of a speeding cab and had to throw myself back on my ass. A well-dressed older black man near me shook his head as if I were a careless child. Something in my brain was jogged by the close call because I strained to remember something the poet Jack Spicer purportedly said on his deathbed, "My alphabet did this to me." It was on that order but then it had been thirty years since the seediness of my M.F.A. days, the only period of my life where I drank too much. I lived in an old house with two other aspiring writers and it was "de rigueur" to drink too much, smoke a great deal of pot, though I avoided LSD. Anyway, one of my housemates had a considerable library of "Beat" writers and knew all the gossip surrounding them. I was drawn to the work of Spicer, and his relatively early death caused by alcohol led him to say, "My alphabet did this to me," or so I remembered immediately after my brush with death-by-cab. It seemed sufficiently profound. All of his perceptions, the totality of the way he received the world, had congealed into this private alphabet which led him to his early death.

Jesus Christ, but this made me hungry for my late breakfast at the Papaya King. I rushed along, a bit wary at the cross streets, hit Schaller and Webber for my well-wrapped slice of head cheese, opening it with trembling hands. A passing, very attractive young woman frowned as I took my first bite, more in curiosity than disgust. Once you are over fifty they usually look just over your head as if you were a janitor and not worthy of registering in their senses. I read a lot of magazines and newspapers to keep my finger on the not very vibrant pulse of the culture but I couldn't recall anything memorable about the young women these days. I only knew two, and not very well. Not to be disingenuous, I see a young woman in France on my two- or three-day trips each year over there, which I basically take for a break in my routines (though I generally work every day in my hotel rooms) and for reasons of culinary freedom of choice. This young woman of twenty-five, Claire by name, is kind enough to accept about a thousand bucks a month from me to help support herself as a burgeoning artist. I'd have to describe her as interesting rather than charming. She thinks of a man's penis as "banal," which is disarming. She lives, with my help, over near the Jardin des Plantes, which is why I was able to use the name of this garden to reach Cindy. I'm so accustomed to being lied to when I do interviews for my Bioprobes that I have a tendency to lie to myself, not to speak of small meaningless lies in my work. To be frank I send Claire closer to two thousand a month. Why not? She has the prettiest butt I've ever seen, though I've been far too busy to have that many lovers. Of the dozen or so lovers in the past thirty years she is dead last at making love. I'm unsure of my motives with Claire. Perhaps her mediocre energies and skills in bed are reassuring? That's a refreshing notion. Once while I was going down on her I caught her glancing at a magazine on the bedside table. Why should sex be yet another unpleasant challenge in one's life?

How can I shatter language at my age? The ball bat meeting the bottle was wonderfully easy. At the counter facing the street at the Papaya King an attractive, waspish woman eats her unadorned hot dog with moist eyes. She is having some real emotions. I want to say, "It can't be that bad," but it probably is. She is my sister's age but then my sister has certainly limited her exposure to anything that could cause her grief.

A quick stop at my travel agent made Cindy a great deal closer. I thought, "I'm actually doing it." How I loved this woman though such specific emotional density becomes distorted into something else over the years. It's hard to weigh something you can't specifically identify except by tremors, pangs, longing. When I first brought her home my sister said, "Jesus, she's just a kid."

Here's what happened on the ninth and last viable day of our marriage. We had started driving to Chicago from Iowa City to announce our marriage to her parents. When we hit Joliet her plans changed and she decided it would be better if she delivered the news alone. We went to the apartment of a promising writer-teacher where we would be staying. He has since disappeared. The last I heard of him, maybe twenty years ago, he was teaching English in Taiwan, his single volume of verse so slender that it has doubtless disappeared from the bookshelves of our nation. Anyway, Cindy took a cab from the apartment to her parents' house and after only eight days of marriage I was liberated for a night on the town. In those days we writers all drank a good deal and between bars we'd have a toke or two of a joint. It was intended to be a sedate evening because we were going to a reading by Stephen Spender, the English poet, whom my friend claimed to know, but at a small reception before the reading Spender seemed not to remember my friend and ignored him. In fact, when my friend attempted to introduce me to Spender the poet turned away toward a small table of glasses of sherry, cheese, and crackers, and my hand was left hanging in the air. I can't say that I was particularly upset because I had so long been tortured by the formal study of English literature that I was itching to run off to a blues club to see Muddy Waters who was in town. We made our way to the door of the reception room where my friend turned and bellowed, "Fuck you, creeps" to the crowd. At the time this struck me as poetic rather than childish.

I stood on the corner of Eighty-sixth and Third rehearsing what happened during those twenty-four hours which, while not a horrifying trauma, was at least tinged with navy blue shame. Thirty years is not quite enough to comfortably gloss it over. I have searched mightily for some viable excuses. The best is that it was spring, the sap was rising, and I have often noted that I'm light-activated, like migrating birds. For instance, standing on this busy corner I have seen five women who have added at least a teaspoon of blood to that circulating in my loins. That's spring for you. It wouldn't have happened in November.

Anyway, after the Stephen Spender exposure we were off to a series of Irish bars which abound in Chicago. My friend claimed to be part Irish but like many of the faux Irish in the Midwest he proved this by adding a Scots burr in the tavern. Of course he was a horrid fool but then he had published poetry in the *Paris Review*, *Sumac*, *Tri-Quarterly*, and a half dozen other magazines that were thought to be important at the time. To me he was heroic and could do no wrong.

We listened raptly and drunkenly to Muddy Waters and Otis Spann, went to an after-hours place where we unsuccessfully threw dice, and were kicked out when we ran out of money. At dawn we were cooking breakfast for two decidedly non-extraordinary women my friend had called up at about three in the morning. They lived close by and were fans in his Chicago literary circle. Anyone less than totally anonymous tends to attract followers and my friend as a major literary light in Chicago at the time had many, though these two women were beckoned mostly because we had run out of beer, wine, booze, anything. In the spirit of the evening, about four A.M. by now, my friend took off all of his clothing hoping the women would do the same. They didn't, and one made a comment about the peculiar, radical crook in his otherwise normal penis which made him morose, and led him into a long disquisition on his lifelong suffering of various sorts, ending, as always with writers, with his severe mistreatment at the hands of his publishers. The prick mocker was impressed enough to take off her blouse and shoes, but then seemed to forget what she was doing when he launched into a virulent attack on Robert Lowell and the "eastern establishment," including, of course, the Englishman Stephen Spender.

The other woman, Rachel by name, was smoking an enormous joint she had pulled from her purse with a flourish. We crawled out on the fire escape and did a little necking, but luckily I was too drunk to commit adultery on the eighth day of my marriage, or at least that's how I remember it. Years later when I ran into Rachel in a Chicago bookstore she recalled our "fabulous" night on the fire escape and I fled. She was still cracking her Dentyne.

Anyway, I awoke on the sofa at one in the afternoon with two pieces of bacon clutched in my right hand, and when I went to the bathroom I saw through his bedroom door that my hero had managed to liberally piss his bed. You could say that he was in the tradition of Dylan Thomas and a thousand other writer-drunks. It was some time before I could eat bacon again. Naturally my hangover was shattering and the taste of Rachel's Dentyne on my lips burned them with guilt. It was a good thing I quit my heavy drinking by the time I was thirty because hangovers tended to flood me with rather self-righteous anger, not exactly the emotional nexus you want to carry around on your first meeting with your in-laws. There was so much to be angry about: the roach wallowing in the congealed egg yolk on a plate in the kitchen, the "fuck you guys" written in the pan's congealed brown grease, my friend's typed "Rodentia Suite" which he had read to us at six A.M. that could not match the song of the sparrow on the fire escape. The shower water was tepid. The only coffee was instant. My shoes looked old. My friend had fallen asleep when I had tried to read one of my own poems. I had felt pleased when he tripped on his way to bed. I had a mild case of diarrhea and somehow had burned my tongue. I envied my friend who got up and rather merrily had two warm beers and popped both a Dexedrine and a Darvon, announcing sententiously that he didn't believe in pain.

I was nearly to Hinsdale in my miserable DeSoto, trembling a bit when it occurred to me I shouldn't have worn my blue velvet bell-bottoms and my orange flowery shirt. I pulled off in a mall parking lot about a mile from my in-laws' home and stuffed a nubbin of hash a student had given me into the end of a cigarette. I brushed

my very long hair while feeling the drug calm my trembling. I rehearsed a number of answers to the obvious questions, prime among
them, how was I going to support their daughter? This was easy as
there was a fair amount of money left from the deaths of my father
and mother. The fact that Cindy was only eighteen was a bit of a
sore point as I had already been teased about it by my buddies in
the M.F.A. program. "Many girls of eighteen in Indiana marry"
seemed a bit weak.

I was walking faster and faster as I told this grim story to myself. High
ideals were missing so the comic nature leapt to the front. I was mindful of cab traffic as I crossed Fifth into Central Park, still moving
rather quickly but passed by a man in his seventies, a racewalker who
flapped his arms seagull style, grinning at me with the tolerance of
an expert, his bony ass wobbling on its hip pinions.

     Again, how can my language match walking up the steps of
that capacious porch in Hinsdale, the yard bee-loud with lilacs from
the warmish spring? My skull was sore, my mouth dry as the soles
of my shoes. My heart a snare drum. The door opened before I
reached it, her knobby brother on spring break staring at me as if
I were a new species of rodent.

     The four sat there at an overlong dining room table, old oak
and Victorian kitsch. Cindy and her mother looked as if they had
just fled from a smoky, burning house, eyes red and rheumy, faces
swollen from rubbing, the father's face a pink storm cloud, the
brother a patina of Ivy League bored disgust.

     The upshot was the cagey dad had two dozen photos of my
night on the town, starting with departures from Spender's reading, Irish pubs, the after-hours place, arm in arm with two ladies.
And somehow through the fire escape window my host with his
pants down and unimpressive crooked dick, and somehow an up-

ward shot of me on the fire escape with the woman's plump, bare butt pressed against iron rungs.

Now I was aware our government had spied on the Chicago Seven but such personally based spying was purely fictive. Naturally I had read Chandler and Hammett, but these photos that were tossed at me, with a few falling in my lap, were beyond my ken. To this lumpen bourgeois family they apparently proved I wasn't marriage material, an illusion indeed in that I had been raising my brother and sister for the past five years.

Sobs began. Cindy wouldn't look at me. Her father actually said, "You goddamned cad," though even at that time, in 1969, "cad" was archaic. He was hyperventilating when he added, "You goddamned filthy hippie." The brother chimed in, "You raped my little sister!" then walked around behind me which added to my discomfort.

"One of your buddies screwed her when she was twelve," I bravely taunted, though Cindy had told me she had cooperated out of "scientific curiosity," even then a nascent biologist.

That was that. I was jerked by my neck from the chair, the brother grappling me in a choke hold, the father coming swiftly around the table and falling on his ass when he tried to kick me, Cindy and Mom with unearthly, piercing screams. Dragged out the door and tossed from the porch and landing partially on a honeysuckle bush which partially broke my fall. Stung by a bee for good measure. To her credit Cindy tried to run to my prone body as I tried to regain my wind but her father grabbed her arm. Or was it her mother?

I drove home to Bloomington, Indiana, forgetting my suitcase was still at my writer friend's apartment. It took him a full month to U.P.S. the suitcase though I sent him money three times to do so. One of my poems was missing and three lines of it eventually ended up in one of his efforts published in the *Partisan Review*. In the meantime I spent two days in the hospital suffering from my most virulent eczema attack yet. In a way this total experience was an apt preparation for writing about the great and near great for reasons I'll reveal later.

At the children's zoo in Central Park I was drawn, as always, to the seal pond and also the penguins frittering their time away against a hokum Antarctic backdrop. Wobbling to and fro waiting for meals. At zoos I always think of Thoreau's notion of quiet desperation. On this day I quite literally ached with empathy for the penguins. The seals at least seemed able to amuse themselves, while I avoided the polar bear whose behavior was decidedly repetitive and autistic with hours spent as if pulled by an invisible wire.

I continued on across the Park to the West Side which, though occasionally full of fungoid self-congratulation, is less provincial than the East Side and its silly self-promoted aura of the world center of art and money. The hot dogs weren't holding up so I had a brief lunch at a Chinese-Cuban place I favor. While I ate my delicious stewed oxtails with garlic it occurred to me that I had fibbed a bit in this little auto-Bioprobe. I do fly first class but usually on an upgrade from accumulated mileage. Business class is good enough for Europe. Claire my French lover (sic) cost me three grand last month due to unspecified medical difficulties, which I doubted. I did fuck the woman on the fire escape so many years ago, partly because I was so amazed by my hard-on what with being that drunk. One of the photos indicated the act. How could I do such a thing on the eighth day of my marriage to my true love? I'm not sure why. I was dislocated in the rapture of the Chicago night. I was a "hundred-proof fool" as a country song I heard on the radio said. My eczema doesn't just strike if I dwell on art and literature but also when I finish a Bioprobe. There. The truth will set you free, but free for what? Laughter arose when I thought of my erstwhile editor cooling his heels at the Four Seasons. There was a real cad. He was an unworthy thought as I regarded the mighty Hudson, then turned toward home. And the chore of cleaning up the shattered wine bottle.

On the way back to the apartment I decided to stop at the wine store and see if Rico had plans for dinner. I was a scant thirty-six hours from leaving to see Cindy and I didn't want to sit around alone and change my mind. Rico had helped me a great deal back in 1994, my "best" year when I had made over nine hundred thousand dollars and had switched my wine buying from the more expensive Bordeaux and Burgundies to Côtes du Rhônes. Thrift is a pleasant sedative. Spending exacerbates. My sister is a puzzle who loves to create puzzles and come up with inane oddities. She has figured out that Bill Gates' fortune would fill seventy-seven thousand caskets with tightly packed hundred-dollar bills, newly minted at that. She has done so much research for me on bio subjects, including fifty or so discarded by agreement between myself and my publisher, that she has become outrageously cynical which is not a Hoosier virtue. Occasionally this cynicism can be a corrective. If I'm perhaps identifying too closely with a subject she'll send a fax with "Donaldson" in the center of an otherwise empty page, referring to the newscaster who presumes to be the equal of any poor head of state. Probably her main defect is that she considers all human activity to be mischief. Several years ago she convinced me and my editor-publisher, whom I'll call "Don," to write my first Bioprobe on a literary figure, Gabriel García Márquez, admittedly a great novelist. I have a phobia against using the word "great" but Don is kind enough to spread the word liberally in my manuscripts before publication. Anyway, I flew to Mexico City and booked into the Camino Real where the first evening I watched two striking women playing tennis on a rooftop clay court. In the morning my ten minutes at the author's apartment was comprised of a delicious cup of hot chocolate his impressive wife brought me, and watching the great man leaf through a couple dozen of my Bioprobes Don had sent ahead. He finally looked up from my work and said with a smile, "Would you mind if I donated these to the poor?" I bowed and fled.

At the wine store I'm allowed to use the service and shipping entrance, a matter of some pride to me. Rico and a salesman were simmering on a hot plate both *boudin blanc* and *boudin noir* the salesman had smuggled into the country from France. I tried one of each with blistering mustard and a glass of simple Crozes-Hermitage. Rico had dinner plans with his newest conquest but called her to see if she had a friend and a double date was arranged.

Back at my studio after my sturdy three-hour walk I surveyed my shattered-wine bottle damage with pleasure though I did recall my sister saying, "If you ever start leaking you'll sink in a day." This was a little squirmy but was allayed by the three messages from Don on the service. "Where the fuck are you?" he barked on the last message. That's one of the drawbacks of first class. Self-important men talking in muffled barks. It is the cryptic language of success, these barks. It used to include braying until magnum success included less drinking.

Certain splotches of wine on the wall seemed to border on the artistic. This was lucky as the spray cleaner and paper towels didn't quite do the job. There were still violet Rorschachs here and there: river deltas, pussies, clouds, sharp fingers, stalagmites. Sweeping the glass raised a musical tinkle in the air. I sent a fax to Don's office saying I had had a malaria attack and turned off the phone. I rejected the idea of a second cigarette. The package sat on the kitchen counter like a lonely sentinel, as young writers say, which can be followed by a prayerful squirrel.

In the shower I barked to myself in the language of my class, a small class but nevertheless an identifiable class. My laughter walking home the night before came from the purposeful strides in and out of the restaurants, the nonchalant self-importance, the gauche expensive tailoring, the hundred-dollar neckties and custom shirts, the diffident assurance of potency. I suppose in antique Marxist terms we are lavishly paid because we are perfect tools for the class even higher up, those who own the ballpark. You can occasionally have some sympathy for those frequently unhappy souls with big inheritances from birth. This was fate in which the sense of victimization is always possible. But my own class is undeserving of a mote, a mite, a filament, an iota of sympathy. We are self-made barkers, toy dogs, prime weenies. I snarled at the steamy mirror. How dare it make me look exactly as old as I am. The mirror rudely watched me apply the pine pitch, the tarry salve that is best for the first itching signs of eczema, invariably around the genitalia, the crotch to be exact. I heard the magical whir of the fax machine. "You too can be replaced. Yrs., Don." Barkers are usually bullies.

I had a long and unbelievably sweet nap that ended late in the afternoon with a brief dream of the time I visited my grandmother, my father's mother and the last alive of my grandparents. Cindy was with me just before we were married and I wanted her to meet old Ida whom I revered. Cindy was far more interested in the local flora than the old lady and had wandered down to a tiny creek on the small farm in far southern Indiana. I sat in the kitchen with Ida watching Cindy out the window. "She doesn't look old enough.

What are her people like?" Ida asked. I couldn't admit I hadn't met
them so I only said, "They're fine." All through my youth this woman
had been far more motherly than my own mother who was bent on
finishing her Ph.D. in her late thirties. In the summer I was often
excommunicated to the farm from Bloomington for being a "trouble
maker" which meant anything that distracted my mother from her
dissertation on the Gilded Age. Oddly I was a fistfighter and
fistfighting causes more of the same because if you keep winning
then everyone wants to knock your chip off. This was during my
years from ten to fourteen. My sister was even more contrary, refusing to have schoolmate friends unless they were black. And little
Thad settled for never taking his thumb out of his mouth so mother
whined about expensive orthodontia. Ida's husband, my grandfather, was a remote fellow, far older than she, a retired high school
science teacher who had inherited his own parents' small farm. The
only pleasurable activity we had together was fishing on a small lake
a few miles away. He was normally taciturn but fishing made him
talkative. He'd drink cheap A&P beer and we'd stay out on the lake
until we caught enough panfish to fry up for supper.

"Well, don't fall down a hole you can't climb out of," Ida had
said as I watched out the window where Cindy was climbing up
the hill from the creek with something in her hands. As she drew
closer I could see it was a large black snake she had lovingly patted
into submission. I turned away before she could catch my eyes
through the window. Ida was also watching Cindy with a smile. She
decided it was prayer time and we went to the parlor and knelt with
our arms on the sofa where she asked God's blessing on my intended
marriage. Her prayers and Bible reading were part of my youth and,
curiously, I never regarded them with irony. I was startled by the
refusal of James Joyce to pray with his mother. Why not? While
Ida prayed we heard Cindy call out from the porch, "Come see what
I got." Unfortunately by the time we reached the porch Ida's old

burly tomcat Ralph was in full threat display. For a cat he was pretty close to a watchdog and was prancing around the porch with guttural yowls. Cindy was backing up fearfully and the thickish snake had become active in her hands. Ralph acted as if he were going to leap and I tried to kick him away but missed. Cindy jumped down the steps and tossed the writhing snake into a grove of lilacs where Ralph quickly nailed it with great drama as if he were fighting a python. Ralph dragged the snake away for lunch and Cindy wept piteously. Ida who was Lutheran rather than a teetotaling Bible Belter insisted that Cindy have a whiskey to calm her nerves.

That incident started the first quarrel of our love affair. She hated cats because they were wanton killers while I rather liked them though I've never owned one. Our second quarrel was that she wanted to go to the Covent Garden Flower Show in England on our intended honeymoon while I wanted to spend a month in Barcelona and Seville, not to speak of Granada where I intended to visit the murder site of the great Federico García Lorca.

My nap's dream had included brave Ralph dragging off the snake. While I dressed for dinner it occurred to me I could scarcely have expected the great leftist García Márquez to be impressed as he held my Bioprobe of Henry Kissinger. Afterward, it was hard to imagine dozens of poor Mexicans sitting in a park reading my Bioprobes in a foreign language. No, the problem while sitting there with the great man is that I hadn't even been to Spain, and Mexico's uncertain relationship to Spain had been nagging at me since I had arrived the day before. When I went to the Mexico City airport that afternoon I was quite literally trembling as I noted flights to Madrid and Barcelona. I was a free man, why didn't I board one?

Thinking this over I lit my second cigarette of the day. At fifty-five I was still capable of living dangerously but not nearly as much so as your average Indiana opossum who hasn't quite learned to recognize headlights.

We all met at Rico's apartment in the East Village, a fearsome place when I had lived there from 1969 to 1972, soon after gaining my flight from the porch and my M.F.A., similar experiences in the long run. The M.F.A. replaced the B.A. in English as the zenith of value-less degrees. Now the East Village had been at least partially gentrified and when I got out of the cab on Avenue A and Third Street I recalled being told of the scandal about W. H. Auden's poem "The Platonic Blow" which had been written locally in the sixties. It was a rather vivid poem about gay blow jobs and at the time the police were eager to prosecute but the mayor's office held them in check. I was trying to think of another time when a poem had excited such interest in America.

Rico's apartment is quite spacious and a little strange with nineteenth-century Italianate furniture he trucked over from his deceased parents' house out in Queens. The kitchen, however, is as fabulous as my sister's in Indiana. Rico is an Angelo Pellegrini–type traditional cook, always seeking out the roots of what he thinks as "genuine." He collects nineteenth-century ethnic cookbooks and has allowed dozens of food fads to pass him by without apparent notice. Occasionally Rico has bursts of bad temper but of late they are mostly about Mayor Giuliani whom Rico claims is a third cousin. "*Giuliani ho sempre ragioni,*" Rico yells, reflecting the famous notion that Mussolini was always right.

The women were already there, both in their mid-to-late twenties. Gretchen, the secretary from the World Trade Center, was rather sturdy and half-Italian from Troy, New York. Donna, my date, was as unprepossessing as possible with thickish glasses and a rather dumpy corduroy suit under which you couldn't detect the shape of her body. "I can't stand anything touching my eyes so I don't wear contacts," she said, shaking my hand and anticipating the question I wasn't going to voice. I was startled to learn that she was a second-year graduate student at the Union Theological Seminary up near Columbia where she had a "ratty" room on the edge of Harlem. It was the kind of announcement that made me nervous about money. I quickly learned that these were bright girls from relatively poor families whose fathers worked for the railroad. They had been friends since kindergarten, in fact, but were polite enough not to talk in the private language of longtime friends. And both had been divorced after brief marriages. They were amused when I topped them with my own nine-day wonder though I withheld the information that I was flying to see Cindy the next day. By magazine standards Gretchen and Donna were rather homely but on this particular evening that made them attractive indeed. My fetish for beautiful women, actresses and models, had exhausted itself by the time I hit fifty and had begun cringing when I touched a fake tit. I certainly didn't blame women for having them, given our culture, but they made me uncomfortable. A feminist I met at Elaine's once asked me how long the lines would be if men could buy a perfectly operable big dick? I am dark complexioned enough not to show my blushes.

I went to the kitchen to open a Lynch-Bages I had brought along as a treat and when I came back Rico was showing Donna and Gretchen his complete collection of my Bioprobes, and also my first book, the one I refer to as *Murgatoyd in SOHO*. I immediately burst with itchy sweat. Gretchen turned to me and said, "You must be a whiz." Donna sensed that I was stricken and withheld comment as she fingered the bindings of *William Paley* and *Warren Buffett* but pulled *Linus Pauling* from the shelf. Gretchen read a back-cover quote: "Well written and beautifully researched. Take one on your next business trip." Donna reached for *Murgatoyd*, which Rico had located at the Strand, a used-book emporium, right after we met ten years ago. She flipped to a page where the prose was interrupted by poetry and where my character's feet become so heavy he can't get them over a curb, but manages to get down the stairs at the Lionhead Tavern where he misses the barn swallows of an Indiana farm. "I actually prefer poetry to biography," Donna said, dismissing my last thirty years. "I mean you're doubtless an exception but I grow bored with all of this false sincerity, this lavishness toward famous people and the petty details of their lives. It's really just an adjunct, or fertilizer for the Disney fascism of our time, don't you think?"

"Fucking A," Rico said, "politicians are mostly two hundred pounds of pus in ten-pound sacks. They leak all over the place."

I poured the Lynch-Bages, affecting a pensive mood. No scintillating "bon mot" was in the offing. Rico was clearly trying to help but this wasn't dollaring up as a fun evening.

"Of course my dad said you shouldn't look down at a gandy dancer until you've laid down some track yourself. I've only lived in New York for a year and I'm already an expert carper. There are hundreds of thousands of brilliant folks here who can sum up their accomplishments each year by saying that they took a shower and read the *Times* every day."

This said, Donna sat down rather snugly beside me on the sofa. She wasn't quite as acerbic as my sister but close. She peeled a shrimp from a bowl Rico had set out. "Would you fuck Giuliani for a million dollars?" I lamely joked.

"Of course," she fairly shrieked with laughter. "For you it would be exactly a dime but men never carry dimes. There's no nature in New York and the closest you can get is an orgasm." She popped the shrimp in her mouth and closed her eyes as she chewed with pleasure, her eyelids magnified by the glasses. My heart went out to her scuffed shoes. Rico and Gretchen were sitting on chairs and wondering if they should try to bail out the situation. I knew very well I didn't have a dime in my pocket, as I habitually drop all my change on sidewalks for bums and children to find. Donna drank her wine rather quickly so I finished my own. The wall clock tick-tocked. Rico cleared his throat and announced that we better head out for dinner. When Donna got up she gave my thigh a friendly squeeze and offered her hand. "If you can't stand me I can go home now." I thought this over. "I adore you. And it's my Christian duty to fill your tummy. I want you to go through life making it hot for assholes like myself," I said.

"She always breaks the ice with a tank," Gretchen said, squeezing Rico's ass so hard he flinched.

At an Italian place on Delancey, Rico and I continued our "head motif" with a half calf's head apiece roasted with garlic. The girls ate chicken and veal. I continued to be disturbed about Donna's perilous neighborhood but limited myself to a passing remark which, nonetheless, lit a fuse. Donna looked up from swabbing a goodly amount of butter on her bread but not all that much more than I used on special occasions.

"You're twenty times as likely to die from butter than be murdered," she quipped. This again had an uncanny resemblance to the kind of information my sister collected. I looked down at my buttered bread, which had the specific charm of not resembling a gun. Her comment started a brief quarrel with Rico who doubted her butter stats. A New Yorker always questions while I immediately believed, in the manner of rural Indiana which sees fibbing as a sin.

"Okay, I'll throw in transfatty acids," Donna said. She put down a roasted drumstick and began searching in her purse. "Dammit, I forgot to take my lithium earlier."

The rest of us stared at the ceiling while Donna took her pill, then I signaled the waiter for a third bottle of the pricey old Barolo.

"We're eating so much better than Dietrich Bonhoeffer did in a German prison," I quipped. I had been searching for a name of a theologian, but not the obvious Paul Tillich whom some fans had garroted for womanizing along with Krishnamurti and nearly everyone else of prominence. After a couple of decades of being ignored adultery has become nearly as fascinating as money.

The bait worked. Donna launched a disquisition on Dietrich Bonhoeffer, also Barth and Simone Weil. Rico and Gretchen started their own conversation. We had two grappas with our coffee and were all quite suddenly well oiled and tired. I asked the waiter to call us a cab and he said his "cousin" in the bar at the front of the restaurant had his town car free. Why not. I went out in front, paid the bill, and complimented the chef who, done for the night, was sitting there all sweaty with a monstrous glass of whiskey. I've often thought of starting a restaurant that would only seat four people at a time. The cousin didn't really want to drive way up near Columbia so we settled on a hundred bucks which I figure was less than each of the bottles of Barolo. I've always used inane comparisons when I'm being economical.

Dropping off Rico and Gretchen was the easy part, then I decided to make the long ride with Donna and be dropped off last. A gentleman walks a lady to the door. That sort of thing. I began to doze off in reaction to the startling midnight speed of the driver, but at several traffic lights on the West Side there was the shattering sound of car alarms which must equal butter as a cause of Manhattan coronaries. Donna was still babbling about Bonhoeffer and Weil, but at a slightly slower pace as if the lithium might have kicked in. Given the theological nature of her chat I was doubly surprised when she gave my wiener a tweak to see if I was awake, or so she said. I put my arm around her and she snuggled close. Wine was creating its own questionable magic, not to speak of the grappa. My sister likes to tell me I'm only a prosperous wino but then I've easily learned to accept this character flaw.

Disaster struck quickly when we reached Donna's room, though the word is a bit strong for a mediocre pratfall. After walking up two improbably shabby flights of stairs and watching Donna unlock three locks on her metal door with three keys, I thought I heard a shout from the street. I went to the window of the room just in time to watch my driver speeding off. Perhaps he'd return but probably not. Two young black men were kicking a soccer ball back and forth, doubtless the threat that sent the driver packing. He had already pocketed my hundred so he had nothing to lose.

"Don't worry, I'll carry you home," Donna joked. The grappa rose in my gorge. Oh fuck, I want to be home in my own bed. The room was larger than I expected with a full wall of books, a two-burner hot plate, posters and prints and some hanging fabrics, a chair and a desk piled with folders. In short, strenuously bleak unless you are in your twenties. The bathroom was across the hall and when I peed I heard moans. Back in the room Donna laughed and said the moans came from a diminutive gay man who hankered after large blacks. This seemed graphic enough so that I sensed my modest hemorrhoids. The gay man, also a theological student, was a close friend of hers. She poured me peppermint schnapps and plopped down her cell phone to help me sort out my problem. I still hadn't quite taken in the room and my breath drew in sharply when I saw the Seville bullfighter poster above her narrow bed. Oh Jesus, but I thought everyone had long since abandoned these posters from my college years.

Donna picked up a robe and nightie and went out to the bathroom, leaving the door open so I might be entertained by the moans just down the hall. What is to become of this fifty-five-year-old child with feet of ice and the uncertain power of a calf's head in his stomach, a slightly wacko theological student at her hygiene across the hall? My editor Don would have given the driver fifty bucks down payment and fifty on delivery. Mordant thoughts of midwestern simplemindedness arose with the grappa. This wasn't exactly Kosovo so I drew up my courage and stared at the Seville poster.

At nineteen my youthful, intended year in Spain was to be split evenly between Seville and Barcelona. I even planned on talking my way into spending a night in Miguel Hernandez's jail cell, wherever that was. The grim walls would inculcate me with the spirit of his poetry. The most viable research of my life had been devoted to these two cities and it gradually became apparent to me sitting in Donna's spartan quarters that I had owned the selfsame Seville bullfighter poster. I had fully intended to walk the banks of the Guadalquivir from Seville to Córdoba, not quite leading a friendly donkey, the idea of which was pushing it even in the sixties. I would have inevitably lived in the Triana neighborhood of Seville, probably with a beautiful gypsy girl. On warm spring afternoons she would sleep naked wrapped lightly in her mantilla with a pink rose in her hair. I recall devouring Théophile Gautier's *A Romantic in Spain* and believing every word, though a professor of Spanish had told me it was largely nonsense. I tortured my graduate school roommates silly with playing both Spanish classical and flamenco music. By a vote of two to one my musical taste was exiled to my room rather than our living and dining area.

Donna came back into the room interrupting my reverie and I impulsively picked up her cellular phone. I intended to call Sean or Michael, old-time bellhops at the Carlyle Hotel, and have them send a car. I had stayed there over the years before acquiring my apartment, and had spent a month there the year before when my apartment had been redecorated. Fatefully enough Donna's cellular needed recharging.

"Have you been to Spain?' I asked, gesturing at the poster.

"Of course. Everybody's been to Spain. I was stationed there in the WACs." She massaged my shoulders and neck, which relaxed me somewhat, then ran her hand through my hair, pronouncing it "flossy wossy," which tightened my neck up again. "With your sort of person nothing is supposed to go awry and now it has," she accurately commented.

"I've never been to Spain," I said plaintively.

"Then go tomorrow." She resumed her massage.

"I have to go to Wisconsin tomorrow."

"They're definitely not the same place." She led me to the bed. "You go to sleep. I'm going to read for a while."

I felt embarrassed and childish taking off my sport coat and tie and shoes. I slumped back on the bed as she sat down at her desk and began reading. She poured herself a schnapps and said that she felt too woozy to read epistemology. She turned off the desk light and now there was only a smallish night-light over near the hot plate. She lay down beside me and pushed at me to move closer to the wall.

"You're becoming less fun than an average corpse. I didn't run off with the fucking car either. Either be amusing or go to sleep."

"You could nurse me," I suggested, only half in jest.

"You're fucking kidding," she shrieked with laughter. "How many times have you used that line?"

"Never," I said honestly. She was up on her elbow looking down at me, then unloosed her robe and nightie and put a breast in my mouth. How sensitive of her. There was a startling smoothness to her skin. She had said she was Irish-Czech and one wondered because the much used "satiny" was a euphemism. I was abruptly excited and went down on her with an energy I normally reserve for a fine French meal. This woman had my ears flying off and hers too. What man is not proud who quickly brings a woman to thumping orgasm by whatever means, with chafed chin and bruised nose, versatile tongue, even forehead in play. I couldn't remember being so utterly thrilled until she turned and moved down, pulling at my trousers.

"Have you been fucking pine trees?" She sniffed.

"Argh," I said, remembering my salve. "That's pine-pitch salve I use for eczema." I bolted out of the bed and door and opened the closed door of the bathroom in a rush. I was not alone. A very tall and muscular black man and a very short and thin white man were looking at themselves in the mirror. At least they were wearing colored bikini skivvies. I covered my erection with my hand.

"I'm with Donna," I said. "Pardon me."

"Are you? Not now. Donna, is he with you?" he called out.

"In a way," she called back and they left me to soap off my salve. It was all too much to bear. She made a diffident attempt at raising my now thoroughly limp noodle, then gave up and promptly went to sleep with a purling little snore. As a light sleeper who keeps a notebook ready on his nightstand for important ditties like "Over the years Castro has diminished his cigar smoking," I dreaded a long night of consciousness but quickly passed out.

It was half past three on the clock near the night-light when someone tested our door. "Beat it, fuckhead!" I roared with a voice swollen by instant adrenaline.

"My hero," Donna whispered and then we were at it with a quiet rapture. It wasn't a fuck equivalent to a fifteen-round fight that Norman Mailer had written about back when I was in college, but sort of a three-round Golden Gloves struggle toward fruition.

My face stretched tight in the broadest smile I could remember. Down the street a beautiful car alarm joined our mutual end. For some reason I murmured "Oomgawah" from an ancient cartoon.

I awoke to Donna saying "A priori" and then a German phrase. She and the gay-blade neighbor, Bob by name, were at the desk fast at their books. Bob saw my open eyes and saluted. He brought me coffee and a glazed donut which is what my face felt like.

I drank my delicious coffee, and the unhealthy donut was equally good. They chattered on about a "dialogue" they were going to present to a philosophy class. Some dirty but merry little sparrows were on the windowsill feeding from a bowl of seeds Donna had put there as a female Saint Francis. If Bob hadn't been there I might have said something otiose like the night had been in the top ten of my life, but then I loathe the anal fascism of lists that my guilty profession creates. I settled to dressing quickly to the tune of their Hegel, Schlegel, Heidegger, and Leibniz. When I finished dressing Donna arose from the desk and gave me a polite buss, then a licky kiss.

"Would you like to go to Spain?" I asked.

"No. You go ahead. If you like, call me when you get back." She rummaged through her books and gave me a biography of John Muir by Frederick Turner, at least four times as long as my own products. "You'll love this," she said, opening the door.

I caught a cab on West End Avenue and stopped at my travel agent on the way home to re-ticket for a later flight. I was experienced enough to know that my euphoria would disappear by mid-morning, and a hangover might descend. I'd need a good nap before heading to LaGuardia.

At the apartment the super had put a Fed Ex from Cindy on the counter plus a note, "Did your walls have an accident?" The wine stains still didn't look all that bad to me. Cindy's package contained a book called *Humanistic Botany* and a note that asked me to read it so I wouldn't ask her stupid questions. How kind. Homework. I called Don for damage control and he was solicitous about my malaria attack which I had forgotten, and reminded me that my Eisner was due in three weeks. Michael Eisner is, of course, the chairman of Disney. My sister had delivered the usual large folder of well-ordered research but I hadn't begun the writing. I had never missed a deadline and quickly toted up that I'd have to do five pages a day for twenty days. Kid stuff assuming that I could begin with a stirring first sentence. Soon after he was born Eisner began breathing. Part of my self-training is to actually remember what people say. Sometimes I do this with visual cues. For instance during Donna's theological babbling at dinner I was slicing the calf's tongue when she said that you have to willingly wish without knowing what to wish for, the meaning of which lacked lucidity. There was more after the first bite of tongue with its juicy freight of garlic to the effect that the best examples of the human race allow their hearts to break. This had brought a nervous glance from Rico who was picking at a jowl.

I went to the front window from which I could see a slice of the river. The night had seemed to be a stunning achievement of life herself and, as a not altogether willing participant, I wondered if I could better be drawn along if I did not continue to think of life in five-page segments. There had been this urgency for thirty years to get something done only to start something else fresh. If you worked too fast and hard, then what? You were free to go ahead. I recalled a grade-school lesson that said Thursday had something to do with Thor, a Nordic deity of sorts. The chair at my work desk in the corner might very well be electric, but then the reception of

complaints about work is properly based on how much the com-
plainer received for the work. How could I complain? I'm mostly
puzzled. Writers are only people who, above all else, write. The
catchphrase, almost sadly, is "above all else." I doubt most plumbers
plumb above all else, or farmers farm—add several dozen profes-
sions. They leave room for something else, or so I suspect. Maybe
the justifiable trap is when we call it the "art" of writing so that ever
afterward any hack may feel himself raised to a mysterious domain.

These troublesome thoughts might have given me a headache
if I hadn't been hungry which takes precedence over everything
else for men and beasts. I made a hasty cheese omelet and recalled
my grandmother's prayer that I become a Lutheran minister, but
then ministers never get to stop being ministers and the similarity
to writers ruined an entire bite of omelet. I glanced over at the Eisner
folder and thought of giving it an East River burial. From the evidence I unwittingly gather, men my age are worried about their
jobs as I am now, but also about their adult children which I don't
have, their health and the health of their wives, and also about the
impending end of the story. You don't hear about these much on
daytime flights with meetings in the prospect, but on evening flights,
and after a drink or two, it becomes a burbling brook or, better yet,
a roiled mud puddle. Dropping dead at any minute is not discussed
directly but is as present as the earth far beneath the plane, in short,
reliably obvious. Maybe the best response is always "Please tell me
something I don't know."

As if to prove me wrong my seatmate on the Minneapolis flight was
a nerdish computer whiz who had just spent three days in New
York art museums. I had been struggling along with my homework,
Humanistic Botany, and had envied the large art book on his lap,

however ungainly. He turned out to be a divorced father of a twelve-
year-old daughter who was an art obsessive. He was unable to "com-
municate" on this level so in the last month he had visited the Walker
in his own city, the Chicago Institute of Art, and now he had "covered" New York. He was thinking of buying a set of paints and
having a "go" at it.

     This was curious enough that I wanted to prolong the conver-
sation but was only on page 9 of *Humanistic Botany* and had six hundred to go. There obviously wasn't a Classic Comic available that
covered the subject. You would think that having had a botanist
father I would have absorbed something substantial but such was
not the case. Once I had idly opened a book in his library and out
fell a photo of Ava Gardner clipped from a magazine. I was about
fourteen at the time and was a little startled, though Ava was a great
deal more winsome than my mother.

     I was struggling with the idea that the root, stem, and leaf of a
flowering plant are referred to as "organs," tripping on the fact that
organs had loomed large only recently, but more so, a very Big
businessman across the aisle (physically large) had closed his laptop
and was talking to a Big partner about Big business in a Big voice
just as the Big pilot (I had seen him) announced that we were passing Big Chicago ("stormy, husky, brawling") a ways to the south.
I recalled that before its economic Big decline the top officers of
General Motors were generally over six foot two. I had sensed a
love of Bigness in Detroit early in my career when I did a Bioprobe
on Henry Ford II, widely referred to in Big Detroit as "Hank
Deuce." Soon we would reach the Big Mississippi. Struggling with
the "alternate, pinnately veined leaves of sassafras" I began to think
of how many time I had witnessed Big florid Texans board a plane
with really Big voices. Once one had insisted on trading seats in
order to sit next to a Big friend but I stuck to my habitual 3B much
to his apparent disgust.

All of these thoughts made tiny flowers most interesting for the time being. I had a glass of cheapish syrupy California Cabernet which the stewardess said was the best available. Oak smoke and Hershey with almonds, worthy of being served with a Whopper at Burger King.

I leafed through the whole book but there were no photos of Ava Gardner. A stewardess with a fine fanny stooped to pick up an errant napkin, surely the highlight of the flight. Far in the back a baby was crying, a far sweeter music than the Big businessman's Rottweiler voice. I suddenly longed for smallish France, my small walks, small coffees, small baguettes, even small Claire who required Biggish money. How rarely lovely-looking women like Claire had the sexual energy of Donna. Never in my experience.

When we landed in Minneapolis before dinner I was delighted to realize that I had never been there, though unlike Barcelona and Seville there was no emotional content to the realization. I was ready to bolt from the plane per usual when a woman with two young children, one crying, rushed forward. She was desperate and loaded with carry-on crap so I carried the child she had been dragging off the plane. The stewardess with the fine fanny thanked me and for a moment I felt warm all over in the manner of those *Reader's Digest* anecdotes I had read as a child. The kid was a plump little bugger, weighing as much as my Eisner-loaded briefcase and the light garment bag I held with my other arm. It was a relief to turn over the wriggling tyke to a sullen father at the gate.

There was a brief, somewhat frightening moment when I got in my rent-a-car and rehearsed, as I always do, just what I was doing. Cindy tomorrow near La Crosse by dinnertime. Read the book. I had written down where Rico had told me to eat dinner. Rico was terrified of flying but had driven throughout America on his vacations. He had asked me to join him many times but I never seemed to have the time what with my Bioprobe projects. His travel notebooks, however, were invaluable for restaurant advice.

    After rehearsing what is called my "game plan," and coming up short this time, I usually try to learn how the car functions while stationary rather than in traffic. I held the key in my hand but failed to find the ignition. Others in the rent-a-car parking lot were wheeling off with gusto, including the Big businessman and his Big friend who had rented a maroon Lincoln. Plugging in lamps tests the outer limits of my technical abilities. I reached in the glove compartment for the manual which was in five languages, including Japanese. The car was overwarm but I couldn't open the windows or turn on the air conditioner and it didn't occur to me to open the door. My eyes became moist with frustration, the dashboard an inscrutable collection of high-tech gizmos that blurred with my tears. Maybe I should take a few days off, but then in the remaining time before my deadline that would gradually increase my Eisner quota from five a day, to six, to seven, to thirteen, and so on until I was down to doing the final hundred in a single day. At last a passing black attendant in a natty uniform opened the door and aptly said, "These motherfucking Jap cars are pure Greek," then showed me the ignition. I tried to give my savior twenty bucks but he refused and walked off laughing.

At the hotel there was a plaque in my suite announcing that Gorbachev had slept here. This caused only the briefest moments of turmoil bound up in the question of what are we to believe nowadays? To avoid further leakage I lay on the bed and burrowed ever deeper into *Humanistic Botany*. Without my previous knowledge auxins, gibberellins, and cytokinins were hormone and regulatory

substances essential to cellular growth in plants. This was a hal-
cyon announcement, and I meant the pill. I slept.

By coincidence, when I awoke in a half-hour, there was a brief
child's cry in the hall. Why hadn't I become a father? Raising my
brother and sister from twelve and fifteen had been enough. My
mother's sister hadn't been much help and we drove her away
after a year. She had been married twice, the second and longest to
an Italian stevedore, and her entire emotional contents, limited as
they were, went into cooking. She had all the bad aspects of her
sister, my mother, and none of the few good ones such as humor
and forbearance. The last straw for me was when she beat Thad
over the head with a wooden spatula for eating raw cookie dough,
then pushed up the volume by accusing him of spending his study
time masturbating over his *Playboy*s and *Penthouse*s. Poor Thad was
convulsed with embarrassment, then burst into tears. We were all
in the kitchen at the time and my sister who has always loved swear-
ing yelled, "Shut up, you stupid old cunt." There was no retreat and
she was gone the next day, never to be heard from again though I
regularly sent her a Christmas card.

I checked the room-service menu's wine list and was pleased
to be able to order up a good Pomerol. I found the name of the restaurant and the concierge made a reservation for a half-hour before closing. Time to boogie down to work. There was a struggle
between Eisner and botany but fierce Cindy was in the offing so I
plopped the book on the desk with a resonant thud. Stern duty calls.
The wine came in a trice but a corkscrew was a foreign object to
the slack-jawed young woman who brought it so I took over. She
was new at the job and didn't know who Gorbachev was so I told
her, adding a description of his birthmark that looked like a wine
stain on a pale wall. Ten minutes of solid reading caused mental
discomfort so I called Donna but only got a message to the effect
that she was not to be called unless it was a matter of utmost im-

portance. I recalled a terrifying line from the postscript poems in
Pasternak's *Dr. Zhivago,* something about it taking a lot of volume
to fill a life. Like Kennedy's death I could remember what I had
been doing when I read the line. It was a warm summer evening
in Indiana and I was listening to the raucous love songs of a thousand cicadas. My father told me that whippoorwills ate cicadas
but I hadn't thought it important at the time. For some reason I
did now. Perhaps calling Cindy and the night with Donna had
opened a window which at normal times would have required a
crowbar.

I reached page 50 of *Humanistic Botany* and the discussion of
Carolus Linnaeus before I was interrupted by dinnertime, and the
raw notion of an old girlfriend from Rye, New York, a devout
Catholic and Sarah Lawrence graduate (magna cum laude when it
still meant something): to wit, my talents were limited by excessively subdued grief and a mediocre education. This young woman
could make your mental teeth chatter. She had interrupted her
Ph.D. in the psychology department at New York University to
help edit a series of do-it-yourself mental health books for my publisher. She was delicate and remote about her psychologizing but
it was always there. Why could I only have my coffee in the morning after I shaved? Why did I only smoke excessively while writing? Only I knew that she was an off-again, on-again heroin addict,
a matter New York neglects to discuss about its higher minds. She
even researched the accident reports on my father's death which I
had never managed to deal with: the Ecuadorian boat captain, under
the influence of rum, had failed to balance the ballast tanks of the
research boat. The only two survivors, excluding the captain, had
been sleeping on deck. In my mother's case it was merely announced
that there had been a five hundred percent increase in brain cancer since World War II for those born and raised in industrial
areas of New Jersey.

Still, I had loved this young woman for her antic wit, however melancholy. Her father was an insurance actuary and a terminal depressive and I suspect I was second choice in someone she could cheer up, having failed at the first. Our final quarrel had begun with my notion, over her superlative macaroni and cheese (made with twelve-bucks-a-pound English cheddar from Dean & Deluca), that her psychology series was bound to raise the suicide rate and, failing that, would be a boon to pharmaceutical companies. She threw my favorite Bioprobe thus far (*Linus Pauling*) out the window of our West Tenth Street walk-up.

But how do we get at the ice that is possibly nestled in our hearts? *"Fais ce que voudras"* (Do what you want) was far from adequate. I used to construct sets of worthless rules, worthless because I had followed these rules before I wrote them down. A later girlfriend, a pediatrician in Chicago, said that "He got his work done" should be engraved on my tombstone.

On the short walk to the restaurant Rico had recommended (D'Amico Cucina) I was amused by the idea that my psychology girlfriend scorned the human-potential movement to the degree she was a victim of it. She had been thoroughly pissed off one Sunday morning when she demanded that I pick the favorite activity of my life and spend the day doing it, rather than working. I said hoeing my grandmother's garden on the farm back in Indiana. Since this was plainly impossible she requested my second favorite and I offered fucking my first wife Cindy dog-style in a cornfield on a July afternoon. She suggested we drive to the country and try it but I pointed out that it was late May and the corn wouldn't be high enough. Sure enough, in her mental health series, also edited by Don, there was a depression-preventive chapter called "Pick Your Favorite Things and Do Them."

At the restaurant I ordered an older Barbaresco and had a plate of prosciutto and imported figs to start with. The waiter frowned

at the idea that I was reading a book and I inwardly agreed. Life
overexamined also seemed an unworthy idea in the face of good food.
I wondered where the Mississippi, that watery knife that cuts our
country in half, was located so that I could drop the book in the river.
I knew that John Berryman, a once famous poet in the poetry world,
had jumped from a local bridge and it might also be a good grave for
the book. Inside the front cover it said, "Cindy McLauglen, 1977,"
the year the book was published, with an added note, "please return."
Here I am at fifty-five years old with a couple of million bucks doing
a homework assignment. Any smart person would lie and say he'd
left for the airport before Fed Ex delivered, or somesuch fib.

It was during my pasta course, a simple but perfect puttanesca,
that I had an epiphany of sorts. The damnable book on the table
beside my radicchio salad was making me suffer because of the
voluminous nature of its contents. Since my father's heyday, the
thirties, forties, and fifties, we have seen the gradual triumph of
process over content. For instance my Bioprobes are full of fact but
not an overwhelming amount, actually an underwhelming amount,
and I've long since understood that their popularity is due to pack-
aging. Of course this isn't profound, and the fact of the matter could
be easily sensed by anyone with a three-digit I.Q., but the rage for
computers is based on process. The nation and its people got plumb
tired of learning so it turned to process in the manner of the hundreds of teachers colleges whose students, the future teachers,
largely can't pass any test that requires substantial knowledge, thus
our students habitually finish dead last among the twenty or so
Western nations.

Frankly I didn't give a flat fuck about any of this except inas-
much as I could extrapolate the core of the notion for my own life.
It was clear, however, that my sister had the contents and I was
the process, and my brother Thad merely doctored the shell of the
process.

Evidently my lips were moving nervously because my waiter came trotting over. He glanced down anxiously at an illustration on page 109 of a longitudinal section of the apical meristem in the ash stem. From a distance of a few feet it did look possibly sexual in nature like those old cross sections of women's parts in biology class. He said that my veal chop was nearly ready and I asked about the location of the Mississippi River as I had passed over the Minnesota River, or so I thought, on the way in from the airport. The question spooked him.

"All around us, sir," he said and I nodded.

Back in my rooms I turned the television on and noted the many stations lacked any particular contents, and opted for radio classical music that dealt with emotions I've never had. Back in college I at least presumed I had similar emotions when I listened to the great Carlos Montoya. I rankled, but only for a moment, at the idea that Cindy was pushing me through a whole college botany course in twenty-four hours. At this time the night before, given the hour difference in the zones, Donna was scenting my pine-pitch salve. I thought of her perineum in the muted shadows thrown by the nightlight. Our sexuality, of course, has content but is invariably written about in terms of process. "And then I and then she . . ." I thought this over and remembered Molly Bloom's soliloquy, then the memory of my mother's voice prating, "The exception proves the rule."

With the help of a pep pill and a pot of coffee I read until five A.M. when I finished *Humanistic Botany*, albeit hastily. I would have flunked the simplest retention test but when I finished I hugged the book and rolled over in the bed as if we had been wrestling. I've given up the practice in recent years but back when I took my work more seriously I used to give the occasional lecture to journalism students on the nature of my success. I told them that you

had to absolutely disregard your moods to get your work done. If
you put all of your moods in a shoebox and placed them on a scale,
you'd only get a reading on the shoebox. Moods are only self-
indulgent emotional whims and the fuel for sloth. I had to keep these
Calvinist inanities in mind in order to finish the book and then I
was able to face the dawn with a moderately triumphant smile. What
I had tried to teach students was the most egregious lesson possible
for happiness.

    The singular high point of the night was when Donna returned
my call. The conversation was brief because she was studying but
she did say she was willing to see me again. That had to be enough,
though there was a trace of sexual teasing that made me anxious. I
told her I wasn't very versatile and was incapable of making love
to anyone I didn't care for. Sad but true, I used to think, but no
longer. It's impossible for me to look at my own sexual behavior
except in comic terms, no matter how occasionally wonderful. At
one time I revered D. H. Lawrence and might still if I re-read him,
but then Henry Miller was more accurate.

To be frank I've been fibbing a bit for reasons of clarity. Another
fib! Is there a chain of fibs that encircles and binds us? You know
who you are when you wake up more than when you go to bed when
your filigree abilities are at their highest. The autobiographical hoax
is not different from the biographical hoax. Donna and Rico and
wine and food are true. So is Cindy whom I'll see in six hours for
the first time since the honeysuckle porch, the hashish smoke in the
dirty DeSoto. When a man, a subject, tells me that he separated
from his first wife and married another it is glossed over, and it
would be impolite for me to probe, yet this is the most momentous
event in the man's life. He sees his spawn, his two children, frequently, then less frequently, then frequently not at all, and the

grandest love of his life, his first marriage, is gone forever. This is true entropy. The largest share of the emotional content of his life has fatally vanished due to the usual plenitude of mutual inconveniences. People even used to say, "We grew but in different directions." The fact that the divorce was necessary, destined, plain inevitable, doesn't make it less consequential.

Here I am avoiding the back wall a dozen feet from the end of the bed. I've never really been married so what do I know? Nine days, really eight, doesn't add up to a hill of frostbitten beans, as Grandmother would say.

Let me begin again. I awoke at eleven A.M. in a sweat with sun pouring in hotly from the southwest window, my brain a whir of flower dreams and large, deep green plants that opened showing green plant intestines, my eyes dry, red-hot balls. I had smoked half the pack of cigarettes I had tucked in my briefcase and had drunk two beers and three half bottles of wine from the mini-bar concealed underneath the television set. I had used the TV clicker to raise three different porn movies at nine bucks apiece but none stirred my loins one little bit. Through all of this I continued my not so studious reading. I hadn't had a night like this in the seven years or so since I was forty-eight and had put myself in a discreet Arizona clinic for a month's rest. Before this downshift I couldn't get my work done without between three and five bottles of wine a day, though well before that I had abandoned my cocaine chasers because a doctor had told me I was going to permanently blow out my gaskets, meaning death. To save myself I had become unfashionably religious, saying my prayers morning and evening as I had done with my grandmother.

Everything is after the fact. That morning I could only croak with a diffident hard-on pointed toward Donna in a different time zone, and domestic jet lag from rising at eleven rather than seven. A snake

loses its skin and doesn't recognize itself. Such is the nature of consciousness that you can lose several skins at once. At such times I
try my hand at fiction, a few poems, ten days or so of musing before I head to the dermatologist who would never give me anything
as primitive as the black pine-pitch salve which came from a young
woman in Coconut Grove who had caught fish poisoning in the
tropics, nearly lost a finger, and had been given the salve in St. Bart's
by a French sailor who had been "mean" to her. God knows what
that meant. With the continentals we xenophobes have learned to
suspect prolonged buggery.

     With my fifth cup of coffee I dozed in a chair with my heels
on my luggage. The language with which I talk to myself had fled
so far into the interior it had disappeared. Buckle up or buckle
down. Gird up thy loins. The worst is to walk tall. We are raised
on a whole school of "guy talk" that leaves out our own sensibilities.
A recent perverse stepfather of the Midwest was Vince Lombardi.
It's at its most absurd when an announcer praises "good ole face-
smashing Big Ten football." We could hear the roar of the stadium
for miles in Bloomington. But on a more malignant level there was
the implicit cultural language of forbearance, bravery, grit, hard
work, thrift, "sticktoitiveness," of getting to work early and leaving late. This has allowed me to save a couple of million which is
not nearly enough according to an article in the *Wall Street Journal*
which said I would need five million to guarantee a "pleasant retirement." This made me long for the real money I earned as a paper
boy pedaling my Schwinn on the icy streets of the city in February, or the quarter an hour I earned hoeing gardens.

     Anyway, I sat there trying to figure out the sentence you use
to call a bellhop, gave up, and carried my own stuff down to the
lobby, my mind still a void with flowers. I recalled something I heard
on NPR about the formation of "dark parks," areas without ambient light so people could see the stars, and that after the L.A.

earthquake many people who had never experienced the lack of electricity were confused and alarmed by the Milky Way, the misty sash of stars that I loved in my youth but haven't much seen since then.

Important businessmen were click, clacking around the lobby with possibly leaky asses. Two of them shook hands with the out-sized vigor that made our nation what it is today. I was pleased to note that my language-numb mind didn't prevent me from navigating through checkout, getting directions from two quarreling bell-hops who had different ideas on my routes. When the parking valet pulled up with my rental car I was thrilled that he left the motor running and I wouldn't have to repeat my ignition search. The cars in the future will start when you pull your dick and whisper, "Bongo."

I felt curiously buoyant having run out of negative interior chatter. I headed toward the Point Douglas Parkway, slowing to miss two very drunk Native Americans who were crossing the street against the light. My brain reeled off whole segments of American history, the questionable gift of my mother whose repertoire of injustices was longer than anyone could listen to. Because of her I tend to avoid thinking of history but perhaps I should forget her and do what I wish. Why reject anything offered? Let it slide. My night-long botany churning was doubtless a hesitation over entering my father's business. I had to wonder how many times he had seen Ava Gardner in *The Barefoot Contessa*, an absurd movie but Ava walking pitty-pat barefoot in her gown across the marble floor buzzing the groin.

Moving toward Point Douglas I passed Pig's Eye Park, a truly enchanting name. I hoped to figure out why the park was called that all by myself, its greenery doing quite well in a world without people with splotched pastels of flowering trees. There was a distinct relationship between the greenery and the book I had read in the night but it would take some time to figure it out.

I took the first of several bridges back and forth between Minnesota and Wisconsin, with the mighty Mississippi looking excessive and disordered. I pulled off into a tourist stop so I could look
down into the water, recalling T. S. Eliot's line to the effect that
this river was a "great brown god." There were the usual vertiginous tremors but the habitual bridge question "Should I throw
myself in?" didn't arise. There was the suggestion of a song in my
heart, however muted, as if unconscious but benign decisions were
being made in my behalf.

Now that I was in Wisconsin I recalled that in the scant hour's
interview Michael Eisner had allowed me, he had told me that as
young marrieds he and his wife had camped in northern Wisconsin and a bear had hassled their tent. This didn't seem possible in
the life story of a man who inhabited such a grand office, from which
he directed an immense corporation, but it was doubtless true. Mike
faces bear in dark. "At age twelve Henry Kissinger was pushed into
a mud puddle by a chum and resolved never to go outside again,
and if that wasn't possible, he would at least avoid the vicinities of
mud puddles. Once while drinking Cristal champagne high above
the city of Gotham, he had told this story to Bob MacNamara, who
had chortled. However, isn't it true, Kissinger had added, that cities
with proper drainage don't have mud puddles."

Fact can be enough to gag a maggot, I thought, driving south
on Wisconsin Route 35, a smallish but delightfully scenic river road.
"They knelt at twilight before a naked Oriental pussy and begged
pardon for Vietnam." Possible but unlikely. Perhaps I could vomit
up enough inanities to raise the river, now on my right, on which
barges headed south.

Near the bridge between Nelson and Wabasha I stopped at a
wildlife area to take a stroll down toward the river, or at least one
of its channels. There were hordes of mosquitoes but enough of a
mid-day breeze to keep them at bay. The path was muddy from a

recent rain and it quickly became apparent that my Bally loafers weren't proper footwear. There was a fat black snake wriggling in the grass which drew up an image of Cindy's poor snake from so many years ago that had become cat food. Cindy's cheeks had been tear soaked and her hands trembled holding the small whiskey old Ida had poured to calm her. Sometimes she cried when we made love because it was so much "pure fun."

At the end of the bush-enshrouded path was a mudflat and the river. Two boys about twelve were fishing and turned in alarm seeing me, as if I might be a truant officer if such creatures still existed. I waved, smiled, and asked the usual question, "Catching any?" They had two smallmouth bass of decent size and I immediately imagined the fish in a frying pan. In a knapsack up the bank I saw a copy of the Victoria's Secret catalog peeking out but pretended not to notice, definitely a better-quality erotica than when I was their age. I moved off upriver on the mudflat and one of the boys yelled, "Don't," but it was too late. My foremost foot plunged up to its knee in mud. My other foot was still fairly solid but the awkward position collapsed me to my butt. I held out an arm and the boys tugged me out with some effort but my left shoe was gone. They were willing to try to retrieve the shoe but I said, "Fuck it," and we all laughed.

On the clumsy way back to the car it occurred to me that the lost shoe left me with only fuzzy bedroom slippers, but in Winona I found an Army and Navy "war surplus" store where I bought socks and a pair of Marine combat boots and was directed to a nearby restaurant where I could get fried fish. It is difficult to find simple country-style fried fish in Manhattan or Chicago. You simply douse it pink with Tabasco and wash it down with a beer or two.

I stood with legs spread wide athwart a sidewalk crack in the manner of a Marine since I was wearing brand-new Marine combat boots. I was recalling my interview with Colin Powell prior to my Bioprobe on him several years back, and wondering again as I had at the time about the evolution of military mannerisms: the hypererect terseness so crisp that even shuffled papers were expected to respond. The rasping of crisp khakis in the halls of the Pentagon, the interior of the building so profoundly ugly you wondered if we were entitled to win a single game of international Scrabble. At the time it seemed apparent that a phalanx of officers striding toward lunch was not unlike a phalanx of pissed-off chimps in remote Gombe. These noble thoughts did not diminish my concern over the sign in the restaurant that simply said, "Fried Fish." There had been a past, silly experience in Kansas when I never did find out what kind of fish was available. The waitress said, "You know, fish fish." When I said that the ocean contained many types of fish she said, "This is Kansas," closing off further discussion.

The catfish was fair to middling but then Dad used to say that "a saltine is a feast to a hungry man." There was the specific regret that I had faxed my sister in Bloomington to say that I would be at Cindy's near La Crosse for the weekend and giving the number. Though it was unlikely, that meant Don could track me down. To be frank it was Don who sent me to the rest clinic years ago with company money. He told me I was his golden goose and he wanted me to keep laying golden eggs, not really very flattering. He had been to this clinic several times and likes to tell me that the Mexican staff called him *El don Don*. Don has the irritating habit of repeating stories, knowing that he is rich and powerful and can get away with it in the same manner that he accepts incoming calls when you are having an important meeting, important being his term.

I slept in the car in the restaurant parking lot, baking like a Sunday chicken, until a kind old man rapped at the window to see if I was alive. During my sleep I had actually made a decision to ask for a month's extension on the Eisner manuscript. I wondered how it was possible to receive instructions in your sleep when no dream was involved. Don is a real killer on the subject of deadlines and once when I had a bit of nervous collapse during the writing of my *Donald Trump* Don had had the bulk of the manuscript ghostwritten.

Frankly, I've never been one for vacations but sensed I was ready for one now. Quite early in my career on the ample monies supplied by my first three Bioprobes I took up tennis and skiing but soon gave them up as simply too banal against my early literary backdrop, though my literary sensitivities were certainly evaporating in the heat of my Bioprobe labors. I skied at Stowe, Vail, and Aspen, and went to expensive tennis schools in California, Texas, and Florida. I almost forgot but I also had a few days of deep-sea fishing off Key West. There is something nearly offensive about the company of other people on vacations. The many long evenings with others who are exhausting mind and body trying to buy high-paced fun: dancing with a woman who was sweltering in a hand-knit Norwegian sweater, eating elaborate and expensive and mediocre resort-town meals that suffered horribly from the latest food fads, and all of the stupidly expensive equipment, the seven-hundred-dollar skis and the four-hundred-dollar tennis rackets, when the level of my abilities would have made Wal-Mart junk more appropriate. In Aspen you could always hear braying Texans a block away. Once on Little Nell a big-deal socialite shit her pants after a bad fall and her friends scattered. I loaned her my parka to tie around her waist but that evening she ignored me in a bar and I never got my parka back. This was more comic than grim I had reflected over scallopini with a cup of vinegarish capers and some tainted frozen raspberries. I shouldn't neglect to say that Don has played the fifty "greatest golf courses of the world."

Life is work, or so I have thought, or "done," since there were no really appealing alternatives. Claire was appalled when we had a tiff in Paris and I spent three days riding the train back and forth to Marseilles to get some work done. The trip was four and a half hours each way and I was too angry and restless to work in a hotel room when I was paying for a high-rent apartment. A lovely train stewardess would bring me coffee, wine, hard-boiled eggs and I'd fill victorious notebooks with workable prose about Warren Buffett.

Sitting there in the hot restaurant parking lot near an exhaust fan pumping out redolent but unpleasant fried-fish smells I thought, "Fuck Don, I'm taking a break." I squealed the tires leaving the parking lot, my heart not exactly soaring but far lighter than usual.

Cindy was far too sun-chafed, wiry, muscular, her speech much more rapid than in the old days. We stood in the jungle-like yard behind her farmhouse that needed its half-done paint job completed. I had been met at the door by a blocky young woman whose voice I recognized from the phone, and in the backyard this young woman had brought us each a two-ounce glass of mediocre sherry. I already had begun to suspect the woman might be Cindy's "companion" in addition to assistant, but then I'm frequently wrong on such matters. I was pleased when Cindy poured out her sherry on the grass and decided my arrival might merit a martini, though when I poured mine out I was chided about directing it on a plant that the sherry might injure. At least I had not yet asked any stupid botany questions though I had verged on one. The fields behind the house were disappointing unlike the photos of blooming flowers in the airline magazine. Easy. It wasn't time for the flowers to bloom yet (though *Humanistic Botany* hadn't dwelled on the matter) but this wasn't quite enough to make me smug. When I followed her up the back steps and into the house I couldn't help but note her ass lacked something in the way of contents, the polar alternative to the middle-age spread.

We sat in her den and had two martinis in two hours, an adequate but not precipitous rate. I never totally recovered from her announcement when we first sat down that she had made a reservation for me at a motel in La Crosse a dozen miles farther down the road. I mentally paused, trying to think just what I had expected. She also turned down my offer to hoe for a couple of days because the flowering plants were now too small to be treated by anyone but "professionals." I was, however, welcome to attend her wildflower workshop in late June at seven hundred bucks for five days, vegetarian meals included. She found it quite comic that I had spent the entire night reading the book she had sent. "So ask a stupid question if you're still capable," she said.

"Why are there so many plants in the world? It's like God couldn't make up his mind," I suggested.

"You got all that dreadful God stuff from that cranky old lady, your grandma," she laughed.

I was pretty nearly offended but it was too early in the evening for a snit, and besides I hadn't had any dinner. I suggested she offer her life history and she demurred though a good deal came out in casual conversation. She had two "real" marriages, discounting our own, and two dead husbands which she implied was lucky in that both men were wanting in quality. Neither were "soul mates" as we had been, which warmed my heart for a minute or two. The first husband, who she'd married soon after college, had already been forty years of age. Two children were born, now both doing quite well, but when they were in their early teens and her husband was a good jump into his fifties, he fell apart in every respect, whatever that meant. He was a C.P.A., a senior partner in a Chicago firm, and had lost his job in a scandal involving certifying the books of a semi-criminal firm. He began drinking too much, was abusive to her and the children, so she left him. He was dead by sixty-two but before then, in her late thirties, she had married a comparative high roller and moved to Santa Barbara. He was in his late forties when they married and into his fifties when her children left for college (Northwestern and Oberlin). At this point her husband's "flagging hormones" had driven him into being a sexual adventurer and he had dragged poor Cindy through all sorts of "humiliations." This, of course, intrigued me but after a number of subtle probes it became apparent that she wouldn't become more descriptive. She ended her narrative by saying that so many men seem to become "pathetic" in their fifties, adding with a weak smile, "Present company excepted."

. Now it was my turn and I wasn't eager despite the normal buoyancy of martinis. This was because I sensed none of the warmth I had hoped for coming from her. I pretended to be bored and successful and then it occurred to me minutes later that this wasn't far off the mark. I fibbed relentlessly as I described tactfully my affair with a theological student whom I seemed to love. If Cindy had given me a soupçon of hope I wouldn't have done so. Sweat beads of enervation popped on my skull as I described the delights of my life, including my prolonged affair with my "mature" French lover, Claire. To add to the credibility of my story I included slight details about Claire's sexual boredom and the high expenses of maintaining her.

Well, shut my mouth as we used to say. Cindy was outraged more than halfway through her second martini. I should have remembered that a single glass of beer could make her hypercritical in the old days. How could I throw that kind of money away on a "lazy slut" when her not-for-profit rare-flowers organization was crying out for funds, and when without more money certain flowers would disappear from the face of the earth creating an actual hole in creation. This is what is called being hoisted by your own petard. I could almost hear the rare flowers bleating out their needs in the American night. Within five more minutes of pleading I had made a pledge to rid myself of Claire, not a bad idea, and give Cindy an amount commensurate to what would be saved, not necessarily a good idea.

Miss Blocky called us for dinner and on the way to the kitchen table (the dining room table was stacked with papers and books as was every surface in the den) it untypically occurred to me that the only reason Cindy had told me to come ahead was in her fund-raising capacity and perhaps the idlest of curiosity. Not only was my continued presence out of the question but there was the suspicion that she wouldn't sleep with another man in this life at gunpoint.

Adding to this confusing state of affairs I was served a massive plate of pasta primavera, a dish I loathed, and as it sat there on a pinkish Formica table I envisioned a bovine struggle to get through half of it. If this wasn't enough I was also given a bowl of carelessly chopped vegetables and a glass of California jug wine that bespoke its screwtop roots. Rutabaga and maple syrup aftertaste, a hint of tag alder and algae.

For the first time in decades I felt lucky when Don called. How could he be so unwittingly kind? I stepped into the hall with the portable phone, suffering from the raw sharpness of uncooked life. Don likes to show his power by calling at inconvenient times, but then his voice was more attractive than the pasta primavera, not to speak of the idea of giving up Claire for flower ideology. As I spoke to Don I stared at a framed photo of a rather vulvic rose which added to my uncertainty.

The upshot of Don's call was that there was an open window for an earlier and cheaper press run, thus I had sixteen days to finish with Eisner rather than twenty. Time doesn't fly, it jumps. To avoid a quarrel I said I would try my best but "try" wasn't good enough for Don. He had never nagged or cajoled and this time he just said, "Get the work to me, kiddo." What kind of man would still be in his Manhattan office at nine on a Friday evening? I lamely said that I was having family problems and he told me I was lying because he had just talked to my brother and sister while tracking me down and they sounded "great." I said I was in the company of my estranged and only wife (he knew the story) and we were thinking of resuming the relationship. He said something to the effect that she had waited thirty years and another two weeks wouldn't hurt her. Then he hung up his phone. My ears were ringing and I wondered how you puke up a hundred pounds of your life. My eyes became misty and my heart fluttered.

I came back into the kitchen and nearly walked out the door, a decisive move, but it suddenly occurred to me that it was the back door and in my present condition it was unlikely that I could struggle through the greenery to my car out in front. Cindy and Blocky looked at me with a perceptible compassion having heard the local half of my waffling chat. I sat down trying to think of a witticism about highly paid slavery but couldn't trust my voice to be manly like my new boots. I stuck my fork in my pasta primavera, which had begun to congeal. Cindy reached a hand across the table and patted my own.

At this exact moment a tall man came up the back steps and in the door looking grimy and distracted. I assumed he was a worker on the farm. He patted Blocky on the head, then leaned over and kissed Cindy with a quick interchange of tongues which didn't immediately record on me even though she ran her hand up the inside of his leg. He offered his hand and I shook it, judging him to be in his late thirties. He talked about irrigation and water problems as he wolfed his pasta. I was still short of my first bite, my innards tightening with total comprehension. For some reason I actually thought of Shelley drowning in Lake Como. I bolted up and whispered that I didn't feel well, then headed briskly toward and out the front door.

Cindy caught up with me at my car where I had paused quite dumbstruck by the beauty of the twilight, the way the river flowed southward through two sets of giant green hills that were dimming to black. I was the macerated piglet in the valley who felt as unreal as is possible without simply floating away. Cindy gave me a peck on the cheek and told me to call. I looked at her shadowed face and tried to ponder the thirty years in between the last sighting but they had floated away.

Despite my silly romantic grief and confusion I ate an enormous cheeseburger at the bar of the Best Western, my motel beside the river which in itself had an unexpected consolation. Travelers were out on the lawn staring at the river, actually a channel of the main Mississippi, or so the waitress told me. She was cheap, pudgy, and brassy, but I liked her. I was so tenderhearted I limited myself to two beers. It wouldn't do to sob over my french fries or leave a tear-wet pillow for the maid in the morning.

I was up and on the road at dawn, just after five A.M., having left messages with Thad and Martha, my beloved brother and sister. I reached Chicago for lunch in one of Thad's yuppie hellholes and made a delicate attempt to fire him. He said he had sensed that I was "on the skids" and reminded me he still had five years left on his employment contract at a minimum of a hundred grand per annum. This is the kind of thing I don't read but trust my lawyer to read, though I never listen closely to my lawyer. After a wretched chicken-breast concoction with fruit, Thad announced pompously that he was part owner of the establishment and that I wouldn't have to pay the tab. I said that dog shit is also free which he seemed not to hear, looking fondly out over the full restaurant with people talking about themselves at a greater volume than in New York.

When we parted out on the street Thad gave me an extremely un-typical hug and told me that if I needed any advice on how to be a failure to give him a call. This was a startling thing for him to say and we both smiled uncomfortably. A stunningly attractive girl approached and gave him a kiss. She looked far too young to be in the company of an adult male. Thad didn't bother introducing her and when they got into his Porsche parked comfortably next to a fire hydrant, I caught a glimpse of her blue undies. This was a far more palpable form of success than my own.

The Chicago River didn't quite dollar up in comparison to the Mississippi for which I felt a slight pang as the latter was the first dominant presence in the natural world I had noticed in quite some time. All that water dropping down the skin of earth from Minnesota. Too bad the water is opaque or one could wear scuba tanks and walk slowly south on the bottom of the river, saying hello to fish and the bottoms of passing boats. On Interstate 65 a semi-truck passed that was the same color blue as the undies of Thad's girlfriend. Another pang and the taste of dank papaya on the wretched luncheon chicken. Cindy's kiss with her farm laborer reminded me of when my dad said that reality was when you were peeking through a keyhole and someone came up behind you and kicked you in the balls. I was in the ninth grade at the time, and he was counseling me on my moping, lovelorn behavior. I was barely eating and totally ignoring my homework because our high school had a senior exchange student from Portugal named Leila who had visited our geography class with a guitar and had sung us love songs from her native land. To say I was stricken is a euphemism. I was in the second row (no one ever wanted to sit in the front row except jerks of both sexes) and she sat on a high stool in a short skirt, which added to the enchantment. This first experience of falling in love was terrifying. Between classes I'd locate her and follow her around the halls as secretively as possible. In the lunchroom I'd give her meaningful glances from several tables away but I can't say she ever noticed. Once by accident I walked by a popular drive-in and she was leaning against a rich kid's new Chevrolet convertible and necking with him. He had his hands on her butt. I wept. In April that year she flew home suddenly for good because there was an illness in her family. I entered mourning and my alarmed father finally took notice and I mumbled out the truth. To his credit he took my dire straits seriously though he had no particular wisdom to offer.

While weaving out and in between trucks in my peppy rent-a-car I was humming de Falla's *Nights in the Garden of Spain.* Of course Leila was from Portugal but on the map Portugal was right next to Spain, sort of like Canada and the U.S. I had decided way back then. In English class we had been reading the love poems of Robert and Elizabeth Barrett Browning but they seemed snuffy and quite pathetic compared to the monstrous, surging love in my heart, not to speak of my pecker, for the dark-haired Leila. A large Bloomington record store managed to get me an album of Portuguese love songs and they drove my family witless until my mother bought me a cheap phonograph for my own room.

My parents weren't noteworthy examples of romantic love. Later, when I saw Elizabeth Taylor and Richard Burton in *Who's Afraid of Virginia Woolf?* I was uncomfortable. My parents when arguing would hurl little etiolated epithets at one another, complicated word firecrackers, so that a working stiff, or a normal child, would have no real idea what the tiff was all about. But then the children of academics aren't intended to be normal. It is a tiny world where everyone is expected to be exceptional, or at least well above average. It is odd that by and large academic parents are unaware that their word daggers cause permanent damage, or it would be called "damage" in a more perfect world. In the actual world this might be good training as nothing is meant to be clearly understood. Don, for instance, can put a dozen types of spin on the word "the." Don is on his fourth marriage and some fools think he had been going downhill in regard to women but I've noted that real estate is central, the whim for good digs. Number three owned a pleasant but not spectacular brownstone in the East Sixties, but number four has a house on one of those private lanes up in Greenwich, Connecticut. I was up there one Sunday afternoon for an editing session but I wasn't asked for dinner. This was fine by me, as a specific division of labor is better in the long run. Earlier in my career I had an obnoxious young woman as an agent but the pro forma nature of the Bioprobe series made an agent unnecessary, especially after Don had a brief, unpleasant affair with her. She was simply too bright for her job and later rose quite high in the bureaucracy that allows the U.N. to function. Before dying of breast cancer a few years ago she wrote me a note suggesting I buy a pistol and shoot Don through the heart, then escape to Spain and do something serious. When we first met I had shared some of my grander ambitions with her.

Just before Indianapolis I turned off into the Lebanon rest area because I was feeling thumpy. My interior monologue had begun stuttering of its own accord. I was hyperventilating and didn't have a paper bag to breathe in, the most immediate remedy for the condition. I walked in elongated circles around the rest area and then back and forth along the back fence that abutted a plowed field. It occurred to me with horror that I had forgotten to take my DynaCirc, my blood pressure medicine, that morning, an item I hadn't forgotten to take in the twenty years since the condition had been diagnosed. It was probably a sign of mental health to finally forget taking the pill but I returned to the car and swallowed one with a swig of warmish water said to emerge from an alpine spring. I felt a specific envy for a small group of bulbous truckers who were smoking cigarettes in front of their enormous rigs. Now I was bathed in my own rank sweat and walked to the far end of the rest area and said firmly to a flowering crab tree, "I quit." Back in my car I allowed myself a single, heartfelt sob.

Afternoon rush-hour traffic around Indianapolis was grotesque but I enjoyed it. Like the others, I was also driving home from work but then I didn't intend to work anymore. It also occurred to me that the enormous vigor with which I had approached my work could now be applied to doing nothing, or something else. I can't say that I was ready to sing the "Hymn to Joy" but I was quite pleased to nudge along in the miles-long traffic jams, glancing at other cars and catching faces contorted with anger and impatience, or simply lax with boredom. The scenery of urban sprawl makes Harlem and Brooklyn look lovely.

I reached my sister's by seven in the evening. Martha had insisted on buying out Thad and me years ago so now our ancestral home (two generations) is truly her own. It had been more than twenty years since I stayed there when visiting Bloomington for research purposes, a difficult few days when Martha lays out the possibilities of the Bioprobe at hand. I stay either at a motel or in the guest house of my broker and investment counselor, a friend since high school named Matthew, but he is currently under chemo and radiation for prostate cancer and Martha told me his second wife was having an affair with a gas station owner we both know. It was Matthew who indiscreetly told me that Martha had a great deal more money than I did because she was smarter. He hastily added that he meant smarter in terms of investments, buying heavily into the technicals even before the advent of the ten-year-long bull market while I stayed conservative as a Kansas schoolteacher.

I felt a trace of sentiment driving through an older section of Bloomington, mostly because academic communities aren't so hysterically venal as the rest of our culture. There are cranky people who don't watch television and maintain a distance from popular culture. On my occasional visits I am charmed by their laconic indifference to most current affairs, which is largely pundit gossip anyway.

The real reason, though, that I don't stay with my sister is that she is a doyenne of the arts, and her house is a virtual salon. I've mentioned that she rarely leaves her home but then painters, sculptors, musicians, poets, and young fictioneers visit her for her acid tongue, food, and wine. She has two three-by-five cards, one green and one red, tacked by her front door depending on whether visitors are welcome or not. I had been pleased in Chicago when Thad told me that she had lately taken to walking a few hours after dark with a group of her arts cronies though the daylight hours were still too raw for her. Something very bad had happened to Martha during her junior year at Wellesley when she had spent three months in London. No one but Martha knows what except, of course, the other possible participants, singular or plural. She returned home when I was gone for my M.F.A. and that was that.

I frankly don't feel comfortable with her visitors. There is nothing haughtier than an unsuccessful person in the arts and Martha's evening living room often abounds in them. When I'm there I'm the toad in the soup tureen. Of course everyone is polite depending on the quantity of the wine served, and even then, the attacks are not personal but directed at the art and literary "establishments" of Chicago and New York, and the vulgarity of the large sums of money directed to unworthy artists and writers. For some odd reason the locals always know the inner gossip of gallery and literary circles in New York and Chicago better than I do living there. I really don't know how accurate this gossip is but everyone moderately successful is lumped into one stew, the contents of which lack parity.

Luckily the red card was out on the bush-shrouded porch and no cars were parked in front of the house. Martha hasn't driven a car since her late teens when she began referring to cars as "nasty items." Her specialty is the human race and anyone's mental condition is thoroughly acceptable to her if it's interesting, thus she's able to indulge the most outrageous nitwits that are likely to saturate the arts community in any academic setting. Her only bête noire has been "minimalists" of any variety, probably because she's big, about one hundred seventy pounds or so.

Only she wasn't that big anymore. I embraced her on the porch and thought she might be down to one forty.

"I'm missing to watch you eat meals with such justice," she said, quoting Claire's garbled English which I had shared with her. Over her shoulder through the screen door I could smell *pot au feu* which she makes expertly whenever I arrive. At my request she made it for my friend Rico when he passed through town which caused him to propose marriage. When he tried to seduce her she laughed for several minutes before telling him to go back to his motel. Last year when we had been drinking a great deal of wine I had asked Martha to tell me what had happened to her in England more than thirty years before and she had told me not to worry, that she would fully recover on her deathbed.

"Get your luggage. I want you to stay with me," she said firmly.

"No thanks." I felt sweat begin to emerge from wherever it comes from.

"Then go away, you fucking coward. I talked to your child bride and she says you're in extremis. Her words, not mine."

Martha helped me find the mysterious keyhole to the trunk after watching me fail from the vantage point of the porch. It was

still practically daylight and she studied the street in both directions
before coming through the gate of the picket fence we had painted
together as youngsters, though scarcely with the brash innocence
of Tom Sawyer. I've never understood why she feels the games of
night are less threatening. She's often said that noon is her worst
time of all.

"I've been thinking about hiring a boat to take me down the
Mississippi," I said, trying to delay any trunk-side discussion of my
sanity.

"Those are wonderful," she said, pointing down at my Marine
combat boots.

Over our delicious dinner I began to create a funny rendition of my
evening with Donna as I spread beef-shank marrow on French
bread with a liberal sprinkling of sea salt. I should have known she
wouldn't bring up anything as banal as sanity. She's just a little
flighty about suicide after having lost a number of friends over the
years. I had passed the test rather quickly and she was delighted
with my theologian Donna.

"Where will you go and what will you do?" she asked while
we were eating our crème caramel, one of the few desserts my
mother could make competently.

I looked around the connected living room–dining room. If it
weren't for the paintings, many of them obnoxiously bad, the year
still could have been 1958. The only additions from our childhood
had been a love seat, and oak end tables with marble tops from Ida's
house. My father's favorite easy chair still had doilies on the arms.
The only jarring note was a faint green light that peeked out of the
door of Martha's office. This woman had been torturing me about
integrity ever since my single little novel had come out thirty years
before, albeit with subtlety. She had stayed the course, as the "great"

Reagan liked to say, never having uttered a single positive word about any of my thirty-six Bioprobes. She was well beyond the concepts of compromise. Some things were worth doing. Others weren't.

"I only know what I'm not going to do," I finally said.

"Just don't turn simpleminded on me," Martha said. "That's a natural inclination for someone in your position. They take up photography or making pot holders and in your case the product would be the same. You're too much of a premature geezer to find something reliably ordinary and you don't learn very fast. Remember when you were playing father and I had to teach you how to dance so you could take that big-titted moron down the street to the prom. What was her name?"

"Sylvia," I said. Her perfume had smelled similar to an over-ripe watermelon.

"Maybe you could do something sensible like learn another language." Martha had always been irritated by my total ineptness at other languages. "And why spend so much money on floozies that treat you like shit? Matthew told me about that French plane trip last year. The accountant called him and then he called me to see if you'd gone batty."

So much for discreet help. It's hard not to resent it when people show concern for you. What happened a year ago was that I was in Paris and having a reasonably unpleasant time with Claire when she got a late-night phone call from her mother that her father had pneumonia. Claire became so hysterical that I was frightened. I made a call and hired one of those small French business jets, a Falcon, to fly us at dawn to Montpellier down on the Mediterranean, not all that far in American terms from the Spanish border. In fact when her brother picked us up at the airport I saw road signs for Perpignan and Barcelona! This was the closest brush with Spain in my life. Of course it was ungodly expensive and her brother

pointed out with humor that a commercial flight from Paris was
due in an hour. Also Claire had been so fascinated with deluxe travel
that she'd never mentioned her sick father during the flight. Within
two days her father, a school principal, was walking around, drinking wine, and treating me with amiable cynicism. I stayed at a hotel
on the water and at night I could see a strong patch of lights way
down the beach to the southwest. I asked a bellhop if they were
the lights of Spain and he said, "Narbonne," shrugged, and walked
away. I didn't know what this word meant having had only three
years of high school French, two years of college French, and two
dozen trips to the country. Later I found out Narbonne was a city
down the coast. On our trip back to Paris, Claire seemed slightly
pissed off that we flew commercial.

"Intelligent people aren't intelligent across the board," Martha
teased, intent upon my brooding. She lightened up by asking what
we should make for dinner the next day. Martha thinks we both
fell into food because it was one of the few barely permissible sensual expressions for midwesterners. Frowned upon but allowed.
How many times has one heard, "We should eat to live, not live to
eat." You're more likely to hear this mental drool in the Midwest
than any other place on earth. Martha is kind enough when I visit
to cook dishes rarely found in restaurants. It was a toss-up between
poule au pot, a simple stewed chicken, or *bollito misto*, a rather involved
Tuscan multiple-meat dish, probably the former rather than the
latter, because it was senseless to make *bollito misto* for only two
people and I doubted I was up to having company.

"You should give up pronto the idea that your situation is anything out of the ordinary. I'd bet half the people in this fucked-up
country snare themselves in a life's work that they know isn't right
for them. The trouble is there aren't enough right things to do. I
just made it less of my life than you did. You simply lacked the
character to follow through on what you dreamed you should do.

I'm surrounded by people who followed through and probably shouldn't have. There's nothing new in this, is there?"

Martha's reassuring little speech was truncated by the door-bell. It was time for her night walk and one of her companions was a burly, surly metal sculptor I had met before who scorned words as inferior metal and favored meaningful grunts. The other, by odd coincidence given Martha's speech, was an old acquaintance and near friend from my Iowa days who had written a half dozen novels about a hick from Missouri named Hokey Pokey. The first one was well received and sold moderately but better than my own first effort of the same year. He went along in the mid-list for a number of years with several different publishers, but the last two of the Hokey Pokey series have been regionally published in small editions. He's had a drinking problem which has made him unable to hold the usual creative-writing job, which would produce more of his own kind. In the last decade he has supported himself by cut-rate travel writing where you get a couple of grand for the piece and the maga-zines help you weasel free air tickets and accommodations. I've always thought that we could have become friends except for the money I've "loaned" him which makes him nervous despite my assurances that it doesn't matter. On this evening his speech was ever so slightly blurred and he looked especially threadbare. An-other pang hit my sternum as I said good-bye and off they went for their endorphin walk.

I thought of having a nightcap but knew it was inappropriate. I walked down the long dark hall of the big house, once a farm-house before the First World War but now totally encroached by a suburb. My parents loved the occasional plaster cracks and the way the entire structure was out of plumb. I looked into Thad's room and the dusty model airplanes still hung from the ceiling. He did a lousy job. Once I tossed one from a high campus building for him so he could see it crash. On another occasion he tipped our gasoline lawn mower back, then lowered it on a model plane to imitate a "space typhoon," or so he said. Model plane making wasn't the sort of hobby my parents approved of, thus he continued.

When I turned out the light in Thad's room there was the idle thought that sharing the money I'd made on my Bioprobes might not have done my sister and brother all that much good. This was an errant and unpleasant consideration. It reminded me of my sister's question, "Could you describe someone you actually know?" Maybe, but it would be damned hard work. My Bioprobes actually depended on me not really knowing the subject at hand, and I expect that in journalism, except of the highest order, truly knowing the person presents a barrier. Anything I've ever read about anyone I've known well has proved to be blithely inaccurate, a bit silly, and could only be considered interesting to someone ignorant of the emotional contents of the person. If you add the physical image as you do in television news you're in real trouble.

Jesus Christ, I'm sinking in a bog like that mudflat on the Mississippi, only this time over my head. I impulsively returned to the living room, found one of Martha's innumerable Post-it pads, and wrote, "I'll learn TWO languages if you'll buy another pup." I pasted it to an urn of ashes on the fireplace mantel, all that remained of her little female mongrel Sash who had died the year before. She kept saying she felt too emotionally timid to get another dog. My note was only to return her friendly meddling.

Before I went to my own room, which I had been delaying, I opened the door to my parents' bedroom, flicking on the lights for a full second. It was supposedly now a guest bedroom but I doubted Martha ever let anyone sleep in it. It seems to be sudden death that creates ghosts. Did my father have a spirit capable of emerging from that sunken boat? Was there anything left of my mother after she took her life from herself? That seemed to be the question.

❊ ❊ ❊

I'm not sure what I expected from my own room which I hadn't slept in since I was thirty-five and so arrogant that, to reverse Henry James, I was one on whom everything is lost. A man in his mid-thirties on a full-tilt-success boogie is as self-referential as the pancreas which is doomed never to know it is a pancreas. My room was absolutely chock-full of the comedy of youthful expectation and, as opposed to science fiction, maybe the only true time machine is when we revisit the signal locations of our far past that resonate so deeply we are drawn out of our shoes back to the emotional content that still resides there.

Glued to the inside of the door was the only arrowhead I had ever found. The creek at my grandparents' farm, beside which Cindy had found the snake, drained into a marsh of forty acres or so. At the juncture of marsh and creek there was a small knoll of high ground that must have been an Indian encampment. I used to know what tribe of Indian but then both D. H. Lawrence and William Carlos Williams had pointed out that this is the first thing we Americans like to forget. Anyway, one day my father took us to the farm to give my mother a few clear days off, then my father abandoned us to botanize on Indiana's southern border. I was fifteen and it was up to me to look after Martha and Thad who were twelve and nine and both capable of nightmarishly bad behavior, but then my grandparents were too infirm to keep track of them. I was sitting on the knoll trying to feel poetic like Vachel Lindsay. Martha found an arrowhead and we all started digging around. Martha ended up finding seven and Thad four. I only found one, which pissed me off because it punched a hole in my presumed superiority. Now millions of people have found arrowheads but at the time it gave me my first little glimpse into living history and confounded me. All of the writers of the books I had been reading were dead like the makers of the arrowheads.

Turning from the door and glancing at the bookshelf I could see the books I favored in my late teens and early twenties, mostly nineteenth- and twentieth-century Spanish and French poetry, and novelists like Faulkner, Melville, Dostoyevsky, Turgenev, Joyce, Sherwood Anderson, also a peculiar book a French professor had given me, Bachelard's *Poetics of Space.* I took out the somewhat tattered volume of Lorca's *Poet in New York,* knowing the absurd photo that lay within. In the ninth grade I had taken my Brownie camera to school and persuaded a vain friend to stand near a group of girls on lunch hour, including our Portuguese exchange student, Leila. It was the only way I could get a picture of her but in the photo she's a bit blurred and half-turned away. In volumes of Roethke and Robert Duncan's *Roots and Branches* there were a few photos of high school and college girlfriends, including an electrifying nude Polaroid of Cindy, but none, including Cindy, had the ineffable power of Leila out near the front steps of the high school, out of focus with a hand raised as if gesturing toward the sky on a sunny but cool day in mid-winter.

What a freaky-deaky fucking romantic, I thought, sitting down on my narrow bed. How could I be such a goddamned nitwit that I could offer such substance to a youthful infatuation that had no substance. But it apparently did.

And maybe these former beloved books were only an immature young man's prized fetishes, once magical arrowheads or a hick's bedraggled rabbit's foot, carried until it was soiled bone and sinew. The room was shimmering slightly like in one of those loathsome horror films on television that I am occasionally drawn to. In a single volume of Hemingway, *In Our Time,* was a short letter from old Ida about the biblical figure Lazarus that I had once thought very funny. Early in my teens I had told Ida I didn't believe the story of Jesus bringing Lazarus back from the dead. She was so shocked she said nothing at first, then wrote me a note a few days later that said, "Young man, if the Bible says it, it's true. Signed, Ida Price Shotsworth." At the moment the controversy didn't seem funny. Ida could "see" Lazarus and I couldn't. She had different eyes. As a senior in high school I had become too finicky to read Hemingway. This was soon after I had gone into a woodlot with two friends and we had shot eleven squirrels with our .22s. We were going to have a fried-squirrel feast, but instead left them in a bushel basket behind a garage until they stank.

The room began wavering again so I turned off the light. On the far wall from my bed was a large map of Spain that was barely visible in the illumination from the streetlight that dappled through trees and bushes that moved in the night breeze. Seville, Córdoba, and Granada flickering with the leaves. I thought of pulling the shades but the streetlight turned out to be the moon, quite visible without the high buildings of New York and Chicago. Is life accessible? Is life inaccessible? Can I only write down what I have made some sense of which leaves out the other seven-eighths or more, the sometimes juicy void that whirls around us, or the darkness bleached with color that closes in, the high noon that suffocates Martha. She hates artless sincerity. She hates sincerity. She loves art with two rooms upstairs full of art books. I said they'll collapse the living room ceiling and she said good, with the art books flopping down and bruising us. Maybe parents should protect their children from poetry not pornography. What disastrous ideals I've had. Guillen said, "Your childhood, a fable for fountains now." I think he said that. Martha caught Thad with these dirty eight-pager comic books and screeched and Mother saw them, then she showed them to Father. Thad lied and said he found them in my room but they didn't believe him. I was sitting out on the grass figuring out my relationship to the moon and stars. Mother and Father were on the porch with poor Thad between them. Mother said this points a finger at something but I'm not sure what. Father said I agree. They were straining for the single evening drink they allowed themselves. Father said, Thad, we'll burn them in the fireplace. Thad said okay, I didn't mean nothing. Anything, Mother said. Say it right. I didn't mean anything. Better that they burned my poetry collection. It was designed for another culture no longer our own. Early ideals can kill you but they deserve to. Early ideals were designed with great pain by everyone through the centuries, from Góngora to Cela, from Villon to Char and onward, from Emily Dickinson down to all of us Bartlebys. The *Times* said, I think, that there are thirty-nine thousand writers in New Jersey. Toil and grow rich and see the girl's flared bottom at the Cajou. I wept today at the rest area and now with the moon on my bare belly for the first time my parents disappeared wherever. A man began weeping in a restaurant just after a fire truck passed by. He couldn't stop and the maître d' asked him to leave. I sat there wondering why he wept and was slightly tempted to follow him and ask. Maybe it is a sign of character.

It was after midnight when I heard Martha's footsteps pausing outside my door. Then they went slowly away. I doubted a new language, or even two, would change the alphabet of my life, but then I'd no longer have to string together fibs, those fuzzy cousins of the lie. "Bob Famous Person toyed with his egg yolk at breakfast, using the end of a piece of bacon and the yolk to paint the fate of nations on the white Wedgwood. He could have been Dalí, he thought, but he was Bob, and he stared down at the hands that held hundreds of millions of destinies, hands that he washed every morning in sheep's milk, a habit taught to him by his mother in an alpine canton in Switzerland because they lived too far up the mountain to fetch water."

The moon passed upward through the top of my window. I heard Donna sleeping in New York. I heard Cindy listening to the river in Wisconsin. I heard myself breathing in and out or out and in. I raised a hand upward from the moonlight on the bed and into the darkness until it waved across Spain. I forced myself to believe that I was more than I had written. It was very hard and took until two A.M. when I won and slept.

A sense of a plan was afoot though without particulars. I awoke at five A.M., left a modestly loving note for Martha, unloaded my brief-case of ten pounds of Eisner notes and three pounds of *Humanistic Botany,* replacing them with a few volumes of bilingual poetry an-thologies with their precious (seriously) Penguin colophons. I drifted out of the house quietly like a large cat burglar, well dressed and confident for no particular reason, thinking there might be a way to fence my life.

I made Indianapolis in time for a feeder connection to Chicago, and caught a lucky booking for New York at American's Admirals Club, a name I have loved, not ever having seen myself as an admi-ral. I still felt miserably full, not with Martha's excellent food but from eating too much of the world and with a particular, monstrous appetite for the world's garbage. There was an urge to make notes on how to vomit up these thirty years of garbage but I didn't want to write anything down before I could make full sense of it which might take God knows how long. I once heard on NPR a bright man describe how you can chat to God but those Hubbell space photos withered my tongue. If the afterlife is so wonderful why did Jesus bother bringing Lazarus back from the dead? To show us the dead are really dead, or the dead aren't really dead? How would I know? The question was certainly a reason to call Donna in ad-dition to holding her gracious, glorious butt in my arms again with the night-light making it improbably beautiful. Butts and Lazarus, not a far reach actually.

O'Hare Airport is our silly, unimaginative hell. In the Bible they were always telling stories about a rich man who had three cows, two camels, and a granary full of grain. What the fuck could we mean by rich nowadays? What month is it? Early to mid-May? In the lounge a man salutes my Marine boots on his hurried trek to his plane.

    In the cab from LaGuardia I reached in my briefcase for a notepad, then seized my own hand with a Frankenstein gesture. The last fucking thing I needed to do at the moment was to write anything down. When we crossed the Queensboro Bridge at Fifty-ninth Street into Manhattan, which never looked fairer, I thought of traveling to a truly far-off and exotic place then decided that the exotic would ill prepare me for the rest of my life. I asked the cabdriver why the traffic was so light and he said, "Because it's Sunday, sir," in a lilting West Indian accent, grinning into the rearview mirror as if accustomed to carting the daft around the city.

    At my apartment I looked at the wine stains with the fondness that a young man might have looking at his first poem. I called Donna who wasn't there. I called Rico who wasn't there, but then why would anyone be in an apartment on a fine Sunday afternoon? Why should anyone be there when you called, as a matter of fact? I called Don the Whiz, as the office girls called him, but his wife in Greenwich said he was playing golf for the day in North Carolina. I told her that I resigned and she said, "It's Sunday but I'll give him the message tonight," a mysterious answer. I threw away the perishable contents in the refrigerator, carrying them down to the stoop. I nearly opened my mailbox but discarded the thought. I called Air France and managed to trade in some of my three hundred thousand miles for a seat on an evening flight. I packed a sturdy bag, then slept sitting up on the couch for a couple of hours, head lolling, drooling on my shirt, dreaming that there were dogs no bigger than my fist hiding in the apartment and they were trying to tell me a vitally important secret. When I awoke this dream was not too absurd to give serious consideration, but then how was I to comprehend dog language?

At Kennedy I bought a half dozen maps of Spain and France to give my nearly empty briefcase some important contents. There seemed to be no real crisis other than that I had had the wrong job and needed to create a new one. I just couldn't sit there and deliquesce like the "boulevardiers" who circulate from bistro to bistro on a schedule that depends on the luncheon specials. I needed to get rid of the timid fibber that wrapped around my spine like the dread green mamba. On the plane I remembered a bold but fraudulent move I had made in the month before I gained my dubious M.F.A. My "creative thesis" wasn't quite long enough so I added ten poems by a young Spanish woman poet I claimed to have met in Bilbao and whom I was translating into English for the first time. Of course I hadn't been there and she didn't exist but the poems had been written faster and slicker than goose shit. One was even about how to cook codfish cakes with a white, cream garlic sauce. My professor-adviser liked these faux translations very much, thinking them much better than my own more serious work. This man had once been thought to be an "exciting" formalist in the early fifties but teaching us "clods" had struck him dumb. Unfortunately he asked for the originals, but a two-day trip home and Martha's expertise with Spanish did the job. She was a bit goofy at the time and thought I might be "many people" like Joanne Woodward had been in a particular movie.

High above the Atlantic I had the idea that I might carve out a modest career writing poems, and perhaps novels, in the personae of a number of different people. After eating a piece of sole that was a lesser experience than the Wisconsin catfish, not to speak of drinking two full bottles of wine, this writing project for a new life seemed admirable indeed. Why be one person when you could be several? I was not disturbed by the apparent fact that novelists were already doing this because my version was obviously fresh and original in ways that would momentarily rise to the surface. My names could vary from Alberto Dorado to Monique Senegal.

There was a problem or two at the luggage belt at De Gaulle that made me lose a little cabin pressure. There had only been one other passenger in first class, a dour New York banker with loose facial skin. Despite our "priorité" stickers our luggage was the last to emerge from the dark hole in the floor, doubtless a prank of leftist baggage handlers, a political persuasion of which I had always half-seriously numbered myself. During the hour wait I had called Claire and reached Oliver, a friend of hers I had met several times, a young man so thin he appeared to be made of Tinkertoys. Oliver had spent two years at Oxford, spoke excellent English, but had the irritating habit of calling me "old chap." The upshot was that Oliver had been subletting the apartment from Claire who had been in Prague for the past four months. She had called me a few times and the connection had been a bit Balkan though she had never said where she was. Claire had neglected to send the landlord any of the money Oliver had been sending her for rent. She was thus consuming a double dose of money, Oliver's and my regular bank draft. Oh well. Anyway, Oliver said, he was being kicked out and I was liable. How so, I asked? Oliver had seen my signature on the lease. Since I had never signed any lease this meant my signature had been forged.

This wasn't exactly what I had in mind for the start of my new life. It was reality in the form of the kick in the balls Dad had so accurately described. One reason to make money is to buy your way out of such soul-crippling bullshit. Before I hung up Oliver suggested that the way out was to pay up the remaining six months of the lease and sublet the apartment directly to him, at least that is what the landlord suggested, refusing to have anything more to do with Claire. With quaking head I told Oliver I'd get back to him soon.

Luckily there was an Air France attendant loitering nearby. With luggage in hand I asked her if there was a flight to Barcelona fairly soon and she said yes, and directed me to another terminal. When safely on this plane my spirits rose with somewhat manic fuel, feeling the plane lift off and head in a direction far from the problems of Claire. There was even a lunch of codfish fritters somewhat similar to those in my poem so many years ago. My aforementioned leftist sympathies did give me a troubling thought that if I hadn't concentrated so hard on the work that yielded big money, I would have had the wit not to get involved with the wretched bitch Claire in the first place.

And one more perilous fuckup awaited me before I could properly start my new life. I rather liked the light red Rioja served me on the plane in some quantity. This admittedly caused a little grogginess and when I disembarked I merely floated along following the other passengers, all of whom were decidedly European. Suddenly I was out in front seeing a few palm trees in the hot afternoon sun and not having passed through customs, an obligation for Americans and others, but not Euro passengers. "Give no thought for the morrow, because the morrow will take care of itself," Jesus had said, so I stood there until I found the driver to take me to my hotel, both arranged from De Gaulle by phone.

Unfortunately my own neglect began to bother me by the time I flopped on the bed in my splendid hotel room, after first looking down from the balcony at the busy crowds of the Ramblas. I was sure my customs fuckup might cause problems, hopefully not including the dread Guardia Civil rousting me from my bed with cocked truncheons. A well-composed, intelligent American citizen would merely have called the consular office for advice. I took a nap. On the way in from the airport I hadn't seen any peasant poets leading donkeys but I was, nonetheless, very happy to be here. As I dozed off my brain played me some favorite Carlos Montoya riffs.

❀   ❀   ❀

My first trip to Spain lasted only forty-nine hours, which at least was
seven times seven, and seven had always been my lucky number.
To my credit I didn't shit my pants or lose my wallet. That first
evening I walked for several hours until the chafe sent me back to
the room for my pine-tar salve. I saw innumerable beautiful dark-
haired women, and spent a full hour in a market looking at all of
the food possibilities. I could even tell that most people were speaking Catalan rather than regular Spanish. In short, I had myself
firmly in hand, but still knew that my foreboding midwestern back-
story would make me continue to probe at my airport error. I've
often noticed that natives of our East and West Coasts are less likely
to have envisioned a perfect world, thus are more generally forgiving
of their own mistakes. When I re-enacted my airport departure I
could even remember the neglected signs.

Before I went out for a late dinner I took a shower, and after
the shower I walked into a hall closet rather than back into my bedroom as intended. The closet was large and I was well inside it before I realized my mistake. This frankly wasn't a funny experience
but it was an immediate help in making me understand that I wasn't
in Spain yet despite my physical presence there. Actually being in
Spain would take days and days, if not weeks and weeks. Right now
I was in the middle of a collapsed accordion like any tourist where
time rolls cinematically past the viewer with scenes that can't be
digested.

Help came in the form of an Irish bartender in a pub a few
blocks from the hotel. The proprietor of the restaurant told me on
entering a dense crowd that despite my reservation it would be
better if I came back in an hour, thus I cooled my heels in an un-
crowded pub that was convincingly Dublinish. After a single drink
I told the bartender my problem which he kindly considered with

high seriousness. He said that if I was just an American tourist fool-
ing around for a few days there was no problem, but if I wanted to
rent a place for a while and settle in I'd best take a bus back into
France, say to Narbonne, have lunch, and come back into Spain
with a properly stamped passport. Barcelona had friendly officials
but there was a chance I might run into an unfriendly bureaucrat
elsewhere.

At a simple dinner of cod stew with tomato and garlic, and a
portion of roasted piglet, the bartender's advice, however possibly
misinformed, put me at ease. I was packed to the hilt with mis-
information but this item was relaxing. And by coincidence I had
seen Narbonne's lights from my balcony in Montpellier, a fine experience if you somehow detached Claire from the trip.

The next morning I became miserably lost for an hour, ducking into
alleys and holding my city map sideways, right side up, and up-
side down in an attempt to get perspective. The only consolation
was watching the crowded sweep of sidewalks with millions of
heads tilted forward on their way to their jobs. By ten in the
morning when I re-found my hotel, I was drenched with sweat,
hastily cleaned myself up, and got myself a car and driver for the
day. Again, was I really there as I made my eight-hour city tour
in an air-conditioned Mercedes? A little bit but not much. Once
the leaving and coming solution to the customs problem had been
resolved Claire's apartment came into being like the dog shit you
can't quite get off your shoe. The driver, actually Pedro by name,
was excellent in every respect but the only sights that penetrated
me worry free were the works of Gaudi. Even the mighty power
of my various neuroses couldn't withstand this genius. Gaudi
made Claire's apartment disappear into the shimmering heat and

smog above the city. Gaudi easily excluded himself from any sense of the travelogue what with personifying the most attractive aspects of our imaginations.

Sad to say the city tried to carry me away but couldn't quite do the job, my fault not the city's. I simply had to turn around and clean up my little messes, however bourgeois the notion. At that moment of realization I was at a Basque tapas bar making a pig of myself. I was very much like the geese I had seen in a courtyard of Barcelona's grand cathedral. I was a goose in grand surroundings but still a goose. I was also a little embarrassed when the owner of the tapas bar shook my hand for so obviously enjoying his food. It turned out I had eaten twenty-one tapas, another multiple of seven which did not make my eighth seven coming up, age fifty-six, a more understandable prospect.

By mid-morning I was back at De Gaulle and went directly to Claire's apartment where I woke Oliver, and then to the glorified delicatessen owned by the landlord where he was braising some leeks for leek vinaigrette. This in itself was disarming. He noticed I was staring at a tray of Bismarck herring and quickly whipped one on a plate with onions and a piece of bread. Back in his cramped office, Oliver was forced to stand up looking all the while like our midwestern bug the walking stick. We all had a cup of coffee, also a glass of white wine for our digestion. The white wine made me feel agreeable and I had the immediate fantasy of commuting back and forth between Paris and Barcelona on alternative weeks and learning French and Spanish at the same time. Why not?

Meanwhile, the landlord showed me the lease. My signature was forged but it was an excellent forgery. For a minute or so the world came down on my head and not lightly. The landlord's position was that though Claire was clearly banished I was still liable unless I wished to call in the cops and go to court. Oliver was in a state of anguish and I gave him my chair where he sat with his face in his hands. There was a definite possibility that this scene had been rehearsed. I knew Oliver was studying to be a doctor but I doubted that he intended to imitate Albert Schweitzer. The banality of it all threatened to become suffocating. I took out my checkbook and paid up the entire year until the lease ended, an amount equal to five pages of my Bioprobe of William Paley who had said near the end of his life when fatally ill, "Why do I have to die?" as if he might somehow be exempt. On the way out Oliver said, "I'll send you a monthly check, old chap," and I said, "I won't hold my hand over my ass," a piece of midwestern slang.

That evening I had dinner at Recamier with the French tutor I had found. She was my dumpy counterpart in age and I had only intended to have coffee with her in the lobby of my hotel on Rue Vaneau, the Hotel de Suede. She was originally from Auvergne and had briefly been married to an American when she was a graduate student at the University of Chicago. I invited her to dinner because she appeared to know more about the history of American literature than anyone I had ever met. She told me frankly that my intention to study French and Spanish intensively at the same time was "utterly stupid." Certain aspects of her character made her an older version of Donna. After dinner I put her in a cab. We had agreed to meet in eight days after I'd had my first full week in Spain. The silliness of it all made us both a little breathless and I gave her hand a courtly kiss as she got into the cab.

I walked over to Rue de St.-Jacques to a jazz club where I frequently have a nightcap while in Paris. I felt jaunty and pleased not to be with Claire, a nightly chore I had faced for the past few years while in Paris. Modern jazz is lonely and strident, perfect for

a middle-aged white male who has cut the tethers with which he
has tied himself. It's sort of metallic and blue but it's still music. I
didn't expect, after all, to become one of those men who can enter
a bar, throw his hat, and hit the hat rack every time. As a matter of
fact there are no more hats and hat racks. You might wonder what
listening to Miles Davis tunes at midnight in Paris has to do with
anything but the question emerges from our vain effort to make
everything fit together. Hopefully I was heading elsewhere.